Impossible Beginnings
A Love Story

Impossible Beginnings
A Love Story

Richard S. Johnson

ARPress
ILLUMINATING IDEAS,
EMPOWERING VOICES

ARPress
45 Dan Road Suite 5
Canton, MA 02021

Hotline: 1(888) 821-0229
Fax: 1(508) 545-7580

Ordering Information:

Quantity sales. Special discounts are available on quantity purchases by corporations,associations, and others. For details, contact the publisher at the address above.

Printed in the United States of America.

ISBN-13:   Softcover   979-8-89389-329-8
                       eBook   979-8-88853-653-7

Library of Congress Control Number: 2024916135

Love is patient, love is kind.

It does not envy, it does not boast,

it is not proud. It does not dishonor others,

it is not self-seeking, it is not easily angered,

it keeps no record of wrongs.

Love does not delight in evil but rejoices with the truth.

It always protects, always trusts,

always hopes, always perseveres.

Love never fails.

1 Corinthians 13:4-8 NIV

ACKNOWLEDGMENTS

Many thanks to my wife Sandra for reading, editing, and other support for this book.

Thanks to the people who read earlier copies of this manuscript and made suggested changes.

Thanks to the mountain people of the Allegheny Mountains in Cameron County, Pennsylvania who make excellent examples of how country folks live and support each other.

Thanks to the many people of ARPress for their patience and most helpful support in getting *"Impossible Beginnings"* published.

CHAPTER 1

W hy me? Why always me?" Merry screamed in desperation, fear tightening her throat as reality slammed home. This day that began with the promise of an exciting adventure became ever more challenging with mile after mile of darkened forest, dense fog closing in, and a miserable rain beating her windshield making driving miserable.

Never before had she been in such a godforsaken place, and she was alone in these mountains. Panic grabbed her thought process; her hands shook as she folded the map. The desire to be her big girl self had long passed.

"What have I done to myself?" Merry screamed as she pulled out of the Medix Run Hotel parking lot heading east on route 555, her tremors of uneasiness growing more intense. "Why was I so stubborn when Arianna bailed out of this miserable trip? I could've said I wasn't going. But no, I jammed my head in my armpit and took off. Couldn't let anyone think I was afraid to tackle this alone. Oh no, not me. Merry, it's not too late to turn around."

Entering the village of Benezette, she watched a bearded man loaded with tattoos, streaming long, greasy hair, and wearing ragged clothes stagger out of a bar and climb into a beat-up pickup truck. Pipes roared as he fired up. Her pulse raced when he quickly rode her tail, headlights flashing and his horn demanding, "Let's get moving."

"What's wrong with you," she screamed, pounding her steering wheel. Fear grasped her until they came to a place wide enough for him to pass. He flipped her an obscene hand gesture on his way by.

The Hicks Run Road sign loomed in the growing darkness. Merry turned north onto the narrow mountain road with mud splattering her fenders. She was shocked by nothingness. *Doesn't anyone live in these godforsaken mountains*, she wondered as miles slid by with no sign of human habitation.

Turn back, Merry; her mind screamed as the fog grew in intensity.

"Damn you, Arianna Troup. You put me in this mess."

A dark figure bounded across the road. With brakes jammed tight, she slid sideways to a stop on the muddy road a few feet away from a huge pine tree. In two leaps, the deer disappeared into the woods on the other side of the road.

A few destitute miles later, the road unexpectedly dropped steeply, and she was traveling too fast to control her car. She slid sideways down the muddy hill onto an old blacktop road before gaining control. Nearing panic, she pulled into the parking lot of a small, remote building. A sign provided its name, "The Hill Church."

Hands shaking, she checked her maps and looked for potential cabin roads. Finding no indication of Bucky's cabin, she drove a bit further. A sign stating "Game Commission Parking Lot" appeared at the top of the next hill, and she pulled in to turn around. Nothing looked right. Sweat broke out on her forehead as the reality of her dilemma slammed home. She admitted Arianna didn't get her into this fix; her big girl self decided to make this trip.

She turned her car around and found herself facing an old cemetery. She tried her GPS and received no signal.

"Why me?" she screamed. "What did I get myself into?"

Her stomach boiled as she considered camping alone in this godforsaken wilderness.

"It's time to head for home while you still can," she mumbled, realizing it could be five hours before she would slip into her Sleep Number bed.

No one would know she tried this camping trip and chickened out. She stopped at the parking lot exit allowing a car to roar past in the fog but filed to see see the vehicle rolling toward her from the opposite direction. Seeing lights at the last second, she slammed on her brakes and slid into the path of the oncoming truck. A tremendous blow threw her into the windshield. She struggled to sit up. Then all went black.

CHAPTER 2

Where's Hackett? Doc Adams nervously wondered as he walked towards his office after the change of shift meeting with his plant superintendents. Hackett called this Friday meeting with no set time. The message "Just be ready for a serious talk" shouted trouble's coming. Hackett was a bully who found great enjoyment in making others squirm in his sit-downs when he dumped a load of nastiness on attendees. Maybe this is my set-up meeting as he closes in for the kill.

Doc was weary from little sleep and an early awakening in his recliner with a half-read newspaper on his chest and an empty whiskey glass on the table. The day wore on with Hackett's threats tearing through his mind. He promised himself Hackett wouldn't make this a one-sided war, but it held ramifications he didn't want to face. His termination agreement amounted to almost 200 grand, something he didn't want to throw away.

Regardless of cost, George Hackett, you won't run over me today, Doc told himself.

As he approached his secretary's desk, Jane flashed the halt signal, ran her hand across her throat, and mouthed, "Monk." George "Monk" Hackett remained the major shareholder of MELCOR

Industries since he took it public, and he was the father of Doc's recently deceased wife, Billy.

Doc repressed an angry smile when he saw George sitting in his chair smoking a fat cigar with a nasty look riding his face. The plant's "No Smoking" policy Hackett initiated didn't apply to him.

Hackett's bushy eyebrows almost hid his dark, hooded eyes, mean eyes that recently saw little good in anything or anyone. He was an imposing man with a muscular body that bore witness to the hours spent in his home gym. This day he sported a menacing, tear-off-your-head look.

"Good afternoon, George."

"Close the door and sit down, Cowboy!" George ordered using his malevolent name for Doc, his jutting chin and furrowed brow stating he was searching for a fight. "We need to talk!"

"About what?" Doc asked as he slid into a chair in front of his desk.

"You, Cowboy. You haven't drawn a sober breath since the funeral. And that's only part of your problems. You're wasting tons of money on BS programs."

As Hackett talked, his throaty voice grew ever nastier.

"Your buddies at the Rotary Club might think this apprenticeship crap is a great idea, but they ain't paying for it. Hire people who don't need training. Your planned employee raises don't sit well, either. Employees already make more than they deserve. Then there's your bonus plan. Our workers don't need bonuses for the little extra they do. Nobody ever gave me bonuses. That crap bankrupts companies."

Doc wanted to say maybe you didn't earn any bonuses, but instead, he said, "Billy put our apprenticeship program together, and you bragged about it. When we put the bonus plan in place, productivity and profitability both improved."

"That's BS, and there are other problems. Late shipments go out of here every week because you spend half days sleeping off hangovers."

An angry smile grew on Doc's face as he took a deep breath with clenched fists.

"Are you listening to me, Cowboy?" Hackett demanded, slamming a fist on Doc's desk, sending a family picture smashing to the floor. "This ain't funny. You better be hearing me. Bad things happen when I'm –"

Doc angrily gripped his chair. "Caught every word, and I don't agree with much of anything you said."

"Don't get cute, Cowboy. I don't take crap from anyone. Got it?"

Nothing.

"Cowboy, I asked you a question."

You wouldn't want to hear my answer, Doc thought.

"Did you hear me?" Hackett demanded.

Doc grabbed his picture off the floor and tossed the broken glass in the trash without answering.

"Did you hear me?" Hackett screamed, standing behind the desk.

With a mean half-smile, Doc softly answered. "I heard you. Half the plant heard you. You don't want to hear what I'm thinking. You can't handle it."

Hackett screamed with chords sticking out on his neck, "I don't care what you're thinking. The only intelligent thing you ever did was marry Catherine. She made you into something you're desperately trying to throw away. Your boozing shows how little you cared about her. You —."

Rage flooded over Doc. In a low, clipped voice, he said, "George, you have no idea how much I love Billy. If you have anything positive or important to discuss, I'll listen. If not, this conversation's finished."

"Finished my fanny. You forget who runs this company? It's me, George Hackett," Hackett said, thumping his chest with his fist. "I'm giving you a week on the street to sober up while I get this operation back on track. If you don't get off the booze, think unemployment. Any questions?"

Doc glanced at the calendar on his desk. "I'm due back Monday, May 14, 2018, at 7:00 A.M.?"

"I'm not done talking."

"I'm done listening," Doc said, picking his cell phone off the desk and grabbing his jacket.

As he opened the door, Hackett screamed, "You better sit yourself down if you know what's —"

Doc angrily slammed the door behind him and headed for his truck.

When the door banged back against the wall, Hackett bellowed, "Get back here while you still have a job!" But he was talking to himself.

"What now, Lord?" Doc asked as he climbed into his Ford F-250. "The only thing keeping me in this job is the termination contract. Walking out on George might have ended that."

Doc drove off feeling like the end of the world was jerking him in. It would be so easy to end it all.

"My life's about over, Lord," he muttered, "and I don't much care. Maybe it's time to pack it in."

Feeling rough with the rain increasing and fog closing in, Doc headed to Kitty's Place restaurant where the owner, Billy's friend and classmate, met him.

"Hi, Doc," Kitty greeted with a warm smile. "I'm caught up. Mind if I sit a bit?"

"Please do. I'm finding a deep need to spend time with nice people."

Kitty slid into the chair across from Doc and looked him in the eye, her hand resting on his. "How ya doing, Doc?"

"OK," Doc muttered.

"Let's be honest. You're not the Doc I know, and you're not doing OK! You look rough and slug down alcohol like you're trying to kill yourself."

"Are you a friend or a friend beater?" Doc asked. "I don't need anyone making a bad day worse."

"It must be hard. You two were so close. How can I help you?"

"Just shoot me!"

Kitty grew a nasty expression, anger gripping her voice. "In case you haven't noticed, I'm trying to be your friend," she snapped as she stood and stalked away.

Mind-movies of the Hackett meeting stampeded through his memory. He knew his drinking was getting worse. *It doesn't seem like it's affecting my work*, he thought, but he acknowledged self isn't always the best judge of personal performance. What's next, Doc wondered as he thought through his day. Hackett isn't happy, and he's known to be a set-up engineer who was generally several steps ahead of people when he planned their demise. *Oh well, it won't be the end of my world*, Doc told himself. *That ended November 12, 2017.*

Kitty soon arrived with his menu and an angry look. "Can I get you something to drink while you review the menu?"

"I'll have a Coke," Doc replied. "And I don't need a menu. I'll have the baked Cajun."

Kitty arrived with his beverage and salad with no chatter. It was unlike her, but he hadn't given her reason to be friendly.

"You're getting busy. You can bring my fish when you get time."

Doc worried through the day as he consumed his meal, finishing with the feeling of a round of heartburn coming. When Kitty arrived, he turned down dessert and waited while she made out his tab. After telling her how great the meal was and paying, he departed.

CHAPTER 3

For months after Billy's passing, Doc stopped at the VFW for a double rum and Coke after Friday dinners. With time passing, it became two drinks and often more, with stops on other nights. Something told him not to stop this night, and he rolled by.

He turned up Moore Hill Road at Howard, thinking *George won't fire me without reason. It would cost him too much. He'd have to prove misconduct that reflects poorly on the company or poor MELCOR performance and the companies on a roll.*

"Ta hell with George Hackett," he screamed without knowing why.

"Oh Lord, please help me before I go crazy," Doc prayed as he climbed the hill. "Grief is turning me into a drunk."

Near the top of Cemetery Hill, a fast-approaching car almost hit him head-on. "Slow down, idiot!" he muttered, looking in the mirror. That glance caused him to miss the vehicle pulling out of the parking lot. He slammed on his brakes at the last second but crashed into the car.

The other driver slumped over the steering wheel. Headlights came on in the cemetery, followed by the red and blue flashing lights of a police cruiser. Doc backed his truck away from the car and turned on his four-way flashers. He limped over to the driver's door and knocked on the window.

"You OK?"

The driver struggled upright with a confused look on her face. She was a beautiful, young woman with wet sand tan colored hair.

"I didn't see you coming," the woman moaned.

"We need to get out of the road before someone hits us."

She tried to move her car but it didn't want to move. "I can't back up."

"Just gas it."

"Here! You try," the woman screamed as she stumbled out of her car holding a Kleenex to her bloody nose.

The cop trotted toward them, but Doc ignored him and struggled into her car. He found reverse and gassed it back accompanied by the sounds of spinning tires and screeching metal. When he was back far enough for other vehicles to get by safely, he climbed out.

"Hold it right there," the cop ordered.

Doc pretended he didn't hear him and ran to his truck. He pulled around the wrecked car and into the parking lot, where he grabbed his flashlight and the spare handkerchief he kept in his glove compartment. Heading for the woman's car, he noted his truck's bent fender and broken headlight, but the thick steel bumper he had installed protected the rest of his truck.

"Didn't you hear me tell you to hold it?" the cop asked as he walked up. "You drunk?"

"Funny you'd ask that before you checked to see if anyone was hurt," Doc replied.

Without answering, the cop stomped around Doc to find the driver sitting with her head on the steering wheel. "You OK, ma'am?"

"If you mean will I live, the answer's yes. I waited for another car to pass and pulled out in front of this guy. It's my fault."

"You may want to reconsider accepting blame for the accident until we finish our investigation. If you're all right, I have things to discuss with the other driver."

"I'm OK."

Doc stood wondering why state police would be sitting in the back of the cemetery. The hill road saw few people at night other than residents and a few people spotting wildlife.

The officer approached Doc. "May I see your driver's license, insurance, and registration?"

"Sure," Doc said as he retrieved them for the officer. "Let me give this hanky to the lady for her nosebleed."

When Doc returned, the cop said, "Forest Adams, I'm going to administer some drinking tests."

"You're wasting your time, Officer," Doc said, recognizing the officer as the one who had spoken about drinking and driving at a Rotary Club meeting some months before.

"Everyone says, 'I'm not drinking.' Folks stop for a few drinks with friends, suddenly realize how late it is, and say their goodbyes. A question overloads their minds as they head for their car. Am I too drunk to drive? The next thing they know, they're in a wreck on Cemetery Hill, and Trooper Ogden is there with a Breathalyzer to catch them driving under the influence."

"Nice story, Officer, but I haven't had a drink today."

"And we're going to check that statement for accuracy. Let's get in my car for a Breathalyzer test."

Doc took a deep breath and expelled it into the analyzer. He continued until the officer said, "OK. That's plenty."

After checking the results, the officer muttered, "I'll be. No alcohol."

"That's what I told you?" Doc said quietly.

"I heard you . . . ah, skip it. It's not important."

"You get a call from George Hackett?" Doc asked, thinking Hackett's threats were already coming true. Drunk driving could be the misconduct charge Hackett needed to cause Doc's forfeiture of termination pay.

Ogden didn't answer as he headed to the woman's car, where she remained sitting on the side of her seat, holding the handkerchief to her nose. "You sure you're all right?" the officer asked.

"Physically, yes, but I tried to make a call and have no reception here."

"Reception's spotty in Cameron County. I need to check your driver's license and registration, Miss . . . ?"

"Merry Morehouse," Merry answered as she retrieved her cards and handed them to the officer.

"Hmmm. First time I saw Merry spelled that way."

"I was born on Christmas."

"Do you have someone to give you a ride?"

"I don't have a ride, but I have a place to stay if I can find it," Merry said as she handed the officer her map and directions.

"I don't recognize this place. Maybe Mr. Adams knows where it is located."

Trooper Ogden motioned Doc over, and they looked at the directions with his flashlight. "I think you're holding the map upside down. The tree farm is on the north side of the Hicks Run Road, and Quail Run Road is on the south side. That road's easy to miss. I can get you there and arrange to have your car picked up for repairs."

"What's the ride going to cost? I'm not loaded with money."

"Maybe a smile. It's been a rough day."

"I can vouch for Mr. Adams," Trooper Ogden said. "He's trustworthy."

"But not trustworthy enough to take his word about drinking," Doc inserted.

"Come on. I have a job to do," Ogden pleaded. "Merry, if you're OK with his help, I'll be going. If not, I'll call a trooper to assist you."

"If he's willing to help a stranger, I'll happily accept."

Merry stumbled as she turned toward Doc's truck, and he tried to steady her, "Let me help you."

"Get your hand off me!" Merry screamed.

Surprised, Doc jerked his hand away, and shrugging his shoulders, he walked her to the truck. "Merry, the camp you're looking for is nowhere to go in the dark, especially on a night like this. You can stay at our place, and we can go over in the morning."

"If it's all the same to you, I'd like to go over there tonight."

"You got a gun?"

"Gun?" she asked, angrily crossing her arms. "No, I don't have a freaking gun." Her voice grew louder as she took off on guns. "Nobody should have guns. They kill people. They should all be collected and burned!"

"They also protect people when they're out in the middle of nowhere on a stormy night like this with a wrecked car, no idea where they are or what to do, don't know anybody, and their phone won't work.

"You sound like an NRA spokesman," she said, slapping the seat with her fist.

"Just a member," he softly replied.

"One's as bad as the other."

"Lady, you don't have to holler. I'm right here beside you."

"You weren't listening."

"Heard every word. Look, I'm not trying to scare you. Just hard to believe you came here alone after dark."

"Coming here is the dumbest thing I've ever done," she muttered through clenched teeth. "Wrecked my car. And this gun crap drives me nuts. They should be collected and melted down."

She has a lot to consider, Doc thought. Nobody might ever know if I raped and killed her. While she considered the mess she was in, Doc quietly asked, "Can I offer you a place to bunk tonight?"

After a deep sigh and a few moments of consideration, she softly said, "I'd appreciate your help, but what's your wife going to say?"

"She passed away last year," Doc muttered with pain in his voice.

"I'm so sorry," Merry muttered with a face drowning in fear. She'd be alone with a stranger in this desolate place.

"Let's get your clothes in the back seat and the other stuff in the back. Our son runs a body shop in Emporium. We can try to call him. My phone grabs a signal when others don't. Maybe he can pick your car up tonight."

"Sounds good if you're willing to do that."

"Been a rough day. A little friendly company might feel good."

CHAPTER 4

"What's next?" Merry muttered as she stared out the window at her car, her arms crossed.

"Thank the Lord," Doc softly answered.

"What?" Merry asked, her voice dripping anger.

Doc quietly answered, "I'm thankful you weren't hurt any worse than you were. My truck's drivable. We didn't get arrested."

"Well, goodie for us. What was I thinking when I decided to come to this godforsaken place?"

"Can you grab my phone in the glove compartment?" Doc asked, softly changing the subject.

Merry did as asked and cringed with pain when she bent over. When she turned toward him, he noticed the welt on her face. "You got a pretty good banging. Are you sure you don't need a doctor?"

"Maybe a psychiatrist. I had to be nuts to come here. But otherwise, I'm OK."

"Merry, isn't it?"

"Yeah."

"We shouldn't leave your car sitting here. Can I call a tow truck?"

"Guess there isn't anything else to do."

Doc ran down through numbers without comment until he came to Ronnie's. "Sarah? Doc here. Ronnie available?"

"Hi, Doc. You sound upset. Problem?"

"Nothing earth-shattering."

"Ron just got home. Hang on! I'll get him."

"Yeah, Dad," Ron soon answered. "What's happening?"

"Had a wreck and —"

"You hurt?" Ron interrupted.

"No, but we need a wrecker."

"Where you at?"

"Game Commission parking lot across from the Moore Hill Cemetery."

"Two vehicles?"

"One. I can drive my truck. Got a broken headlight. Can you bring one along?"

"What's the other vehicle?"

Doc looked at Merry and asked, "Your car a Chevy Cruze?"

"A wrecked Chevy Cruze," Merry answered, emphasizing "wrecked."

"Did I hear Chevy Cruze?"

"You did," Doc replied. "Sarah said you just got home. Had a chance to eat yet?"

"No, but Sarah said she'd make me a sandwich to eat on the way. See you in about 45 minutes."

"Can you stop at Kitty's and grab a dinner? I'll order one for you too. Baked fish work for you?"

"Always, but are you gonna eat in front of him?" Ron asked.

"I already ate. The dinner's for a her."

"Ooooh. A her?"

"Don't get any ideas."

"Gotcha."

"We'll wait where our road hits the Hill Road?"

"See you ASAP."

"You like fish, Merry? Kitty's Place has the best-baked fish around. Their New Orleans is special."

"That'll do," she answered crisply.

Doc dialed Kitty's Place, and when Bud answered, he asked, "You still serving?"

"This you, Doc? Thought you ate earlier?"

"I did, Bud. Ran into a friend who hasn't eaten yet. I'd like to order two New Orleans baked fish dinners to go. Ronnie'll pick 'em up shortly. Put 'em on my tab."

"We'll have 'em ready."

"Ran into a friend? What's that about?" Merry demanded.

"Just making conversation," Doc said. "Wanta see if we can spot some wildlife on the way home?"

"Whatever," Merry said.

Her comments screwed Doc's face in wonderment as he reached under his seat for the spotlight. Putting the truck in gear, he mentioned she hadn't buckled her seat belt. Plugging the spotlight in the lighter, he waited for her to buckle up, and when she didn't, he mentioned it again.

"I heard you the first time. I don't use seat belts. They wrinkle your clothes and confine you."

"Like Billy told complaining kids, 'They aren't nearly as confining as wheelchairs,'" Doc said in a soft voice. "We fasten belts in our vehicles before we move! Keeps faces from smashing into windshields."

Merry breathed loudly and buckled her seat belt. "You happy now?"

"Merry, I've had a difficult day," Doc quietly explained as he pulled onto the Hill Road. "I'd like to have a more pleasant evening."

"Wanta see if we can spot some wildlife on the way home?"

"Whatever."

With a scowl riding his face, he drove off. Running the spotlight along the first field, he saw grazing deer. "Five deer."

"I see them."

He continued scanning another clearing and came across two bull elk feeding. "Elk."

"I see them."

Disgusted, Doc spotted the fields along the way, stopping without comment to look at feeding animals. He turned into Spring Brook Road and pulled off to the side. Ronnie soon arrived in his wrecker, and Doc walked back to meet him holding Merry's car keys.

"Novel way to get dates, Dad. Run into them on the road."

"No date, Ronnie. Can't even call 'I see them' a friend."

"I see them?"

"That's about all she said on the ride over from the cemetery. Looks like a long night. Can you haul her vehicle in and look it over? Order the needed parts. She has insurance, or she couldn't keep a license. Here's her key."

"I'll check it over tomorrow evening. I gotta pack for an art show tonight. Oh, here's her dinner. Your headlight too."

"Thanks, buddy. I'll pay ya next week."

"Guess I can trust you that long." Ronnie smiled.

Doc shook his head as he walked back and climbed in, handing the boxed meal to Merry. "If you can wait, we'll be home in a few minutes."

"How far is it?"

"About a mile and a half."

"On this dirt road?" she asked, her fear evident.

"On this dirt road."

Three-fourths of a mile later, Doc stopped and opened his gate.

"We aren't there yet?" she asked as he struggled into the truck. Her voice carried more fear than anger, and her face showed white in the interior lights.

"Halfway," Doc answered as they rolled down the steep wooded mountainside toward home.

"Why would anyone choose to live back here?"

"Guess we wanted to punish ourselves."

"We're here," he announced as they pulled in, the motion detector turning on the spotlights, and a big German shepherd came running. The dog waited, noticed the passenger, and barked. Doc ordered, "Jack. Sit!"

Merry jumped back in the truck when she saw Jack. "C'mon," Doc urged. "He won't hurt you."

Merry hesitantly climbed out with a worried look. Jack remained sitting and pointed with his right paw when she rounded the truck.

"He's going to attack me!" she screamed, holding the dinner over her head.

"He's welcoming you. Wants to shake hands."

"With a dog?"

"Not just any dog. Jack, the dog who lives here."

Hesitantly, Merry ever so lightly touched his paw. Jack stood, whining gently, and turned to Doc. "Good boy. Meet Merry. She'll be staying with us for a while."

"Just the night," Merry said with a forced smile. "I have a place to stay after tonight." Looking around and seeing the house with little else in the dark, she muttered, "Big house for an end-of-the-world place."

"Not quite the end of the world, but you can see it from here," Doc offered as he unlocked the front door and turned on the lights. Holding the door for her, he said, "Bathroom's on your right, and the kitchen's straight through the living room. You'll find silverware in the top drawer beside the kitchen sink. Beverages are in the reefer. There's a microwave if you need it. Make yourself at home. I'll be back."

"Where are you going?" she asked.

"Think I'll go to town for a while. Doesn't seem like I'm welcome here."

As he watched fear rising in her face, he smiled, "I'm going out to feed the horses."

"You have horses?"

"Three. I give 'em grain when I come home. That's why you hear 'em stomping."

Doc turned off the switch that ran the dog security system and headed for the barn where the motion sensor turned on the outside lights. The horses stood nickering in their stalls. He grabbed metal cans in the feed bin, filled them, and talked to each horse as he poured feed into their boxes. "Sinbad, you've been rolling in the mud again, you darned heathen."

Sinbad whinnied as if he understood what Doc was telling him.

After throwing hay in their mangers, he grabbed a curry comb and brush and walked into Sinbad's stall, talking as he worked him over, first with the comb and then the brush. With him completed, he decided to go over the others to allow Merry time to eat. Finished, he headed to the house. Jack quickly sat by Merry, and she just looked at him.

"You act like you've never petted a dog before."

"We weren't allowed pets. You're the first person I ever met with horses."

"Maybe that's why you weren't impressed with deer and elk."

"No, I was just an ignorant ass, and I'm sorry."

"Apology unneeded but appreciated. Hey, is that a pie dish?"

"Apple pie. It came with the meal. Thanks."

"I'll be. Kitty never threw dessert in for me. Wait'll I see her."

"What do I owe you? It was delicious."

"We can go there for a fish fry next Friday if you want," Doc answered.

Seeing her body tighten, Doc added, "I'm thinking as friends, not a date."

Merry loosened a bit and said, "I won't be here Friday."

Doc knew it might be Friday or a rental car if she decided to head home because it would take time to get the needed parts.

"Let's bring in your things. We'll set your cooler and food inside and take your clothes upstairs. My bedroom's on the left at the top of the stairs. The first door on the left going down the hall is a bathroom, and the next door on the left is a bedroom Billy uses for her office. There are two bedrooms on the right side of the hall and another at the end. You'll feel most comfortable in the second bedroom on the right. It's Cindy's. The door locks."

"Cindy's not home?"

"She teaches in Harrisburg."

"Oh. Why did you mention the door locked?" Merry asked in a concerned voice.

"Telling you there's privacy, and you don't need to be afraid."

"Should I be afraid of you?" she asked, her arched brows drawing together.

"No, but a rapist might say the same thing."

When they carried her cooler in from the truck, he said, "We better put this in the pantry."

"There's nothing in there but stuff to eat."

"Bears and coyotes live here. They tear up coolers and eat the food when it's left outside."

"Really?"

"Really. Let's get your stuff in before the noseeums get us."

"Noseeums?"

"Tiny insects that cause burning skin rashes. We'll soon feel 'em if we don't get movin'."

The thought of bug bites spurred Merry into action, and they quickly carried her things inside. Doc carried her suitcases up, sat them by her door, and headed downstairs, wondering why she needed two suitcases for a one-week camping trip. She stopped to check out a bedroom, and turning on the light, she screamed.

"Help!"

Doc was limping downstairs when she streamed into his arms, almost knocking him over. "What's wrong?"

She trembled, looking up at him with frightened eyes with pain bringing tears to her eyes. "There's a... a. . . a bear in that bedroom."

"He's stuffed."

He held Merry, and looking at him, she whispered, "A stuffed real bear?"

"Yeah. Ronnie got it when he was fifteen. Live weight was about 550 pounds. He taxidermied it himself."

"Taxidermied?"

"As in stuffed."

"I'm sorry for grabbing you," she whispered in a hoarse voice as she moved away. "I was so scared. I turned the light on, and the bear stood there ready to eat me."

You want Cindy's room, the next one down the hall. Three times being scared should be enough for one night."

"Three times?"

"Getting run over by a hillbilly, attacked by a wolf in the front yard, and scared by a bear. It's the rule of threes."

Merry smiled lightly at his inferences, her first smile since they met. "Can I change and meet you downstairs?"

"Sure. Shower if you want. Towels, washcloths, and Billy's smell pretty stuff are in the closet behind the bathroom door. There's also Biofreeze in there to help with your pain. I'll be downstairs when you finish."

The fireplace held a large Kodiak wood stove insert capable of heating the home in the coldest weather. He soon had a beautiful fire dancing red that eliminated the spring chill. With the fire burning, Doc moved to his old green swivel rocker, the first piece of new furniture he bought with Billy. Though well worn, it remained comfortable. He often read himself to sleep and rocked two kids to sleep in it. Billy wanted to replace it, but memories wouldn't allow it.

His mind rambled through this night since the cemetery accident. He rode across the hill with this young woman whose life seemed to be falling off a cliff, a person suffering obvious pain from the crash and maybe something more from the fear she exhibited. The bear-induced hug ran by, and he decided he had better think about something else.

Picking up his Bible, guilt grabbed him for not reading it like he should during this challenging period. This night he badly needed the Lord. The Proverbs chapter he opened to talked of a woman coming out to meet a man, and Merry pictures streamed through his mind. She was a beautiful woman with long amber hair and hazel eyes. The one time she offered a genuine smile, he noted perfect white teeth. Something about her reminded him of Billy, but he couldn't put his finger on it. Sure wasn't Billy's warm, easy-to-get-along-with personality. When she charged into him on the stairs, he could feel her breasts against him, and he found it difficult to let go of the thoughts of her.

"Sorry, Lord. You know I love Billy."

Chapter 5

A door opened upstairs, and a woman emerged, first tan slacks and a dark green blouse, and then Merry's face. An attractive, unblemished, but sad face, Doc thought as his eyes followed her down the open stairs.

"It's nice in here, and the fire's beautiful," Merry announced as she walked over to watch the dancing flames. Rubbing her hands, she added, "You didn't have to do this for me."

She's more than enough to light off any man, Doc thought as she walked to a chair. "We have fires most nights in cooler weather. Makes a house home."

"My parents have two fireplaces. They lit one on Christmas Eve years ago. My father considered them messy and said wood cost too much. They converted to gas but still didn't use them."

"We love to watch the fire while we read and discuss things. Not much we enjoy on TV. We watch Blue Bloods, Bull, maybe an NCIS, and now and then a Hallmark always-ends-right movie. Sometimes Billy watches HGTV. Provides ideas for her Honey-Do jar."

As he watched Merry studying her surroundings, Doc viewed the room in a new light. The furniture selection was unplanned, with holdovers from Billy's parents and cherry benches from her grandparents. Furniture sat on oak flooring partially covered by a faded American Indian pattern carpet and throw rugs. The swivel rockers they sat in were well-used. Another chair and a hide-a-bed sofa sat against one end wall with a coffee table loaded with family pictures under glass. They faced a large stone fireplace surrounded by bookshelves and a TV. Framed artwork, photos, and various awards covered the walls. Spotting his book, she asked, "You reading anything interesting?"

Doc nodded. "My Bible."

"Really? We never had a Bible in our house."

"Sorry to hear that."

It was quiet for a bit while Merry processed his comment. Deciding to change the subject, she said, "Thanks for the shower. There were so many suds it seemed like I was in a TV commercial. What do you do to your water?"

"Spring water. Comes out of the mountain that way."

Merry watched Jack move from lying beside Doc's chair to sitting at attention beside hers with his right paw resting on her knee. Concerned, she looked at Jack and gently touched his head. Jack licked her hand, an action she didn't know how to handle. "Things are different here."

"Different?"

"Yes. Water. People. Life. I entered a nightmare when I exited I-80. I was turning around to head home when I ran into you. To say I was terrified is an understatement, but it's getting easier. Jack's a gentleman. Then there's you. I wrecked your vehicle, and instead of cursing and threatening me with a lawsuit, you helped me. You didn't seem to notice I was scared of being alone with a man I didn't know."

"Oh, I noticed. Your face was an 'I need help' billboard with fear stalking it. Noticed your pain too."

"You always help people?"

"Don't you?"

"Maybe a few. Some have taken me for a ride. I'm in the middle of a ride right now," Merry said, crossing her arms and rolling her eyes.

"Can't judge everyone by the actions of a few. Gramp said if you help folks needing help, you'll receive help when you need it. Maybe not from people you helped but from someone. I've received a lot of help in my life," Doc responded.

"From strangers?"

"Some."

"What do you expect from me?"

After searching for an answer, Doc said, "Maybe a smile. You had a pretty one the only time you used it."

Merry smiled and shook her head. As she considered his comment, a blush came to her face. "Do you think a smile will work for your son? He rescued my car in the middle of the night. Brought me dinner too. It's hard to believe."

"Ron's a good Samaritan. Takes after his mother."

"Good Samaritan?" she asked with a puzzled look.

"Forgot. You don't read the Bible."

"Only went to church five or six times. Let's see, three weddings, no four. Yeah, four weddings and two funerals."

"That's it for church and no Bibles?" Doc asked, shaking his head.

"My father said Bibles contain unbelievable garbage written by BS-ers to give hope to the weak. He said our family takes care of itself. Even mentioning Bibles brought on one of his curse-laden speeches."

"Hard to believe."

"What's hard to believe?" Her face darkened, and with clipped words, she began, "Come on, Mr. Adams, you're smarter than that. Don't you think if there were a concerned god, she'd do away with pain, poverty, disease, and other human sufferings?"

After thinking through her statement, Doc softly replied, "No one ever accused me of brilliance, but my life's complete with a caring God who's lifted me out of life's swamps. You're His latest helper."

"Me? How can you believe that?"

"Easy. You cannot believe where my mind was when we collided. Something else. It's hard for me to believe one could think the Bible is unbelievable garbage if one hasn't read it. I find the Bible easier to believe than some science-type stuff."

"Such as?" Merry asked, recrossing her arms with a disdainful look on her face.

"Stuff like the evolution of humans beginning with lightning flashing on pond slime. I'm more into the Bible's creation story."

"Can we talk about something else?" Merry suggested while glaring into the fire. Jack laid his head on her leg as if he felt sorry for her. She paid no attention to him at first, but when he whined and looked at her with sad eyes, she stroked his head until he laid down beside her.

Time passed quietly until Doc asked, "Can we still talk with each other?"

"As long as it's not about Bibles."

Merry's eyes followed Doc when he added wood to the fire. "Almost let the fire go out. You'll be thinking I'm from ... Where'd you grow up?"

"Outside Philly."

"You'll be thinking I'm from outside Philly."

"I don't think so. You're from Cameron County?"

"Sterling County, Texas."

"Texas? Really?" she carried a puzzled look and asked, "How'd you get here?"

"Brought by an angel, but that's a story for another time."

They sat watching the fire until Doc asked, "How'd you get here?"

Merry smiled. "Maybe you forgot. You brought me here."

"Ok. Why'd you come to Cameron County?"

"My supposed friend Arianna discovered I hadn't been camping and decided to show me the ropes. A guy with a cabin permitted us to use his place. I'm here."

"Where's Arianna?"

"Good question. Everything was a go until she called and said something came up. She dropped off the stuff for the cabin at my place."

"And you came by yourself?" Doc asked, shaking his head in disbelief.

"I gave myself a big girl talk, packed my stuff, and here I am."

"Pretty fancy outfit, but it doesn't fit here."

"This happens to be very comfortable."

"Look great too, but it doesn't work for camping. Folks here don't dress that fancy for church."

"You would've gone ape if I'd have come down in a dress."

"Tell me you didn't bring a dress on a camping trip."

"I can't," she said, smiling shyly.

"You bring any Levi's?"

"No. I thought the place we were visiting would be like my family's place in the Poconos."

"We'll look through Billy's things in the morning. You two seem to be about the same size."

"You've been checking me out for size?" Merry asked with a wry grin.

A flush came over Doc's face. "Hard not to notice a pretty woman."

CHAPTER 6

Merry caught a case of shivers looking at the deadbolt and sliding bolt locks on Cindy's door. Maybe Cindy and I share the same problem; Merry speculated as she used both locks and braced a chair under the door handle for additional protection.

I'm scared, Merry thought. Doc could be a sexual pervert. Being nice could be part of his game. He seemed safe, but appearing harmless and being safe could be worlds apart. She discovered that truth years before.

Merry, your big girl self has you in a mess, she told herself as she looked in the mirror, noting the pain riding her face. Leaked rumors suggested significant changes were in the wind at WLDZ. I could be job hunting, and I so hate that. There goes my wrecked car and condo if I'm out of a job very long. I got lost, wrecked into a hillbilly, and petted my first dog. Then there was that darned bear. Only his incidents in my entire life scared me more.

Struggling away from those problems and back to her current dilemma, she asked herself, What possessed me? I was unprepared for a week in these god-forsaken mountains, and now I have no car.

Even more, how am I going to pay my accident deductible? For sure, I can't rely on Doc.

Thoughts of this square-jawed man with thick, black hair and blue eyes grabbed her and wouldn't let go. There's something very different about him; she rationalized and couldn't decide if it was a peaceful or scary difference.

Where's my life headed, she wondered as she turned out the light and cracked the window. A million stars drilled holes through the black night, a site this city girl wasn't used to. She slipped into bed and soon heard noises sounding like wolves howling. Others joined from different directions. Doc's shushing followed Jack's growl. After a while, it went quiet.

Real quiet. And somewhere in time, sleep came.

But sleep didn't last long. Merry awoke to a man screaming. A dog barked, more yelling, and then it got quiet again. She fell back to sleep, and night passed until she was jerked awake by a strange noise. She opened her eyes, squinting in the sunshine cascading in the window. Where in the world am I, she wondered as she looked around the strange bedroom, a bedroom with beautiful photos adorning soft green walls. Animals. Flowers. Birds. Scenes.

The noise began again, and she remembered where she was and what brought her here. The scratching sound at her door must be the dog; she thought as she struggled painfully out of bed, carefully slid into her robe, and headed for the bathroom. Opening the door a crack to check, she found no sign of Jack other than the noise running down the steps. It had to be the dog.

CHAPTER 7

After completing morning chores, Doc fired off the old cookstove, chasing away the brisk breath of spring. He washed his hands and began working on breakfast.

"Doc?" a low voice called from the stairs a bit later.

"In the kitchen."

Coffee and freshly cooked food smells grabbed her taste buds as she rubbed sleep bugs from her eyes. "Wow! I smell something good."

Doc stood over the stove cooking. "How do you like your eggs?" he asked without turning.

"Any way someone is willing to cook them."

"How's over easy on rye toast sound?"

"Great. How'd you know I was up?"

"I didn't. Knew you'd be getting up. Sent Jack to get you."

"That's why he was scratching on the door and whining?"

"He's getting bacon treats for doing a good job."

"You get out of bed early to cook breakfast?"

"Fed Jack and the horses, installed a new headlight in my truck, carried in some firewood, and built a fire before I cleaned up for breakfast."

"I didn't even hear your alarm."

"Silent alarm. Jack's paw at five. Pour yourself some coffee. Cups are in the cabinet above the pot. Sugar's there too. Might be a little hard. We seldom use it. Milk's in the reefer."

"Was that wolves howling last night?"

"Coyotes," Doc answered as he turned, noting she was wearing a beautiful robe that presented a sensual body. "You're looking good this morning."

"What?" Merry asked with a look that said she was unsure how to take his comment. Looking around, she asked, "Do you always cook like this? I see potatoes, bacon, and eggs."

"Pancakes are staying warm in the oven. Billy and I take turns cooking breakfast on weekends," Doc said as he carried food to the table. "She's a great cook. I make up for lack of ability with tonnage and variety."

Merry managed a grin as he pulled out her chair, nodded for her to sit, and helped her slide toward the table. He sat beside her and reached for her hand to ask the blessing, but she jerked away.

"Keep your hands off me," she barked, fear evident in her voice.

He gave her a puzzled look. "What's that all about?"

"I don't trust men, and I don't want to be grabbed by one!"

After shaking his head with a 'what gives' look, Doc prayed, ". . . and keep us ever mindful of the needs of others. Thank you, Lord. Amen. And now, please pass the pancakes, Merry."

Merry handed him the pancakes, and when their eyes met, she acted like she held a question that needed answering.

"What?" he asked.

She paused, getting her ideas in order. "Do you always pray before you eat?"

"Don't you?"

"I never pray about anything."

"You didn't pray when some old hillbilly talked you into his truck out in the middle of nowhere?"

"Should I have?"

"I prayed," Doc said, shrugging his shoulders. "Asked our Lord to make it right for both of us. News reports suggest a woman can get raped anywhere, while others yelled rape when it didn't happen. If you need to move, I'll understand."

"I'll be fine right here," she growled. "What are these?" she asked, pointing at the daffodil, narcissus, and hyacinth bouquet.

"Hill folks call 'em posies," Doc replied with a silly 'what gives' grin.

"Alright, smarty, what are you up to?"

"Up to as in what?" Doc demanded.

"Are you trying to tell me something?" Merry asked with embarrassment crawling across her face.

"Billy always has in-season posies."

Merry smelled the flowers. "They're beautiful. Smell great, too. We never had flowers on the breakfast table." Looking past them, she asked, "What's with those over there, the ones that are all dried out?"

Hesitating, he shook his head, searching for words. "Billy's last bouquet. Haven't found the strength to throw 'em away."

Doc tossed Jack food, and together they finished firsts. When he finished loading his plate with seconds, he glanced at Merry.

"What are you looking at?" she asked with a disapproving scowl.

"A pretty woman," he answered with a smile.

"I don't think so."

"Some learned scholar said beauty's in the eye of the beholder. I'm the beholder."

She shook her head with a mean look and glanced back at her plate. The next time Doc looked her way, he found her checking out the kitchen with an 'I can't believe this' look of wonderment. She stopped to stare at the old cookstove.

"Not used to a kitchen like this?" he asked

"It's different," she answered, her face red with embarrassment.

"It ain't your usual city kitchen. The thing grabbing your attention is a wood cookstove that's making it warm in here. It belonged to Billy's grandparents. Comes in handy when we lose power."

"My parents have an emergency generator that comes on when the power goes off," she replied with a disdaining look.

Smiling, Doc said, "We have a generator but use kerosene lamps until it looks like power will be off for a while. That wood stove cooks great meals. Takes the chill off when we have cool mornings like this one."

While they ate, they discussed plans for the day. Merry looked at him and said, "I think you'd like me out of your hair, so I'll clean up and be on my way. I've caused you enough problems."

"Let me remind you of a conversation we fought past last night. It concerns staying alone in the mountains with no protection, no car, and a phone that doesn't work. Even if your phone worked, it would take cops most of an hour to get out there."

Merry's eyes watered as she crossed her arms. "Why do you paint such horrifying pictures?"

"It's life out here. That trooper filed a report that says a young woman wrecked her car looking for that camp. Then the people the trooper talked to mentioned it to a half dozen other people in a 'can you believe what this good-lookin' woman is doing to herself' manner and then —"

"Stop!" Merry demanded. "I get the idea. What would you recommend? I'm not interested in handouts. I don't even know you."

"Let's try this again," Doc said smiling. "I'm Doc. You're Merry. Now we know each other. I'm not offering handouts. I'm offering a hand up."

"What's the difference?"

"One's welfare and the other's paid-forward support. We have a daughter. I hope someone is around to help her if she finds herself involved in a problem. Maybe you don't get it. You ain't fixed to protect yourself."

"You didn't ask for my problems."

"No, and I didn't ask for your company, but I got it. Might get to enjoy it if you lighten up," Doc said, shaking his head. "Together, we can tackle your problems. My first recommendation is to go up to my bedroom after breakfast and look for some hill country clothes. I left Billy's closet door open. Levis and flannel shirts are hangin' in there. The drawer in the chest that's pulled open contains various kinds of socks. What size shoes do you wear?"

"Eights, but are you sure you want someone wearing Billy's clothes?"

"She shares. You're in luck with the shoes. I think she wears an eight-and-a-half. If you're afraid of catching some terrible foot disease, I'll spray the shoes with smell good kill bad stuff spray."

Merry grinned. "I think I wound you up. Sorry. Merry will do as told. I'll be down dressed as ordered. And Doc, thanks for helping me."

After breakfast cleanup, Doc stood in front of the house throwing a stick for Jack when Merry arrived on the porch looking great in

Billy's clothes. They fit better than Doc imagined. The yellow flannel shirt lit up hazel eyes that provided beauty few women enjoyed.

"Merry, I've been thinking. Someone set you up."

"What gives you that idea?" she grumbled, crossing her arms.

"What if I told you a supposed friend wanted to take me on a trip to a city when I was never in a city before? At the last minute, he tells me something came up and suggests I go by myself. Notice any problems?"

"Oh, man, I must be blind!" Merry said, shaking her head in disbelief.

CHAPTER 8

"Merry, you can call people to let 'em know you're ok."

Her crossed arms and tightened lips shouted, 'No way.' "Right. I'm not calling anyone who is a part of this. I feel more than a little dumb coming here."

"Maybe yer too trusting. You climbed into a wrecked truck with an old derelict at night in the middle of nowhere —"

"Stop!" she snapped. "I'm not talking about here here. And I was desperate, not trusting."

She smiled lightly, and Doc noticed her smiles were coming easier. "You may want to call your insurance agent today. Tell 'em you had an accident and your car's at a garage in Emporium. Don't volunteer information. Just answer their questions and stop. If they ask if other vehicles were involved, tell 'em, yes, but the State Police investigated and deemed it no-fault. Once again, don't —"

"— volunteer any additional information." After a thinking pause, she asked, "Why are you so interested in helping me?"

"I owe for all the help I've received. Grab your cameras and camp package. You'll want a jacket."

When Merry turned to leave, Doc remembered the insurance call. "Better call your insurance company."

"Can't we do that when we come back?"

"Let's do it now. Agents may only work until noon on Saturday."

"Man, you act like a parent!" she said, shaking her head.

"I am a parent, just not yours. By the way, who do you have for insurance?"

"State Farm."

"Us too. Their local number is on the cover of the phonebook."

After making the call, she went for a jacket while Doc changed legs. After checking his stump, he pulled on his work boot leg, adjusted the elastic sleeve, and then pulled a boot on his good foot.

Merry called from the coat closet, "Sure takes men a long time to put on boots."

"Just some men," Doc answered, trying to stand without her noticing his problem. "After you," he said, waiting for her to turn toward the door before he took his first steps. With everything working, he grabbed his jacket before heading out.

Doc pulled out his keys as he opened her door. Merry eased into her seat and set her cameras and camp package by her feet. Jack jumped into the back seat, his tail wagging happily. Crawling in, Doc noticed Merry watching him flip his right leg in and slide into his seat. Squinting against the morning sun, Doc asked, "Got any ideas about what we might find at the camp?"

"I'm anxious to get there but afraid of what we might find. Charlie's comments seem like warning signals."

Doc took his time across the mountain so Merry could view her surroundings. Arriving at their turn, Doc said, "Be easy to miss this road, especially after dark."

"This it?" Merry asked, looking at her directions.

"Yeah."

"Not much of a road."

Doc stopped in front of a small cabin with a big front porch. Merry jumped out and had the key out of the camp bag when Doc walked up and saw the muddy porch. "Took a real hog to leave this mess. Oh, and look, bear tracks. Big bear, too."

"A bear? Let's get out of here. Had enough of the stuffed one."

"He's long gone. That key work?"

"No."

Looking at the key she held, Doc said. "This is a padlock key, not a door key."

"It says 'Door Key' on the tag."

"Maybe someone switched tags."

"Charlie used it last. He'd delight in screwing us up. Maybe that's why he volunteered to come up on Saturday. Figured we'd be sleeping in our car."

With hands-on-hips and a nasty facial expression, Merry watched Doc thinking through the problem. "Let's go," Merry said. "We can't get in without a key."

"Ya know, you're beautiful when you get torqued."

"Get what?" Merry asked, her anger showing.

"Like you are right now. You want to get in here?"

"Not if we have to wreck the place."

"Let's check the windows and back door. Maybe one is unlocked."

They found all of them locked. "We might as well leave."

"Not yet. Most people have hideout keys."

"You have a hideout key for your place?"

"Yeah. Remind me to show you when we get home. You might need to know."

"I'm not planning on staying that long," Merry said, her hands squeezed into fists.

Doc considered her comment and smiled, then tapped the porch for her to sit beside him. She paused before reluctantly sitting down, leaving plenty of space between them. "Think where you might hide a key."

"I don't hide keys because I don't lose keys."

"You might someday and wish you had one hidden."

After checking under the porches and the porch rafters, Doc walked back to what looked like the outhouse and found it locked.

Working around the back, he checked the roof rafters for a key and found one hanging out of sight. He tried it in the outhouse padlock, and it worked. Success, he told himself and looked skyward, mouthing, "Thanks."

Opening the door, he discovered what had been an outhouse was now a storage shed. Feeling over the door, he found a key that looked like it might fit a door lock.

Merry was sitting on the porch when he arrived. "You ready to give up?" she asked.

"I think we're in," he said as he tried the key in the door lock. "Sure enough. Let's check it out."

"Really?" Merry asked, surprise evident in her voice.

Doc stepped aside so she could walk in. "What a mess," she fumed when she flicked on the lights. "No wonder Charlie was so happy to know we were following him. He's such an ass."

Muddy boot tracks ran everywhere. Dirty dishes crowded the table with messy pots and greasy frying pans lining the stove. Unmade beds announced someone was proving a point.

"Let's get out of here," Merry said. "The place stinks."

"Let's think this through. You planned to be here all week and leaving when?"

"Sunday morning, and Bucky's brother's using it next?"

"He'll believe Bucky allowed this to happen."

"So be it! Let whoever made the mess clean the mess. I wrecked my car hunting for this shanty and couldn't even get in when I got here."

"Merry, you're in. I see you standing right there."

"Right! Nobody will know I was in here. I'll tell Bucky about the key when I get back."

"We'll know."

"Whatever?"

"You said Bucky went out of his way to prepare you to use his place. Do you want his brother upset with him after he tried to help you?"

"All right, Smarty, what would you do?" Merry asked, arms crossed.

"Me? I'd take a video of the mess before I began cleaning it. And while I was cleaning, I'd be thinking how to let the people who did this pay for their prank."

"Yeah, right!"

"Look, I'll do this myself. Just sit on the porch. I'll have this place cleaned in no time."

"I didn't see any cleaning equipment."

"The shed's full."

"Bucky's kit contains directions for turning the water and propane on."

"By the time we get the water on, fill the tank and water heater, and bleed the air out of the lines, we'll have it cleaned and be heading home."

"You taking charge of my life?"

Doc broke off the conversation and went to the shed, leaving Merry with crossed arms and a scowl on her face. She doesn't seem happy, he said to himself with a brief smile, realizing he enjoyed kidding her. He found two empty buckets in a plastic bag and a large steel pot to heat water. He placed the pot on the porch on his way to the spring. After filling the buckets, he stumbled some because the weight bothered his stub. He saw dirty bedclothes on the glider on his way in to heat water.

"I'll sweep inside until the dishwater's hot. I'll wash if you dry."

"I can't believe we're doing this," Merry said, shaking her head in disbelief as she watched Doc opening windows.

Doc and Merry washed, dried, and put away the dishes, swept and mopped the floors, and piled the dirty towels and washcloths with the bedclothes. "I'll mop the porches with the rinse water. We'll wash the dirty laundry at home and bring it back tomorrow."

"I don't know why we did it, but the place looks good."

"We're paying forward like the Guide Book directs us."

"Guide Book?"

"Yeah. Remind me, and I'll show you a copy on the way home. Now you might want to take an after-cleaning video while I scrub the porches? Before and afters may come in handy."

"For what?"

"Might lead to an opportunity."

"Are you nuts?"

"Winston Churchill said a pessimist sees the difficulty in every opportunity; an optimist sees the opportunity in every difficulty," Doc answered and prepared to sweep the porch. "Ever have an idea you didn't pursue, and someone else made it work? Billy and I saw opportunities in video presentations that interested us and held the potential to be quite profitable. We created them, and they supported our work at MELCOR. Billy's brother used them at his plant too."

"You might not believe this, but we just had a meeting at the TV station where I work looking for ideas on how to increase viewer percentages and corporate profit. I suggested ideas that had to do with video projects."

"What kind of video projects were you talking about?"

"Not dirty porches."

"Ok, not dirty porches, but what?"

"New York State and beach cities such as Ocean City, Maryland run endless commercials on our local TV stations showing recreational opportunities in their areas. I suggested we make videos for Pennsylvania and maybe a video about Hershey Park. Things like that."

"Were your ideas accepted?"

"My mentor liked them. I hope we'll discuss them when I return to work."

"You might want to get started on them while you're here."

"Right!" Merry said, ridiculing the idea. "I'll make a career out of videoing dirty cabins."

"Not dirty cabins. Why not these beautiful mountains and the animals that live here? People come from all over to see this place."

With that comment, Doc completed cleaning the porch and returned the stuff to the shed. Merry was sitting on the front steps holding her camera when he returned. "Two forty-seven," Doc said as he sat down beside her.

"What?"

"It took us two hours and forty-seven minutes to turn the mess into a castle."

"Charlie should have done it."

"Charlie wasn't here. We were. And don't cross your arms."

"What?"

"You always cross your arms when you're upset. Clench your fists when you get torqued."

They both smiled. "I think you're spending too much time looking at me."

"You're easy to look at. Got a beautiful smile when you use it. Lights up the room and me too." Smiling inside as her face grew red, he asked, "Aren't you glad you came to Cameron County? Look at all the things you would have missed."

"Like what? Getting lost, wrecking my car, and sitting here in dirty clothes that belong to someone else that I got filthy cleaning up someone else's mess in a shanty belonging to someone else. My parents wouldn't walk into the place now that it's clean. If I knew more about this cabin and its location before I came here, I wouldn't be here."

"And I woulda missed meetin' you and your company."

Shaking her head, Merry leaned against outstretched arms; her blouse tightened, revealing the figure she struggled to hide. Looking out across the mountains, she wore a ticked-off look. Feeling sorry, Doc gathered an understanding smile.

Turning and catching his smile, she asked, "You laughing at me."

"I wouldn't laugh at you. Just asked the God of hope to fill you with joy and peace."

"Where do you get this stuff?" she asked in a caustic voice, her forehead puckered.

"Book of Romans. You carried a rough look, and I thought that little prayer might help."

"Just thinking what my parents would say if they saw me now. Mother would shake her head, 'Oh Honey, you're so filthy. If I didn't know better, I'd think you were someone else.' My father would blow up in a rage. 'Merry, did you just climb out of a dumpster? I knew you'd make a mess of your life. You had the chance to be a lawyer at Morehouse, Peabody, and Rosenstein. Now look at you.'"

"You're kiddin?'" Doc asked with a look of wonderment on his face.

"Totally serious, but he would be cursing. I'd rather be sitting here in dirty clothes than stuck working with him."

"Your brother must not feel that way? You said he joined the firm."

"He wanted to become a Navy JAG officer. I can still hear our father yelling, 'It takes a real idiot to serve in the military when you can get a medical deferment for a freaking hangnail. I invested several hundred thousand bucks on your education, bought you nice cars, and kept you in spending money.' And he would have loaded up on four-letter words."

"Not in front of his family?"

"Oh yeah, in front of his family," Merry snorted, a mean look sliding across her face. "Sunny Da Morehouse has to be nuts to work with him."

"My family never faced that crap."

"Bet your kids have a different story to tell when Doc isn't around."

"They never heard a four-letter word from me, never saw their parents fighting, and they chose their careers."

"Aren't they fortunate?" she asked in a derogatory manner.

Shaking his head, Doc wondered how to approach the subject of her anger that hounded him. "Merry, this is your life, your one trip through."

"So what?"

"So maybe you should enjoy it. You don't seem to enjoy anything about anything. You're a sharp person who appears to be bent on throwing away what could be a great life in a job you don't like, with people you don't want to be around, with bad memories you won't let go of, and who knows what else."

"Ok, big guy, what should I change and how can I do it?" Merry asked, shaking her head and speaking with forced restraint.

"What would you like to do? What's your college degree?"

"I didn't know what I wanted to do, but I knew I didn't want to be a lawyer working with my father. I ended up with a liberal arts degree with a minor in multimedia studies."

"There you go," Doc said excitedly. "Why not put that multimedia stuff to work."

"Right!" Merry snapped. "I'll grab the next video project that drifts by."

"Didn't you just tell me that was an idea you put forth in that company meeting?"

"Yes, but I have no experience. That kind of project takes more than wishful thinking."

"Everyone has to start somewhere. Why not here," Doc implored, his voice filled with passion she hadn't witnessed before. "You have a video camera, maybe more talent than you realize, and we have the computer equipment."

Merry crossed her arms with her face growing red. "You can't be serious."

"Serious as a heart attack. What do you have to lose?"

57

Chapter 9

Doc slowed on Cemetery Hill. Glancing at Merry, he said, "Do me a favor. When we get home, remind me to send a letter to the county commissioners."

"About what?"

"Changing this hill's name to 'Collision Corners.'"

"Don't you ever let up?" she asked.

"Just wanted to be sure you were awake before I asked you to go to town for supper."

"I have pizza in my cooler."

"Got enough for Jack, the pizza lover?"

"Only ate a few pieces of a Pizza Hut Supreme."

"That should be enough for lunch. After the news, we'll run into Kitty's for prime rib. Bud makes the best rib going."

"My fish dinner come from there?"

"Yeah."

"Let's plan on Kitty's. My treat."

"We'll fight over the bill after we eat. Everybody likes fight scenes at Kitty's."

"Any more great ideas?"

"Yeah, It doesn't matter how much you like their soap; don't come out of their restroom sniffing your fingers."

"You're nuts!" she said, but her smile said she enjoyed it.

They rode along in silence until Doc stopped close to his mailbox and hit the button for Merry's window. "Can you check the second box from the left? That cardboard box on top will be ours too."

Merry opened the mailbox. "Man, when was the last time you checked your mail? The box is full."

"Last week."

After handing the mail to Doc, she strained to get the cardboard box in. "What if someone stole this box?"

"Wouldn't get much. Cindy sends me sections of the Harrisburg Patriot-News, plus the editorial section of their Sunday paper. She also sends sections of the New York Times, Washington Post, Wall Street Journal, and other papers she thinks I might like."

"Why would you want them?"

"Stray cats live in the barn. We spread newspapers out like litter boxes. Makes it easier to clean up after them."

"Are you kidding me?"

"Yeah. I read 'em when I have time. Been considering writing a book addressing how major media reports the news along with the complete story as it happened."

"You think there's a difference?" she demanded.

"Sometimes there are considerable differences between media coverage and witness statements, police reports, and court records."

"I work for a TV station, and we produce the complete story," Merry said, crossing her arms.

"Maybe the local news. What major TV media group do you carry?"

"CBS."

"You ever heard of Sharyl Attkisson?"

"I have, but why should I care?" Merry demanded, her voice displaying anger.

"Attkisson is known as a nonpartisan investigative journalist. I read that she resigned from CBS because of network news bias. She's a multi-time Emmy Award winner and received the Edward R. Murrow award for providing information the networks don't want you to have."

"Oh, she's a female Rush Limbaugh. I should believe her instead of CBS News?"

Shaking his head with a grin, he answered. "Attkisson is not Limbaugh. She provides the facts and allows you to think for yourself. Google her. She's a beautiful woman. You could be sisters. And she earned a fourth-degree black belt in taekwondo."

"Maybe that's so she can beat people if they disagree with her take on the news."

"Merry, how often do you watch Fox News?"

"Never!"

"Why's that?"

"I don't believe their coverage."

"Understood. It's conservative, and your beliefs tend to be more liberal. I seldom watch CNN or MSNBC because they favor the liberal side.

"Enough dammit!"

Doc let it drop and turned around in Beck's driveway. Merry calmed a bit as he turned into the road home. "The box on top of the mailbox amazes me. It could rain and ruin the contents."

"Nah. Wanda would pick it up and put a note in my box."

"Who's Wanda?"

"Bob Beck's wife. Let's thank her for helping me. Leaf through the mail, and we'll put anything that looks like a bill in her mailbox."

"You ever serious?"

"When I'm fighting about the news."

"Darn it, Doc," Merry said with a touch of irritation. "At times, you're difficult to understand."

"Sorry about that"

"Can I ask you a serious question?"

"You want a serious answer?"

"Yes." Pausing for the right words, Merry looked at him, "It's not my business, but I'm going to ask anyway. Why do you drive with your left leg at times?"

"Why wear out one leg when you can trade off."

"I'm serious."

"How about I show you when we get home," he said, hoping she'd forget by then.

Doc pulled in at home and backed around with Jack crying to get out. Merry was out as soon as the wheels stopped turning and opened the door for Jack. "Come with me," Doc waved, heading toward the barn, his limp more pronounced now that the day was wearing on. "Gotta show you something."

Merry stood by as Doc opened the barn door. "Where would you begin looking if you needed a hideout house key?"

"Until today, I had no idea people had hideout keys."

Doc ran his hand behind a nondescript wooden cabinet hanging on the barn wall and retrieved a key. "That's the house key," he said, replacing it. "Wanted you to know where it was just in case."

"In case of what?"

"In case you decided to kill me and locked the house before you stole my truck, then wanted back in the house to get your suitcases. Something like that."

Merry didn't answer but shook her head with a painful look as they quietly walked to the house. Doc grabbed the mail out of the truck and hurried to hold the door for her. As he closed the door, she asked, "Weren't you going to show me something?"

"I showed you the key in case —"

"Something else."

"Only if you remembered."

Doc dropped into the chair, swung around, and picked up his other leg with the matching shoe before turning back around. Without saying anything, he pulled up his pant leg.

"I'm sorry, Doc. This is none of my business. I —"

"You'd know sooner or later."

Merry held a wanting-to-know-more look but changed the subject, "Are you ready for stale pizza?"

"I am. Let's put your cooler stuff in the reefer."

"Reefer? Are we talking marijuana smokes?"

"Reefer's Navy slang for refrigerator."

Doc finished changing legs and washed his hands and face before digging out plates and two beers from the fridge, a Straub Amber and a Miller Highlife.

Merry asked, "Can I put the pizza in the microwave? I like mine warm."

"Make yourself at home."

"Since I'm making myself at home, let's eat in the great room. It has a terrific view."

Doc chuckled as he headed for the great room, which had seen little use since Billy's passing. This addition featured large windows on three sides. A well-used twelve-foot picnic table sat on one end. The other end of the room held two colonial-style sofas and two swivel rockers with a large wood stove separating them from the picnic table. Chairs sat on each side of the stove, and three handmade cherry wood benches sat around the room.

Merry arrived and took a few minutes to check out the beautiful mountain view before placing the warmed pizza on the coffee table in front of their chairs. "Which beverage would be mine," she asked as she sat down.

"I picked a Straub Amber and a Miller High Life. Like 'em both. Your choice. The Amber is great stuff if you like dark beer."

"I'm not much of a beer drinker, but I'd like to try the Amber."

"Great choice. If we go to the Straub Brewery next week, you can tell them you drink their beer and won't be fibbing."

"Who said anything about being here next week?" Merry wondered as she picked up the beers and handed Doc the Millers.

"Better give them both to me," he said, holding out his hand.

"We getting a little piggy?" Merry asked with a wry smile.

"Don't want you messing up those work-weary hands twisting off bottle caps. You beat 'em up for two forty-seven today."

"I grow tired asking, Doc, but don't you ever forget anything?" she asked with feigned agitation in her voice.

"Sometimes. Forgot to let Jack in. He's ready for pizza too."

Merry jumped up and called Jack in, then returned with Jack assuming his begging position between them. After Doc said grace, Merry placed pizza on each plate. The irresistible smell, accompanied by the cheese sticking to his fingers, brought college memories with Billie that he fought to set aside. Taking turns feeding Jack and eating themselves, they soon finished. "Want anything else?" Doc asked.

"This Amber is good stuff. Hope you have lots."

"I can get more. East End Beverage is open until nine tonight. We can pick up a few cases before we eat."

"I was kidding. Thought you'd have a few more on hand."

"Got a couple cases in the basement, but I wouldn't wanta run out. Not sure what kind of booze hound you might be."

"I'm not a booze hound," she said with emphasis. "Afraid some mountain man would take advantage of me."

"Don't worry about this guy," Doc said. "I'm not much for chasing chicks."

"Maybe that's why we didn't hold hands when you prayed."

"Learned my lesson this morning," Doc said, his face gathering color.

With the pizza gone, Merry picked up her beer and walked over to look out the windows. "Such a beautiful view with the four mountains rising above the valley, leaves twinkling on the trees, and flowers blooming around the edge of the lawn."

"We took the animal pictures hanging in the lookout out of these windows. One evening last week, we had sixteen elk and twelve deer in the field. The flower pictures were taken around the yard from early spring until late fall. The people pictures are folks who visited here. Hope to have yours up there soon. Maybe a 16 X 20."

"I don't think so."

"You don't want anybody to know you were here?"

"I don't want to scare your friends away," she said, smiling.

It was quiet while Merry walked around looking out the windows. "Man, this is a big room," Merry announced. "Ron's bear would be a great addition down here."

"There are two bears up there. There's a coyote, a couple of elk racks, Ronnie's twelve-point buck, and other stuff."

"Where did all these critters come from?"

"Mostly here on our property."

"I'll help you bring animals down if you want?"

"Maybe when we get back from Kitty's, that is if you can handle it."

"I'm catching on to you, Buster," Merry said with a grin. You mentioned I could sit on the porch if I didn't want to help clean Bucky's place, but I was soon drying dishes. You can bet I won't forget about moving animals when we get home."

"Think we should wash the stink off before we go?"

"Are you talking about showers?"

"I am. How about if I'm downstairs? The lady stuff is mostly up. Help yourself to anything you need."

Man, she's beautiful, Doc thought as he watched her walk toward the steps. He remembered his prayer as Billy was slipping away: "Please, God, don't take her from me. She's most of what I have." Guilt rode in on a dark horse canceling his thoughts of Merry.

Doc found the shower water relaxing and enjoyed it for some time. He dried off, sprayed on some smell-good, dressed, attached his leg, and headed for the laundry with his dirty clothes. Remembering Merry, he yelled up the stairs, "Bring down your dirty clothes. We'll let 'em wash while we're out."

He was sitting in his chair when Merry came down carrying clothes. "You don't have to wash my clothes," she said, embarrassed that a man had offered to wash her things.

"I'm not. The machine is. Look, you've been wondering if you got shafted at your station. I'll call Cindy and ask her to record your station's programs. She can probably hook us up through her recorder so you can advance through the parts you don't want to watch."

"Do you think she'd mind? I don't want to impose."

"She's Billy trained and will be glad to help."

"Doc, who do you watch for the national and international news?"

"Doesn't much matter. We catch news stories that I then research. I wouldn't watch any major media if someone offered unbiased national and international news programs in the same time slot."

"Like that doesn't happen now," Merry said, shaking her head.

CHAPTER 10

Doc and Merry's discussion about today's happenings had them smiling when they arrived at Kitty's. Doc led Merry to his favorite table, thankful no one was there and helped her with her chair before taking his seat. Kitty's Place featured red tablecloths, small flower bouquets, with dinner music playing softly in the background. Moments after being seated, Kitty arrived with their menus. "Good evening Doc. And you're —"

"Kitty, this would be Merry."

"Hi, Merry. Are you new in town?"

"No, Kitty, she was born here and raised in a coal cellar. She doesn't get out much."

"I was talking to Merry. I don't believe we've met," Kitty replied with a you're full of baloney attitude.

"This is my first visit here," Merry answered sweetly.

"Welcome to Cameron County. I hope your stay's a good one. Could I get you something to drink?"

"Doc's been bragging about your prime rib, so I'd like a red wine. Would you have Cabernet Sauvignon?"

"It's our featured house wine, and that's what Doc and . . . well, Doc sometimes orders with prime rib."

"I'll go with spring water tonight," Doc said.

Kitty departed for beverages, and when they were alone, Doc clued Merry in. "Kitty's friendly. She's also inquisitive and passes on information to other need-to-know people. She's wondering about our relationship, and she'll be asking questions. Miss Kitty will pick up on your answers and follow with a question. Her idea of keeping secrets is only telling a few people at a time."

"Got ya."

"You'll feel people staring at us because they carry the small town need to know. They'll guess about our relationship and then pass on take-your-breath-away stories until their audience's eyes light up. Then these folks will quickly pass the news to other friends."

"And you're not from here?"

"Just know how folks act in small towns."

"If you don't mind my asking, how'd you get here?"

"Kinda like you did."

Merry realized this topic wasn't going any further, at least not now. It became quiet until Kitty arrived with their drinks.

"You folks ready to order?"

"I believe we are," Doc said. "I'll have my usual prime rib dinner."

"That would be a garden salad with house dressing, medium-rare gent's size order of rib, a baked potato, and corn for a vegetable. You have your glass of water," Kitty said with a glad you're taking my advice on alcohol grin on her face.

"You got it, Kitty."

"What can I get for you, Merry?"

"Doc told me to order the same thing he did. I'm following orders."

"Oh, you're staying with Doc?"

The question surprised Merry, and she answered without thinking. "Yes, I am. How nice of you to ask."

"And I bet a late-night fish dinner Doc ordered was for you?"

"It was, and it was great. I loved the apple pie too."

"Thank you. Would you like a piece with your meal tonight? Baked fresh today."

"We'll see."

"I can pack it so you can take it to eat later."

When Merry didn't answer, Kitty smiled and departed.

"Wow, Doc, I see what you mean. She should be a reporter."

"She is. Reporting is the local pastime. You could become the beautiful, out-of-town young woman shacking up with Doc. And to think it's only been a few months since Billy's passing. She doesn't look the type, but maybe he found her on one of those online porn sites and is spending the insurance money on —"

"Enough!" Merry said, crossing her arms. "Darn! You sure trip off on things."

Kitty arrived with their salad and a smile just as Merry finished cutting off Doc. "You two look serious about something."

"Just a little romantic testing," Doc said. "We're trying to get used to each other."

"Your meals will be ready when you are," Kitty said sweetly.

"You can bring them now," Doc said. "You're getting busy."

Kitty agreed and quickly departed, acting like she didn't want to get involved in whatever was happening.

"You're something," Merry said, shaking her head but letting her frown turn into a slight smile. "She won't have any idea about our connection."

"Why should we care? Who knows if we'll ever see each other again? She'll have to admit I was with a beautiful woman. We can share a few laughs about something we can't control."

Doc reached across the table to hold her hands while he prayed, and Merry pulled away. "What will people think?"

"They'll think Doc is holding that pretty woman's hands while they pray." With that, he closed his eyes and prayed.

"Doc, I'm getting a lot of firsts with you. You're the first person I ever ran into who prays before every meal."

"And you did run into me, but that's another story." Doc grinned.

"And you don't let up."

The conversation ended with smiles, and they turned to their salads. Their meal came, and they discussed some of this and that as they ate. After a while, Merry remarked, "This is as good as meals get. So glad you bullied me into coming."

"I take 'Let's get ready for Kitty's is bullying you?"

"Something like that."

They finished eating, and Kitty returned to check on the desserts. When they professed to be too full for dessert, Kitty offered to pack two pieces of apple pie for later.

"We'll take 'em," Doc said, smiling.

"I'll bring them with your tab."

"Please put those pieces of meat we cut up for Jack in a plastic bag. Oh, don't forget last night's dinners."

"Thanks for the reminder. I'll take care of both."

"I'll take care of my meals," Merry said as she reached for her purse.

"They won't take your money when you're with me."

"And why not?" Merry asked in a voice loaded with irritation.

"Let's not get angry. Remember, we're having a wonderful time."

Kitty returned, and Doc handed her the money, including a sizeable tip. Thanking them, Kitty said, "You two have a nice evening."

"Oh, we will," Merry said, smiling. "I'm discovering you don't know what's going to happen next when you're with Doc."

"So they say," Kitty acknowledged with a knowing smile.

Doc opened Merry's truck door, and as she was getting in, he noticed someone looking out of a restaurant window. "She's watching us."

"Maybe we should give her something hot to report."

"You gave her enough to talk about with your 'don't know what's going to happen next with Doc' comment. She'll pass it on as verification of whatever she comes up with."

Doc drove through town, headed south across the Broad Street Bridge, and up over the mountain, prompting Merry to remark, "This isn't the way we came into town."

"Got a surprise for you."

"What's that?"

"I sense fear in your voice. You afraid some old hillbilly is running off with you?"

"Oh, stop!"

They climbed the mountain, and after three hairpin turns, S curves, and more crooked road, Doc pulled off where there was a clearing in the trees. "And why are we stopping here," Merry asked with fear evident in her voice."

Merry found herself looking down over Emporium. "Wow, Doc, this is beautiful. It could be called Lover's Lane."

"Billy and I mow the grass here, and there's evidence many somebodies find love here."

"I don't think I've ever been to a prettier place."

"Cameron County's beautiful. I'll show it to you for your video project."

"I won't be here much longer."

"It'll be a few days until your car parts get in and at least a day to put it back together."

"I'm imposing on you."

"Some imposition. As fast as news travels, half of the men in the county will wish they were in my shoes by tomorrow. Monday at the latest."

"You keep that up, and I'll start believing it."

"Facts are facts."

It grew quiet as they watched vehicles crawling down the streets far below. After a bit, Doc said, "We can have some fun together over the next few days. Make your Harrisburg friends sweat a bit for the crap they pulled."

"What's on your mind?"

"They have to be worried. Charlie knows bad things could happen up here, especially to a pretty woman who hates guns and was never camping who finds herself locked out —"

"Let's not go there," Merry interrupted with angst.

"Think! Arianna and Charlie are bound to be talking, and they have to be concerned."

"Maybe you're right."

"This trip could provide unique career opportunities. What if you had pictures of you sleeping on that old glider on the front porch of the camp? Maybe of a little one-man, no a one-woman tent in the front yard. We'll take a video of you cooking hotdogs over a fire. This could kill two birds with one stone. Make Charlie and Arianna sweat while you create a video that gets you into a new line of work at the station."

"I've never slept in a tent or eaten anything cooked over a fire."

"You're kidding," Doc muttered. "Our kids grew up cooking over fires and sleeping in tents."

"Weren't you afraid they'd burn themselves?"

"We didn't let them toast marshmallows until they were four or five. They couldn't cook hot dogs until they were a couple of years older."

"You let little kids play with fire?"

"They weren't playing," Doc said with a smile. "They were cooking under the watchful eyes of their parents."

Another car pulled in and turned off its lights. The young couple glanced at them and then slid closer to each other.

"This is a lover's lane."

"It's called 'The Lookout,' and lovers come here."

"Good. I hope those kids recognize your truck and tell everybody. That will add to the gossip train."

"I'd like that. Even more, I think we finally agree on something."

"Don't get used to it."

Doc laughed as he started the truck and headed up the mountain.

"Darn. Are we leaving already?"

"I noticed you didn't say anything until we got rolling."

Both laughed. Then Merry asked, "Why no wine with dinner?"

"I don't need wine, and tonight it was just to be safe. Remember what happened last night with the cop," Doc answered. "I believe someone might be paying to have me arrested so they don't have to pay a termination fee. Enough said."

With that said, Doc led the conversation back to the potential video. "If you want people really interested in our video, we could begin with a shot of me in my underwear crawling out of a tent behind you, my hair messed up, with lipstick covering my face. We'd get it on Facebook."

"Not on your life. People gossip in Harrisburg too," Merry protested.

CHAPTER 11

It remained quiet until Merry broke the silence. "I should have paid for dinner. I wrecked your truck; you bought me dinner, put me up for the night, and cooked breakfast. Then you worked half a day cleaning up a mess you didn't create and bought me another dinner."

"Two forty-seven."

"Whatever," she answered, shaking her head. "How do I pay you back?"

"Pay forward. Gramp believed in paying forward when someone helps you, which goes into the Help Chest. When somebody needs something, the Help Chest caretaker opens the lid and pulls out the support they need."

"You believe that?"

"Have to. It's proven true for me. You've done more for me than you might believe."

"Oh, sure! I gave you a few hard times."

"Merry, I was living in real hard times," Doc said in a sick little murmur. "Then the Lord threw me a lifeguard. You! Things I've helped you with can't compare with those I've drawn from the Help Chest. God's been good to me."

"Now God's running the Help Chest?"

"He's the caretaker."

It grew quiet as they drove home. Passing a logging road, Doc spotted a vehicle almost hidden from view. Looking back to the road, he swerved to miss a pothole. As he straightened up, the car's headlights came on, closely followed by the red and blue lights of a police cruiser and the siren's whoop whoop. "It's a cop," Doc muttered as he pulled to the side of the road and retrieved his driver's license, vehicle registoration, and insurance papers.

The trooper pulled in front and walked back to Doc's window. "What can we do for you, officer?" Doc asked.

"You're swerving all over the road. Have you been drinking?" the officer asked with 'I know you have' riding in his voice.

"Water."

"Water and we're going to find out what else."

"How much has George Hackett offered the officer who catches me driving under the influence? Second question: Does your sergeant know his troopers have made me a target?"

"What are you talking about?" The trooper stammered, his face glowing red.

"Trooper Ogden stopped me last night and ran me through drunk tests and the Breathalyzer. He's the first officer I ever saw out here at night. Being stopped twice in two days is not a coincidence."

Without arguing, the officer looked over Doc's papers and ordered him out of his truck. After the walking-the-line test and commenting on Doc's slight limp, the trooper took Doc to his vehicle and administered a Breathalyzer test. He couldn't believe the negative test results. "Well, that's a surprise. When you were swerving around on the road, I was —"

"— hoping I was drunk. Maybe troopers slam their state vehicles through potholes because they don't have a nickel in 'em. Taxpayers paying for their rides gotta be more careful."

"I don't know what you're talking about?"

"Sure you do," Doc bitterly challenged him. "Were I you, I'd let my fellow troopers know I discovered what's happening. Hackett will be upset knowing I discovered this, and your sergeant won't be happy when he learns about this charade."

Doc realized he had upset the officer and decided to add to it. "You didn't answer me when I asked how much money Hackett offered the trooper who arrests me for drunk driving."

"I don't know what you're talking about," the officer said, his voice higher and unsteady as he walked with Doc to his truck.

Climbing into his truck, Doc said, "Oh, you know. If you don't need anything else, I'll head over to check on the trooper waiting on Cemetery Hill."

As they drove off, Merry asked, "Any reason for Breathalysers two nights in a row?"

Doc answered, his voice exhibiting anger. "Billy and I negotiated termination clauses in our contracts with MELCOR so we wouldn't leave to work for her brother. If Hackett fires us for any reason other than poor company performance or something that would embarrass the company, we'll receive large termination payments. The cause that prevented payment of the termination money could be a drunk driving arrest. I had an idea this might happen again, and that's why I drank water with dinner."

"What made Hackett think you were that valuable?"

"We were rapidly growing the company in size and profits. Hackett walked on eggshells thinking we might join Billy's brother's plant in St. Marys. He didn't know we were building a video-based company on the side and planned to leave his employ within a few years. That's what our computer and video equipment is about."

They drove on in silence until Doc asked, "You mentioned Charlie at dinner. What kind of person is he?"

Merry ran memories by before answering. "He's a know-it-all, smart ass whose ego blocks his brain waves so he can't think straight, and his sex drive drips off his tongue. Charlie challenged every idea presented at the WLDZ improvement meeting."

They turned into Spring Brook Road with Doc feeling sorry for Merry. "Merry, it seems like you find little in life that excites you. Your job is just a paycheck. Your father sounds abusive. You —."

"Don't remind me," she angrily answered, crossing her arms.

"Why do you hold such animosity towards your father?"

Moving closer to her door, she mumbled, "Let's not go there!"

They pulled in, and the motion sensor lights exhibited Jack waiting on the sidewalk. When Doc crawled out of the truck, Jack noticed he didn't have a food container and waited for Merry.

Jack sat down in front of Merry, surprising her with his paw in the air. "Shake hands. He's thanking you for the food you brought him."

Merry fed him the meat, and Jack stood and barked once when she finished. "He's thanking you again. Come on. He'll follow us in."

Doc set the pie on the counter and went to the bathroom to wash his hands. Merry was standing in the doorway to the great room when he returned. "Doc, you've mentioned wine. Could we share a glass, maybe with a fire?"

"What changed your mind?"

"You want the truth?"

"No, lie to me," Doc answered, his voice soft but demanding.

Merry hesitantly searched for words. "I was afraid of what your motive might be. Trust is a difficult concept for me."

"And?"

"Doc, I don't know how to say this, but you're different. I was never around anyone quite like you before."

"Guess your luck ran out last night."

"No, Doc, great things began with that difficult situation. I feel my life changing."

Doc looked her a warm smile. "You get wine, and I'll build a fire. Wines on shelves at the bottom of the basement steps. Your choice."

Their eyes met, and they shared a smile before each turned to complete their tasks. With long practice, Doc soon had the fire going.

"Wow. That beautiful fire didn't take long," Merry said as she handed him his wine. "I can't remember having fireplace fires two nights in a year even after we had gas installed."

"We heat with wood during the winter."

"You're kidding!"

"No. This fireplace insert keeps the place toasty. We have a combination wood and fuel oil furnace in the basement, but it doesn't get much use."

"It must keep you broke buying firewood. My father paid six or seven bucks for a little cellophane-wrapped package, and it wouldn't last a day."

Doc laughed. "Wouldn't last more than a few hours here. Sweat provides our firewood."

"Beg pardon?" She asked with a brow wrinkled frown.

"We own more than a hundred acres, and there are always downed trees to cut and split."

Doc added larger pieces as the wood caught fire and then turned down the lights. They sat quietly, watching the fire burn down to dancing blue flames over red coals, creating the classic lovers' fire so often pictured in movies. Doc remembered all the nights he and Billy sat watching fires, reading, and making small talk. Love usually got the best of them, and soon Doc would take Jack out while Billy made coffee and set the table for morning. Their passion would continue in bed, and more often than not, Cupid would shoot his arrow. Then —.

"Doc, you talked about growing up in Texas. Your parents still live there."

"My parents are dead. How about you?"

"Until college, I lived in a five-bedroom, six-bath, zillion-dollar, two-hundred-year-old remodeled sterile mansion that sits off Hagys Mill Road outside Philly. It has a pool, tennis court, and a pavilion that contains a fireplace they never use. My friends occasionally came over, and we'd hang out in the pavilion. One wouldn't want to mess up that maid-cleaned, ever so cold house."

"What about your family?"

"My mother's a beautiful showpiece for my father. She has little say about anything. None of us do. My father's most important concerns are billable hours and what people think of him, as in how much they worship him, his bucks, and the little hotties he keeps on the side. If you're wondering about men in my life, there aren't any. I had a boyfriend during high school and others for short periods. Most of them departed for reasons I didn't understand. Quite truthfully, I didn't miss them. And no, I'm not a lesbian. Right now, I'm being taken care of by someone I hardly know because I got sucked into something I didn't understand. Anything else you want to know?"

Merry exhaled as if she were blowing off a lifetime of bad memories. Searching Doc's face, she said, "Let's talk about you, Doc."

"Not much to say. My dad died before I was born, and my mother died when I was ten. I'm an orphan raised by my dad's parents. I joined the Navy for the GI College Bill. I considered becoming a journalist, maybe a writer for the Abilene Reporter-News, or working for one of the TV stations in Abilene. I didn't think I'd live anywhere but Texas."

"What happened to your father?"

"See that flag box?" Doc asked as he pointed at the hand-hewn oak mantle. "That's about my dad. Behind it are pictures of my parents."

"Do you mind if I look at them?"

"Guess not." Doc hesitantly answered. He seldom shared family experiences.

Merry carefully carried the flag box and album to a sofa. "Why don't you join me?"

Doc told himself this wouldn't be easy, but maybe it was time to face life.

"Tell me about the box."

"Gramp made it for my dad's burial flag and medals," Doc said his voice barely a whisper. "The flag-draped his casket. When the funeral ended, the Military Honor Guard folded the flag and presented it to my mom."

"What happened to your father?"

This part of his life proved most difficult, and he had trouble discussing it.

Merry sat quietly beside him and placed her hand on his. She spoke quietly. "It's okay if you don't want to discuss it. It's none of my business."

"Gotta think about it sometime. When I was maybe fourteen, my grandfather and I were sitting on the porch sipping iced tea when a retired Marine gunny sergeant stopped by. Said he was with my father when he got wounded the first time. They were members of a Marine Reconnaissance Team inserted by helo to check enemy activity west of Khe Sanh. That night a large enemy force discovered them. They killed two Marines and wounded my dad. Gunny said my dad kept Charlie off them with an M-60 machine gun until a dust-off helo rescued them. They awarded Dad a Silver Star and a Purple Heart."

"What are they?"

"These medals," Doc said, pointing to them. "The Silver Star Medal signifies gallantry under fire, and the Purple Heart wounded in action."

"What are these other medals for?"

"His second tour. He was on Operation Dewey Canyon, the last major Marine battle in the Vietnam War. It was supposed to stop the flow of arms and supplies coming in from North Vietnam. They killed Dad on February 19, 1969. He received the Navy Cross and another Purple Heart. The other awards include a Bronze Star, Combat Action Ribbon, Gallantry Cross, Navy Commendation Medal, and some other stuff."

"Is that enough for tonight, or can we look at the pictures?"

"We can look at pictures."

"This first picture is of a happy, young couple, my parents, dressed up for a high school dance. Gramp told me they were already talking about marriage. The next pictures are their high school graduation, followed by one taken a day later when they announced their engagement."

"They look like they loved each other."

"Gramp said they were crazy about each other since sixth grade. Dad's cousin joined the Marines, and Dad went with him to beat the draft. They talked about being Marines for years. This is Dad's first official Marine Corps boot camp picture, and the next is on his boot leave with Mom. They were married four days later. These are pictures of their wedding at First Baptist Church in Sterling City. They had a reception at my grandparent's ranch. Gramp said there wasn't much to it because Dad and Mom made it plain they needed to get going. Didn't have much time for a honeymoon."

"Are these your grandparents?"

"They are."

"They look happy together."

"Very happy. They usually sat on that porch swing holding hands on summer evenings after a hard day's work. I received my first real look at what love could be watching them."

"We never saw that look," Merry softly murmured.

"Too bad."

"Your grandfather looks like there's something wrong with his right arm."

"His arm and hand weren't much good for him. He got wounded in WWII. Gram made him a padded holder that slipped over shovel and pitchfork handles. He'd place the pad on a tool and slip it under his armpit. He could pitch hay and shovel rock about as good as anyone. Always apologized for his handwriting because he had to learn how to write with his left hand."

"How'd he get hurt?"

"He got wounded on Tarawa Island the first time. His arm got screwed up on Iwo Jima. That was the costliest battle in Marine Corps history. The Japs killed about eight thousand Marines and wounded many more."

"My gosh. They killed that many Americans?"

Merry turned to the last page to find a young woman's picture lying face down in front of a tombstone. She was crying with her face buried in the grass. Her Bible lay nearby. A sad-looking little boy sat beside her.

"Before you ask, that's my mom and me one Sunday after church," Doc softly said, looking away. "Mom went to the cemetery after church on Sundays. She often cried herself sick in front of Dad's tombstone. Gramp would pick us up for supper. We lived with them from the time I was five."

"How old were you when you lost her?"

"Ten. Mom lived in a yesterday she couldn't have. Died from a broken heart."

Merry wiped her eyes with a Kleenex as she wondered what to say. "Doc, I'm so sorry."

"I remember a woman from church on Memorial Day telling my grandmother she was sorry our family had suffered so much because of wars. Gram said, 'Irene, that's the price we pay for freedom.' That woman didn't know what to say."

"You lose your leg in a war?"

"Ya."

"Your family paid heavily for the freedom many take for granted. Three generations wounded in wars."

"Four. Gramp's father got gassed in World War One. He died when he was in his forties. Lungs burned out. Gramp said he was in bad shape, always wheezing and coughing."

"Man, Doc, that's tough. It makes me wonder why that would happen to so many people in one family?"

"Guess we didn't get hangnails."

Chapter 12

Jack licked Merry's hand before lying in front of the fireplace. Merry shook her head, looking at her hand and back at the dog. "He's the first dog I ever touched. We weren't allowed to have pets. My mother believed they were mess creators, and my father said they were expensive nuisances. He said, 'The dumbest thing I ever witnessed was a goofball in a suit walking a dog with a bag of dog crap swinging in his hand. I saw another idiot holding an umbrella over a mutt while it took a dump. No damned dogs here. My family's above that!' We never got a dog."

"I had dogs until I joined the Navy. When you're a kid, and no one understands you, your dog does. Billy used to say, 'Whoever said diamonds are a girl's best friend never had a dog friend.' They love you."

"How do you know that?"

"They know when you're feeling down and put their head on your leg. They wag their tail when you talk to them. They go crazy when they recognize the sound of your vehicle coming home. The best story about a dog's love involves a wife. If you want to know who loves you, lock your dog and wife in your car trunk on a hot summer day. Go back in an hour and let 'em out. See who's glad to see you."

Merry laughed, shaking her head. "Sure wouldn't be this woman."

"Point made."

It was quiet for a bit as they watched the dying embers in the fireplace. Merry spoke first. "Are you still into bringing those animals down?"

"You checked the time lately?"

"I have, but so what?"

"How's your back?"

"Ready to carry a few stuffed animals."

"Okay. You go up and get started, and I'll fix the fire. Mounts aren't heavy, but we'll carry the big ones down together. Remember, they go in the great room."

Merry smiled and hurried upstairs while Doc scraped hot coals on a large shovel and carried them to the great room stove. He added wood and watched the fire sizzle into life, burning flickering shafts of orange. He looked up at the family picture, remembering Billy's last night with him. She was about out of strength and communicated in a shallow whisper. "Doc, I'm sorry to leave you alone. I love you so much, and I know you love me. But please, when I'm gone, find a nice woman to love and care for you. You both deserve that." Doc remembered telling her there wouldn't be another woman, that he couldn't love another. Tears ran down her face, and as he kissed them away, she whispered, "Please, Doc, for me. You're a good man and deserve another woman; some good woman deserves time with you.

We'll meet again on the other side." He kissed her lightly. He couldn't forget their talk, and it hurt to think about it. They held hands until her grip loosened. It was over.

He watched the fire come to life, knowing her memories would always be with him. Sorrow rolled over him like a hurricane. How could a loving God do this, take so much of your life? He went over her dying words again, which brought tears he couldn't fight off. Doc was drying his eyes on his handkerchief when Merry arrived with another load, saw him still staring into the fire, and felt what he was thinking. He wasn't over his Billy. Might never be.

"You deeply miss Billy," Merry softly said.

He thumbed his wedding band Billy placed there. Slowly, he turned to face Merry with teary eyes, "It hurts to think about Billy. When Billy became terminal, life as I knew it seemed doomed. The blinding snow the day she died accompanied bucketfuls of my tears. I deeply believe in God and his miracles. I prayed earnestly for her recovery, and Billy got worse. Then she was gone." Time crawled as they stood looking at each other. "Merry, I loved her deeply. We have children we love. We grew loving experiences I couldn't forget." Tears slid down his face as he relayed her last words. "Losing Billy was the first time I remember crying. Guess I'm crying now."

"Doc, this is the first time you talked about Billy in the past tense as if maybe you realize she's gone. Maybe it's healing time for you and ..." She stopped, realizing the conversation had gone past too far.

Staring into the fire, Doc wiped tears on his sleeve. Maybe it was healing time or perhaps sharing time. Without thinking, he replied, "I haven't done very well with this healing thing. I read about coping with grief trying to crawl past my loss, and it provided more reasons for my sorrow. I received sympathy cards that ate holes in my mind. Church folks dropped by, and their prayerful condolences multiplied my grief. I read my Bible seeking answers, which wracked me with questions I couldn't answer. I asked God what I did wrong to make Him take Billy and received no response. I tried booze. It was a bust that was ruining my life, but I didn't care."

Silence ruled, broken only by the crackling firewood. "One evening after a difficult day at work, I was praying on the way home, telling God I couldn't handle living this way much longer. I asked Him for help. God pulled you out of His Help Chest."

Merry couldn't answer and, with tearing eyes, headed upstairs. Doc followed to help with the animal migration when she suggested, "Let's get the guy that scared off my pants."

"Man and I missed that."

"Missed what?"

"You with your pants scared off."

"Glad to see you're coming back, Doc. You were in a different world when you were staring into the fire."

He often entered that dimension and had trouble returning. With Merry, it became different. For the first time in months, he found peace. Together, they carried the massive standing bear down and stood him on one side of the stove. He looked alive, standing there with his mouth open and those huge teeth showing. It was no wonder Merry screamed when she saw him.

They returned for the second bear, who stood on all fours with his tongue hanging out. At times, he seemed to hold an it's too hot smile, and at other times, a thankfulness for just eating your leg. They sat him near the slider that opened to the deck until they could decide on the right place for him.

"Man, there's a lot of stuff here. Ronnie must have been a busy kid."

"He still is," Doc replied as he carried Ronnie's owl and a coiled rattlesnake down before returning for the deer fawns on his dresser."

"These little guys are beautiful," Merry said. "I didn't know you could hunt fawns."

Doc grinned. "You can't. Ronnie rode his bike out to catch the school bus one spring morning and saw a car stopped on the hill road with a woman leaning against it crying. She killed a pregnant doe with her car. Ronnie called the game warden from the Becks. The warden let the woman go and gave Ronnie the deer. Even hauled her into our place, and they put her in the barn."

"Did the wreck cause the fawns to be born?"

"No. The fawns died inside their mother."

Merry walked over to study the pictures and artifacts hanging about. "Is this you and Billy standing in front of that old house?" Merry asked as she pointed to a photo.

"That's us with Billy's parents and a lawyer. That old house is this place the day we bought it."

"Wow! You've had a lot of work done on it."

"Rebuilt it ourselves. Then we added this room down and our bedroom, a sitting room, and a third bathroom up. Got a walk-in closet too."

"Your family is so talented. Contractors did the work on our house."

"Limited funds encourage self-help."

"Your son is so artistic," Merry said, looking at Ronnie's artwork. "I love his work."

"He received his talents from his mother. I hung her paintings, but she replaced most with Ronnie's."

"Is your daughter artistic?"

"She's big into photography. Took the pictures in your bedroom. The photo of the hummingbird hanging in midair with his beak stuck in that red beebalm flower won her the grand prize at a Kodak exhibit in Rochester.

"Billy used her talents in ways besides painting. She created apprenticeship programs and advertising material for MELCOR and her brother's plant in St. Marys. She didn't tell anyone about helping her brother. Her father would have thrown a fit."

"Is he a bad dude?"

"I hope you never meet him?"

"That bad?"

"Worse at times."

Why'd I mention George Hackett? Doc asked himself. Sure, he has redeeming qualities, but thinking about him drags that hostile face into focus, yelling obscenities, his guttural voice full of hate. Mostly towards me, Doc thought.

Merry arrived at a place that held pictures of a young woman with various awards. Without turning, she asked Doc, "Do you have two daughters?"

"Why do you ask?"

"The name on these awards - Catherine E. Adams."

"That would be Billy."

"How did Catherine Hackett become Billy?"

"Hillbilly got shortened to Billy."

"And Hillbilly came from?"

"Being raised in these mountains."

"What kind of nickname do you have planned for me?"

"None right now," Doc replied, his face reddening. "Do you always ask so many questions of strangers?"

"Never talked this way with anyone before you. Not sure what's happening, but anyone who knows me wouldn't believe it."

"Doc, I have another question, that is if you don't mind."

"Let's hear it, and I won't answer it if I don't like it."

"How'd you two get together?"

"In the hospital?"

"Were you patients?"

"She was a visitor. I was sentenced there."

"For your leg?"

"Yeah."

"Which war?

"Desert Storm."

"What happened?"

"We were part of the ground offensive to kick Saddam Hussein out of Kuwait. Jerry stepped on a mine. Killed him. He died in my arms. It badly wounded Ray and blew off my leg. I got a tourniquet on my leg and went to work on Ray. He was in bad shape. Lost an arm and a leg."

Doc caught Merry looking questions at him as he leaned back against the sofa. "They brought us back to Bethesda Naval Hospital and fit me with a prosthesis. That's where I met Billy."

"Did she come to see you?"

"No." Doc smiled, thinking about it. "Her and two girlfriends were on spring break from Penn State. They had a buddy they thought was in Bethesda and decided to visit him on their way to the beach. They were on I-495 when they saw the Bethesda signs and stopped by, asking if we knew their friend. We didn't."

"You two hit it off right away?"

"If you're asking if she fell all over a one-legged dude, the answer's 'no.' They talked about college and wanted to know our plans.

You know, just something to make conversation. I had completed distance learning college courses plus evening and Saturday courses. I planned to finish college after the Navy. We thought we saw the last of them when they departed. Two of them came back a few weeks later with information on Penn State."

"Billy was one of them?"

"No. It was her girlfriends, Linda and Judy."

It was quiet until Merry asked, "How'd Billy get into the picture?"

"After their visit, I studied the Penn State material they left behind and developed a list of questions. Linda and Billy came back, and we went down to the hospital gedunk to eat. Linda sat by me. She's pushy. Nosey too."

"Like me?"

"Not like you!" Doc growled. "I see you as interested, not nosey."

"And you're interesting. So easy to be with."

"Maybe it's that Help Chest thing."

"Yeah, right, the Help Chest," she said, shaking her head with a forced smile.

Neither of them talked until Merry as ked, "What's a gedunk?"

"Navy slang for a military cafeteria."

After a period of silence, Doc explained how Billy became part of his life. "A few weeks later, the three of them came, and we went back to the gedunk. This time, Billy sat beside me and asked if I had found anything interesting about Penn State. I had. We discussed majors, and she asked if I had considered business management. She said there were always good jobs in that field."

"She was taking mechanical engineering and had missed the girls' last visit because of a weekend seminar. I explained that Penn State might be out of the question with books, tuition, room and board, and other costs associated with attending a major university. I could count on the GI Bill and a small medical retirement check, but I'd have to get a part-time job and maybe two. People might not want to hire cripples. Billy suggested I find roommates to split the costs on a rental home as they had. I told her I'd still need transportation. She said I needed to look at things in a more positive light."

"Billy came down the next weekend by herself. The girls she lived with had discussed me living with them. If I helped with rent, I could set up a bed in the basement and share the costs. I could ride to school with them if I chipped in on gas. They drew up a contract we'd all sign, and I'd find myself out on the street if I got out of line."

"Oh. So Billy had her eye on you?"

"I think it was sympathy. Nothing happened to break the contract."

"You struck out with all three women?"

"Not exactly. Linda made it plain we could become an item. She stayed on campus a few times when the other girls went home for the weekend. Once, she ordered pizza, and we had a couple of beers together. After I was in bed, she crawled in with me. I got out and sat in my chair. She wanted to know what was wrong. Didn't I like her? I told her I had a contract and didn't want to find myself in the street. She said nobody would know. I told her I would."

"That ended it?"

"She came on to me a few other times, but I didn't let it go anywhere. Linda and Judy graduated from Penn State while Billy finished post-graduate courses in powdered metal and metallurgy, and I finished my last semester."

"How'd you get together?"

"I carried a heavy course load and held two part-time jobs. That took most of my time except Sunday morning when I attended church. Billy started going to church with me. One night, we went out for pizza and discovered we liked each other. It went from there."

"What happened to Linda and Judy?"

"Not sure about Judy, but Linda went back to St. Marys to teach school. She married another teacher a few years later and visited us here a few times, absent her husband. Linda dropped by a few months ago. Said she saw Billy's obituary and felt sorry for me. It got late, and she wanted to stay overnight. I turned that off, but she's called since then."

"Sounds like a 'Merry' kind of pest."

"You're not a pest. You dropped out of the Help Chest when I needed a Merry to talk with."

"We're back to that Help Chest again?"

"Not back to it. It's always right here with us

CHAPTER 13

Tired from a day loaded with surprises, Merry took a couple of Aleves, locked her door, and slid into bed, thinking, *It's strange how our lives turn out. Doc considered becoming a journalist and ended up in manufacturing. I didn't want to be a journalist; now it's an essential part of my job. My mother wanted to be a journalist but got pregnant with a someday lawyer. My father, the someday lawyer, became the third-generation owner of a powerful law firm founded by his grandfather. Yeah, and he demanded I become a fourth-generation lawyer at the prestigious law firm Morehouse, Peabody, and Rosenstein, Attorneys at Law that he now leads. I wanted to be an attorney working with him even less than I wanted to be a journalist. I couldn't work with a father who would do what he did,* and there she forced herself back into the real world. *Enough, Morehouse!*

They talked about opportunities, and Doc said never limit yourself to small dreams because great opportunities surround us. Then he quoted Andy Rooney. 'Opportunities aren't lost. Someone always takes the ones you miss.' Could there be something to this Help Chest thing with Merry support in there for new opportunities?

Nah. Don't gather strange ideas, Merry. You better start thinking about how you'll pay the deductible that's coming with your car's repairs. That and your condo payment. None of this mess fits into your real life. You knew better than to make this trip. Now you're becoming more than a little too familiar with this hillbilly. You never made suggestive comments to anyone before, but they slide right out with Doc.

Walk carefully, Merry. He's really into this God business. His Guidebook turned into a well-worn New Testament the Gideons presented him when he joined the Navy. Oh yeah, beautiful flowers on the table for breakfast. What's that about? Yeah, that and his screams last night.

As her back pain eased and memories dimmed about this different kind of day, sleep crept in.

CHAPTER 14

The Sunday morning sky burned from pink into scarlet red with a phoebe bird searching for bugs on his deck rails. The coffee finished perking while bacon and french toast stayed warm in the oven. When he heard her door open, Doc broke four eggs into the bacon grease sizzling in the frying pan and pushed down the toaster lever sending four pieces of 15-grain bread into toast hell.

"Heard you singing. You sound happy this morning," Merry muttered as she walked in, rubbing her eyes.

"Learned our lives are pretty much what we make 'em. Sun's up for a beautiful morning, and you're getting ready to pour our juice."

"Gotcha." Merry answered, and while she was pouring V8 juice, she added, "You won't believe this. Jack scratched at my door like he did yesterday, only this time he waited with his paw raised. I petted his head, and he licked my hand, then headed downstairs on the fly."

"He likes you," Doc answered in his baritone voice as he buttered the toast, placed two on each plate, flipped an egg on each piece, and set them on the table. She poured coffee and took it to the table while he grabbed the bacon.

Doc reached for her hands to pray, and this time she accepted. After praying over their food, family, and friends, Doc looked up and smiled. "Have a change of heart overnight? You wouldn't let me hold your hands last night."

"That was different."

"Not sure how, but —" and he let it drop.

"You cook like this every morning?"

"Yesterday was my first cooked breakfast in months, but we usually cook on weekends. Eat cereal during the week."

"Great, or I'd weigh two hundred pounds by the time I head home."

Doc smiled. "Talked to Ronnie this morning. Hopes to finish tearing down your car after church. He ran out of time last night."

"He's up already?"

"Caught him at his garage."

"You guys don't sleep much."

"I'm beyond beauty rest help."

"You have a hard time saying anything positive about yourself."

Ignoring the comment, Doc said, "I've been thinking about Miss Merry and her dilemma. We need to go over to Bucky's place and fix the beds. Clean bedclothes are already in the truck. Bring Bucky's key. Got a few ideas I want to run by you on the way over."

"We can discuss them now," Merry suggested as she stirred creamer into her coffee.

"Got other things to talk about now." Doc drank a slug of coffee while he gathered his thoughts. "Let's contact Cindy after breakfast and see if you can watch the video to find out what happened at your station."

Doc then hooked Merry up with Cindy on his computer, and while they talked, Merry watched part of the video. At the same time, Doc worked over steaks with his spice mixture and marinated them.

Merry returned wrapped in anger. "I can tell you what happened to Arianna. That witch was the weekend news anchor after she made sure I wasn't available. I could strangle her."

"It ain't the end of the world."

"Could be for me. The station's heading towards layoffs, and this could put me in a real bind. How could she do this to me?" Merry said, pursing her lips as she crossed her arms.

"Sometimes people make spur-of-the-moment decisions without considering their impact on others." After considering what he said, Doc added, "Maybe it happened because the Lord is leading Merry in a new direction."

"How can you say that?" Merry snapped.

In a mere whisper, Doc added, "If I hadn't lost my leg, I never would have met Billy. I had to wreck my truck to meet Merry Morehouse. I don't believe either meeting was an accident. While you're here, we can have fun doing things I believe could further your career. We'll discuss them on the way over to Bucky's. You might want to make another draw on Billy's clothes."

With everything ready to go, Doc waited on the porch. Hearing her on the steps, he called, "Out here. Jack's in the truck. Grab your cameras and that key."

Merry walked out with Bucky's key and her camera bag. "Not sure why we need this. The key doesn't fit the door."

"Bet it fits some door. Might add a few pieces to our puzzle."

They walked to the truck's passenger side, and Doc held her door before crawling in himself.

"You're something," Merry said, looking at him with a smile. "I've enjoyed a lot of life firsts in a few days. You're the first person who ever pulled out a chair or opened a door for me."

"Gramp always opened the door for my grandmother. When I got a little older, I'd quickly open Gram's door. Gramp would smile and whisper, 'Sorry, Frosty, you're wasting your time. The lady's already spoken for.' We'd grin at each other like we held a big secret."

As they neared the hill road, they saw Bob Beck leaning on a fence post watching his Angus cattle, and Doc eased in beside his friend. "Morning. How's Mr. Beck?"

"Happy to see my long-lost neighbor. How ya doing, Doc?" Noticing Merry, he tipped his hat. "Good morning, ma'am. Not sure we met."

Merry smiled while Doc introduced her. "Bob, this is Merry. She dropped by to see me."

Bob smiled. "She dropped by because you ran over her on Cemetery Hill. People can't figger how you knew there was a pretty woman in the car."

"That'd be a secret."

"Yeah. One you won't share. Need a favor, Doc. I could use help this afternoon."

"You can see I'm busy, but I can make a little time for you. Whataya need?"

"Your guitar. There's a church picnic after service with a singin' session when the eatin's done."

"I'll drop my guitar by. It'll give me a chance to introduce Merry to Wanda."

"You know that ain't what I meant. We've been missin' you. Miss Merry," Bob said, looking past Doc, "this man can pick a guitar. Sing too. Don't let him leave without you."

"Who said I was coming?" Doc asked.

"You did. Said you'd make time to help me, and that's what I need help with. See you for the picnic too. Looks like you're headed someplace now?"

Doc smiled as he drove off. "Ya notice how he ended with half a question. He'd like to know where someplace is. It ain't just women who hold a need to know."

"I noticed folks don't get a lot of information from Doc."

Doc looked at her and grinned. "You get more than most. Don't feel forced to go to the picnic, but you'd have a good time."

"What do you wear?"

"Not your fancy city duds. Everybody'd think you're a rich lawyer's daughter from the big city. Get something out of Billy's closet."

After a bit, Doc asked, "Is there any reason why Charlie might have it in for Arianna?"

"Arianna went out with him more than a few times. They acted like they had something going."

"Something doesn't fit. Does Charlie have any reason to play tricks on you?"

"I turned him down for dates, but I always did it graciously and didn't tell anyone."

"He wouldn't leave that mess for Bucky's brother because it would end him using the place."

"Why would he screw with the keys so we couldn't get in if he wanted us to clean up his mess?"

"Maybe something changed after he messed with the keys. What can go wrong will go wrong."

"Doc, why are you helping us when you don't even know us."

"Let's start with Miss Merry Whatsherface. She unexpectedly dropped out of the —"

"Help Chest and Morehouse would be her name," Merry said, smiling at him.

"Yeah, her. I needed help, and she was assigned to be my helper."

"How did I earn that assignment?"

"Maybe as punishment. Only the Lord knows. He says we're to share with his people and practice hospitality. Am I hospitable enough?"

"You're very hospitable, but I haven't been one of God's people. I haven't even —"

"Attended church, but I took that as 'at least not yet.' God comforts us in our times of need so we can pass it on to others who need comfortin'. I needed to be comforted. Here you are. Maybe you don't understand what a blessing you've been."

"I feel more like a pain in your fanny."

"Not so. You're a lifeguard."

It was quiet until Merry asked, "Why did you want me to bring Bucky's key? It doesn't fit the door."

"Wouldn't you like to know what it fits?"

"Why care?"

"Just nosey."

They let Jack out and headed for the porch. "I counted four locks yesterday," Doc said, "front and back doors and two storage sheds."

The key was for a padlock, so Doc headed for the sheds. Luck was with him, and he opened the shed lock and retrieved the camp key. "This can be your door key until you leave for home."

"You throwing me out of your place?"

"You nuts? Guess we can pretend the key doesn't fit the shed and hunt for it each time. When we find it, we can hunt for the house key. You know, leave a little challenge in the process."

"Were you smoking something before I got up this morning?"

After laughing together, Merry asked, "You got any ideas on the lock mixup yet."

"Some. Let's talk about it on the way to Walmart."

"What do we need there?"

"We'll make a list on the way."

After making beds, they headed to St. Marys Walmart. It was quiet until Merry asked, "Weren't we going to discuss some things?"

"Guess I'm used to being alone. I was running stuff through my head. Got any ideas on the keys?"

"Maybe they just got mixed up."

"Let's say there were several keys in Bucky's package, and Charlie switched key tags to give you ladies something to fret over. Then Bucky simplified the package with one door key, not knowing the shed key was tagged 'front door'."

"Think we should change it back?"

"We could get keys cut, and you can lay the shed key on Charlie's desk. Give him something to think about."

"I like the way you think, Doc. What else are we getting at Walmart?"

"Food, and you'll need a small two-person tent in case Arianna shows up or we decide to sleep together."

"Right?" Merry sarcastically returned. "Arianna isn't going to show, and I wouldn't know what to do with a man in my tent."

"We could learn together," Doc replied. "We'll get a tent, sleeping bag, and an air mattress. Some paper plates and plastic eating utensils. Some camp-type food to add to the stuff you already have. Some eggs. Whatever else we see that we need."

"Who's paying for all this stuff? I have a wrecked car, and I'm strapped for bucks."

"We'll put it on my credit card and hope the bill gets lost in the mail."

"You're crazy," Merry said, shaking her head.

"I'm thinking we can have fun with a video for Arianna and Charlie, making you appear to be a lost soul, and another version for your TV station's new programming plan."

"Where do you get this stuff?"

"I'm a sailor who spent most of his time with Marines. You can grow a lot of imagination working with crazy guys who love to pull goofy tricks on each other. Then I got a brain concussion in Desert Storm. That can do bad things to your thinking machinery."

"A beginning camper's first trip doesn't seem that exciting."

"Did you forget you made me move animals last night? Can you imagine making a movie of a huge bear sniffing around the porch where you happen to be sleeping? Or how about one peaking into your tent with his mouth open? There are loads of rattlesnake and coyote possibilities. Tonight we'll look over our animal inventory and develop a master plan. I'm getting excited," Doc finished with a lilt to his voice.

"You're nuts," Merry said with a chuckle.

"Yeah, but who else could make this camping trip video? You don't want to be a journalist. Here's your opportunity to use the adversity of being wrecked in the big woods to build an exciting new career. Merry, we go through this life one time. Make your trip a great one."

"You talk like a career could be built on goofy videos."

"I believe videos present a great career opportunity, and Billy has the computer and programs. Consider shots with the coyote running under the porch with your sausage or the bear peeking in your tent. You could dub animal sounds into your video. Even better, wait until Charlie sees you had to sleep on the porch or in a tent you bought because he switched keys. People will beg for more after they preview your first video."

"What makes you think there's going to be a preview?" Merry questioned.

"Your boss will view it, and then she'll get station management together to view it," Doc answered enthusiastically. "They'll make sure everybody sees it, so they know the types of improvements the station is seeking. You'll have several more project ideas lined up, and they'll place you in charge of the operation. You'll get assignments like tours of the Straub and Yuengling Breweries, the Elk Center, state parks with waterfalls, Amish farms, and other stuff. Other TV stations will see what you're doing for WLDZ, and your phone will ring off the hook as they try luring you away with the promise of big bucks," Doc added with sparkling eyes.

"Doc, as my friend likes to say, you're a few fries short of a Happy Meal."

"It's called positive thinking, and you haven't heard all my ideas yet. You could stay with me when you shoot them. By then, I'll have expanded my ideas to other projects in the area so I can see you again and again."

"You'd be so tired of me," Merry said, shaking her head.

"Don't even think you're a once-and-done visitor. I believe you're loaded with bucks.

"Did I mention you're nuts?"

"Maybe, but I didn't listen."

They pulled into Walmart and began shopping in the camping area where they loaded their cart. "What are you going to do with all of this stuff?" Merry asked, showing more than a little concern.

"I'll carefully store it, so it's available for your next assignment, that's if you still talk to me after you get a huge pay raise and all those Hollywood offers. Can't tell if a woman's fickle until they add you to their heap of forgotten poor souls," he added with a fear-filled tone.

"Did I mention you're nuts?"

"Maybe, but I didn't listen. Men are known for that. Let's get our food."

Doc grabbed two eighteen packs of eggs prompting Merry to ask, "Doc, why so many eggs? There are two of us, and you mentioned cereal on weekdays."

"You could get tired of cereal, and you can't ever have too many eggs. Let's get the coyote's sausage, some juice, and milk. Oh, and we need some big cans of beans."

Merry shook her head as she looked over the heavily laden cart. She was amazed when he handed her two giant jars of pickles to carry. Even more, she couldn't believe they filled that cart in just under twenty minutes. Doc had to be the fastest shopper ever.

The lady at checkout casually asked, "Find everything you needed?" as she worked her register.

"We left a few things until next time. This little lady likes to shop, so we try to do this a few times each week."

"Really?" the cashier asked. "Kinda looks like you got one or two of everything in the store."

All three laughed until Doc asked the cashier if he could borrow her credit card. She shook her head with a 'how dumb can you be' look while Doc and Merry reloaded their cart.

They were soon in the truck heading home. "Doc, what's your plan for all this food? No way we can eat all of this stuff."

"Share it."

"With whom?"

"The people attending the picnic. We can't go empty-handed. They'll be expecting beans and deviled eggs. Pickles too. You're going with me, aren't you? I'll make all those dudes jealous when I have this pretty young woman with me."

"Doc, I don't know," Merry said with a worried voice. "I won't know how to act. I'm not a churchgoer."

"This ain't church. It's a picnic songfest."

"You'll stay with me?"

"Don't try to get away. I'm not sharing. These dudes can wreck their own trucks trying to find pretty women."

"You're crazy, but I like it," she said with a smile.

Both were quiet until they headed up Moore Hill Road. "Who's going to make the eggs and bean stuff?"

"You can do it while I take a nap."

"You're nuts, but then I —"

"Said that before. Not much to it, Merry. I'll put the eggs on to boil while I get the beans ready to bake. Hey, I'm on it."

CHAPTER 15

The kitchen smelled like a picnic as Doc placed the deviled eggs in the cooler. Finished, he tuned 'Old Tex,' his Martin guitar, and with eyes closed, he cradled the guitar like a lover, picking a favorite from his Texas years.

Merry came down dressed, "Well, does my choice fit a church picnic?"

"That outfit works for anything, Miss Merry," Doc answered. "You look great. You're so ..."

"So what?"

"Not sure what I was going to say," Doc answered. Unable to be truthful, he picked through a few chords, thinking about Billy and the deep love they held for each other. He couldn't let anything replace that.

"What's the name of the song you were playing?" Merry asked, endeavoring to return to their conversation.

"This?" Doc asked, picking a few chords.

"That's it."

"I'll Be All Smiles Tonight," Doc answered. "It's an old Carter Family song. My grandmother could pick that baby. Had a beautiful voice too. Gave me her guitar when arthritis kept her from picking. Said stiff fingers weren't going to turn her into a strummer."

"I understand why Bob wants you to come. You can play that guitar."

"Got any songs you'd like to hear?" Doc asked, changing the subject. "They'll take requests."

"I don't know any hymns or country songs. Most of the singing-type parties of my age were drug-related. I stayed away."

"Better pack our food," Doc suggested, struggling to his feet.

Merry climbed into the truck after the food was packed and said, "As ordered, I brought both cameras, but I'm not sure why."

"This shindig might fit into your video. Best to be prepared."

Heading for the picnic, Doc asked, "If you could have any career, what would it be?"

She replied with a slight smile, "Not sure, but it wouldn't be a journalist."

"What's your favorite family memory, something you call up when you're alone and want to be happy?"

She rubbed her cheek as she paused to think. "Don't have many family memories that make me happy."

"What's your favorite hobby?"

"Don't have any. I work and ...well work."

"Who's your best friend?"

"With this Arianna mess, it looks like I don't have one. Why do you ask? You looking for a job as my best friend?" she asked, her voice trailing away.

"I wanna be your friend. Can I say something without ticking you off?"

"Let's give it a try," she answered with a puzzled smile.

"I don't wanna annoy you, but it seems you have no real life."

With pursed lips, Merry crossed her arms and said, "OK, mister counselor man, what's your ideal job and favorite family memory? Yeah, and what's your hobby? Oh. And who's your best friend?"

"Merry, do you want to know, or are you upset 'cause I'm nosey?"

"Maybe a little of both, but go ahead."

"My favorite jobs have been those leading people to improved lives. Real family memories begin with my grandparents. I acquired my understanding of life through them. Many of those moments still whisper to me. I have great memories of working with Billy on almost any project. We rebuilt our home, and the things we did with our kids make great memories. My favorite hobby is playing the guitar, and my best friend was Billy. She pushed Gram and Gramp into a second-place tie. I recently discovered I needed to find a new best friend."

"Doesn't look like it can be me."

"Why's that?"

"I annoy you."

"We annoy each other, but it doesn't have to stay that way. Billy and I didn't always agree on everything. We discussed our thoughts and how we came to think that way. We allowed each other to hold different viewpoints and opinions without arguing. We agreed on big things like our kids and our home. And we enjoyed kidding each other without taking offense."

Merry gently placed her hand on Doc's arm and smiled. "Doc, I'm a different me when I'm with you. I can't describe how I feel. You treat me like I'm special."

"Merry, you are special." Doc's heart fluttered as he glanced at Merry. She was growing on him, but they had little in common. Her job surrounded her with media news people and their ideas, ideas that were vastly different from his. Then there was her moneyed, anti-Christian background. And she carried something from her past that crept toward the surface when they discussed serious family things.

"Doc, I've learned a lot in a few days. Life doesn't always have to be a serious, end-of-the-world happening. We make fun of things without hurting people. Laughter feels good."

Doc silently nodded in agreement. She was picking up on things he grew up with, like kidding. Might as well show her another example of how that works. "Merry, you might want to get a little prayer together. They usually ask a newbie to say grace before the meal."

"You're crazy," she stormed, angrily pounding her legs with her fists. "I don't pray. Take me back!"

He glanced at her angry face and recognized her pain. "Ease up. No one will ask you to pray."

"Right! Take me back!"

"Merry, I was kidding," Doc said as they topped Cemetery Hill, "and I'm sorry. I forgot you're not into kidding. Look, they say picnic grace inside the church at the close of the service."

Thinking about it with a scowl on her face, Merry finally said, "That better be true, Buster."

"It's true, Merry, I apologize. I thought you could take a joke."

"Wasn't funny for me!" she replied, arms still crossed, accompanied by a hateful stare.

"I'm sorry. Things are different with you. I'll be more careful with my comments. Promise."

People were filing out of the church toward the pavilion when Doc drove into the parking lot. Someone called, and Doc saw the Pastor walking hurriedly toward them. Seeing a worried look sliding back over Merry's face, he assured her it was OK. "Merry, this is the Pastor. He's coming to say hello."

"So glad you could make it, Doc," Pastor Mike said with a big grin. "We've missed you. A cheer went up when Bob said you might be here today."

Doc shook his head with a smile. "Bob must have told you about Merry. Let me introduce you. Merry, this is Pastor Mike. Pastor Mike, this is Merry. Oh, and Pastor, can you carry our beans over to the table? We'll get the cooler."

"Nice to meet you, Merry. I can see you haven't yet had much of an effect on him," Pastor said with a knowing smile as he picked up the beans.

Doc unloaded one plate of eggs and a bowl of pickles at the food table and set them beside the beans. Curious, Merry asked, "You're not putting everything out?"

"Regulars know when the first plate's empty, set out the second one. Keeps 'em cooler. Let's get in line."

"Bring your guitar, Doc?" a man named George asked as they filled their plates.

"Merry will be picking this afternoon."

"Why do you say things like that?" Merry begged when George walked away.

"They expect it. You'll discover that over time."

"Over time?" she demanded.

"I'm sorry, Merry. I know my comment about prayer, and things like this upset you. That's the last thing I want. Please forgive me."

"Doc, I was thankful everything seemed to be going more smoothly. I want that."

"I want that too. Last night was special for me. I'll be more thoughtful."

"You're different, Doc," Merry said, shaking her head as she filled her plate. Finished, she searched for a place to sit, pointing at an empty table near the rear of the pavilion, but Doc shook his head.

"Good choice, but we won't get that far."

"Why not?"

"Somebody will ask us to sit with them. They'll want to know how we met, how serious we are, and whatever else nosey people need to know."

A couple soon invited them to their table. "So glad to see you, Doc," the woman said. "Please sit with us."

"Thanks. Clair. Edna. Meet Merry," Doc said as they sat down.

"George stopped by and said Merry would be playing with our group today," Edna said with a welcoming smile.

"Doc fibbed," Merry said, shaking her head.

"And I shouldn't have," Doc admitted, trying to keep things calm.

Edna smiled knowingly. Clair proved to be the investigator. He asked Merry questions, trying to complete his knowledge of their relationship without much luck. He finally gave up and turned to his plate.

"Merry, you've only had half of your meal," Edna announced as they finished their plates. "The desserts are on that table," she said, pointing to another table. "Follow me. I always get Clair's desserts," Edna said as she stood up to get desserts.

"Oh, Edna, I wouldn't know what Doc likes."

"He's a man, Merry. He'll like whatever you bring him. Put some things you like on your plate and add a little something you can trade. Do the same for Doc. He isn't picky. He'll be thankful you thought of him."

When they returned to the table, Merry handed Doc a plate, and he gave her an appreciative smile, "Thanks. Man, some good-looking stuff. Lots of it, too."

"Edna told me to get lots and a variety. That way, you won't be trying to steal mine," Merry said as she worked at the kidding stuff.

Edna smiled. "Did I hear my name misused?"

"I don't think so," Merry answered with a mischievous smile. She was catching on.

"Merry, I need help," Doc said. "I can't eat sticky desserts when I'm playing. Can you cover mine? We'll eat them at home?"

"Why don't I put them all on one plate and cover them with the empty plate for later?"

"You don't need to wait for me."

"No room. I never eat this much."

With their meal finished, Doc and Merry placed their combined dessert plate in the now-empty cooler before making their way to the truck to get his guitar and her cameras. Parting, he handed Merry the keys. "You might need these while we're playing."

"I'm not sure I'm ready to take videos of people I don't know," Merry said apprehensively. "I don't know how I'd use them, but I know what you're thinking. It's better to have the video and not use it than to want the video and not have it. See, I'm catching on." After Doc's smile and approving nod, they went their separate ways.

Merry returned to their table to get her cameras ready when Clair said, "Wow, that baby looks expensive. Movie camera?"

"Video camera. Same thing. Doc suggested I take some pictures of the group."

"Can I do it for you?" Clair asked in a pleading voice. "I never used a camera like that, but you could show me how. I'll be careful."

"Great! I'll set it on automatic," Merry said as she provided instructions.

Clair stood and shot a little footage and then said, "Think I got it. Merry, I'll get shots of people eating and catch the band when they get going. Maybe some of the kids playing too."

Clair took off looking for picture material, leaving Merry to work with her other camera. He seemed happy, talking to people as he moved around.

Merry seated herself at a table close to the musicians. An older man took a seat across from her and introduced himself as Chuck. "Are you saving these seats?" When she shook her head, he said, "Great. My Nora will be along soon. We don't hear so well and like to sit closer."

The musicians set up in the pavilion and played "Blessed Assurance," an old Fanny Crosby hymn. Some people used folding chairs, while others sat on the grass. Most kids ran to the playground with one mother yelling, "You kids watch for snakes."

Merry held a shocked look as she asked Chuck if there were snakes around and was more than a little surprised by his answer. "Snakes are almost everywhere. Blaine Jensen gets several rattlers every year at his tree farm. A big rattlesnake struck at Ronnie Adams right there behind the church. Missed him. Ronnie had it behind the neck before it could recoil. Man, that kid's quick. Big snake, too."

"What did he do with it?"

"Dropped it in a burlap sack and put it in Doc's truck." Chuck stopped talking momentarily and added, "Snakes are just one of the reasons people carry guns around here. With all the drugs and rapes, somebody has to protect us, and it's us. Some kids staying at a camp were high on drugs and stopped Edna Mason on her way home from work. Hate to think what would have happened to her if she didn't carry."

"Do you think she would use a gun?"

"Oh, she used it. She took their gun and called the cops. They're still in jail."

"Oh," Merry answered, her eyes wide with surprise.

Doc's guitar case lay open by their table with sheets containing the words to songs. Reading through some, Merry decided she understood why it was difficult for him to sing some for her.

The group played a few hymns and then a couple of old country songs. Someone yelled, "Hey Doc, can we have one of them Carter Family tunes?"

He began picking 'I'll Be All Smiles Tonight,' and Edna sang along. She saw Merry mouthing the words and called her. "C'mon, Merry, give me a hand." Several others urged her on, so she hesitantly walked over to Edna carrying the song package. Doc picked through the chorus again, with Edna singing. Hesitantly, Merry joined in. Doc began singing, and Merry gave it a little more power as they sang it through. She was shocked and grew red-faced when listeners clapped when they finished.

Bob Beck called out, "Any more requests?" Before anyone else could answer, Edna requested 'A Winding Stream.' When the group started playing, Edna said, "Merry, help me with this one too." Merry sang with a little more energy this time. When they finished, Edna remarked, "Merry, you have a beautiful voice. Where'd you learn to sing like that?"

"From you."

"Me?"

"Must be from you. I've never even hummed through a whole song with anybody around."

"You keep singing, girl. You're good." She smiled and added, "Maybe I should get paid for your lesson."

The group played for another hour and a half before quitting. Doc packed his guitar, placed it in his truck, and locked the truck. He joined people at the food tables and discovered Merry had his utensils in the cooler when he arrived. "Not much to take home, Doc. Beans and eggs are gone. Pickles too."

"Usually are."

"Hey, Doc. Wait," Clair yelled as he hurried toward them. "I have Merry's camera."

"So glad you're honest. Find anything to shoot?" Merry asked.

"Did I ever. You gotta be about out of film. Hope we can view it together sometime." Before she could answer, Edna called, and Clair hustled away.

Doc looked at Merry as he struggled into his truck. She was smiling with a happy face. "I'm glad I came, Doc. Everybody was so nice. Your group was great, and I enjoyed singing. Now you'll have to teach me how."

"You gotta be kidding. Somebody told me I sound like a jackass with a toothache."

"You're good. Bob Beck stopped when I was packing the cooler and said I now knew how Merle Haggard sounded. I don't know who Merle Haggard is, but I know he sounded great."

Bang! Bang! Doc quickly glanced in his review mirror to see who was banging on his truck, and the who was Pastor Mike. He was waving his arms and running up along Merry's side. "I forgot your newspapers. They'd be a week late when you got them next Sunday."

"He wouldn't even notice, Pastor," Merry said. "He has a box full of month-old newspapers."

"You're kidding."

"Doc might kid you, but not me."

"It's a long story, Pastor," Doc said. "And thanks for bringing the papers. How we doing for money?"

"Lot's left, but I'm afraid to talk money with you. You might stay away another six months."

They laughed as Doc rolled off. Merry looked at the papers and asked, "Does he always bring you newspapers?"

"You can bet Bob Beck called him this morning. Told the Pastor I'd be there this afternoon with a new girlfriend, so he brought the papers."

"Do you think people believe I'm your girlfriend?"

"Sure hope so," Doc answered, watching to see what her reaction might be.

"You may want to be careful. My father threatened boyfriends with everything including death. 'Merry, you hook up with someone I disapprove of, and woe be unto him. I have ways to make people disappear.'"

Doc looked her a wondering glance. "Was he serious?"

"I was afraid to find out," she said with a strange look on her face. It was quiet as they drove toward home. After a bit, Merry broke the silence. "Did Ronnie catch a big rattlesnake by the church?"

"He did. Had it in a cage, but it wouldn't eat. One day I saw it mounted as the coiled snake."

It grew quiet again as they rolled down Cemetery Hill. Merry broke the silence. "I hate to bring the gun topic up, but I'm getting mixed feelings."

"Are we getting ready to argue after such a nice day together?"

"I hope not. Chuck and I were talking while you guys were tuning up. He said most adults out here have carry permits. He told me about druggies stopping Edna. Said they didn't stand a chance. She seems like such a nice lady."

"She's nice, but don't fool with Edna. She's a Marine."

CHAPTER 16

Merry read newspaper headlines aloud as they drove home, "White cops killed another black man. The cops claim the dead guy pulled a gun, and they acted in self-defense. That's what cops always say."

Merry looked up at him as they turned toward Doc's place. "Did you hear me?"

"I did," Doc quietly agreed.

"You didn't say anything."

"Because I don't know anything, and arguing without knowing is like juggling hand grenades. I don't want to ruin a beautiful day with an argument that carries no importance."

"No importance?" Merry barked, slapping her legs. "I closely —"

"Please stop!" Doc begged, with white knuckles gripping the steering wheel. "Merry, there's a difference between discussion and argument. With the first, you're helping someone understand a different side of things. With arguments, you're fighting to prove you're right. One helps, and the other hurts. Arguing leads to anger, and anger leads me to horrible dreams I can't control."

Neither talked until Doc was backing around in front of the house. He grabbed Merry's arm as she was getting out, "Look, I keep promising myself that's the last argument. Then it happens again. Can we shake and be friends."

"There's nothing I want more. Today was wonderful until I read about that killer cop."

Doc ignored her comment and climbed out of the truck. "I'll get the cooler if you unlock the door," Doc said, handing her the keys.

While they finished cleaning up the mess, Merry noticed the marinating steaks. "Look. Our steaks," she said with excitement in her voice. "Not sure I'll have room?"

"We'll fire up the pit and be ready with the steaks when we have coals. You'll find room."

Doc soon had a fire going and sat chairs on the smoke-free side of the fire as Merry arrived.

"I turned over the steaks and made sure they had liquid on top just like my teacher did," Merry said.

"You might want the experience of cooking your steak on a handheld grill."

"I would. Is the fire ready?"

"I let the fire burn into coals before I start grilling. Takes a while, but the meat tastes better."

They reminisced about their day, all except the brief exchange about cops and guns, as they waited for the fire to get ready for steak cooking. Doc wrapped four russet potatoes in aluminum foil and carefully placed them in the coals when the fire was ready. Doc retrieved a handheld grill and explained how to use it. A while later, they cooked their steaks and moved to the deck table to eat.

After the prayer, Merry picked up her water glass and offered a toast. "We had guests at our house, and their son tried to hook up with me by offering this toast.

"Here's to the red and sparkling wine,

I'll be your sweetheart if you'll be mine,

I'll be constant; I'll be true,

I'll leave my happy home for you."

"Did he move in with you?"

"Not hardly," Merry said. "My father, being the generous soul that he is, calmly said, 'Randall, I'll have your cot put up in the storage room down by the pool.'"

"Now that you toasted Randall's memories, can you toast us?" Doc asked, grinning.

Smiling and looking Doc in the eyes, she offered the toast again. When she finished, Doc seriously asked, "Did you mean that, Merry?"

"I must mean it," Merry answered without hesitation. "I'm moved in."

Doc nodded, grinning without comment, and clinked her glass. He held the smile, and she smiled back. They touched glasses again and began eating. Following the meal, Merry said, "The food was great, and I enjoyed the company. Too bad we don't have a dessert."

"We have Kitty's apple pie and the plate from the singalong, but I have a better idea," Doc said and headed for the house. He returned with a bag of marshmallows and a sweater for Merry. "Better put this on. It's getting cool, and we have to cut toasters."

They walked out to a patch of young birch trees where Doc cut sticks. It was growing dark when they headed home. At the salt block set out for wildlife, Doc walked over to a tree and unhooked a box fastened there.

"What's that?" Merry asked with a puzzled look.

"A trail camera. It's pointed at the area around the salt block and picks up animal visitors. The other box is a security camera picking up travelers on the road. We'll view the photo card for the trail cam and put it back tomorrow."

Heading back, an owl hooted overhead. Alarmed, Merry grabbed Doc's arm. "What was that?"

"I'm thinking dinosaur. If that isn't scary enough, I'll try something else."

"Okay, Adams. What are you telling me?"

"I like you holding my arm." Glad it's dark, Doc thought as he felt his face warming. He said nothing more until they reached their chairs by the fire, where he placed two marshmallows on the end of each sharpened stick. "I like mine nicely browned," Doc offered. "How do you like yours?"

"Don't know. Never tried this before."

Merry immediately caught hers on fire. "What now, Doc?" she asked in a begging voice.

"I don't like burned ones, so I'd throw those cremated babies in the fire."

She tossed hers and watched Doc toast two. A few times, they caught fire, but he quickly shook them out. He held out his stick to her when they were brown, and she took one. He took the other and said, "Here's dessert."

Merry said nothing as Doc put more marshmallows on their sticks. Looking at her and noting a dark look, he asked, "Something wrong?"

"Not wrong, Doc. So right. I had a beautiful day doing things I never dreamed of doing before. I was in a foreign bedroom making beds with a man I didn't know two days ago and wasn't scared. I went to a church picnic where I only knew one person and him for just two days. Sang songs I hadn't heard before in front of people I didn't know. I cooked my first steak over a fire, and it was my best steak ever. I burned my first marshmallows. Oh, and I was scared by a —. It wasn't a dinosaur; what was it?"

"An owl."

She squeezed his arm and laughed. "You like to kid me, and I enjoy it. Most of the time, anyway. I have another question. Are all the people around here as friendly as the ones at the picnic?"

"They are to me."

"Doc, you're two days past being a total stranger, and you're already the easiest person I've ever been around when I'm not picking fights with you. But is the you of today really you?"

"Merry, it's how I live my life."

"Yeah, but why?"

"I was an orphan who had most of nothing and nowhere to go. My grandparents took me in and loved me. This is how they lived."

"With everybody?"

"Almost everybody. A few people crossed Gramp."

"And?"

"It wasn't good for them."

After a quiet time with Merry's hand resting on his, she said, "Today was a day I won't forget."

"I had a great day, too, but don't tell your father. I don't wanta disappear."

CHAPTER 17

What a great day, but why can't I let anything slide? Merry asked herself as she slipped out of her clothes and stepped into the shower. *Maybe I should have been a lawyer. You don't have to be correct to win, just the most persuasive.*

Closing her eyes, she tipped her head back and allowed the water to spray her face. Using the Suave shampoo found in the shower, she quickly learned a little bit goes a long way. As she soaped down, Merry looked back through the day and had difficulty believing they had done so many different fun things. It began with a great breakfast, finishing the Bucky job, a whirlwind shopping trip, a songfest feast with Christians, and finished with cooking steaks over a fire with marshmallows for dessert.

Maybe he's on to something with this video thing. It sounds good, but then he makes so many things seem right. It might become a future opportunity, but I need something now.

I wish I could have met this 'Gramp' of his. He sure had an impact on Doc's life. Merry, admit it. Doc's affecting your life, too, like it or not. He's quite a man. Must be six two or three with big arms. Good looking with black wavy hair, a square jaw, and those blue eyes, man,

With her shower completed, she dried off and slipped into PJs.

Bedtime.

CHAPTER 18

After a cereal breakfast on a rainy Monday morning, Doc loaded some of Ronnie's animals and camping equipment into his truck for video efforts. Heavy black clouds streamed by with lightning blazing across the sky, followed closely by the ear-piercing crack of thunder and the smell of ozone. Looking at the sky, Doc wondered if they might have too much planned for the weather they faced.

Doc walked Merry to the truck with an umbrella and opened her door. "Doc, you don't have to open the door for me. I'm a big girl who can get in vehicles by myself."

"Hey, remember being your big girl self landed you here in Nowheresville."

Doc jumped out at the state police headquarters and picked up copies of their accident report before stopping at Ronnie's garage, where Merry's car sat outside. Giving Merry his umbrella, Doc grabbed her camera and shot a video of her assessing the damage.

Seeing them, Ronnie came out, and Doc made introductions. "Merry, I'd like you to meet Ronnie."

"Ronnie, I couldn't wait to meet you. Love your artwork and stuffed animals," Merry said with a warm smile.

"Thanks," Ronnie said, his embarrassment showing. "About your car, body parts will be here Wednesday morning. We'll install them when they arrive and get her painted. The mechanical part is another story. We'll stay in touch and go from there. If you don't mind my asking, who's your insurance company?"

"State Farm."

"Great. The State Farm agent's right down the street, and they're easy to deal with," Ronnie assured her.

"I know. Your father made me call them," Merry said with a smile.

"That's Dad. He always wants to get things done now."

While they talked, Doc videoed them with the wreck in the background. When they said their goodbyes, Ronnie watched his father open Merry's door and grew a broad smile. When Doc walked by, he said, "Noticed you remembered how to act around ladies."

"Not sure where this is heading, Ronnie. I'm concerned."

"Dad, like mom said, you gotta give love another chance. Remember what you told Sarah and me? Do what your heart tells you today. Tomorrow will take care of itself."

Doc shook his head and headed for the State Farm office. When he started to get out, Merry smiled. "You don't have to come with me. I'm a big girl."

"And a pretty big girl, but I'm part of this wreck, too. These reports ask questions you might need help with."

Doc watched her eyes and smile, full of sparkling white teeth, as he helped her out of the truck. And yes, he noticed the rest of her, too.

Doc held the office door for her and introduced her to the staff. "Bill, Ginny, this would be Merry Morehouse. I tried to run over her Friday night. It was dark and raining when we crashed at the top of Cemetery Hill. She turned around in the Game Commission parking lot, and we didn't see each other. Trooper Ogden investigated and found no one at fault."

"That's Shippen Township, isn't it, Doc?"

"It is. Route 3001."

Merry gave Doc the I don't need help look as she handed Bill her accident report and driver's license. Bill then completed the accident reports with Merry answering questions. "Merry, this looks like an easy one. No injuries, and you're both insured by State Farm."

Cold wind and rain chased pain up Doc's spine as they departed. "We better stop at the grocery store. Anything you might need other than a newspaper full of fighting stories?"

"I can't think of anything. My babysitter takes great care of me." Their eyes met, and she winked, bringing an amusing grin to Doc's face.

"Grab the umbrella and come in anyway," Doc said as he parked the truck. It'll keep young, handsome dudes from hanging around my truck. Can't tell what they'll do if they see a beautiful woman such as yourself all alone, one who doesn't carry self-protection."

"All right, Adams, enough. I'm trying my best to have sweet little discussions instead of hateful arguments."

Both laughed as they exited. Grabbing a shopping cart someone left in the parking lot, they headed for the store, where they ran into an older man with his arm in a sling fixing a flat tire. Doc took over and asked him to wait in his car while he sent Merry under the awning out of the rain. With the tire changed and rain dripping off his face, Doc said, "Your flats in the trunk. The spare looks like it could use a little air."

"Thanks so much. What do I owe you?"

"Help someone who needs a hand," Doc suggested as he walked away to meet Merry.

Doc exchanged the shopping cart for a dry one and dropped in a Bradford Era newspaper as they maneuvered through the store, grabbing some greens, sausage, and other things. Moseying over to the ice cream freezers, he announced with a grin, "Merry, we're in luck. Perry's ice cream is BOGO. Any special flavors you like?"

"I shouldn't be eating ice cream."

Doc grabbed cartons of peanut butter chocolate and French vanilla and headed for checkout. "We need to get in the first lane if you need snuff or chewing tobacco," Doc teased.

"We'll be okay in either lane, Mr. Adams," Merry answered in a disapproving voice.

"Well, lookee here. None other than Doc Adams," the cashier said in greeting.

"It is, Polly, and this young lady is Merry."

"Nice to meet you, Merry. You Doc's friend?"

"Just an accident victim so far," Merry answered with a pleasant smile.

Doc said nothing until they returned to the parking lot, where he asked, "So far?"

"Am I beginning to sound like you, Mr. Adams?" Merry chuckled.

"Yeah, and I like it," Doc agreed. "So much nicer than arguments."

"I like it too."

The rain had almost stopped when Doc finished putting food in the cooler. Merry was already seated in the truck when he pushed the cart back to the store. Opening her door, he said, "When Billy jumped in by herself, I opened the door and gave her a kiss just to show her she wasn't stealing my job."

"You don't have to change traditions for me."

Pushing back temptation, he walked away, blushing, wondering what would have happened if he tried to kiss her.

They headed home and drove up the mountain with the rain slowing. They pulled in at the lookout, where Merry got out and shot a video beginning with the long valleys coming into Emporium and the mountains towering over the town. Zooming in, she captured landmarks such as the old brick courthouse. Climbing back in the truck, damp from the light rain, she said, "Even on a rainy day, it's a beautiful place."

CHAPTER 19

Arianna slumped over her desk after calling Merry again with no answer. "What's going on? I call, and zip, nada, nothing," Arianna said aloud, looking around to see if anyone heard her.

Maybe Charlie knows something, Arianna wondered and buzzed him. "I was wondering if anyone heard from Merry."

"Dear Arianna, wait until that young lady discovers what the person she trusted pulled on her."

"What are you talking about, Charlie?" Arianna asked with her stomach knotting.

"Everybody knows you sent her up to Bucky's place when she was never camping before, then shafted her out of the weekend anchor spot. Something bad could happen to her up there without anyone knowing."

"I'll tell her you put me up to it because you're tired of her cold shoulder."

"I'm concerned. The big woods country can be dangerous when you know what you're doing. When I talked to her last week, she was getting cold feet and didn't know you weren't going."

"Stuff it, Charlie."

"We better see if anyone knows anything about her. Can you talk with women who might know? I'll check with Bucky and some others."

"Sounds like you pulled some crap on her."

"Just trying to help!"

"Baloney, Charlie. I'm not sure how you're involved, but the truth will out. In the meantime, I'll talk with Jaylene Carter and Maggie Ward."

"Merry won't talk to you again when she finds out what you pulled."

"Drop off a cliff, Charlie," Arianna said with a clenched jaw. She wasn't proud of what she'd done, but the terrifying changes hanging over the company made it initially seem okay.

During the morning, Charlie and Arianna contacted others but discovered nothing. The people Arianna talked with had more questions than answers, making her more fearful. To make matters worse, the morning crew called twice to see how she was doing on their project, and she had barely started it. What was I thinking, she asked herself, but no answers came.

Charlie called at 11:45, "Arianna, let's get out of here so we can talk."

"I told you I wasn't going —"

"Forget that crap. You're in this mess deeper than I am. Let's go to Wendy's for lunch. I'll be out in my vehicle."

"I can't stay long. I'm already late with this assignment."

"Whatever."

Arianna locked the project in her drawer and headed for the parking lot where Charlie waited. He was talking before the door closed.

"Man, Arianna, I talked to Bucky, and he gave me information that flattened me. And no, he hasn't heard from Merry."

"What did you do, Charlie?"

"Let's talk inside."

Inside, Charlie headed toward the food ordering line. With a fearful look, Arianna grabbed his arm. "Charlie, I'm too nervous to eat. I'll save our seats."

Arianna walked to a table near the exit, looking around to ensure she didn't know anyone. Charlie was soon back with two sandwiches and two Cokes. "Charlie, I told you —"

"I know what you told me, but you need to eat something."

"Let's get on with whatever Bucky told you so we can get out of here. I have an important deadline staring me in the face."

"Remember a couple of weeks ago when we had that fight? You had —"

"How could I forget, Charlie? I said I wasn't going anywhere with you again, but here I am."

"Arianna, please hold down your voice. Everybody's staring at us."

"Tough. This thing's driving me nuts."

"Look, after you gave me crap, I —"

"You had that and more coming. I'm tired of your arrogance."

Charlie allowed her to finish before he answered in a fearful voice. "Okay, so I'm arrogant, but we still have a mutual problem. After our argument, Ike and I used Bucky's place. It rained the whole weekend, and we tracked mud all over the porch and inside his camp. We ate like hogs and didn't clean up our messes or make the beds. We believed you two would clean up the place because if you didn't, Bucky would think it was your mess."

Glaring at him, she said, "You idiot."

"Bucky always puts three keys in the cabin package he gives people, with each key tagged with the lock it fits. I mixed the keys and tags up. Today, Bucky told me he simplified the directions and just put the door key in the package. Merry can't get in the cabin because I swapped keys."

"She's going to be very upset, Charlie."

"That's not the whole problem. There were bear tracks all over the place. One was a big sucker that had been on the porch looking in the window. If Merry can't get in, she's sleeping on the porch where anything could happen. I'm worried."

"Serves you right. You're such a know-it-all. You had smart-ass comments about every idea anyone offered at the company's improvement meeting. You embarrassed Merry when she suggested producing Pennsylvania videos in line with those New York and the beach communities advertise on our channel. You said that would be so uninteresting and —.”

“It wasn’t that bad.”

“Charlie, it was worse than that.”

“I get your point, Arianna,” Charlie said. “I was out of place, but that’s not the problem now. You talked Merry into going up there, stood her up, and took her job.”

“Merry said, ‘I need to do a few big girl things myself.’ It’s on her, too.”

Fear rode Charlie’s face, and his hand shook as he took a bite of his burger. They sat quietly for some time with Arianna sipping her drink until Charlie suggested, “The state cops should know if she ran into a problem.”

“Better call Charlie. I see this more your problem than mine.”

Charlie pulled out his cell phone and Googled ‘Pennsylvania State Police,’ then dialed the Cameron County barracks. When the officer answered, he began. “Good afternoon, officer. We have a problem and hope you can help us.”

“What’s your problem, sir?” the desk trooper asked.

“Our friend is a first-time camper, and she’s staying by herself in a Cameron County cabin. She promised to call but hasn’t. We’re wondering if you know anything about her.”

“What’s her name?”

“Merry Morehouse.”

"When was she supposed to have arrived here?"

"Friday evening."

"Let me look through the log."

After several minutes passed, the officer came back on the line. "We have a Merry Morehouse listed for Friday night at 8:47. She got hit by a truck on Moore Hill. Cameron County is a remote area. They often remove critically injured people in helicopters."

"Can you tell us anything else?" a panicked Charlie asked.

"I probably told you more than I should without clearing it with the sergeant."

With the call complete, Charlie turned to Arianna. His colorless, fear-ridden face said trouble, and his hands shook as he reached for his Coke. "We're in deep trouble, Arianna. Merry got hit by a truck. Probably a loaded triaxle log truck. Those babies weigh over forty tons loaded. The duty cop said they take critically injured people out in helicopters because there isn't a hospital in the county."

"I'll try to get her parent's phone from personnel. Maybe they know something."

"That could open up a whole new problem. Merry's old man's a big-shot lawyer. Who knows what he'll do? Look, I'll try to get some advice from someone in the know. I know you said you wouldn't do it again, but let's meet for dinner at Applebees. I should be there a little after seven."

On their return to the station, Arianna nervously asked, "I wonder if we're criminally liable for this mess, Charlie?"

"You suckered her into going up there when you knew she couldn't take care of herself. All we did was leave the place dirty, and that was to get you, not Merry."

"Hey, bozo, you screwed up the keys too. If a logging truck didn't get her, the bears might. Wrap your conscience around that, Charlie."

CHAPTER 20

Merry looked herself over and asked, "Why'd you ask me to dress in the clothes I brought from home?"

Doc smiled. "You had no idea how to dress for a camping trip. People viewing this video will only know what you show them. TV viewers will find it interesting, while those who set you up find it disturbing. You can introduce other clothing with video shots when you're shopping."

"Whatever," Merry muttered in an unconvincing tone.

"Let's place your video camera on a tripod and take pictures with you reading directions and setting up the tent."

Merry soon had the tent up. She grabbed a large stone and pounded in the tent pegs following Doc's signaled advice. Doc procured newspapers, matches, and Merry's video camera and headed to the fire pit, where he shot video of Merry breaking dead hemlock limbs and lighting her first fire.

"Let's cut some cooking sticks while the fire burns a bit. I'll operate your camera."

They walked down the road until they came to a patch of beech brush. Doc took out his pocket knife and cut a sample. Taking the camera, he gave Merry his knife and took video as she grabbed a limb of the right size and carefully sawed it.

"Put more pressure on the knife, but be careful. It's sharp."

She stuck out her tongue at his smiling face. Snatching the limb tightly, she made slick cuts, trimming the end to a point. The thicker limb for the braut went easier with her newfound skills, and she soon had sticks cut and sharpened. "What next, partner?" she asked with a grin that said I'm proud of my accomplishment.

Doc located himself by the fire pit to video her cooking sausage. She stuck the braut on her stick and, holding it over the flames, slowly rolled it around until moisture bubbled out. She soon ate the sausage and began toasting marshmallows.

"How's that, camper buddy?" she asked as Doc finished the video.

"Looked good," Doc said as he retrieved her pillow and blanket from the porch and placed them in the tent. With the bear standing on four legs outside the tent, he said, "You're waking up to find this bear inspecting you. Act scared and start rolling the video. Zoom into the doorway after you shoot with the bear's shadow seen through the tent. I'll turn the bear allowing its head to stick into the tent. That will make it look like he's getting ready to have you for breakfast."

"Okay. Here goes." Merry screamed, "Help me!" in a terrified voice, acting like she was trying not to cry as she continued shooting. Doc turned the bear to appear like it was coming into the tent, and she screamed again. Soon, she yelled 'Done' and crawled out smiling. "This is starting to be fun."

"Let's do a run with the rattlesnake." Doc placed the coiled snake in thicker grass by the spring, where it looked as if it were ready to strike.

"It looks so doggone real. I'd be scared to death if I didn't know your son stuffed it."

"I'll film, and you say something like, 'You won't believe what I saw when I went to get water.' Walk toward the spring with me filming, and you say things like, 'Gee, I don't see him anymore. He was right over here and point to a location away from the snake. Then act as if you see him. You're scared. We can film it several times until you think it's right."

They ran through it twice, and some parts didn't satisfy Merry. On the third try, she said, "I think we got it that time."

"Review it tonight. If you aren't satisfied, we'll do it again tomorrow. Let's get this stuff in the truck and head down Hicks Run. Be ready with your camera. Can't tell what we'll see."

As they neared the bottom of the valley, three bull elk were feeding by a beaver dam. Doc stopped in the road, and Merry began shooting. The bull's new racks were in velvet and already massive. After tiring of watching Merry taking videos, they laid back their heads and trotted into the dense brush.

"Man, they're big!" Merry said, her voice radiating excitement. "I wouldn't believe it if I hadn't seen them."

They came to a place where they could park off the road near the stream. "Grab your video camera," Doc said as he struggled out of the truck.

They walked to a place where a large oak tree had fallen across the stream and eased across on it. They worked along the creek to a rock outcropping, where the stream widened and deepened into a huge hole. Doc turned over stones below the pool, searching for something to tempt a trout until he found a crab.

"You're quite a hunter. A real live crayfish."

"They call 'em crabs in Cameron County, but we'll call this one bait. Let's climb up on those rocks overlooking the pool. Maybe you can get a picture of a brookie grabbing this guy."

Merry sat camera-ready on the rocks. Doc said, "Here goes," and tossed the crab. A large brook trout lying in the shadows grabbed it when it hit the water. "Wow, Merry, that guy's a beauty."

"Yeah, but we took a life to get his picture. It's the first time I saw anything get eaten alive."

The sounds of the fast-moving stream churning below and the birds calling from the trees surrounded them. "Remember this spot, Merry. You're going to need to take baths. Maybe wash a few clothes, too."

"You kicking me out? I'm doing quite well showering at your place. Washing clothes there, too."

Chuckling, Doc looked at her. "Not kicking you out. Just thinking about bathing for the video."

"Oh sure, you want to take nude pictures of me. I was beginning to think Doc Adams was different from other men."

"Can't lie. I'd sneak a peek if you were nude, but I was thinking of a swimming suit with the camera on a tripod."

"Oh, now you plan to send me here by myself where a bear might eat me. Maybe the truth is coming out."

"Great idea, Merry. We'll bring a bear. Let's head home so we can celebrate."

"Celebrate?"

"We haven't argued yet today."

After a busy day at home, Doc cooked dinner with Merry perched on a stool. They discussed additional video shoots until dinner was ready. The mixed aroma of onions, garlic, and potatoes wafted about as Doc and Merry ate their meatloaf dinner. "Great food, Doc. How about teaching me to cook?"

"You don't cook?" Doc asked with surprise spreading across his face. What do you eat?"

"Afraid you'd ask. Breakfast is cereal or Starbucks, lunch at the cafeteria, and dinner is something frozen, stop for pizza to go, or something like that. Weekends are touch and go."

As they ate, Merry's cell phone rang. "It's Arianna. She can leave another message. She's called several times every day, but I haven't listened to her messages. Somebody suggested two can play most games."

After discussing the Arianna and Charlie situation, Merry asked if she could take him up on the email offer to explore files on subjects that caused their arguments. He explained how he filed articles under Biased Media Coverage with subtopics such as Second Amendment, Climate Change, and Police Incidents. "Each folder includes media and email messages along with the email addresses in case one wants to research for accuracy. If you need to take notes, you'll find tablets and pens in the top left-hand desk drawer. Sharyl Attkisson's email address is on a paper clip hanging from the desk light. She often provides eye-popping information. My email address is docnbil@ aol.net. The password's hanging on the same paperclip from the desk light. Holler if you have questions."

Doc showered and retreated to his favorite chair to look through Cindy's papers. He had articles of interest placed in boxes when Merry came downstairs.

"Find what you wanted?"

Nodding, she answered with arms crossed, "Read the info on some of the police shootings. It's hard to believe the difference between national media coverage and the materials in those emails. I assumed, 'Hands Up. Don't Shoot' was the real deal, but on-site witnesses report it never happened. It seems there's a common theme running through the bad cops-killing minorities articles. Most perps were known criminals resisting arrest when they ran into problems. I have a question. Why are you saving those emails?"

"I've considered writing a book on differences between what reports say happened and media coverage."

Merry crossed her arms and shook her head, letting a smile light her face. "After knowing you for a few days, I can believe that. During our meeting to increase viewership, a new staff member suggested changing our news coverage to include all sides of current events. The station manager cut him off and said we were affiliates following company guidelines aligned with our national media reports. After reading coverage of several stories, I feel I've betrayed our viewers because of the way I presented some stories prepared for me. I need another favor, Doc. Can you set me up on Billy's machine so I can begin reviewing our videos?"

They retreated upstairs, where Merry looked over the program list, "Wow. Her programs will do everything I need and more."

"Yell if I can help," Doc said and departed. He soon finished the box and placed the saved articles in boxes containing article descriptions on the lids.

Sometime later, Merry returned to find Doc reading. "Can I interrupt?" When he nodded, Merry continued. "Billy was into some great stuff. She created advertising pieces along with educational and training support products. She was also working on a mentoring series for schools. How'd she do all that stuff and still work a difficult day?"

"She's Billy."

Merry hesitated, wanting to ask Doc something else but couldn't decide how to phrase it. "Doc, can I ask you a question? You can tell me it's none of my business, and I'll understand."

"Ask away."

"Do you realize when you mention Billy, you talk as if she's still here?"

Doc thought through the question, taking his time before answering. Staring into space, he replied in a low voice. "Merry, you hinted at this before. Maybe I'm afraid to let her go. She gave me a wonderful life. During her funeral, Pastor Mike said something to the effect that she's still with us but living at a new address."

They discussed Billy until Merry mentioned the picture frame messages she viewed on Doc and Billy's computers. "Doc, Can you tell me about the 'COMMITMENT' message hanging by both your computer and Billy's? If it's none of my business, tell me."

It was quiet while Doc thought through what to say and how to say it while Merry waited prayerfully.

"Merry, Billy and I loved each other and wanted a happy marriage. Before our marriage, she read and kept a little pamphlet by Charles Swindoll titled 'Commitment.' It was a giveaway at the little church we attended together. We reread it together and decided we would never allow anything to get in the way of our love and life together. We agreed our lives weren't our own; we belonged to each other. When our kids came along, we agreed we belonged to them too. The pamphlet meant so much that we placed it in my frame. Those three lines became our continuous reminder never to allow anything to get in the way of our love and marriage. That's why we both signed both copies. I still carry a handwritten copy in my wallet on the back of our wedding photo."

"COMMITMENT

. . . FOR BETTER OR FOR WORSE. . .

. . . TIL DEATH DO US PART."

"Did it always work?"

"Almost always."

"What happened when it didn't?"

"We got our 'commitment' pledge and read it together—a few times with our kids. We knew what we had to lose. It wasn't always easy, but it was right for us."

"Maybe every married couple should do this. It could be a guide that lessened the divorce rate," Merry suggested.

After a quiet spell, Merry asked, "Can you handle another question?"

"I can try."

"I've noticed you always try to sit on my right. You set the table that way, sit to my right on the porch, and did over at Buckys. When you drive, you turn toward me when I talk. Is there a reason for that?"

"I want to hear what you say. Isn't that why you talk to me?"

"All right, smarty. I guess I deserve that for being so nosey."

Doc thought through her question and then answered in a soft voice. "When I lost my leg, my eardrum blew out, and they diagnosed me with TBI."

"TBI?"

"Traumatic Brain Injury. I should warn you I sometimes wake up screaming."

"You paid a heavy price for this country."

"There's a payoff."

"Oh?"

"I met Billy at Bethesda."

CHAPTER 21

At 7:15, Arianna nervously rechecked her watch. *Where is he?* she anxiously asked herself. *He should have been here by now.*

"Trying to hide?" Charlie asked a few minutes later as he walked up from the opposite direction.

"Stuff it," Arianna said with tightness in her voice. "I didn't think you'd ever get here."

"Geez, it's only seventeen after seven," Charlie answered as he checked his watch.

She shook her head and gave him a mean look. "I got a booth away from people so we could talk. All I could think this afternoon was she got run over by a truck. Then I missed a project deadline."

Chills chased fear up Charlie's spine. "I'm learning I have difficulty passing up chances to act like an idiot."

Arianna rolled her eyes. "Charlie, you finally uttered a truth we can agree on."

Their waiter brought menus and asked if they'd like something to drink. When the waiter walked away with their beverage order, Charlie took out his cell phone and pulled up the State Police phone number in Emporium. When the desk trooper answered, Charlie said, "My name is Charlie Williams. Is Trooper Ogden in?"

"He's is. Let me transfer you."

Shortly he was on the phone. "Trooper Ogden here."

"Charlie Williams. I understand you covered an accident Friday night that involved my friend Merry Morehouse. We've been unable to reach her. Do you have any information on her?"

"Trooper Gornick said you might be calling. Are you a relative?"

"Very close friend."

"Trooper Gornick is relatively new and shared more information than he should have. Is there anything else we can help you with?"

"If someone needed a hospital, where might they be taken?"

"It depends. Cameron County has no hospital. St. Marys and Coudersport Hospitals are closest. If accident victims are in bad shape, they could be life flighted to Dubois or Pittsburgh."

"Could you tell me which hospital Merry might be at?"

"Sorry. I don't have that information."

"Do you have phone numbers for the hospitals you mentioned?"

"Can you hold a minute?"

Charlie drew circles while he waited.

"Are you ready?" Trooper Ogden asked as he came back on the phone. With hands shaking, Charlie wrote the phone numbers on a napkin and thanked the officer.

"Wait until Merry discovers you and her are close friends," Arianna quipped.

"Stuff it! I'm trying to get information. How about helping me call hospitals. I'll try Coudersport, and you hit St. Marys.

Charlie turned the paper so Arianna could read the numbers while he dialed the Coudersport hospital. The receptionist came on the line, "Charles Cole Memorial Hospital. How may I help you?"

"Good evening. You sound friendly. I appreciate that."

"Thank you, sir. How may I help you?"

"My friend was in an accident Friday evening in Cameron County. Her name is Merry Morehouse. I'm wondering if she might be there?"

"Are you a family member or an official party?"

"Just a worried friend."

"I'm sorry. I'm not allowed to release that information."

"I live in Harrisburg. I'd hate to drive four hours to Coudersport if she isn't there."

"I'm sorry, sir. Our privacy policy is specific about the information we can provide."

"Okay," Charlie answered dejectedly. "Thanks anyway."

Arianna had completed her call when Charlie hung up. "Some old bat answered the phone. I couldn't get anything from her."

"I'll dial Pittsburgh and just ask to be connected to her."

The waiter arrived to take their orders before Charlie completed dialing the call. "I had a grilled chicken caesar salad last week and loved it. I'll have the salad again and the glazed baby back ribs."

"Have you been able to select a dinner yet, ma'am?"

"Yes. I'll have the dinner of the day."

"We have two delicious fish choices: blackened Tilapia or savory cedar salmon. The Tilapia is lightly rubbed in Cajun spices, grilled and drizzled with garlic and —"

"I'll have the Tilapia," Arianna murmured.

"Great choice," the waiter murmured. "Can I get you anything else while your dinner's prepared?"

When both answered 'No,' the waiter departed and soon returned with their salads.

"What next?" Arianna asked as she fixed her hair again.

"Well, my friend, I came —"

Rolling her eyes, Arianna snapped, "Don't call me your friend, Charlie. I'm not."

"All right, smarty, how about accomplice in crime?"

"Whatever."

"Let's call the other hospitals. Nothing there, and I'll call the owner of Jensen's Tree Farm. It sits across the road from Bucky's place."

Charlie called Pittsburgh, and Arianna tried Dubois with no luck. Charlie pulled up Jensen Tree Farm and dialed the number. After four rings, a recording came on requesting the name and phone number for a return call. Charlie left his information along with a message, "This is important. Please call me ASAP."

"Can you try Merry's phone again?" Charlie requested.

Arianna nervously scratched her head and dialed. After Merry's announcement message ended, she said in a tight voice, "Merry, this is Arianna. I'm so worried about you. Please call me."

"Well, Arianna, I'm out of ideas. I'll talk to Bucky and maybe Warner's secretary. Can you try Maggie Ward and perhaps Jaylene Carter again? Somebody has to know something."

Their meals arrived as they discussed what to do next. After picking at their food for some time, the waiter dropped by to see if they wanted dessert. When they didn't, he made an effort to help them, "I see we're having trouble with dinner. I hope the meals were okay."

They both nodded, and Arianna said, "The meals are great. We're the problems."

The waiter asked if they wanted boxes, and when they didn't, he prepared their bill and laid it on the table. Charlie grabbed it and said, "Please hang on a minute," as he fished out a credit card.

When the waiter departed, "Arianna snapped, "Charlie, I don't want to owe you anything. I'll pay for my meal."

"You want to pay for your meal, and I want to find Merry. Let's see whose want is received."

CHAPTER 22

Merry talked excitedly as they strolled to the barn for her first horseback ride. While Doc saddled Dolly and Duke, she examined her surroundings. Tipping her head, she smelled the air, sniffed a wad of hay, looked into the feed bin, and glanced out the window at the manure pile. A grin spread over Doc's face as he watched. "Find anything interesting?"

Surprised, she answered, "Everything. This is my first time in a barn. I thought it would stink, but it smells, well, interesting."

After leading the horses outside, Doc said, "Let me help you on, and we'll get out of here. Put your left foot in the stirrup. When I say 'go,' push off with your right foot. GO!"

Merry pushed off, and Doc's boost threw her over Dolly's side, where she hung upside down with Doc hanging on to her leg. Surprised, Dolly started dancing with Merry screaming, "Help me!"

Doc pulled her upright, and she slid off the horse, falling to the ground. Her eyes quickly shifted from fear to anger. "Dammit, Adams! You did that on purpose."

"Merry, I'm sorry. I didn't —"

"You don't look sorry."

"Let me help you up," Doc said, reaching for her.

"Keep your hands off me," she demanded with tear-filled eyes.

Doc sat down beside her with both horses looking at them. "I didn't think that could happen."

They sat with her crying and him wondering what to do next. Duke stomped impatiently, and Doc stumbled to his feet. "Let me help you up."

Merry climbed to her feet with a touch of pain on her face. Fearfully, she said, "That's enough horses for today. Probably forever."

Doc shared his handkerchief while softly asking, "Is your back still bothering you?"

"Some, but that's not the problem."

Not knowing what else to say, Doc suggested, "Do it for your big girl self!"

Merry handed back his handkerchief. She shook her head and said, "I'll try it, but keep your hands off me."

Merry tried again and struggled aboard. Doc handed her the reins, hung her video camera on her saddle horn, and mounted. "Our horses neck rein. Hold the reins in one hand and pull them against Dolly's neck in the direction you want her to turn. Pull back to get her to stop and loosen up to let her go. Dolly will teach you everything you need to know."

They rode side-by-side across the field toward the state road. Hitting the blacktop, they rode single file until they turned down a dirt road toward a farmhouse. A magnificent log home sat on the ridge top to the left. "See that log cabin," Doc pointed. "Billy's parents live there."

"That's nice. Your kids could visit often."

"Cindy, some. Ronnie, not much," Doc answered in a tone that told Merry he didn't want to discuss it.

Before they got to the Hackett gated driveway, Doc took a trail down into the woods that continued into a hemlock tree-lined valley. Merry leaned back sniffing the forest scent flooding over them. Birds of all kinds and colors moved about, keeping her video camera humming.

After they had ridden for about an hour, Doc stopped. "Had enough for today?"

"I'm enjoying this, both riding and the video shots."

Doc nodded and smiled as he turned Duke and began retracing their trip. When they hit Spring Brook Road home, Doc moved Duke over and allowed Merry to ride beside them. "Would you like to try a little higher gear?" he asked.

"Do you think I'm ready?" Merry asked with a frightful grin. "I don't want to hang upside down again."

"We'll canter," Doc replied. "Dolly's a gentle ride. Just keep the reins up and heel her sides lightly. She'll know what to do. Anytime you want, you can pull back on the reins and drop back to a walk."

"Let's give it a try."

Doc nudged Duke, and they cantered toward home. After a bit, Merry slowed to a walk, and Doc noted pain on her face. "Back hurt?"

"Some."

They dismounted at the barn and, after removing their saddles, turned the horses loose in the pasture. Duke bucked a bit before lying down and rolling on his back. "Don't have to wonder how he gets dirty," Doc said, shaking his head. "You did good, Merry. Anybody seeing you cantering wouldn't know it was your first go on a horse."

"Oh yeah. Tell that to my fanny."

"You hurting?"

"The Aleve's wearing off. Hanging upside down gave me a new perspective on life."

"I'll bet," Doc answered, hoping she wasn't holding a grudge.

They were eating an early hotdog lunch when Merry announced, "Good thing I washed upstairs. I'd have missed another important call."

"Did you answer it?"

"Nope. You want to listen to the messages with me?"

"Why don't you listen to them out on the deck? They may carry information I shouldn't hear."

Merry went to the deck and returned, laughing about the calls. "You'd bust a gut listening to my messages. Arianna and Charlie exhibit ever-increasing concern for my well-being. They're fearful with a need to know while I'm enjoying the best of times. It sounds like they're thinking of the worst possible scenarios. "One message was from Maggie Ward. It was pleasant, hoping I was having a good time. She asked me to drop by when I get back."

"You'll have video material ready for her review."

"Do you plan everyone's life for them?"

"Nah. I let some stumble around on their own."

After lunch, they headed to Buckys for some video efforts. As they passed the Hill Church, Merry remarked, "I feel hypocritical saying this, but I had a great time Sunday."

"Maybe we can attend church next Sunday."

"I never worshiped before."

"Has to be a first time for everything."

As they turned down the Quail Run Road, she studied the tree farm to see if anyone was there. "Bucky suggested I introduce myself to the owner in case I needed anything."

"Might not want to do that. Your friends might call him, and your disappearing act will end."

"You're right. I don't want anyone to know what's happening."

Doc stopped across from Bucky's place with a suggestion. "Why don't you take your video camera and wait here? I'll set Mister Foxie by the road down at Bucky's place. Take videos from here and then zoom in slowly. Stop now and then. Wave and I'll move him to make it appear like he's turning his head. Walk down the road shooting videos and whispering things such as how beautiful he is. Stop shooting, and I'll move him out of there. Take a little video saying something to the effect of 'Darn, he ran away.' You can edit out anything you don't like."

With the fox video complete, Doc ran the camera while Merry built a fire. She then went for water for coffee. Doc was setting up the coyote when screams lit the air. Merry stood petrified by the spring with a giant yellow rattlesnake stretched out nearby.

"We aren't within striking distance," Doc said, slipping his arm around her. "He's as scared of us as you are of him. Look how beautiful he is." Doc released her and took snake videos for several minutes before handing the camera to Merry. "Shoot some pictures, so you have a truthful story to tell."

She moved back, drawing the snake's attention. They allowed him to escape when it became difficult to get good shots.

Doc placed the coyote behind the fire pit so she could shoot a video of him running off with sausages. Merry began filming the coyote, pausing now and then so Doc could place sausage in its mouth and move it, allowing Merry to capture it from different angles. They worked in video of Mister Coyote by the porch and again in the woods behind the building, taking long-range shots of him looking back at the fire pit as if he were wondering if he could slip in later.

After the shooting, Doc put the coyote back in the truck and joined Merry at the fire. "What a day. My first try at riding a horse and my first live rattlesnake. What could top this?"

"Maybe a video of you hanging upside down from a horse."

"I'm trying to forget that so I can forgive you!"

Doc and Merry discussed the rattler on the way home. "I was so scared. He looked big enough to eat me."

"I appreciate Mister Yellow."

"Why's that?" she snapped, her brow raised.

"I got to hold Miss Merry. Again."

Guilt crept over Doc. One moment, he was helping her, and the next, loaded with lustful thoughts. The truth might ruin a blossoming friendship or generate something beyond his ability to handle.

After a while without talking, Merry asked, "Doc, why are you so quiet?".

"Guess I was thinking about supper," he lied as they turned down the hill to home. "Can you handle meatloaf, day-old salad, and potatoes two days in a row? We could sit out on the deck. Maybe see some wildlife for video shots."

"Sounds like a plan. Who knows what I might discover to fight about."

They laughed until Jack began growling as they traveled down the hill. "Grab your camera. He hates bears."

Merry was sitting camera-ready when a large sow walked out of the laurel, followed closely by three cubs playfully attacking each other. Seeing the truck, they quickly disappeared into the hemlocks on the opposite side of the road.

"Wow!" Merry whispered excitedly. "Got them. They're beautiful!"

At home, Jack growled as they walked onto the porch. He sniffed the porch and door handle. "What's wrong with him?" Merry asked with fear grabbing her voice.

"Merry, get back in the truck and lock the doors until we look things over?"

Doc walked to the driver's side, pulled his Ruger 9MM out from under the seat, and cautiously followed Jack inside. Jack searched about growling softly, stopping now and then to smell things.

Bristled up and snarling, Jack headed upstairs. The intruder's shoe dropped a piece of leaf and some dirt in the master bedroom. Doc observed that the chest and nightstand drawers were slightly ajar, the computer desk was fooled with, and there were other indicators that someone was looking for something while they were gone.

He returned downstairs and carefully inspected the doors, finding no signs of forced entry. Ronnie had keys, but he wasn't a snooper. Cindy was in Harrisburg. That left the Hacketts with keys. What could they want?

Doc placed the pistol back in its holster and stored it in a drawer until he could replace it in the truck without drawing Merry's attention. He searched the road for tire tracks and found none. Scratching his head, he wondered how much he should tell Merry.

"What's wrong?" Merry asked, grabbing his arm, hesitant to leave the truck. Her face was drawn and worried, her eyes fearful.

"Not sure," Doc lied.

Merry calmed as they worked unloading the truck. While food heated for supper, she picked up glasses and asked, "Are you having water tonight?"

"Yep," Doc replied.

"You serious?"

"Yep. You can have something else if you want."

Doc was unloading the microwave when Merry quickly filled the glasses. "Can we eat on the deck?"

Doc suggested, "You may want to set up your video camera on the deck. Deer will be coming out. Maybe elk too. We might even see coyotes or bobcats."

Merry set up her camera on the deck, where they shared a great view of the bottom yard and the field beyond. They ate quietly, watching as deer began to infiltrate the field. A pair of bull elk followed the deer with Merry running video.

Merry sat thinking through the day they had shared. Neither of them spoke until Merry asked, "Did you and Billy argue?"

Doc struggled with Billy's memory. "We had differing opinions, but we discussed them without arguing."

"Do you think we can learn to discuss things without arguing?"

"Sure. We don't need to hold the same beliefs or argue to discuss different opinions or ideas. Believe what you want, but I think we should understand why we believe the way we do."

Without pausing, Merry asked, "Great! Why do you believe in God?"

"As opposed to what?" Doc asked.

"No, God."

"Merry, I believe in God because of experiences like your arrival."

"Are you crazy?"

"I was in a terrible hole Friday night. Down and almost out. The first peace I've had in six months came with you showing up."

After a period of silence, he muttered, "Don't even know why I told you that."

After another period shared without talking, Doc asked, "Why don't you believe in God?"

Merry searched her mind trying to create an answer. "It's hard to believe in something your father made fun of from your earliest days. My friends weren't into God. I didn't go to church. My mother's parents are believers, but my father often made fun of them and their beliefs."

Merry sat with her arms crossed, leaving Doc wondering what to say. So he said nothing.

"Doc, I've never spent time with anyone like you. You help people like it's your job and treat me like I'm special. I was so afraid when we headed back in here the first time, but I felt comfortable around you before that night was over. It's hard to believe."

CHAPTER 23

A vehicle noisily banged toward them as darkness closed in. Hackett's Ford King Ranch 4X4 truck slid to a stop with stones flying. The driver slammed the door as he got out.

Doc realized his world was about to erupt. "Run in the house, Merry," Doc ordered. "Lock Jack in my bedroom."

Merry ran for the door with Jack, and being a news person, she clicked on her video camera and swung it toward Doc's end of the deck.

Storming angrily onto the deck, Hackett spotted Doc sitting in a chair with Merry running away and charged him like an out-of-control locomotive. Shaking his fists, he bellowed, "What were you doing riding your freakin' horses on my property, Cowboy? I followed two sets of tracks here. You musta had that little whore with you."

Gripping the chair arms with chills chasing up his spine, Doc readied himself. He clenched his fists as a mean smile tightened his face. What was about to happen had been in the works for a long time. He was ready and answered in a low, dangerous voice, "Please

172

watch your mouth, George. The lady is anything but what you called her."

"I'm telling you to stay the hell outta there," Hackett yelled, the veins on his neck standing out. "Something else, I want my stock shares back. I don't know where you hid them, but Catherine told me she was giving them back before she died."

"Ransacked my place an' couldn't find 'em, could ya George? You may want those shares, but that doesn't mean you're gonna get 'em. Billy made sure of that."

"You lying piece of crap. You didn't love Catherine. Those shares are all that kept you two together. Deliver them, or you'll have hell to pay."

Anger burned into Doc's mind as memories of Hackett's many intimidations ran wild. "You bring on that hell to pay."

Hackett kicked Merry's chair out of the way and grabbed Doc's shirt, "Cowboy, I'm done fooling." He swung, and Doc ducked away, taking a glancing blow on the head. He swung again, but Doc rolled away, sliding Hackett's fist to the side. Grabbing Hackett's arm, they landed on the deck with Doc's foot catching in Merry's chair. Hackett scrambled to his feet and kicked Doc on his shoulder. He jerked the chair away, tearing off Doc's prosthesis.

Hackett jumped on him, hitting him in the mouth. Doc grabbed his arm on the second swing and deflected the blow into the deck. Hackett cursed with pain. Holding Hackett's arm, Doc rolled sideways, forcing himself on Hackett. He hammered Hackett in the face. Swinging again, he hit him in the throat, knocking him back into the deck. Hackett sucked hard for breath.

Grabbing Hackett's throat with one hand, Doc hammered his face. Hackett's head slammed into the deck. Doc rapidly pounded him again and again until Merry grabbed his arm, fearfully screaming, "Stop! You'll kill him."

"That's the plan," Doc muttered, wiping his bloody hands on Hackett's shirt. Drenched in sweat, he gasped for breath as he crawled off Hackett. While the fog cleared, he touched his mouth to see if he had lost any teeth. All were where they should be, with one bottom tooth loose and his lips hurting.

Gaining strength, he crawled over to his leg, his shoulder pain growing. He tried to attach his leg and discovered Hackett had broken it. "Merry, can you grab my other leg?"

"The one in the box?"

Doc offered a weak grin. "The one behind my chair."

Merry brought him his work leg, a wet washcloth, and a roll of toilet paper. She cleaned the blood off Doc's face while he rolled toilet paper, packing his nose to stop the bleeding.

Hackett grabbed a table trying to get up but fell back on the deck with the table landing on top of him. "He needs help, Doc. He's in bad shape."

"Should be dead," Doc groaned. "You saved him."

With his leg on and gaining strength, Doc stood with Merry's help and struggled into the great room, where he dialed 911. He explained George Hackett needed help, how to get to Hackett's home, and hung up. Then Doc and Merry got Hackett on his feet and struggled to his truck. Merry opened the passenger door, and they crammed him inside.

"Merry, we gotta do something," Doc said in a low, pained voice. "I know him. Put Jack and your cameras in my truck. The keys are in the truck. Lock the house and follow me. Hurry! An ambulance is on the way to his place."

By the time Merry returned, Doc was sitting in the driver's seat of Hackett's truck with Hackett partially in the passenger seat and partly on the floor. Pain screamed through Doc's hands when he grabbed the steering wheel.

"You're in no shape to drive."

"Hurry."

Merry jumped in Doc's truck and bounced down the lane behind him hitting most of the potholes as dusk rolled in. Hackett was struggling, and Doc wanted him home for the ambulance. They parked outside Hackett's house, where Doc laid on the horn until his wife ran out. "My gosh, Doc. What happened?" she asked when she saw his face.

Without answering, Doc pointed to Hackett. "He's upset with me. An ambulance is on the way."

"Oh my god," she screamed and ran around the truck.

Doc shut off Hackett's truck and climbed out with Merry's help. "Drive Merry," Doc said, struggling to stand.

Merry carefully examined Doc's face using the interior light. "Your lip's split, and your nose is bleeding."

Backing around, she drove toward the blacktop road. "Turn left and head for MELCOR." Traveling down Moore Hill, they passed the ambulance speeding toward Hackett's with its siren blaring.

When they arrived at MELCOR, Doc said, "Park around back by the lighted door. When the night superintendent opens the door, begin taking videos of everything that happens. Don't stop until we're back in the truck."

They rang the bell at the entrance door and waited for Brian Ryder to arrive. When Ryder saw Doc's face and bloody shirt, his face went white. "My gosh, Doc, what happened?"

"Ran into a problem. I'll tell you about it while I grab some things. Oh, Brian, this is Merry, a new friend."

"Nice to meet you, Merry."

Doc unlocked his office, turned on the light, and motioned Ryder to enter first, handing him the ring of plant keys as he passed. He retrieved his personal computer from a desk drawer, grabbed a flash drive, and turned on his company computer. He selected five items and copied them to the flash drive. After Ryder reviewed the files, Doc shoved the flash drive in his pocket.

He took a bottle of water out of his little refrigerator and asked, "Anyone else want one?" When neither did, he closed the door. "Brian, you don't have a fridge. I own this one. Wheel it over to your office. I'll send you the receipt."

"I'll pay for it."

"You already paid with super support."

Brian asked, "Aren't you taking anything else?" and Doc walked to his file cabinet, where he retrieved a prosthetic leg.

"Don't want to forget my just-in-case spare," Doc said with pain riding his face.

"You're leaving all your other stuff here?" Brian asked.

"I'll get my things when George fires me," Doc answered. "I copied those document folders in case something gets changed or removed. Thanks for everything, Brian. You're appreciated."

"Same to you, Doc. You brought us a breath of sanity." With that, Brian hugged him.

With pain running through him, Doc struggled out to the truck with his leg and computer and waited for Merry to get in.

"Home?"

"Yeah."

Going up Moore Hill Road, Merry broke the silence. "Why'd we bring Jack?"

Doc exhaled loudly before answering. "Wouldn't want to lose Jack if Hackett torched the place."

"You think he'd burn your home?"

"George Hackett is capable of almost anything. That's why you videoed my actions in the office. After moments of silence, Doc added. "He was in our place earlier when we were gone."

"What makes you say that?"

"He asked me where I hid Billy's stocks before he started hammering me."

"Do you think he'll cause more problems?"

"Cops'll be out tonight."

"You're kidding?" Merry asked as she looked at Doc.

"It's the way Hackett handles business."

"Why don't you just quit."

"The contract clause. Tonight is part of George's just cause. He lost on the drunk-driving fiascos. Now he'll claim he fired me because I attacked him. He'll want me arrested for assault in addition to stealing stuff."

"He'll lose the assault charge. I turned on my camera when I ran upstairs. It ran the entire time you guys were fighting."

"Let's not tell anyone about the video. It'll support our story in court. George will demand that I get charged with everything, including attempted murder. This mess could tie you up for days."

"That's okay. It's going to be hard for me to leave. Could you help me understand something? Why'd you let him hit you?"

"Couldn't plead self-defense with no marks on my face. I've been expecting this day for years. Merry, he'll implicate you, and they'll force you to testify in court."

"If I can stay with you, bring on the trial."

"You can always stay with me."

"Hope it's a long trial."

Merry studied Doc's face with the interior light. "You need a doctor."

"Can't hurt my face much more than the Lord did when He created me."

"Stop! You're a fine-looking man."

"Have you seen your optometrist lately?"

"I see perfectly, and tonight I see a need for medical support." She grinned and added, "I also see a guy wearing two different shoes. You replaced your broken leg with your boot leg and you're still wearing your dress shoe on your good leg."

Doc looked down, then at Merry, and they laughed together.

As they exited the truck, Merry asked, "How'd you learn to fight like that?

"Marines. It's called the Line System for hand-to-hand combat."

"You almost killed him," Merry said with fear in her voice.

"As Merle Haggard would say, 'He was walking on the fighting side of me' when he called you a whore."

When they reached the deck, Merry discovered both water glasses had spilled. Holding them up, she said, "Now we have a reason to be upset. He spilled our expensive water."

"With annual taxes the water comes to a little over two grand.."

"And that isn't cheap," Merry remarked as she watched Doc pick up his prosthesis.

"Meet you in the living room," Doc said as he headed in with his broken leg. He stopped in the bathroom and carefully washed the blood off his face, noting a cut over his swollen eye. He carefully removed toilet paper from his nose and discovered the bleeding had stopped.

They talked about the run-in with George until Doc turned the light off and whispered, "There's a vehicle coming. Guess who."

"Cops?"

"Yep. Their cop lights are on."

A trooper got out with a flashlight and shined it around before ringing the doorbell. Doc waited until the bell rang again and went to the door. "Who is it?" he questioned, looking out the peephole at the officer.

"State Police. Open up."

Jack stood by the door, growling lightly, the hair on his neck standing. When Doc opened the door, Jack moved up to the screen, sniffing the officer and still growling. "How can I help you, Officer?" Doc asked with a strained voice.

"Are you Forest Adams?"

"I am."

"I hold an arrest warrant for you. George Hackett filed a complaint against you and a female accomplice. He said you two attacked him without provocation. After badly beating him, you went to his factory where you stole a bunch of things and destroyed other stuff."

"What if Hackett's lying?"

"Is your accomplice here?"

"Miss Morehouse is here, but she isn't an accomplice; she's a witness."

"Could you and Miss Morehouse please step out and leave the dog inside?"

"Merry," Doc yelled as if Merry was somewhere far away.

"Coming," she softly answered.

When she arrived, Doc said, "This officer wants to talk with us."

"What would you like to know, Officer," Merry sweetly asked.

"Could you please step out?"

"Man, the bugs will eat us out there," Doc complained. "Why don't you step inside to discuss your problem?" Doc asked.

"What about that dog?"

"He's a German police dog. He'll think you're family," Doc answered with a straight face.

The officer stepped in after Doc had Jack sit. "Can we sit down? I'm not feeling well tonight," Doc asked and took a seat in a chair.

"You look beat up. Did that happen when you attacked Mister Hackett?"

"Nobody attacked Hackett," Merry retorted. "He came roaring in here and called me a whore. I ran upstairs and looked out the window when he started beating Mister Adams. He knocked Mister Adams down and kicked him. He just kept pounding him. I thought

Mr. Adams was going to be killed by that mean brute. Hackett even broke Mister Adams' leg."

"You seem to be walking on both legs," the officer said.

"I had a spare."

"A spare leg?" the surprised officer asked.

"It's a prosthesis. I had a leg blown off in the war."

"See what kind of person that Hackett is," Merry said, sounding even angrier. "He attacks wounded vets and crippled people."

"This isn't the story Mister Hackett reported."

"I bet not," Merry said. "I witnessed the whole thing. He's such a mean, hateful person. If I hadn't run upstairs, he'd have beaten me too."

"I'm going to have to take you in to sort out this mess."

"Officer, we want Hackett there, "Doc said. "He assaulted us, Merry, verbally with filthy language, and me physically. The leg he ruined is right there by the fireplace. Look at me. You can't believe I did this to myself. And look at this young woman. Does it look like she would attack anyone?"

"Mr. Adams, I have arrest warrants for you and your accomplice. I have no warrant for Mister Hackett."

"What's it take to get one?"

"You'll have to file a complaint."

"You going to haul him in tonight after we file a complaint?"

"That will be up to someone besides me? The judge knows Mister Hackett, and his word goes a long way."

"Can I quote you on that?" Doc asked, pounding the table beside him. "Folks might like to know some people get breaks because they know judges. Law enforcement's already on the hot seat, and this won't help your cause. Merry's a newscaster for a TV station. Maybe you can understand how this might play out."

"Maybe I should call our station commander."

"You can use the phone in the kitchen. It's hanging on the wall."

Doc winked at Merry as the officer walked to the kitchen. Doc caught bits of conversation that made it apparent the station commander wasn't happy with a midnight call. The officer finally stepped into the doorway with his hand covering the phone. "The station commander would like to speak with you. His name is Sergeant Richardson."

"Good evening, Sergeant Richardson. How may I help you?"

"Trooper Bates explained the situation as you claim it to be. If I can trust you and the woman to come to the barracks in the morning, we can try to get to the bottom of this situation."

"What time would morning be?"

"How about eight-thirty?"

"We'll be there. Will Mr. Hackett be there with a list of the things he claims we stole and pictures of the things he claims we destroyed? We'll need them for Merry's father. He's an attorney."

"Is he from town?"

"No. Merry's father is Howard Morehouse, head of the legal firm Morehouse, Peabody, and Rosenstein."

"From Philadelphia?"

"You know 'em?"

"Any officer ever stationed anywhere near Philly knows that firm."

"Merry will be happy to hear that. When you're a child, you don't realize your father is famous. Is there anything else we can do for you tonight?"

"Please put Trooper Bates back on the phone?"

Doc handed the phone to the trooper, "Sergeant Richardson would like to talk with you."

"Yes, sergeant." After listening for a bit, the trooper said, "Yes, sir, and goodnight, sir."

The trooper hung up the phone, thanked Doc for its use, and said he was sorry for any inconvenience he might have caused. As Trooper Bates drove out the lane, Doc smiled at Merry, "You sure laid it on that poor cop. Couldn't believe you'd get that hot about anything other than things I say or do."

"It was a put-on. My father talked like that on the phone. Then he'd laugh when he hung up. I thought I'd give it a try. Another subject. My father told clients to make sure they had their stories straight. Anything we need to talk about?"

"When we appear before the district judge, we gotta tell the truth and not dispute each other. Let's request a trial by the judge for Elk and Cameron Counties. Hackett invested a lot of time and money to get the Magisterial District Judge reelected, which might make him move favorably on Hackett and MELCOR matters. We'll act like we're going forward based on advice from your father. You may even want to call him before we go to town."

"Not on your life. I can hear him already. 'Dammit, Merry, what the hell are you doing in Cameron County? You need to start using your head, and soon.' Thanks, Father. I knew I could count on you if I ever needed help."

Doc was smiling as Merry finished. "Maybe you should try out for a comedian slot. That was great commentary."

"I listened to many of his advice-giving sessions growing up," she angrily replied.

CHAPTER 24

What a day, Merry thought as she rubbed her eyes and gingerly climbed into bed waiting for her Aleve to take effect. *Howard Morehouse is not the only big-headed ass in the world. George Hackett could be his brother. One could stand around making life difficult for people, and his brother could represent him in court.*

Merry, you learned something today. Doc seemed like a saintly, bigger-than-life nice guy until he mauled Hackett. He might have beaten Hackett to death if you hadn't intervened.

Where's all of this headed? Merry asked herself, her stomach knotted. *I've never really wanted any man before, but something's happening with Doc. Too bad he isn't over his first love. His Billy.*

She found herself talking to a God she didn't know and wondered if He was genuine, would He help her despite her past. *If you're there, Lord, what's your plan for me? For us? Please help me understand. Is Doc even safe? What if I push him past his tolerance level when we disagree? Would he trip off the line and come after me? What then? Oh yeah, Lord, why do I find it necessary to fight about things we can't change? Please help me, Lord. And Lord, what if Doc discovers what my life's mess is all about? What then?*

186

These considerations prompted Merry to get up and check her door locks. No telling what might happen. She had found herself becoming ever more comfortable with this Doc fellow until tonight.

187

# CHAPTER 25

Merry ran her fingers through her hair as she watched Doc working on entry door locks. "What are you doing," she asked, her voice carrying a puzzled tone.

"Woke up thinking about Jack sniffing his way through the house after Hackett went through the place looking for Billy's stocks. I talked to Sergeant Richardson about fingerprinting the place. He asked who had keys. When he heard the Hacketts had keys, he said if they discovered Hackett's fingerprints, he'd say he had permission to be there. You gave him the key. Knowing the DA, he won't accept the case. The locks I installed came with a rekey kit. I'm changing them to the other key."

"Hackett terrifies me, Doc. What can we do?"

"I don't know," Doc said in a pinched voice. "I'd be lying if I said I wasn't concerned."

Merry's screwed-up facial expression told Doc it was time for anything that didn't include Hackett talk.

After a quiet breakfast, Doc and Merry gathered their things and headed for the police station with Merry's cameras and a video copy of the Hackett fight in a sealed envelope. Stopping on the road into Hackett, Doc took videos of their horses traveling well short of the Hackett property. Back in the truck, Doc handed Merry a list. "I plan to go over these questions with the sergeant. I'll tell him we're supposed to ask these questions before we sign anything."

After reviewing the list, Merry crossed her arms with anger flooding her face. "Don't tell me you called my father."

"I wouldn't call anyone connected with you without your permission. I woke up thinking about this mess. Those questions came to me. I typed them into an email, sent it to myself, and then copied it, minus my email and name."

Merry smiled as she read through the list. "It sounds like advice from an attorney."

"That's what we want the sergeant to think."

"I'm nervous," Merry said with uncertainty as they pulled out and headed for the police barracks. "Can you handle the sergeant's general questions? I'll answer questions directed to me."

"That's the plan. Answer with the minimum amount of information possible."

They pulled into the police barracks, where the duty officer asked them to have a seat. Within minutes, the sergeant met them and was surprised by Doc's facial problems. "What happened to your face, Mr. Adams?"

"George Hackett attacked me. Let me introduce Merry Morehouse, the person George Hackett called the accomplice. She's not what he called her."

"I wasn't aware Mr. Hackett called anyone names," the sergeant said, inviting them into his office, where he gave them a copy of the charges and briefed them on the arrest warrant. Doc placed it so Merry could read it as he took notes. When they finished, the sergeant asked them if they had questions.

"Sergeant, this report states we stole things and damaged equipment. Where's the description of the things we allegedly stole or damaged, how much they cost, and pictures of them in the plant? Hackett claims my accomplice and I assaulted him, and he just tried to protect himself. Does my face look like he was just protecting himself?"

The sergeant's face reddened. Most people wouldn't ask for this type of information. "No, it doesn't, and so far, we have no evidence of any kind. The Magisterial District Judge called and said Mr. Hackett had a problem. Asked me to work with him."

"If someone charged you with stealing their vehicle, wouldn't you want that vehicle identified by name, year, color, and body style, things like that?" Doc asked with a puzzled look.

The sergeant who usually asked the questions showed angst on his face. "Yes, I'd want the items I supposedly stole or damaged identified," the sergeant agreed, visibly annoyed.

"Please help us understand why you would consider an arrest warrant without having this information."

"As I mentioned earlier, we acted on a late-night call from the judge. When the DA called, we asked him for such details. He said he'd have them here this morning, but we haven't seen him or those lists."

"Could your officers visit MELCOR this morning to acquire those lists along with copies of the sales receipts that prove MELCOR purchased the items reportedly stolen or damaged and are no longer on-site? While the officers are there, they could take pictures of the damaged equipment along with their nomenclature plates to prove the equipment was there and damaged. Receipts for damaged equipment are needed to verify the damage cost estimates."

"I'm afraid our operational schedule precludes that type of visit. Why is it important that we get there this morning?"

Doc's voice grew cold and tight. "Sergeant, our freedom and who knows what else is at stake. How well do you know George Hackett?"

"I've met him a few times."

"Was it personal meetings or police matters?"

"Always police matters."

"Were different opinions presented in those matters?"

"I'm not sure what you're getting at Mister Adams," the sergeant asked brusquely, his anger evident.

"Did the people on the other side of those police matters agree or disagree with Mr. Hackett's assertions?"

Clasping his fingers, the sergeant leaned back as his face reddened. After rubbing his mouth with his hand, he answered, "Now that I think about it, there were disagreements in both cases."

"I've reported to George Hackett for twenty-five years. He's also my father-in-law. As a plant superintendent and plant manager, situations arose where what I believed happened and what George Hackett said happened were quite different. I don't know what your schedules might be, but I wouldn't think he's had time to damage anything, remove anything from the plant, or anything else he might claim we did. But if you wait until tomorrow, he'll have that time. The MELCOR plant normally operates two shifts a day, and there are people there from about 6:30 A.M. to 12:15 A.M. There is just one security person on duty from 12:15 A.M. until some time before 7 A.M. when the day shift begins to arrive."

"That would seem secure enough," The sergeant suggested. "I'm under the impression that there are security cameras throughout the facility."

"Security cameras are limited to external sites, and the external camera security system has failed before at key times. When called, the company that services the system couldn't find anything wrong with it. Do you think there could be some security personnel who might bend the truth to protect their jobs, and do you think management might know who those people are?"

"What are you telling me?"

"Hackett can't be trusted."

"Maybe I had better revise our schedules," the sergeant agreed.

"Your officers will need a camera that dates pictures and a search warrant to collect a copy of the security system videos that show all plant access up to the point your officers get there. Last night your officer informed us the safe had stuff stolen from it. If the safe's open, have the plant superintendent on duty check to see if the cash is still there."

"What would you suggest I do with this arrest warrant, Mister Adams? It contains the assault charges in addition to the theft and destruction charges."

"Have one of your troopers take the warrant and us to the magisterial district judge. We have one stop to make on the way."

"Where might that be?"

"Citizens & Northern Bank on Fourth Street to transfer bail money to my checking account."

"Mr. Adams, Miss Morehouse, I'll have an officer follow you to make it official, and we'll go to MELCOR and take care of business."

"Great. There's just one more request. Please sign this envelope as evidence, and keep it under lock until the trial. Then prepare a letter for us that says you received the item into state police custody with the date and time."

The sergeant smiled and shook his head. "You folks came prepared. One last question; does Mister Hackett know who Merry's father is and what he does for a living?" the sergeant questioned.

"Mister Hackett didn't seem interested in finding out anything about Merry. He called her a whore and started pounding me in the face."

"This will be an interesting case."

After transferring bail money to his checking account at the bank, Doc and Merry met the trooper at the courthouse, and they proceeded to the judge's office where Judge Bailey's secretary met them. "Good morning. Let's get you signed in so we can visit the judge."

The secretary led them into the judge's inner office, where Judge Bailey took over. After swearing them in, he said, "I discussed this case with Sergeant Richardson minutes ago. He added some interesting concerns. Before going over your charges, I must inform you that George Hackett and I share a friendship that goes back many years. If you'd like someone else to hear this initial hearing, you may request that."

Doc looked at Merry, and when she shrugged, he continued, "Let's go over the charge sheet. It could present ideas on how we should proceed."

Judge Bailey began. "I talked with a very disturbed Mr. Hackett last night after his alleged assault. He's adamant that these charges go forward."

"Without Mr. Hackett's presence?"

"We have his sworn statements. This hearing is solely to determine how to proceed with this matter. Do you wish to have legal representation at this time?"

After looking at each other, both declined legal representation. Judge Bailey then read the filed charges. Upon completion, he looked at Doc, "How do you plead to these charges, Mr. Adams?"

"Not guilty to any of them, your Honor," Doc said, his brows drawn together. "None of them are true! Your Honor, look at my face. Does it appear as if Mr. Hackett might be the aggressor?"

"You'll have the opportunity to prove that, Mr. Adams. Now, Miss Morehouse, how do you plead?" the judge asked, his anger with Doc apparent.

"Not guilty, your Honor."

"These charges are serious. I'm setting bail at twenty thousand dollars each."

"Is bail necessary," Doc asked. "Miss Morehouse has no previous record of any kind. I'm not going anywhere other than home in Cameron County."

"Many criminals say that and fail to show up for trial. How do you wish to pay your bail?"

"With a personal check for both of us."

"I prefer cash or cashier checks in cases like this," the DA announced.

"I can be back in fifteen minutes with the cash."

"We'll go with your check this time," the judge said with displeasure showing.

Doc wrote out the check to cover their bail. He handed it to the judge and said, "We're hoping there isn't any next time."

"Let's discuss hearing dates," the judge said as he checked his schedule.

"Judge, I believe with these serious charges, our lawyer will suggest we go to trial. Is it possible to request that at this time?"

"Highly unusual, but possible."

The judge checked his computer. After a review, he answered, "District Court is being held here in Emporium on May 24 and 25. It appears the schedule is relatively light. The next scheduled dates are June 20 and 21."

"Let's go with the May dates. We want a bench trial if possible."

"Mr. Adams, Miss Morehouse, caution is in order. If I can get you on the docket at this late date, it gives you little time to prepare for a trial. The charges include felony assault for the beating you gave Mr. Hackett, felony theft because of the value of the items taken, and a felony for damaging equipment. Mr. Hackett also claims you refuse to return property that belongs to him."

"None of these charges are true. We'll be ready if we get the May date."

All present could see the judge was upset with their decision. "I'll put you down for May 24 and 25 dates. I'll try to get you on the docket. You said you had another question for me."

"Do you conduct weddings, and if so, do you do it on short notice?"

"Are you two planning on getting married?" the judge asked with a strange look on his face.

"We may be."

"Would that be because spouses don't have to testify against each other?"

"No, sir."

They signed the required papers, said their goodbyes, and headed for the parking lot. When Merry crawled behind the wheel, Doc noticed her 'we need to talk' smile. "Let's have it," he said as he climbed in.

"You asked the judge about marriage. What's with that?"

"I was screwing with the judge, but would you be shocked if I asked you?"

"At this point, nothing would shock me."

After a period of quiet reflection, Merry said, "You requested a bench trial. Isn't that a trial without a jury?"

"It is."

"Wouldn't a jury be more sympathetic to our needs?"

"In most cases, it would be. However, George Hackett invested considerable money in Bailey's campaign for District Judge. He also donates to many different charities. People involved in those charities could end up on our jury and might feel they owe Hackett something."

"I'll have to trust you on this," Merry whispered in a fear-laden voice.

After court, they had Bucky's door and shed keys made at the hardware ststore before stopping at the used clothing center operating at a local church. "Last week, I would have laughed at anyone suggesting I buy second-hand clothes. Now I'm looking forward to it, but it's doubtful I'll find anything I'd wear."

"You might. Grab your video camera so we can shoot shopping pictures."

She agreed and shot videos of the church's exterior and the 'Lightly Used Clothing' sign before entering. "Who knows how one might use them in a camping video," she said with a fake smile as they walked in.

Merry's mouth dropped open as she gazed at the packed clothing aisles. Doc videoed her struggling to get through the cramped spaces, holding things out in front of her, examining both sides, before placing some in her cart. She had a dress, two skirts, blouses, slacks, a scarf, some everyday camping outfits including Levis and flannel shirts, a beautiful white robe, a boyshort swimming suit with a bikini top in the cart, and continued looking. She saw a wedding gown, held it to herself, smiled at Doc, and after noting his nod, put it back.

"What do you think, Doc?" she asked after an hour and a half of shopping for the right things. "Do I have enough for the video?"

"Getting close. Hold out your arms, and I'll pile on your stuff. You can stagger up to the cashier with me taking videos."

Merry uttered a soft ooohh of pain as Doc piled clothes on her arms. "I was planning on putting this stuff back after we got our videos. I don't have a lot of money."

"I'll put it on my credit card and figure out how to handle it later."

"My gosh, what happened to you?" Missy, the cashier, asked at the register. "You get hit by a train?"

"This pretty young woman said she'd beat me if I didn't bring her down here first thing yesterday morning. I should have listened."

"That didn't happen," Merry innocently countered. "The cashier down at County Foods mauled him when she caught him stealing a can of snuff."

"Guess I'm not going to get any serious answers out of you two," Missy said with a smile dancing across her face. "Find everything you needed?"

"I'm not sure I needed anything, but I'm a woman," Merry said. "We're shoppers. I shopped."

Doc and Merry were soon in the truck, with Merry talking excitedly about her morning. I can't believe this day," Merry said, shaking her head. "I've been arrested, attended a criminal hearing, and had a great time shopping for used clothing that someone else paid for."

"You appear tired and in pain. Maybe you'll need help trying stuff on."

"You'd like that, Mister Adams," Merry said, with a lilt in her voice.

"Helping a beautiful woman out of her clothes is every red-blooded male's fantasy."

"Play your cards right. Can't tell what might happen," Merry teased.

Upstairs alone, Merry stood in front of the mirror in her underwear, trying on clothes. A smile danced across her face as she let the current selection drop, wondering what Doc would say if he saw her like this. *This isn't like me*, Merry told herself as she stared at the well-endowed young woman smiling back from the mirror.

There was something different about this Forest Adams, something she couldn't put her finger on. *I've only known him for five days, and it seems like we've enjoyed each other for months or years, not days.*

She tried to shake away her thoughts as she considered what might happen given the right circumstances. She discovered a need for Doc deep within, but her eyes teared as disturbing memories of the past crowded out those pleasurable ideas. Sweat beads broke out on her forehead as the problem that ate at her flashed through her mind. Could she fully love any man given her history of what had happened? She wondered if Doc would want her if he recognized this dilemma that ate through her life. Then, too, he might never get over his Billy. How would it be if he couldn't let her go?

Backing away from this self-destructive conversation, she tried on the low-cut red dress that fit perfectly, showing that she was a woman in all aspects of the word. What would Doc do if she went down to eat looking like this? Even more, what would she do?

She liked what she saw when she slipped into a red T-shirt that covered to mid-thigh. There was just enough room inside the shirt so it didn't appear as if she were showing off, yet it was revealing enough to catch his eye. She fought off concerns about Doc and got serious about trying on the clothes, laughing when she considered what those who knew her might think if they saw her modeling used clothing. She slipped into the swimsuit and, after smiling with satisfaction, worked on down through the pile. She was dressing when Doc called up the stairs, "Supper's ready."

With the clothes separated into two piles, she placed the first load on the washer, washed her hands, and met Doc in the kitchen. He was dishing up food, so she got a platter for the meat and set the table. "Water, Doc?"

"Twist my arm."

As Merry walked toward him, he held up his hands in mock fear, "Stop! I can't take a lot of pain."

"That might be the first lie you told me, mister. I saw you with Hackett."

Back with glasses of water, Merry beamed as Doc pulled out her chair. She appreciated his gestures and held out her hand as he offered the prayer. This time he thanked the Lord for their friendship and the warmth they shared this day.

When the prayer ended, he still held her hand. She liked the feeling as she watched the warm smile come over his face. "We made it through what could've been a tough day, Merry."

Still holding hands, she said, "Each day with you gets a little better. Maybe you could play a few songs on your guitar after dinner."

"You forget what happened the last time we sat out there?"

Her forehead creased as those memories flew past. A much different Doc had almost killed another man, and he didn't seem regretful.

CHAPTER 26

After quietly eating, Doc and Merry sat on the deck discussing the Hackett situation when a vehicle drove in. Merry quickly retrieved her video camera on the tripod. "Hope this doesn't come in handy two nights in a row."

Doc recognized the car as Dolly Hackett's. She parked, and as the door closed, Doc called, "Out here, Mom," and stood up to greet her.

Dolly talked in a raspy voice when she reached the deck. "I was so hoping you'd be here, Doc. I hold no part in the hell raining on you. I don't know what —" Seeing Merry, Dolly stopped. "Oh, I'm sorry. I didn't see you. You must be the woman George mentioned."

"Using his words, I'm the whore he heard Doc's shacking up with."

"I'm so sorry," Dolly said with embarrassment burning her face red.

Feeling for Dolly, Doc said, "Dolly, this is Merry. Merry, this is Billy's mother, Dolly. She's one of the nicest people God ever created."

"Pleased to meet you, Dolly," Merry said, smiling as she took her hand.

Blushing deeply, Dolly said, "Glad to meet you too, but I fear Doc is a little generous with my description. I'm so sorry about your run-in with George." With tears running down her face, she added, "Tonight is George's poker night, and I needed to talk with you, Doc. You've been good for us. Catherine couldn't find a better husband."

"We loved each other."

Dolly sucked in a deep breath, "I'm scared. I know George did terrible things to others, and I'm worried about what he might do to you. Yes, and to you too, Merry. I heard George talking to Judge Bailey. George was so angry when he discovered you asked for a bench trial. When he called Dorman Westfield at the plant, Dorman asked him about the hearing. George became furious and went outside with his phone for a long time. He slammed the door and kicked over his chair when he came in. When I asked him what was wrong, he choked me and told me to keep my mouth shut. That's why I'm having difficulty talking. I'm wearing this scarf to hide the bruises on my neck."

Dolly pulled the scarf down and let them see the black choke marks. "I don't know what I should do."

Doc considered the situation and looked at Merry before answering. She met his eyes with fear written across her face. When she shrugged her shoulders, Doc turned to Dolly. "Dolly, please don't upset George. You're important to us."

Turning away, Dolly cried harder. Between sobs, she whispered, "Doc, I keep praying for you. You and Catherine were so close.

I know how you must hurt. Now, this. Please forgive me for any problems that ..."

It was quiet until Doc began talking. "No need for forgiveness, Dolly. None of this belongs to you."

"Dolly quietly looked from Doc to Merry. "I better go. It wouldn't be good if George came home early and found me gone. It was nice meeting you, Merry. Hold on to him, Honey. It seems your coming was God sent."

When Dolly departed, Doc said in a low voice, not wanting to talk about Hackett until he had time to think it through, "Let's go in. The noseeums will be after us soon."

Doc built a fire in the parlor fireplace. As the flames grew, he added wood, then took a seat. "Well, Merry, what do you think of Dolly?"

"She seems nice. How'd she hook up with George Hackett?"

"That's what love can do." After thinking about Hackett and their situation, Doc said, "George Hackett can act like many different people. He has a good side that does a lot for many people. He's heavy into charities. Built MELCOR from scratch. Provided jobs for a lot of people, including me. He can't help himself when he loses. Years ago, we played our last game of cards with him. He lost several heart games and became so mad he tore the cards into pieces."

"There's another George that ran his son and Ronnie off. Ronnie received a college football scholarship, but George talked him into a tool-and-die apprenticeship at MELCOR. Said he'd be a manager someday. When George wouldn't pay him what he promised, Ronnie quit."

"I'm scared, Doc. If it's possible, he's worse than my father."

"Maybe you should stay in Harrisburg until the trial."

"What about you?"

"I'll call Sergeant Richardson and seek advice. That'll provide the police advance notice if something happens with Hackett."

"This mess twists my mind," Merry said, biting her bottom lip.

Doc held her shaking hand as they sat quietly watching the fire. After a bit, Merry asked, "What do you make of Dolly's comment when she was leaving?"

"Not sure which comment you're thinking about," Doc answered, but his facial expression said he understood but didn't want to answer.

"Dolly said I was God sent. Do you believe there's a God who acts this way?"

After running his fingers through his hair as he considered how to answer, Doc replied, "God is bigger than my understanding. Jeremiah tells us God knows His plans for us, plans to prosper us and not harm us. Plans to give us hope and a future. He brought a lot of good into my life. He's there for you too."

"Doc, I don't know who Jeremiah is, but you're sidestepping my question. If there's a God, I think our accident must be God sent. Everything is happening so fast. My heart's running away with me, and I feel compelled to race after it. I know I sound crazy, but I can't help it. You're giving me the first meaningful life I've ever had. My father and his actions and constant negative comments forever ripped away what little good I felt about myself." Merry paused, thinking about what she said, then continued in a low voice. "I'm wondering how you feel about me."

Maybe I'm afraid to face those feelings, Miss Merry, Doc told himself. "Merry, I'm a one-legged, old dude with problems. I shave every morning and see the scarred face of a man who might be ending life when a certain young lady is in her peak. The man and woman in question come from very different backgrounds and see life in vastly different ways. It might be too much to overcome."

"What if the woman in question liked the differences and didn't see an age problem? What if she never before met a man she so enjoyed being with or respected so much? And what if that man turned her on, and they hadn't even kissed? What then?"

Doc's mouth sat in a hard line; a haunted look rode his face.

"Look, Merry, if we're playing what-if games, consider this," Doc replied with his stomach knotted. "What if the man wasn't over a previous love affair?"

Merry stared at the fire and quietly answered. "Doc, that's a question I'm praying about. If you put on some slow music, we can dance while we search for solutions."

CHAPTER 27

Thursday morning broke with a warm breeze slipping through the mountains as the sun crept up out of the trees. Doc had animals loaded on his truck, the stock fed, and several kinds of cereal on the table when Jack woke Merry.

Merry arrived at the table in a set of nicely fitting, green PJs from the second-hand store. They said their good mornings with smiles, and as they held hands and bowed heads to pray, Doc looked at Merry, realizing she made his heart run wild.

With their prayer over and still holding her hands, he looked at her with affection glowing in his eyes. "We had a lot of things planned for this day, but maybe we should sit here and hold hands. Whataya think?"

After an eyebrow wiggle, Merry allowed her smile to slide away. "After our dance party last night and all that went with it, I went to bed with a smile running across my face. Then I had trouble sleeping because an insane idiot is threatening us," she said, and her hand began shaking. "Doc, I'm scared."

Unsure where the conversation was heading, Doc let go of her hands. His skin crawled as he considered what might happen if

Hackett attacked. He let the thought slide and began eating breakfast without talking, wondering what to do.

"Let's do the bear and bath shots today. The bears are in the truck. The weather report for today said it might make eighty. I think late morning light is best."

"Yes, and if the parts don't come in, I'll need to get a rental car."

"While you get dressed, I'll call Ronnie."

Doc waited until she was climbing the stairs before dialing Ronnie, who answered on the second ring. "Any word on parts for Merry's car?"

"The earliest we can get the mechanical parts is early next week. Sorry."

Merry soon arrived wearing one of her new "everyday outfits" as Doc ended his phone conversation. They made eye contact, and Merry flashed a smile. She stopped and, touching his arm, she asked, "See anyone you'd be willing to dance with again tonight?"

"I went to sleep and woke up this morning thinking about our first dance, holding you, and more. Lots more."

Merry removed her hand from his arm and smiled. "We better get going so we have lots of time tonight for all that might continue."

With Jack loaded in the back seat, they were underway. "How were you thinking of using Mister Bear?" Merry asked.

"Couple ideas for Buckys. I threw in your camping pillow and blanket. We could have you sleeping on that lounger on the porch and waking up to see the bear looking at you. You could roll and scream when you heard the noise behind you. The other thought is something by those big rocks with the other bear where you're going to take your bath."

"Great ideas. Maybe we can get shots of Mr. Bear looking out around the shed or something."

They turned down Quail Run Road, parked in the shade, and left Jack in the truck for the shoot. While Merry fixed her bed and got her camera ready, Doc set up a bear, walked away to see how it looked, and walked back to adjust it. Merry shot several minutes with that view accompanied by a few screams, then had Doc move it around and took more video, once again accompanied by cries of surprise. When she had all the video she wanted, she packed her cameras in the truck and helped Doc reload the bear.

Jack waited while they built a fire and cooked sausages. As they ate, they tossed him pieces of meat. After eating, Merry carried water and put out the fire while Doc ran the video. Before departing, they videoed Merry taking down her tent.

Merry talked excitedly as they neared the creek where she would bathe. She got her clothes while Doc grabbed camera gear. They carried the big bear together using a rope sling. Merry showed Doc where to place the video camera at the deep pool. "Doc, can you turn around while I get dressed? No peeking."

"And if I peek?"

"It could turn into a wild afternoon we might long remember."

"What's wrong with that?" he asked, grinning.

"Maybe you remember, it wasn't my idea to stop things last night."

Doc turned around, and Merry dressed in the swimming suit and robe they purchased. "Doc, I'm going to throw my robe and top over that limb, walk further into deeper water, and drop to wash up. Allow the video to run the entire time. I'll cover myself up when I get my towel and robe. If anything's too racy, I'll edit it."

"Merry, a little advice. This water's spring water, and it's always cold. Don't waste time."

Striding into the water, she threw her towel over a tree limb, slipped out of her things, and placed them with the towel. This beautiful woman wearing nothing but the bottom of her suit torched his heart. *Oh Lord*, he prayed, *I'm falling hard. Please help me!*

After soaping down, she waded into deeper water, dipped under and rinsed herself, then swam back to her soap. Doc only saw her back, but his heart threatened to jump out of his chest as she strolled over to the limb, put the soap in the pocket of her robe, slipped into her robe, and strolled toward Doc with a smile riding her face.

"How was that, Mr. Adams?"

"Heart-stopping. Can you handle some bear shots? We'll place him by the boulder we sat on. You wade out, turn and see him, and come running toward the camera, screaming."

They ran through this shot, and it became the most realistic of any taken. Merry tore through the water, holding her robe closed, her breasts struggling to get free. His heart pounded. Could he ever get enough of her?

"Whew!" She whistled, her breath ragged. "That's enough. I'm freezing."

Doc reached out to hold her. She shivered into his arms, and they snuggled tightly. "Doc, You feel so strong. So good. Don't ever let go."

Breathing hard, he kissed her. "Oh, Merry, where are we headed?"

Last night, he discovered that holding her was troublesome. Searching for words to back out of something he wanted ever more of, he clumsily muttered, "I better get the bear."

While Doc retrieved the bear, Merry dried off and dressed. They were soon in the truck heading home. Considering what might have happened after the bathing scenes, Doc thought about how best to spend the rest of the afternoon. "Merry, when we get home, let's take videos of the fawns. Then, while I mow, you can work on your videos. You want them ready to take home with you."

She smiled. "Great. I need to do something calming to help get the hugging scene out of my mind."

As Doc drove, he realized she was thinking about last evening and this afternoon. Merry grabbed Doc's arm at home as they finished unloading the truck. "Please don't think I'm crazy, but how I feel makes me sure there's a God. It's such a stretch to think this camping trip could be coincidental."

"Dolly called it. God sent."

After videoing the fawns, turkeys, and other smaller animals and spending several more hours mowing, Doc headed for the shower.

When he finished and dressed, he remembered the frozen chicken noodle soup.

Merry heard him in the kitchen and came down to eat.

"Soups on," Doc said as he filled dishes.

After prayer, a puzzled Merry stirred her soup. "What's this?"

"Chicken noodle soup."

"Doesn't look like any chicken noodle soup I ever ate. Who makes it?"

"Doc Adams."

"You made this from scratch?"

"Couple weeks ago. I made the noodles from my grandmother's recipe and cooked chicken breasts. Ate half and froze half. Must have known you were coming."

"Man, this is delicious. Are you sure you weren't a chef?

"My cooking's so bad our kids thought I cooked to punish them."

Through a laugh, Merry retorted, "You're so full of crap. Where do you get this stuff?"

"Just report the truth as I see it."

After supper, they looked through stacks of CDs, "Billy and I both liked the late 50s to 90s music along with Alan Jackson and Ricky Van Shelton. She recorded Elvis, Jim Reeves, Merle Haggard, a lot of slow dance music and instrumentals."

"Where's the CD player for the deck?" Merry asked after picking CDs. "I'll set it up."

"Right there," Doc answered, pointing to a cabinet in the hallway. "Place five CDs in it and flip that red switch to the middle position for the deck speakers. Take the remote with you. You can operate the player from the deck."

"Can we share some wine?"

"Guess you need to be half in the bag to stand me."

"Will you stop?"

"Okay, twist my arm, and we'll load up on cheap wine," Doc muttered.

"Beg pardon?"

"I said I'd meet you on the deck."

Charlie Walker was singing 'Pick Me Up On Your Way Down' when he got to the deck and sat down. By the time Elvis was singing 'Anything That's Part of You,' they were dancing together, growing ever closer, her eyes sparkling and her mouth drawn into a smile. As they danced, he went from holding her hand to arms wrapped around her. They danced, barely hearing the words, lost in the intimacy that engulfed them. As another Elvis song ended, Merry smiled and pulled him closer, kissing and holding him tightly. She leaned back, smiling, pressing herself to him, and they kissed again. They were breathing hard when she whispered, "This didn't just happen last night. I wanted to kiss you all week. I love you, Forest Adams."

Her kisses cradled him like flowers in bloom. He didn't want to stop. "Merry, there's so much going against us. We better sit for a while."

After quiet time, Doc suggested, "Merry, we should talk before things go any further. Things are quickly progressing towards—"

"Our love affair. I was never part of one before, but what could be wrong with what we have going?" Merry whispered.

"I'm older than you and have problems. How can this work?"

"It seems to be working pretty well right now."

"Yeah, but can it continue long term? I don't want to hurt you."

"I never dated anyone for more than a few weeks. Then Doc Adams crashed into my life and, as the song said, picked me up on my way down. Everything changed. I love you and want to get married."

"You may want that now, but what happens when I'm an old man, and you're still a hot, young chick? What if some new Mr. Right comes along, and I get dumped?"

"Enough excuses, Mr. Adams. I'm 31. My Mr. Right came along last Friday night, and when, not if I'm married to Forest Adams, nobody else will ever get close. I'm living a love story I didn't know existed. I find myself awake in the middle of the night talking with Jesus, telling him how much I need and want you. I think He's smiling too."

"I'm not giving up a few things that are life essentials," Doc said, his voice serious.

"What might those things be?"

"I can handle our political differences as long as we don't argue about them. Billy and I stopped watching most of the news because they all provided half of the story. I'm not interested in moving to a city, and there's the gun issue. I own and shoot guns. I won't push them on you, but I'm keeping them."

"I've considered our gun discussions... or gun fights many times. I wasn't exposed to guns until you came into my life—just the hate for them. Guns won't get in our way. Now, what are the other subjects?"

"It's more than a subject; it's my life based on Christian beliefs. Too many marriages fail because partners think they'll change the other after marriage. That doesn't work."

"Mr. Adams, you're not listening. I said I've been talking with Jesus. I began seriously thinking about Him when I read the sign over your computer."

"What sign would that be?"

"'Live in such a way that those who know you but don't know God will come to know God because they know you.' I can't get that sign out of my mind. I don't know much about God, but I know you. If you're God-like, everybody should be more God-like. I caused you to wreck, and you got even by buying me dinners, cooking for me, and working with me on a video project that I dearly enjoy. You haul me everywhere and treat me like I'm special. I've noticed you're nice to everyone. You changed a tire for an old guy in the rain. Then there's the note you gave the waitress with a folded hundred-dollar bill wrapped inside. She told us about her daughter's need for an operation. Your note said to call you, and you'd help her. I wondered how you got this way."

"A long time ago, someone told me, always be kind and helpful. You never know how much someone might need it. Someday that someone needing help will be you. Then you'll know.'"

"Gramp tell you that?"

"Yep. Sure enough, you came along when I needed a smile."

"You made me know I need God." After thinking for a moment, Merry added, "And you. I need you, too."

"Maybe now, but will it last?"

"I couldn't sleep last Sunday night. During the night, I felt someone helping me sort through things. I talked with Him as if He were my friend. You might not believe this, but I'd love to live here in these mountains. And this video project has me wrapped tight."

"You make this sound like we're living in a Hallmark movie. Please don't lie to yourself and throw your life away because of a few days in the mountains."

"Doc, listen! Last night was the first time I ever kissed a man and didn't want to let go. And that's not the first time I wanted to kiss that man. Something special is taking place for me. I hope you're feeling the same way."

"Maybe we should head to the courthouse tomorrow," Doc whispered, looking at her with a smile.

"For what?" Merry asked with a quizzical grin.

"To apply for a marriage license," Doc said with the smile slipping away. "If our relationship was God sent, the folks down at the courthouse should hear about it. While you're thinking about that, I'd enjoy the pleasure of another dance."

CHAPTER 28

After little sleep, Doc struggled awake Friday morning with crows chattering at a red tail hawk where they perched in an apple tree. As the sun climbed out of the pink and gray-streaked sky, he relived the incredible night he enjoyed with Merry while admitting that this love must be real, a thought he didn't know how to handle.

That thought landed with a thud. Last night was beyond real. He sat up in bed, pulled on his leg, dressed, and shaved. Unable to get Merry off his mind, he began daily chores with Elvis singing 'I'm Yours' resonating in his mind.

Doc finished chores, grabbed a chicken treat from a box by the feed bin, and tossed it to Jack before heading to the house. He was settling into his chair when he heard Merry coming down the steps.

"You're up early, young lady. What gives?"

"Just nosey. Wanted to see what you do in the morning," Merry answered through a wide yawn accompanied by a hand over her mouth. "Brought down your trail camera. I looked at the chip last night. It contains neat pictures: bull elk, a couple of cow elk with calves, deer, two bears, and us after we cut our marshmallow sticks. You had your arm around me. I love it."

"I'll put the camera back when we ride out this morning."

"I was awake when you got up and watched you walk out to the barn with Jack. I can't remember being excited to see a new day arrive until I came here. My clock radio's snooze button is worn thin from use. There's always exciting stuff to do here every day. I can't wait to go riding horses. If it's still on, I'm excited about our courthouse visit, and then I want to finish the video we're creating. After that, I'm anxious to start on whatever is coming next. Maybe we can dance for a while. I had difficulty sleeping last night after we kissed and danced and kissed and hugged and... well, you know."

"Merry, if you told anyone who knows me that I fell in love with a woman after knowing her seven days, they'd wonder what you were smoking."

Merry held his eyes as she considered what he said. "Last night, I was lying in bed thinking the same things. No one who knows me could believe this. I can't believe it myself."

She smiled and added, "Oh, Honey, I love you. I don't want to leave tomorrow."

"I don't want you to leave. I'm afraid you'll get back to Harrisburg, reality will set in, an' you'll ask yourself, 'What in the world was I thinking?' Then you'll send someone up to get your car, so you don't have to say, 'Sorry, Gramp, that crash screwed up my thinker. Gave me TBI.' Then you'll dump old Doc and head into a bright future with some young, handsome buck. I'm scared."

"Doc, that's hateful," Merry said with a frown. "The last two nights witnessed a Merry An Morehouse I never knew. I don't want to lose any of that me. Lying in bed going over yesterday made me crazy to be close to you. I wanted to get in bed with you. I wouldn't want to live if you didn't love me."

"I understand that feeling. I love and want you badly, but I want a ring on your finger and marriage vows first. I couldn't sleep, remembering the heat we generated. I want to marry you. Please be sure you want the same. I'd hurt a bunch if it ended now, but I don't know if I could handle it if it happened after we were married."

"I want you now and forever, Forest Adams. Be sure of the forever part."

"Will you want the Forest Adams with night problems and terrible dreams, the one with the scarred body you haven't seen, the old —"

"Stop! I want you, and I'll handle all that goes with you. We'll work things out together."

"That might be easier said than done," he replied. "I'll have no trouble telling Ronnie and Cindy about us, but a tough question's running through my mind. How and when do you tell your parents?"

"Maybe I won't tell them. I don't want my father's threats or his 'Merry, don't be so dumb' speech. I've enjoyed more real heart-stopping love and door-opening courtesies in a few days than my mother ever experienced. My father would never do for anyone what you do for me."

"Pray for him," Doc whispered.

"I've been praying for both parents and didn't know what prayer was until you." Then, with a wide grin, she added, "I didn't even know I had the hots for you then. When we get married, I want to share all your worries."

"That's kind of you, Merry, but I don't have many worries."

"Maybe that's because we aren't married yet."

They smiled, and then Doc said, "We better get our breakfast before I get scared and run off."

They laughed as he pulled out her chair, kissing her on the cheek. She stepped into his arms; they embraced and then kissed. They held the kiss and snuggled closer. "Oh, Honey, I do love you, Merry."

"I love you too. Doc, you take my breath away. I never said I love you to anyone before you. I love you. I love you. I love you. If you'll have me, I'm yours forever."

After a warm kiss, they sat down with eyes sparkling and held hands to pray. Merry's being warmed its way into his tender spot, a place Billie's death replaced with the anger and discontent that ruled until Merry crashed into his life. "Oh Lord, our God, be with us. If this isn't real, lasting love, please show us. We think we're heading into a bright future, but please show us if it's a mirage. If it's right, open the doors for us to go forward. And Lord, please help us with this Hackett mess." Doc finished with his standard Adams prayer.

They talked as they ate. "Doc, you asked about my job. My annual reviews report I'm good at my job, but I'm not happy with it. After college, I couldn't find a job, and a friend got me the Philadelphia Inquirer job. Another friend brought me to WLDZ. Neither job excites me like this video we're making. Do you think we can make a living turning out video material?"

I know we can, Honey. You just have to believe."

"Doc, I came up here on a whim, and my life was turned around by a person I didn't think I wanted to know our first night together. When I'm with you, I'm a me I never knew until you. I had no real-life concept of love before, and now I'm crazy in love with you, the person I didn't want to know."

"Remember the courthouse."

"You're serious?" she asked in a voice hovering between 'This can't be happening' and cautious optimism.

"We aren't getting any younger. We might get the urge to get hitched on a holiday weekend, and we'd be out of luck with no license and a waiting period."

Merry couldn't talk for a bit. Wonderment ran across her face as she looked intently into his eyes.

"Was that a proposal, Doc?" she whispered.

"Preparation for a proposal. I can't propose until we get your ring."

"I don't need a ring."

"I need you to have one."

"Can we go to the courthouse when we return from riding?"

"You sure, Merry?"

"Never been surer of anything."

"After a few days with some kisses, hugs, and dancing?"

"After two nights of dancing and lots of kisses and hugs. And I wanted it to happen before that. A long time before that. Several days at least."

"Then, that would be my pleasure."

They smiled and kissed deeply.

CHAPTER 29

Arianna dragged herself to work Friday morning, thinking she should call Merry's family. Her message light welcomed her as she shoved her purse into her desk drawer. *Please don't let this be a terrible message about Merry.*

"Arianna, Charlie here. I got news about Bucky's place. Not sure what it means. Can you come over when you get in? Thanks."

She arrived to find Charlie's door closed. With her light knock, he said, "Come in" and continued "Blaine Jensen just returned from vacation and checked Bucky's place. There was no one there but —"

"That's great, Charlie. Wonder why I don't feel a big surge of relief?"

"C'mon, Arianna. It's not much, but it might be something. Blaine said it looked like somebody cooked meals over Bucky's fire pit. He found two cooking sticks, one for toasting marshmallows and a hotdogs cooker. He also found a bean can used in the fire. Someone set up a tent, but it's gone. He found tracks but couldn't tell if they were coyote tracks or a large dog's, and a man left tracks where it was muddy."

"She could have been attacked by a coyote who could kill her. And the man could be a rapist or murderer."

"Whoa! Let's not add a rapist or murderer to the problems we face," Charlie said, trying to arrest her fears.

"With our luck, anything could happen. Most people don't get run over by log trucks!"

"I don't know what I was thinking when I switched the key tags and left that place a mess." After pausing, Charlie continued. "Yes, I do know, Arianna. I have the hots for you. When you cut me off cold, I decided to get even. Then you didn't even go up there. I wouldn't be a part of this mess if I —"

"You're your own worst enemy, Charlie. You cut people down and run your big mouth when you shouldn't. You should make a 'How Charlie Screwed Up' list. Sometimes you have so much going for you. Then you pull another dumb stunt."

"Maybe I'll make that list, Arianna."

"Do that, and let me look it over. I'll add things you miss."

"Look, I'm trying to change, and I could use your help. Blaine said he'll be trimming Christmas trees tomorrow, and he'll keep watch for people. He said there were truck tire tracks that looked like they had been in and out of there several times."

"Like maybe some druggie kidnaped a pretty woman?"

"Arianna, stop! It's bad enough the way it is."

"I should call her parents. Maybe they know something."

"Better think that over. Remember, Merry's old man's a big-shot lawyer with a tough reputation. What if the worst comes true, and he holds us accountable for her demise?"

"Charlie, culpability is one thing. Saving the life of someone we shafted is another. Bucky thought we were only staying until today, and his brother's going up tomorrow. I didn't know what to tell him, so I didn't tell him anything."

"Oh crap, Bucky's brother is part owner of the place and fights Bucky every time he lets someone stay there," Charlie said with a deep frown. "When he walks into the mess we left, I can kiss off ever using the place again."

"Put that on your list of lessons learned."

"Stuff it, Arianna. You cheated your friend out of the evening newscaster job where she shines. You're so afraid she'll get this as a permanent assignment when Maggie Ward hangs it up. I'm just an accessory that does dumb things."

"Great description, Charlie. Add that to your list. And that isn't the only reason I had for backing out of that trip north."

"I heard. Mister general manager's old lady is out of town, and you two had a date."

"Who told you that?" Arianna demanded, her face tightening into a mean scowl.

"We work in a news organization. Folks investigate and report stuff. It seems you and Warner had a date Wednesday. You had your hair made up real pretty and wore a sexy black dress. You were all smiles as you —"

"Darn it, Charlie, can't you shut up? That dinner meeting came about because my job depended on it. You wouldn't understand."

"Oh, I understand. Mister Big gets to enjoy your company when regular guys don't."

"Charlie, shut up!" Arianna said in a mean voice. "That dinner was dinner and nothing more. He tried to take me to a motel, but I wouldn't go. My future at the station could be at stake because of it. I feel so bad about that night. About Merry. About a lot of things."

"Arianna, there might be lessons here for you too. My big mouth cost me a relationship, but what you did could cost more than friendship."

CHAPTER 30

Tree leaves twinkled in the breeze as they rode horseback past the hill cemetery and headed down Whippoorwill Hollow.

"Hey Doc, this is where your troubles began," Merry said as they rode past the place where they crashed into new lives.

"It's where I began a wonderful new life," Doc countered as they rode side by side. "Did you ever think the cause of this love you're experiencing might be something I'm slipping into your coffee? They just convicted and jailed Mr. TV Family Man for drugging women so he could have sex with them."

"I feel drugged, but not the way you're thinking. Doc, are you serious about going to the courthouse today?"

"You backing out?"

"Never. But I'm scared," Merry said, looking away, her face white and hands shaking. "What if I can't ...can't ...you know? I've talked hot stuff with you, but what if I can't be your total wife? What if past problems get in the way of - well, in the way of us?"

"Merry, we've kidded and held each other until it was hard to stop."

"Oh, Doc, I'm so scared. I can't add to your problems."

"Merry, listen to me. I love you. Totally. We'll work through whatever problems you have."

"Doc, if you're sure you can handle my problems, we'll go with it. You have to be sure."

"I don't know what those problems are, but I'm sure we can deal with them."

Color slowly returned to Merry's face. They shared warm smiles but didn't talk again until they approached a beaver dam. "Get your camera ready," Doc whispered as he spotted a beaver swimming with a mouthful of aspen branches. "We'll get fairly close on horses, and you don't have beavers in your video."

Merry began shooting and soon spotted two beavers cutting limbs from a downed aspen tree. They rode close with Merry running video until a beaver slapped his tail in warning, and they dove into the water and out of sight. After another mile or so, Doc suggested they return home.

It was mid-morning when they off-saddled and went in for showers. As they walked into the house, Doc grabbed Merry's shoulder and kissed her neck. She scrunched up her shoulders, made an 'ooooohhh' sound, turned, and they kissed passionately.

"I so love you," Doc whispered between kisses. "I know we'll be able to overcome any problems."

"I'm praying, Doc. I prayed all the way down and back from the beaver dam. Can we get married today?"

"There's a marriage waiting period and our trial to get past. We'll get a license today. When you're ready, I'll be on the porch. It takes pretty ladies longer to get ready for important dates.

Showered and dressed, Doc headed to the garage to get out the Traverse where it had been sitting since Billy's funeral. He checked the oil, water, and tire pressures, and after placing a little air in the tires, he pulled out of the garage, closed the door, and sat on the front porch with Jack. Merry soon arrived and looked shocked when she saw the car.

"Nice car Doc. What is it?"

"2017 Traverse. Not many miles on it. We bought it for our business. Billy left us five months later."

"You sure you want to use it to get a marriage license?"

"And a ring. Yes, and I'm sure that's what Billy would want too."

"I don't need a ring."

"I need you to have one. I want you to look at that ring and think, 'Some old dude loves me a bunch.'"

"Doc, please stop that old dude stuff," Merry said with a sad face. "It hurts. You're not old, and I'm crazy about you. Every bit of you."

"You'll need your driver's license. I have mine and Billy's death certificate. They're required."

"I have it."

"Great. How about driving for us," Doc asked and helped her into the driver's seat. "Wow. You smell good. Wind song?"

"Billy's Wind Song."

When they hit route 120 headed for Emporium, Doc said, "I have a confession to make. I wasn't supposed to peek when you came out of the water, but I did. You're one beautiful woman."

She placed her hand on Doc's arm and squeezed. Her face was red. "I have a confession too. I wanted you to peek. It started on Bucky's porch when I leaned back against my arms, and my blouse tightened. You kept sneaking peeks at me, and I liked it. It's all so crazy. I buy my clothes loose-fitting, so no one sees much of me. But I wanted you to see. Nobody else has ever seen me as you have, and they won't. Well, maybe the doctor when she delivers our babies."

"Don't you think I'm a little old for babies?" he asked in a shocked voice.

"You're not too old for anything. And that's what happens when people fall in love."

In Emporium, they drove up the hill into the Cameron County courthouse parking lot and headed for the clerk's office. After showing her their documents and paying for the license, they discovered Doc was correct about the three-day waiting period. Doc asked the older female clerk, "Are you sure we have to wait? What if she changes her mind?"

"Mister Adams, the way she's looking at you and holding your arm says you have nothing to worry about."

"Sure hope you're right."

"Oh, I'm right. I can always tell the ones who love each other and those who might not. Your lady's keeping you."

"Thanks, Honey," Merry said with a glowing smile for the clerk.

Walking out of the courthouse holding hands, Doc suggested, "Merry, let's check on your car before we head to the jewelry store."

Grabbing his arm with a worried look, Merry asked, "How's Ronnie going to feel when he sees me driving his mother's car? Yeah, and to get a marriage license? Maybe even an engagement ring."

"Probably wanna know when the wedding is."

"Yeah, right," Merry mumbled, shaking her head.

She hesitated to get out of the car at Ronnie's, but Doc opened her door and held her hand as they walked toward the garage. Ronnie was talking with a customer and winked when they walked in. After closing that conversation, he grew a wide grin and asked, "When are you two getting hitched? Can't be long the way you're looking."

"You tell him, Merry. He won't believe me."

"We just came from the courthouse. Got our marriage license."

"You're serious?" Ronnie asked with a thoughtful look. "When's the big day?"

"Not sure. What weekends do you have free? I'll need a best man, and I'm looking at my choice."

"My next several weekends are open, and I'll keep them that way. I can't wait to tell Sarah. Merry, you may be the only person who won't be happy. How'd he con you into this?"

"It's my idea."

"Guess you haven't heard how poor he is."

"We're planning on welfare," Merry said, smiling. "We heard welfare will even pick up the tab for car repairs."

"Good luck with that. Speaking of your car, I got a call this morning. The last parts should be here on Monday, Tuesday at the latest. I'll have it ready Wednesday night. I'm hoping that doesn't screw up your plans too badly."

"I can get a rental car," Merry said, showing a long face.

Ronnie leaned forward and looked closely at his father. "Okay, son, what are we gawking at?" Doc asked, sounding aggravated.

"Your face. It's bruised, and your lip's split."

"Hadn't noticed."

"Looks like Merry beat you into a wedding. Maybe she told you to shut up, and you thought she said stand up?"

"I'd never hit him, Ronnie."

"Somebody did."

"You'll see it in the Echo police report," Doc growled. "Your grandfather picked a fight, then had us arrested. Said I started the fight, and Merry was an accomplice."

"Wonder what he told Gram. I don't want problems with her. She's always so nice."

"She dropped over the next night when George went to play poker. After we talked a bit, she said Merry was God sent. Said she gave me back my smile."

"I believe that," Ronnie said with enthusiasm. Let me know if we can do anything to help with the wedding."

"Will do. Look, we have to be going. We're off to see the ring wizard."

"What are you and Sarah doing for dinner tomorrow? Merry asked. "Let's do steaks."

"I'll tell Sarah when I call her with the good news."

"Come early so you can look at Merry's video."

"Video? What's it about."

"It's a surprise."

As they walked to the Traverse, Doc explained, "There isn't a jewelry store in Cameron County. Choices are St. Marys or Olean, New York for rings."

"Let's do St. Marys. I can pick up a rental car while we're there."

"You don't like the Traverse?"

"I can't drive your car to Harrisburg."

"Why not? It'll soon be half yours."

"Olean, it is. Give me directions."

"Go east when you pull out of here."

"And which direction would that be?"

"Make a right at the light. I'll give you directions as we go along."

Merry looked over and caught him grinning. "Oh, sure. That's a man thing."

Doc provided directions right into the Kay Jewelers parking lot on North Street, Olean. The salesperson in Kay's asked them what type of ring they were looking for and quickly discovered they were each looking for something different, Merry, something small and inexpensive, Doc, something more significant. She endeavored to please them both, showing them rings in several price ranges until the discussion took on a new look when Merry proclaimed, "We'll take the smaller diamond."

"Do you like the larger stone?" Doc politely asked.

"Very much but —"

"I'm buying the rings. We'll take the larger stone."

"I'm wearing the darned ring, so —"

"Maybe you can compromise with a different ring," the salesperson suggested. "We can look for something that suits both of your tastes."

"Let's compromise with the larger stone size 7. We both like it. Wrap it up!" Doc said, smiling as he handed her his credit card.

Watching her, Doc said, "The credit card should be good. We found it in the parking lot."

The clerk jerked around, "What?"

Doc smiled while signing the credit slip, and after a brief hesitation, she handed the ring to him. As they walked to the car, Merry asked, "Did you have to make a scene about the ring choice?"

"Is this a question or the start of an argument?" Doc stopped and asked. "Look, I hope to be looking at that ring on your finger for a long time. The price tag drew you to one, but your eyes said that wasn't the one you wanted. If that would have been a vehicle, clothing, or furniture purchase and you wanted one over the other, you'd get your way."

Shaking her head, Merry replied, "See why I love you. You're something, Doc. I love the ring you bought, but I bet that poor woman is wondering if this was a sale or a theft after your comment on finding the card."

"If she's wondering, it's because you look like my daughter."

"As I've mentioned, you don't stop. Where to now?"

"Home. I want to propose to a beautiful lady."

As they drove through Portville, New York, Doc saw a florist shop and yelled, "Pull in here."

Merry jammed on the brakes sliding the tires to make it into the parking lot with the horn blowing on the car behind them. "Man, Doc, you could give me a little warning," Merry snapped.

"Sorry, Honey," Doc said as he climbed out of the car. "Didn't see the store until I yelled." He was back in minutes with a bouquet of beautiful red roses in a vase tucked into a box.

"Honey, you shouldn't have done that. The ring was too much."

"I have to replace the dried roses on the kitchen table. Today, I'm entering a new life with a woman I love. We need flowers for our relationship."

The miles rolled quietly by. Doc finally broke the silence with a question. "Honey, do you wonder how we got here?"

Merry thought a bit before softly answering. "Dolly told me. I was God sent — to a world I didn't know existed to be with a man who gave me a life filled with love. I'm doing my best to live up to what I've learned, things like discussion rather than argument. How'd you get here?"

"God allowed me to crash into a beautiful young woman who pulled me out of a drunken, grief-filled existence."

They soon traveled through Emporium and were on their way up the mountain. "Is this really happening?" Merry asked as they pulled into the Lookout, where they watched cars creeping along on the streets below.

"No, Merry, it happened," Doc replied as a freight train whistle drew their attention as it rolled northward far below them. "Sweetheart, this is the first week of our new life."

Doc kissed her softly, savoring her tender lips and touching her cheeks with his hands as he felt his dreams of a love life with her flowing together. "Oh, Honey, your smile lights me up, and your beauty takes my breath away. I so want to be married. I'll love you forever."

"Doc, I'm scared. This Hackett court nightmare scares me. The other thing, the thing with my father tears me to pieces. I pray we can get past them."

"Oh, Honey, we can get past anything together. I love you so," Doc said as he tucked strands of hair behind her ear and kissed it, then kissed down her neck.

They kissed tenderly, gently touching each other's faces, loving each other. Doc reached for her left hand and whispered, "I love you, Merry Morehouse. Will you marry me?"

"I love you too and want to be your wife, now and forever. But I'm afraid of so many things. What if I can't be a... a... a whole wife? You know what I mean ... don't you."

"Like I said, we'll get through these things together," Doc said as he slipped the ring on her finger. They kissed deeply, holding each other tightly.

"Oh, Doc, I love you. I'll work forever to make you happy. My life changed when I looked across the table at you last Saturday night, and I can't get enough of that change."

Life bloomed with love. After kissing again, Merry headed towards home. Holding her ring up, she looked at Doc and smiled.

"Thanks. Oh, Honey, I have so much to learn. You make everything seem so easy."

"It's hard to believe we crashed into this love affair. We haven't known each other a week until nine tonight."

CHAPTER 31

Merry struggled. Sleep refused to come as scenes from a full day roared through her mind. Riding horses. Beavers. Elk. Marriage license. The ring. And love. Then the question ran through her mind again: could love overcome her past?

As she fought through the question, a terrifying scream rang through the home!

"No dammit, Jerry! Breathe. Breathe! Damn you, Jerry, breathe. You can't die."

It was quiet for a moment. The voice screamed louder. "Damn You, Jerry. Breathe! You're dying on me."

Fear boiled through Merry as it grew quiet. Screams filled the air again, accompanied by cursing and Jack barking. Worried, Merry slipped her door open. Something crashed, and the screaming began anew.

"Roof. Roof. Roof." A loud, low-pitched dog bark penetrated the night.

Merry knocked on Doc's door. "Are you all right?"

Nothing. "You all right, Doc?" A little louder this time.

A haunting, fear-filled voice whispered. "It's okay."

"You don't sound okay."

"Please go back to bed."

Merry refused to listen and shook her head as she turned on the hall light and cracked open his bedroom door. "I can't go back to bed, Doc," Merry said as she sat by him. He held his head in his hands and was sobbing. She put her arms around him. "I love you, Doc Adams."

"Please go," Doc begged, tears running down his face.

They sat while Merry tried to wrap her mind around something she didn't understand. She held Doc, feeling him shake. Gradually, he calmed, took a handkerchief from his nightstand, and wiped his face. "Yer gonna hate me," Doc mumbled. "I'm so sorry."

"Nothing could make me hate you. I love you."

After a bit, she tried to talk to him again. "Who's Jerry, Doc?" she asked quietly.

Silence ruled broken by an occasional sobbing-sucking sound. Merry held him tightly until he worked up to an answer. "He was my best friend."

"Was?"

"Jerry's eyes begged for help. He died in my arms." Doc sobbed again for a bit and then quietly mumbled. "I tried so hard, but he couldn't breathe."

"Is that when you lost your leg?"

"I saved me an' Ray but lost Jerry."

Merry held him with Jack resting his head on her knee. Finally, Doc demanded in a low, flat voice, "You can't live with this. It won't let go."

"We'll learn to deal with this together."

After a bit, Doc calmed, and Merry returned to her room, where she sat on her bed, head in hands, lightly crying. She struggled to bring sanity to her night, but it wouldn't come. Breathing was difficult. Through tears, she softly talked to God. "Oh Lord, it was easy talking about Doc's problem until it happened. How do I help him through this horror-filled world?"

After a period of quietness endeavoring to make sense of her life, Merry began whispering. "I love this man. I'm not quitting, but I need help. I can't do this myself." With hands clenched into fists, she pounded her pillow. "Merry, get hold of yourself," she demanded. "You're bigger than this."

Exhausted and shaking, she cried herself to sleep.

CHAPTER 32

Saturday morning spoke of a beautiful day with birds singing, but Doc couldn't feel that truth as he fought through a cup of coffee that didn't want to stay down. Unshaven and disheveled, his eyes carried a haunted look, a carryover from his latest attack. Endeavoring to understand, Merry sat beside him on the porch swing, trying to discuss the previous night's problem. Finally, he half-whispered, "Merry, I can't chain you to an insane life."

"How'd Billy deal with this?"

"Billy understood my problem. We lived in the same house for four years. She helped me when I had attacks. Her roommates were different. Judy wanted me to move out before I hurt someone. When we were alone, Linda told me sex would help, and she could help me."

"Forest Adams, get this straight, I love you, and we're getting married. You're all I have. We must work through this!"

Tears hung in Doc's eyes as he quietly sifted through her comments. "Honey, you're facing a never-ending problem."

"Listen to me," Merry returned with passion and anger rippling through her voice, "I talked to the Lord with no answers. Not yet, anyway. I cried myself to sleep and woke up tired. Still no answer. This I know. I'm leading a lousy life and didn't know how lousy until last Friday night. I know what I'd be throwing away if I listened to you. I'm not listening."

As he put his arm around her, Doc's mouth curved into a slight smile, his first of the day. "You gotta be nuts, girl. You were so scared. How can you be okay with that?"

"If by okay, you mean, am I willing to help with the problem, the answer is yes. If you mean will I cut and run, throwing away the only real love I've ever experienced, the answer is no. Nuff said."

After time passed quietly, Merry asked, "What brings on these nightmares?"

Doc clasped his hands and stared into space.

"Doc?"

Nothing.

"Doc, we need to work on this. Together. I'm discovering personal problems don't fix themselves. I threw away half of my life before I could admit I didn't cause my difficulties. That's when I discovered I needed someone to love me if I wanted to get past those problems. You're giving me that love. I need to help you the same way."

Doc turned to her and noted her tear-filled eyes. Something inside led him to talk, to tell her things he shared with no one but Billy. Struggling, he searched for words and softly began. "I have a hard time with memories. The military. Anger. Love. Deep meaning things."

"How's that?"

After a loud sigh, Doc tried again. "They're memory generators that lead to PTSD problems. It's a long story."

"I need to hear that story so we can tackle this together."

Doc struggled in search of a beginning. Running his fingers through his hair, he hesitantly began. "Yesterday was an ever-so-happy generator until it brought back memories of my mother. My father lost his life in Vietnam before I was born. After that, everything made my mother cry. When I was eight or nine, I hugged her when she was crying. I said, 'Mom, I love you. Please don't cry.' She shoved me away and cried harder. She cried herself to death a couple of years later. I became an orphan."

Really?"

"I was eavesdropping on my grandparents after her funeral and heard my grandmother ask, "What are we going to do with Forest? We're too old to raise that boy.' It got quiet for a bit. Then Gramp said, 'Edna, I've prayed for strength and guidance. While I was shaving this morning, the Lord said, 'Forest needs you. If you turn your back on that boy, you'll never be able to look in that mirror again.' I plan on shaving."

"It was quiet again. Then my grandmother said, 'Honey, our love and our Lord pulled us through many hard times. I think we'll do just fine on this new assignment.'"

"Did you get along with your grandmother?"

"She became the mother I never really had. The morning the Navy recruiter picked me up for boot camp, she hugged me tight and cried, 'Oh Frosty, I love you. You're very much like your grandfather. The Lord took great care of me when he gave me you two men. Be safe.' She emphasized the, 'you two men.' I didn't consider myself a man until then. She walked away so I wouldn't see her cry."

"What happened after you joined the Navy?"

Doc sucked his lungs full and noisily let the air escape. With head in hands, he began. "I became a Navy Corpsman and requested service with the Marines. Saddam Hussein grabbed Kuwait, and President Bush decided he wasn't going to get away with it. During the attack, Jerry stepped on a mine that blew three of us up. Jerry was my best friend. He died in my arms choking on his blood. I still see the fear in his eyes. His blown apart body. He held a 'help me' look and died. That scene won't let go. Bad dreams don't always begin with mines. Jerry can be attacked by wild animals, drunk drivers, whatever, and he's dying in my arms. Realism hits. The mine—" The sound of an approaching vehicle stopped Doc mid-sentence. Merry jumped to her feet and headed for the door. "I better get dressed for visitors."

As the vehicle came into view, Doc recognized the truck. "It's Blaine Jensen. Wonder what he wants?"

"Maybe he heard you have a new woman," Merry said as she disappeared inside.

Doc laughed, and when the truck door slammed, Doc called him out to the screened porch. "Welcome, Blaine. What brings you out this time of the morning?"

"I've been meaning to drop by and see how you're doing. Heard you played at the songfest, and I missed it. With that said, I'm here for another reason."

"Oh. Should I be worried?"

"Man, Doc, you look rough. You get mauled by a bear," Blain asked, looking at Doc's beat-up face and teary eyes. "You okay?"

"Okay, enough. What's on your mind?"

"Folks down in Harrisburg are trying to locate a woman who was supposed to be staying at Bucky Liniger's camp. She ain't there. Her friend talked her into this camping trip and then backed out. The guy who used the camp last is a practical joker. After folks stay there, I check the place for Bucky, and that bird left a mess."

"Really?" Doc asked.

"Yeah. Folks are worried. They've tried her cell phone for days with no answer. They think she got run over by a log truck. They've called hospitals. No word. Requested me to look around. Someone's been there. Cleaned the place. Do you know anything about a woman getting run over by a truck?"

"Can you keep something between the three of us?"

"You mean the two of us."

"No, three of us."

"I can. Would the third person be a woman named Merry?"

"It would. She'll be out momentarily with the rest of the story. In the meantime, can you handle a cup of coffee?"

"I can. Black, please."

Merry came down while Doc was pouring coffee, and after refilling her cup, she moved to the porch. Blaine stood to meet her when she walked out.

"Blaine, this young lady is Merry Morehouse, the woman you're looking for."

"Nice to meet you, Merry. You don't look like you got run over by a log truck."

"That's because I wasn't."

Merry tells Blaine the story, beginning with her decision to come alone and ending by showing her ring. When she finished, Blaine said, "Three questions are running through my mind. What in the world were they thinking when they let you come up here by yourself? Even more, what were you thinking? And are you telling me you went from wrecked strangers to an engaged couple in a week?"

"We did, and I came because I wasn't thinking. Dolly Hackett said I was God sent."

"Had to be to go from strangers to an engagement in a week."

Blaine talked a bit, and after promising not to tell folks about Doc and Merry, he drove off, leaving them holding hands on the swing. It was quiet until Merry asked, "What happened to your other friend?"

After searching for words, Doc quietly began. "Ray was trying to find his weapon, crawling around, missing a leg with his arm just dangling there. My foot was gone. I found my medic bag and got a tourniquet on myself. Crawled over to Ray. Got tourniquets on him. His face was bloody. He was screaming, 'Who stole my weapon?'

Marines got us out of there. We ended up in Bethesda and did months of rehab together."

"Did you stay in touch?"

"For a while. Medically retired Staff Sergeant Ray Benson stayed with us over a weekend while I was attending Penn State. He told us his wife couldn't live with his problems and left him. She hated his sleepless nights. Screaming and seeing stuff that wasn't there. We hugged when he drove off in the morning. Hunters found him a couple days later. He pulled into the woods a few miles up the road. Killed himself."

"I'm so sorry," Merry said, realizing that was all Doc could contribute for a while.

Birds sang on the feeder while a phoebe walked along the deck railing hunting bugs. Doc finally broke the silence. "Merry, CBS ran a special on a vet named Brian Mancini and his fight with PTSD. I saved it in my email. Pull it up when you're in Harrisburg. Know what you're facing. I won't blame you if you change your mind about marriage."

"I hear wedding bells. We're getting married, Doc Adams. Better call Preacher Mike."

"I'll do that," Doc said, and after thinking about it, he got up for a phone.

"Anita, This is Doc Adams. How are you?"

"Fine, Doc, and you?"

"Great. Is Pastor Mike home?"

"Sorry, Doc. He's a volunteer fireman, and he's fighting a brush fire. Can I help you?"

"We're wondering if you two could share dinner with us tomorrow after church? It's important."

"Would this have anything to do with the pretty woman who was with you last Sunday?"

"It would."

"I told Mike she watched you playing as if there was love running through her mind. I can give you a tentative 'yes' on the dinner date. It would take another fire to miss dinner. What can we bring?"

"Just yourselves. See you at church."

"I'm happy for you, Doc. See you tomorrow."

"Well, Merry, let's head for Valley Meats. We need food for Ronnie and Sarah today and Pastor Mike and Anita tomorrow. We'll whip up a batch of potato salad, baked beans, and an anti-pasta salad with a pan of lemon surprise for dessert. That will take care of tonight's and tomorrow's meals. I'll split the leftovers with you when you head for Harrisburg."

Doc and Smitty, the owner and butcher, warmly greeted each other when they arrived at Valley Meats. Looking at Merry, Smitty asked, "Is this another one of your daughters, Doc?"

"Nope, my grandmot—"

"He fibs. I'll soon be his wife," Merry proudly announced, holding out her ring.

"Sorry. I didn't know."

"Doc didn't know either until I got my claws in him. He knows it now."

"Smitty, this is Merry, my soon-to-be. Do you cater weddings?"

"I do. I'll get you a flyer. I give vets a ten percent discount on already rock-bottom pricing. Watching you two walk in holding hands and smiling suggests the wedding could be this afternoon. Now, my friend, what can I get you?"

"I'd like twelve Delmonico steaks."

"Sounds like quite a party. Anything else?"

"Three sticks of pepperoni and a pound each of Swiss, provolone, and that other cheese I always get."

"Monterey Jack? Heard you quit at the plant. You going to have enough money to pay for everything?"

"Hand Merry the bill. She's got money coming out her ears."

"You gotta be kiddin', Doc."

"Yeah, but I like the sound of it."

Their next stop was the County Foods grocery store, where they picked up the rest of their grocery list and two Breyers ice creams. Looking over the order, the cashier asked, "Can I go home with you guys? I love ice cream and salad meals. Light on the salad."

"Glad to have you, Gina, but you'd be so bored with us old people."

"Old? Maybe you, Doc, but not the lady."

"We're the same age. She eats vitamins by the handful and drinks a couple quarts of cheap booze every day. Do that, and you'll look just like her."

"Doc, you can be a real BS-er."

"Says you."

On the way home, Merry pulled into the lookout. "Been a long time since I enjoyed a kiss. I'm throwing a fit if I don't get one."

They kissed until Doc suggested, "We better get going. We have a lot of work waiting for us."

They arrived home and had the salads prepared when Merry's phone began ringing. "Arianna's on the hunt," Merry guessed as she grabbed her phone. "Oh, it's my mother calling," Merry apprehensively said. "Wonder what she wants."

"Hi, mother. How are you?"

"Worried sick. I got a frantic call from your friend. She informed me my daughter got run over by a log truck. Are you in a hospital?"

"Did Arianna ask you to call back if you locate me?"

"She did. She's worried sick. She said you were all alone in some godforsaken mountain place, and she can't reach you up there wherever up there is. Where are you?"

"Can this be kept between you and me? I don't want anyone in Harrisburg knowing where I am."

"Are you in serious trouble?" her mother asked, fear riding heavy in her voice.

"No trouble. Is it a deal?"

"Okay, it's a deal."

With that guarantee, Merry explained her wreck and that she wasn't hurt. They discussed her video and how much she loved the mountains.

"Are you staying at that camp by yourself?"

"No, Mother, I'm staying with a new friend."

"How did you meet her?"

"The person I'm staying with is the person I crashed into. And the person isn't a she. It's a he."

"Is he married?"

"Not currently, but soon will be."

"What's his girlfriend say about you staying with him?"

"She loves it. It's me. We're crazy in love, and we're getting married. We got our license yesterday. He bought me a beautiful diamond engagement ring. We're having the pastor and his wife over for dinner to discuss our wedding. And Mother, don't tell Father anything! Please."

"Merry, are you on drugs? We don't live like this. Your father and I went together a year before we were engaged and another year before we were married."

"How'd that work for you, Mother? I crashed into a gentleman who loves me and always thinks of me first."

"Everything will change when you're married. Your father will go ballistic when he finds out."

"Don't tell him anything. I don't want him messing things up. I'll let you know when the big day is, but I don't want Father there."

"Merry, you need to talk to a psychiatrist, someone to help you make sense of your life."

"Mother, I'm finally making sense of my life. This man has shown me more love and kindness in a week than I witnessed my father showing you in my lifetime. Nothing is going to change my mind."

"You weren't raised to act like this."

"I know. Let's talk about something else."

"I'm too nervous to talk. I'll call you after I try to make sense of this. Goodbye."

The phone went dead. "I'm sorry, Merry. If you're having second thoughts —"

"Frosty, that phone call should tell you why I'm crazy about you and your way of life."

"Maybe I'm treating you nice and keeping you on drugs until we're married. I think you're loaded with bucks."

CHAPTER 33

Doc and Merry stood quietly on the deck after cleaning up the kitchen. Doc placed his arms around her and held her tight. They were watching a doe with twin fawns when Doc suggested, "We better get ready. As excited as Ronnie sounded, they could come early, and I need a shower."

"We talking about showering together?" Merry asked.

"You like to tease, but you'd like to be able to say we waited until marriage when all these kids you want ask questions."

"We could shower together now, and I could lie a little later if the topic came up."

"Perhaps you forgot the pastor and his wife are coming to dinner. Their mission is to discuss marriage with us, and I don't want your face carrying guilty conscience signs."

"I hope I don't find out after marriage that you're afraid of sex," Merry said with a smile.

"Merry, my darling, I promise you that's one area where you have no worries."

Doc finished dressing before Ronnie and Sarah pulled in, and Jack raced out to greet them. Doc yelled up the stairway, "They're here."

"Hey, guys. Good to see you, Doc called out the front door. Let's sit on the deck."

Merry soon arrived wearing white slacks and a low-cut green blouse. Her auburn hair hung loosely around her shoulders, and a heart-shaped emerald necklace lit fire in her hazel eyes.

"Sarah, this is Merry. Merry, this is Sarah," Doc said as an introduction.

As Merry sat down, Ronnie said, "Okay, Merry, hold your hand out so we can see it."

"See what?" she asked, a puzzled look on her face.

"The ring."

"Doc saw the price tags on rings and decided on a bouquet of plastic flowers instead."

"Yeah, right. Let's see it."

Beaming, Merry held out her hand. "Wow," Sarah exclaimed. "It's beautiful. Someone's serious."

"It's a bit of a compromise."

"You wanted something bigger, and he wouldn't do it?" Ronnie asked with a puzzled look.

"The other way around."

"Ronnie has been telling me about you two. He said, 'You may not believe this, but don't be surprised if this ends up as more than friendship.'"

"I've been a huge problem."

"Not what Ronnie thought."

"Here's the short story. Last Friday night, my ill-fated camping trip ended up in a wreck. That led to meeting Doc and Trooper Ogden. The trooper didn't think it was wise for me to go to that camp, and Doc said I could stay with him for the night. I agreed. Terror struck when we started back in here. I believed this was my second very dumb mistake in one day, perhaps my last mistake ever. He could be a sex criminal. The third mistake happened when a wolf met us. I was petrified."

Sarah's laughter caused Merry to pause her story. "You met two harmless, big and easy males when you met Doc and Jack."

"Yeah. I know that now. Saturday was a fun day, but Sunday morning, when we held hands to pray before breakfast, I thought I didn't want him to let go. The magic moments continue to grow. I was never serious about any man before, and in one week, we're discussing marriage."

"As pretty as you are, and you didn't have boyfriends. They must be slow where you come from," Sarah suggested.

Embarrassment slipped over Merry, and she changed the subject. "Let's talk about you guys. How are you?"

"We're great. Couldn't wait to get here," Sarah said excitedly as she flipped blond hair off her face.

"We were anxious for you to arrive," Doc said. "Merry has a video we want you to preview."

"Is it your wrecked car sitting at our garage with no one working on it?" Ronnie asked, looking at Merry.

"It's a video of what people could see if they visit Cameron County," Merry answered.

After a few minutes, Ronnie excitedly exclaimed, "Wow! I recognize many of the animals, but the way you used them doesn't hint that they're taxidermied.

"Wait until you see the coyote stealing my lunch," Merry said.

The beautiful yellow rattler escaped into the brush as the video rolled on, followed by the coyote running away with Merry's sausage. "Oh, my," Sarah exclaimed as the bear rolled into view with shots showing where Merry was supposedly sleeping. Bull elk shots appeared in various places, followed by two huge bulls with several cow elk.

The video included deer shots that included the fawns from over the fireplace. Busy beavers swam by. Later video caught Merry walking into the water to take a bath. When the bear reared by the giant rock, Merry ran for her life. In another place, clothes washed in the spring run and hung on the clothesline provided a different taste of camping.

"Great job, Merry. Everybody should see Cameron County, but only as visitors. As the video ended, he added, "Forty-five hundred people are enough full-time residents."

"How about just one more full-timer?" Merry asked. "I want this to be my home."

"I like the pictures of you whittling the hot dog stick," Sarah said. "Sleeping on the front porch shots are cool, too."

"Some folks at our station won't think so," Merry said. "They believe the worst."

"Hey guys, it's looking like rain. We better eat," Doc suggested. "Merry chose hot dogs for supper. I'll get the grill going."

"If Merry wants hot dogs, hot dogs would be my choice," Sarah said.

"Only Merry didn't choose hot dogs," Ronnie challenged. I saw seven beautiful steaks marinating when I got our beverages."

"Seven?" Sarah asked. "There are only four of us."

"I told Dad we want two steaks each when they're the little things he buys."

"You better never, Adams. He always gets those oh-so-good Valley Meat giants."

Doc smiled and began grilling steaks. When he returned, they held hands while Ronnie prayed, a prayer that included thanking the Lord for Merry becoming a member of their family.

"Thanks, Ronnie," Merry said. "I need to know you accept me. I so want to become a part of your family."

"Our family, Merry. You're in and a blessing. Dad's smiling again. It's been a while since we've freeloaded steak dinners off him, and you're making it possible."

The mountain sky grew heavy with dark clouds as the rain closed in. The wind picked up, blowing napkins off the table. It grew ever blacker as they finished dessert. Rain soon sprinkled over them. "Let me close my windows," Ronnie said as he grabbed food bowls and headed for the kitchen.

"We'll get this," Doc said with a serious tone to his voice. "When old people bore you, eating and running is all right."

"Some things don't change, Dad. Thanks for dinner. It was delicious."

Raindrops pelted Ronnie and Sarah as the bottom dropped out of the blackened sky. Lighting flashed, followed closely by a thunderclap as Ronnie closed the car door. "That hit close," he said as Sarah slammed her door."

"I feel bad not helping clean up. Dad bought the food, they prepared and served it, and we ate and ran," Sarah confessed.

"Just in time to beat most of the rain. Dad wanted it that way."

Ronnie's phone began ringing as they passed the gate at the top of the hill. With the rain beating on his truck, Sarah grabbed his phone, "It's Cindy," Sarah said, handing Ronnie his cell phone.

With wind slamming rain into his windshield, Ronnie parked and answered the call. "Hi Cindy, how ya doing?" he asked with a smile.

"Not good!" she declared, her anger evident. "I received a call from Pappy Hackett that ruined my day."

"What are you talking about."

"Pappy told me about the mess Dad created. Is he crazy?"

"Maybe crazy in love, and who could blame him? Merry's as nice as ladies get. She looks and acts a lot like our mother. Sarah and I had a great day with them. It was like old family times."

"You gotta be kidding. Pappy warned me Dad's problems would be in the Echo. He didn't want me falling off the deep end when my paper arrived."

"You knew Dad had a female friend and seemed fine with her after you talked on the phone."

"I didn't know the whole story until Pappy gave me the rundown. He said Dad and the woman he's shacking up with badly beat him. He said —"

"He told you a bunch of crap, and you believed him. They're not shacked up, but they're getting married. They're so happy together. Remember, Mom told us all she didn't want Dad living alone. Her exact words to me were, 'Encourage your father to date when it's time. He has too much to offer another woman to sit around wondering where his life went.' I agree with Mom."

"Maybe you don't know what happened. Pappy went over there to talk about business ideas. When he saw the woman, he asked for an introduction. Instead, Dad started pounding him. Then that hooker jumped on Pappy's back so he couldn't protect himself. Dad beat him up and kicked him down the deck steps, hurting his back and leg. Then Dad and this chick went to the plant, stole money, and smashed equipment. Pappy had to report them to the police. He said our father's gone off the deep end."

"Cindy, how can you believe that about Dad?"

"I have to. Whoever heard of someone falling in love and wanting to get married in a week? You can stick up for Dad if you want, but are you going to support him when he's in prison?"

"Cindy, George Hackett is engineering our father for a fall."

"How can you know that?" Cindy angrily demanded.

"I'm a George Hackett victim. Pappy ran off Uncle Kevin and me. Just because we don't complain doesn't mean it didn't happen. Pappy plans his crap long before it occurs, so he appears clean. Then he claims everybody does him dirty, and he's so sorry when he has to stick up for himself."

"How could Uncle Kevin think Pappy shafted him? Pappy set him up in business."

"Our parents helped get the money together to get Uncle Kevin going, and I got that straight from Uncle Kevin."

"Uncle Kevin probably said that when he was mad about something. You know he doesn't always see eye to eye with Pappy."

"No, Cindy, he doesn't, and for good reasons. Our mother didn't either. She was actively planning for the day she didn't have to work with him."

"I can see I'm not getting anywhere with you, Ronnie. You won't listen to reason. Dad will need support after his trial, him and that little honey. You won't be so sure Pappy's off-base when our father's headed to prison."

"Cindy, I'll send you —"

With the phone buzzing, Sarah said, "Guess she doesn't want to hear anything else, Ronnie."

Chapter 34

Low clouds hung over the mountains with fogged in valleys and a driving rain slamming against the windows."Good morning, Honey," Doc greeted Merry as he set down their plates of fried eggs, crispy bacon, and toast. They held hands, sharing smiles as they looked into each other's eyes.

"I'm a bit worried, Merry. Are we crowding too much in the day? You have a long drive home. We could cancel dinner with the Pastor and his wife."

"Not on your life. I'm looking forward to this dinner, and everything's ready except the steaks.

The rain slowed as the morning passed. Doc was ready for church when Merry came down dressed to kill. "You have no idea how nice you look. That outfit belongs on you, and your hair is beautiful. Honey, I'm so thankful you're wearing my ring."

They headed to church with the rain ending and a bit of blue sky showing. When they arrived, the Pastor's wife hugged each with a smile. "We're looking forward to this afternoon. Mike even changed his message in preparation for our time together."

"Should we be scared?" Merry asked, sporting a fearful look.

"I wouldn't think so."

They were soon seated in the old oak pews, and the service began. Pastor Mike began his message after initial songs, notes, and Bible readings. "Friends, I'm inserting today's message, 'Love and Marriage,' into the series we're working through. It's one of the most important issues couples face. Divorce statistics tell us this subject impacts all too many marriages, and Christians aren't immune. Our first hymn is 'Softly and Tenderly.' The title provides a hint of something that's missing in many marriages."

As the last notes of the old hymn ended, Pastor Mike began, "Many don't realize the importance our Lord places on love and marriage." The Pastor continued with the theme that the Lord intended marriage to be a lifetime promise. His frequent glances in their direction ensured Doc and Merry got the word.

"Our many Fanny Crosby hymn lovers should enjoy our final hymn. Please turn to page 42 for 'All the Way My Savior Leads Me.' The title models the route for a successful marriage."

After the final prayer, the congregation began departing. As was usual, many stopped to chat. When Doc and Merry reached the Masons, Edna asked Merry, "Do you play an instrument?"

"No," Merry replied with a puzzled look on her face. "Why are you asking?"

"When the Pastor talked about marriage, he looked in your direction. I don't want to lose a music partner to a woman who doesn't enjoy our music."

"That would be my little outspoken Edna, the fiddle player," Clair said quietly.

"Don't worry about losing Doc. I love to hear him play and sing."

Edna looked closer at Doc and, with a hint of a smile, asked, "Has Merry been forceful with you? I see bruises and a split lip."

"That would also be my little outspoken Edna again," Clair added, leaving a smile on Merry's face.

"Okay, guys, we gotta go," Doc said light-heartedly. "We have important business to take care of."

"Looking at you, I'd bet you do," Edna agreed.

"Let's go, Merry," Doc said. "Edna will be announcing you're whipping me into shape, and she feels bad about my beatings."

They could hear laughter as they shook hands with Pastor Mike and Anita. "See you soon," Pastor Mike said as they were departing. "You still live in the same place?"

"We do."

"Does the 'we' include both of you?"

"Until tonight, when she has to leave."

"And it's in separate bedrooms until we're married," Merry assured him.

Arriving home, Merry asked, "Do you mind if I stay in these clothes? I like this outfit."

"I like it too. Sexy but not too sexy, if you know what I mean."

"Maybe it's time to get the grill going," Merry answered.

Smiling inside, Doc departed to change clothes. He was working on the grill when he heard their car. "They're coming in."

"I think the rains over, so I set up on the deck."

When car doors slammed, Doc and Merry greeted them from the deck. "Welcome, and thanks for coming."

"Yes, we appreciate it," Merry added. After greeting, Merry asked, "What can we get you to drink?"

"I'd take a glass of Doc's ice tea if you have some," Anita said.

"Make that two," Pastor Mike agreed.

It became tea around, with their initial discussion centering around the morning sermon. "Guess the sermon surprised you," the Pastor suggested.

"Not really," Doc replied. "Other messages carried more surprises."

"Like what, Doc?"

"Like the time you told us you were an unsaved, anti-Christ hippy before Anita."

Pastor Mike laughed. "She changed my life in a hurry. She grew up living with her grandparents. They're devout Christians who love Anita and gave her a real life."

"We have something in common, Anita. I grew up with my father's parents. They were deeply believing Baptists."

"My father led my mother into drugs, and she gave up on church," Anita began. "They fought continuously and were always threatening divorce. I'm fortunate my grandparents took over my life."

"My father was killed in Vietnam, and his parents took us in. My mother couldn't get over losing him. She had a rough life. And her parents were a bit like yours. It was a popular lifestyle."

It was quiet until the Pastor asked, "How about you, Merry? What was your home life like?"

After hesitation, Merry began, "My father's a wealthy lawyer who has no use for God. I didn't know God or real love until Doc came along. With him, everything in my life warped into a change that is so much more than I ever dreamed life could be."

"Would you marry Doc to protect him?" Pastor Mike asked.

"Pastor, the way you asked that question suggests you talked with Judge Bailey?" Doc observed with bitterness clanging in his voice. "I know he's a member of your church in town."

"I shouldn't have asked that question. Can everything we discuss remain among the four of us?"

When they signaled agreement, Pastor Mike admitted to the call. "Judge Bailey told me you beat George Hackett when he visited to discuss a business plan, then went to the plant, stole money, and destroyed stuff. I couldn't marry you if that's true."

Doc snickered sarcastically before he quietly answered. "Pastor, there's no way I'd marry Miss Morehouse if any of this were true. Our court date is May 25th. We plan to get married as soon after that as possible."

"How did you arrange a court date that soon?"

"Judge Bailey let it slip that district court scheduled for May 24th and 25th had a light schedule. We asked for that date even though the judge warned us we'd have little time to prepare for a trial with such heavy consequences possible. After we made bail, I was funnin' him and asked if he still married people. He asked if marriage was to keep us from being forced to testify against each other. It isn't."

"George Hackett has a winning court record. What makes you think he won't win this time?" the Pastor asked.

"When George sets someone up for a fall, he has evidence in place, trusted witnesses lined up, and in this case, Judge Bailey elected for another four years before he springs the trap. That won't save him this time."

"Judge Bailey said the newspapers would carry the complete story this coming week."

"The complete George Hackett story, but Hackett and Bailey don't know what's coming."

"Doc, I had a hard time believing what I heard. If you say it isn't true, it isn't true."

After a pause, Doc began, "Pastor, I got off track when Billy passed away. That ended with Merry last Friday night. This young woman and I are in love, and we want you to marry us as soon after the trial as possible."

"You're telling me you've known each other for one week, and you're talking marriage?"

Doc looked the Pastor dead in the eyes. "It's hard to believe, but that's what I'm telling you."

"Let's talk about you, Merry. Are you a Christian?" the Pastor asked.

"I am."

"How long have you been active in the faith?"

Merry hesitated as her face turned red. "I got my first interest in God a week ago when Doc held my hand and prayed for us before our meal. We attended the Songfest last Sunday, and that stirred deeper feelings. Today was the first time I ever attended church to worship."

"You never attended church before today?" Pastor Mike asked in a disbelieving voice.

"My father admonished God as a myth for the foolish, and prayer was for the weak who couldn't stand on their own."

"You certainly came a long way in a week, Merry," Anita said. "Your first prayer, your first church service, falling in love with Doc. How do you account for that?"

"It was God sent."

"It was what?" Anita asked with questions written across her face.

"Dolly Hackett visited the night after the George Hackett melee. She believes God sent me to help Doc and for Doc to lead me to Christ. I initially believed Doc was one of those weak fools my father talked about, but I quickly came to believe in the Lord through him. We're ready for a life together."

"How much do you know about Doc, Merry?" Pastor Mike asked. "Have you talked about problems each might hold that could impact your marriage?"

Doc and Merry looked at each other as if seeking permission to continue. When Doc nodded, Merry began. "Doc doesn't know everything about my problems, why I'm thirty years old and unmarried. He will."

"Did he tell you about his problem?"

"If you mean PTSD, we had a live episode, and I was terrified. He wanted me to forget marriage, but that isn't going to happen. My choices are between a life that carries some rough spots or a return to no life at all."

"Don't underestimate this problem, Merry," the Pastor warned. "PTSD generates much of the drug use and alcoholism vets suffer. Many are homeless or suicidal because of it."

"I accept that just as Doc accepts problems that eat at me." Then smiling, Merry added, "You might have to work overtime getting us past occasional rough spots. Can you handle that?"

The mood that had been dropping into the pits brightened a bit. Then Anita had a question. "Either of you can tell me this is none of my business, and we'll let it go. Have you discussed Billy and the life they shared? It was a solid union with deeply shared love."

Again, Doc and Merry searched each other for an agreement on how to proceed. Merry began, "At times, Doc talks as if Billy's still here. Her pictures hang in this home; I've looked at them and asked questions. The positive effect she had on people is evident with Doc and their children. I initially asked myself how anyone could break through that love barrier. Something told me that if Doc hadn't loved a woman like Billy and didn't miss her greatly, I couldn't expect much love from him either. Truthfully, Billy feels like the big sister I don't have. I expect her memory to stay bright with Doc and their children. At the same time, I feel like they've made room in their lives for me and want me in."

"I usually talk with couples several times and see them in church together for four or five Sundays before I discuss marriage." Pastor Mike said. "I consider marriage one of the most serious of all pastoral duties. I've had few failures."

"Pastor, ours won't be a failure either," Doc assured him. "We understand your feelings about marriage, but here's how we see it. We plan to be married as soon as court is over and the world discovers we're innocent. I love Merry, and I know what the Bible says about marriage. If it isn't you who marries us the first time, it will be the first person who can legally do so. When we meet your qualifications, we'll ask to be married in a Christian ceremony."

"You'd go through the marriage ceremony twice?"

"We would. If you can keep something between us, I'll tell you another story." Doc paused and continued when he had everybody's affirmation of secrecy. "Billy and I were married twice. We loved each other but didn't want premarital sex. We were married by a Justice of the Peace but kept it secret. She became a born-again Christian, and we remarried in a church. The only one who knew was the Pastor. If our marriage starts this way, the Pastor and his wife will both know."

"Doc, Merry, I see this in a light I never before considered. Can we wait until after your trial for the answer to your marriage? Merry,

I'd like you to read Luke 8:4 -15," the Pastor said. "The Lord talks about short to long-time believers."

"I'll do that, Pastor. The Lord gave me life through Doc. I'm staying close to both of them."

It was quiet as people searched for anything else that required discussion. Doc broke the silence. "I should put on the steaks. We can talk while we eat. I'm good at cooking medium-rare. I can go less or more if you like."

"That's how I like mine," Anita said. "Mike likes his well done. How much time does it take for a medium-rare Doc?"

"Give or take five minutes to a side."

"Then give Mike's ten. That way, it'll be like shoe leather and just the way he likes it."

Doc was cooking steaks when Merry's phone rang, and she got up to answer it. She discovered it was her father and answered on speaker. "Good afternoon, Father. How are you?

"Angry. You're shacking up with some hillbilly, aren't you? Hooked on drugs and shacked up?"

"I met a very nice man."

"Merry, you met other nice guys like the high school boyfriend who inherited the convertible they found wrecked in the Delaware River or that college boyfriend who ran into law problems. Then there was the guy at the Philadelphia Enquirer who suddenly decided to move on."

"You're sick. I should have known you had something to do with their problems. Maybe I'll report you for things you did to your daughter."

"Don't push me, Merry! Your hillbilly friend might disappear."

"I'd like to push you off a cliff!" Merry shouted.

"What the hell's wrong with you? If you're pregnant, I'll pay for an abortion."

"We haven't had sex, but if I were pregnant, I wouldn't get an abortion."

"Merry, how dumb can you get? Love in a week. Most people don't find love in a lifetime," he angrily screamed.

"He's a Christian, Father. We received a great message on marriage at church today. The Pastor and his wife are eating with us now so we can discuss the marriage ceremony. We're getting married as soon as our court date is complete," Merry said, egging her father on.

"He has you in trouble with the law? I'll take care of this. When's your court date?"

"We'll be just fine without your help, Father. We did nothing wrong."

"Yes, and I'm Santa Claus. Get real, Merry. Criminals all claim they're innocent. Then, the truth comes out in court. I can get you out of this."

"We won't need your help."

"It'll be a cold day when I allow my daughter to get married in a church."

"Sorry, Father, you have no say in this matter. I have to run now. Thanks for calling. Bye."

"Merry, don't you dare —"

Merry hung up, and the phone quickly rang again. She turned it off and returned to the table. As she was sitting down, she said, "I answered on speaker so you can understand the world I'm leaving. I'll pray for my family but won't live like them."

Doc waved, signaling the steaks were ready, and Merry took the beans from the oven where they were staying warm. She pulled the salads from the refrigerator and placed them on the counter. Doc carried steaks in, and Merry said, "Let's dish up in here."

They were soon sitting at the table, and after prayer, they began eating and chatting between bites. "Pastor, We're going to have to hit Doc up for plagiarism," Merry gleefully announced.

"Oh? What did he plagiarize?"

"When you read the love description from Corinthians, I recognized it. Doc has that message hanging over his computer, but it doesn't say where it came from."

"Do you think our Lord will forgive him, Merry?"

"I don't know. He has other things hanging around. One of his signs says

'Live your life in such a way

that people who know YOU

but don't know CHRIST

will want to know CHRIST

because they know YOU.'

"That's pretty serious stuff. I wonder how I can get a copy for my office. It would be a good insert for our bulletins too."

"You'll have them tomorrow," Doc promised.

After the Pastor and Anita finished eating, they departed. Merry asked Doc, "Did you hear my father's call?"

"Hateful people are cancers that eat the lives of everyone they come in contact with."

Tears ran down Merry's face. "Yes, and what can anyone do about them."

"Merry," Doc began in his low, powerful voice, "he may be your father, but he doesn't want to fool with us."

"Doc, I love you so much, but I'm terrified of him," Merry cried, wiping tears on her napkin. After a bit, she said, "Doc, I don't want to, but I should leave so I get to Harrisburg before dark."

Hugging her tightly, he ran his fingers through her hair and kissed her. "I'd say it's only for a few days, but I know how long days can be. This week apart will be packed with video reviews, people trying to make up to you, and who knows what else. I packed your cooler and split the food with you. Made two sandwiches in case you get hungry on the way home. Honey, if you have an emergency, there are five one hundred dollar bills between the vehicle manual's last pages. If you need 'em, use 'em."

Smiling, Merry said, "Honey, you spoil me, and I love you for it. How did I get so fortunate?"

Returning her smile, Doc replied, "First, there was the wreck on —"

"Let's not go there. My life began that night."

"Merry, I can't let something go," Doc said with worry stampeding across his face. "We're talking marriage, and there's more you need to know. Give me five, and meet me in my bathroom."

Doc slipped into a swimming suit, then called Merry. When she arrived, he said worriedly, "You know about my leg and deafness, but you need to know what you have to look at if we marry."

He turned sideways so she could see the ugly scars running up his right side. With tears slipping down her cheeks, she softly said, "Frosty Adams, I want to marry you more now than before. We can go swimming, and I'll be proud to be with you. Don't wait for that phone call, you big, handsome brute. I love you."

They kissed, holding each other tightly. Finally, Doc suggested, "You better go. Wish I could go with you."

With a devilish grin, Merry said, "You're so trusting. What if I don't come back and keep your car?"

"I'll report it stolen and tell the cops where to find it."

"When they find me, I'll tell them you attacked me and gave me the car to keep me quiet."

"Honey, you're catching on with this kidding. Drive safe. The life you save might be the woman I love."

CHAPTER 35

Doc walked Merry to the Traverse, where they kissed, holding each other tightly. Merry's tears announced the hurt she felt. Tears crawling down Doc's cheeks witnessed his difficulties too. Driving off, she saw a sad man waving and a tail-down dog watching her depart. "Oh Lord, I love this man you sent me. Jack too."

Merry mentally reviewed her love for Forest "Doc" Adams, gripping the steering wheel as she considered his scars and their parting. Thoughts of PTSD and the George Hackett fiasco slid in with fear gripping her. Face it, Merry, you're afraid. No, I'm scared to death.

She forced her thoughts to the To-Do lists they had completed. Hers included preparation for a Maggie meeting with the video copies and a list suggesting how to subdivide the video in sales-oriented ways. She also had a plan detailing how the station could license the video for use elsewhere. Her third list contained other videos they might create to increase market share.

Forcing herself back to softer issues, Merry went over the answers Doc helped her prepare for questions she might receive concerning how she spent her time up north and why she hadn't contacted anyone. She also had to inform Maggie and Melvin Warner of their court date.

She spoke bullet notes into the tape recorder Doc gave her as she worked through her plans. She smiled, thinking this was just one more way Doc had influenced her life. He looked ahead, preparing for what might happen, and always seemed ready for what actually happened.

Twilight crept in as she neared Harrisburg and pulled off Route 322 onto Linglestown Road. She was approaching home when she noticed the Susquehanna Township police cruiser sitting near her condo. "What now?" she asked herself. "He's waiting for me."

She hit the garage door opener, drove in, and closed the garage door before exiting, preventing the cop from seeing her run up the steps. Her game was not quite over. Rushing into her bathroom, she grabbed mascara and lightly blackened her eye. She created light mascara bruise marks on her left cheek, rubbing it with tissue to gather the desired effect. Opening a dresser drawer, she retrieved a white scarf to make a sling to hold her arm and fluffed her hair. When the doorbell rang, she turned on the porch light.

"Good evening, officer," she greeted him, acting surprised. "How may I help you?"

"Are you Merry Morehouse?"

"I am."

"Worried coworkers have us watching to see if you arrive home safely. I almost missed you. We've been looking for a red Chevy Cruze, and I believe you're driving a Traverse."

"My Cruze got run over by a truck."

"Looks like you got banged up a bit."

"It could have been worse. I learned city girls shouldn't go camping alone in the Appalachian Mountains."

"Is there anything I can help you with?"

"I'm OK, but thanks for asking."

She closed the door and grabbed her phone to call Doc. He answered on the first ring. "You're home, Merry?"

"I am and already had an interested young man at the door."

"You're teasing."

"Let me tell you about it," Merry said and told him the story. "He probably called Charlie or Arianna with a report, and they could be flipping coins to see who has to call me. Won't they be surprised when I walk in tomorrow with no problems except a long, missing Doc look?"

"I miss you, and we've only been apart for four hours. If someone told me this could happen in a few days, I'd laugh at them. I love you, Merry."

"I now know how missing someone feels. Oh, I just got the beep of someone trying to call in."

"Do you want to answer it, honey?"

"Are you kidding me? Doc, I tear up thinking about us. You're my everything. I'm so thankful."

"Me too, honey. I love you."

"Goodnight, Sweetheart. I love you too."

Merry grabbed the key and headed for her mailbox. She found it stuffed with a box and mail. Wondering who would send her something in a box, she made her way to the kitchen to open it. It contained a Charles stanley study Bible, which had to be from Doc. She grabbed the phone and hit his number.

"Merry, my Dear," he answered. "Long time, no hear."

"Yeah. A couple of minutes. I just picked up my new Bible. Thanks, Honey. I have the guide you prepared. I'll start reading a Proverbs chapter corresponding to the date and a New Testament chapter or two. Doc, thanks for everything. I feel like a teenager. I can't stop telling you I love you."

They ended the call with difficulty, and Merry began carrying in her things. When finished, she emptied the cooler and prepared to eat. Remembering preparing food with Doc brought warm memories and tears. As she ate, her phone rang again. It was Arianna. It was tempting to let it ring, but her conscience wouldn't allow it. "Hello."

"Merry, Arianna here. I've been so worried. I'm sorry —"

"Things are working out."

"Forgive me, Merry. At least try."

"Arianna, let it go. This trip was God sent."

"Did you say God sent?" Arianna asked, surprise running through her voice.

"I did."

"Can we go to lunch tomorrow? It's on me."

"I'll have to take a rain check. I have so much to do tomorrow."

"I don't blame you for being angry with —"

"Arianna, stop! Let this slide behind us. It's OK. I have to go now. We'll talk tomorrow."

Merry briefly waited before clicking off the phone. She'd hear enough of that at work.

After a fear-filled night with little sleep and a stale donut breakfast, Merry headed for the office, rehearsing her sales pitches and hoping to catch Maggie before she became busy. She had been eager to get the videos to her, but now hesitancies scrambled her stomach. What if Maggie didn't want to review them or reviewed them and didn't like them?

She hesitantly knocked on Maggie's open door, and Maggie looked up with a smile, waving her in. "So glad to see you, Merry. Terrible rumors are rolling through this place. I've been concerned about you and your safety. How was your time off."

"God sent."

"Beg pardon?" Maggie asked with a surprised look.

"Maggie, I was unprepared for Cameron County, but the trip led to my new life and these videos. Do you have a few minutes to discuss them?"

"I can give you up to a half-hour. If we need more time, we can arrange another time, possibly lunch together. Execs from New York are here, and I'm scheduled for several meetings."

"I have two videos for your review. I marked the one that might meet company needs 'WLDZ'; the second one says 'for the WLDZ team.' This envelope contains two lists. One list includes suggestions on how WLDZ might use the company video, and the other is a list of additional video projects that could help the station."

Merry provided an overall story of her trip and explained why there were two versions of the video. "A few folks gave me a bum steer. I believe showing the team video will correct this. I'd ask that the video invitation include Charlie, Arianna, and Bucky for sure. You might watch the WLDZ Team video at home."

After explaining that part of her trip in more detail and saying it might be wise to warn Warner about the differences, they both laughed and agreed it would be fun to watch faces during the video.

Merry then prepared to leave. "You're busy, and I appreciate your time."

"No problem. You're carrying a bigger smile than you had before. What took place?"

"Oh, Maggie," Merry began with a beaming smile, "It started rough when I crashed into a big, ruggedly handsome guy who rescued me. One minute he's a leader planning, organizing, and getting projects up and running, the next, a laid-back guy picking his guitar and singing. He's a Christian with a great sense of humor, too."

"Is that an engagement ring you're wearing? We need to talk more about this trip. There may be more to discuss and not just as mentor-mentee?"

"Maggie, I'd love that. Thanks for your time this morning."

Merry departed in high spirits. Arianna and Charlie arrived as she was entering her space. They were loaded with questions and armed with apologies, none of which Merry cared to discuss. After a few minutes, she excused herself, using the need to work on assignments as her excuse.

A little after three that afternoon, Maggie called Merry to her office. She arrived to discover the station manager accompanied by two men and a woman she didn't know.

"Merry," Warner began, "I'd like you to meet our guests from headquarters: Annette Labrozzi, Martin Goldstein, and Joseph Foer. They're reviewing progress on our search for ideas to improve viewer ratings. We reviewed a bit of your video over lunch and have a few minutes to discuss it."

After introductions with handshakes, Goldstein spoke first. "Merry, we've been touring our stations throughout the east, and your video appears to be the best idea we've come across. We plan to watch it this evening with Mr. Warner. If the remainder of the video is as good as the initial section, it will interest viewers throughout our operating areas. Can you share how this came about?"

"It's an unbelievable story. The short version is I planned a camping trip to Cameron County in the Appalachian Mountains with a coworker when I hadn't camped out before," Merry began and gave them an abbreviated version of her week.

"Annette Labrozzi spoke next. "You sound like you're still excited. Maybe there's more to this story."

"There is, but I won't bore you with details."

"Merry, this group doesn't bore easily. We have time to discuss more if it might be of value to the company, Goldstein said."

"I should discuss this with Maggie first. She's my mentor."

"Did you use company cameras and equipment for this video?" Joseph Foer asked. "It looks very professional and high quality."

"I own an excellent video camera and a Nikon P900."

"Taking the videos was one thing. This product indicates it was edited by a professional using professional equipment. Was it edited here?"

"No, I completed the work at my friend's home using his wife's equipment. She had a business creating professional videos."

"She let you use her equipment?" Foer asked.

"She passed away last year."

"How did you learn this skill, Merry?" Foer asked.

"I have a degree in multimedia studies, and I took an advanced multimedia evening course at Penn State-Harrisburg this past semester."

"You haven't sold your skills very well," Foer said.

Merry's face reddened as Foer turned to Maggie. "You need to help her along these lines, Maggie."

"Merry," Goldstein began as he stood, letting her know the meeting was over, "We believe we've discovered a new talent. I'm sure we'll want to talk more with you after reviewing your video."

"Thank you all," Merry returned.

"Thank you. We appreciate your above-and-beyond efforts for the company," Annette Labrozzi said.

It was approaching six P.M., and Merry had phoned in a Pizza Hut order when Maggie called. "Merry, I'm so glad I caught you. Could you come to my office for a few minutes? Melvin and I would like to talk with you."

"Be right there, Maggie."

At Maggie's office, Melvin began. "Merry, Mister Goldstein plans to debrief station personnel Friday before their team departs," Warner informed her. "He would like to speak with you after the briefing."

"I'll be there, Merry said, trying not to show her excitement."

Merry arrived home with her pizza when her phone begged for attention. "Hello."

"Hi, Honey. How'd it go today?"

"Absolutely wild," Merry excitedly announced as she ran through her day, explaining that execs from New York were reviewing their video that night."

"I'm happy for you."

"What if they're looking at a future for me here in Harrisburg or New York City when I want to live on the hill with you? I need a job, but I realized I couldn't live without you when you were disappearing in my rearview mirror."

"Let me tell you about my day. I called Tom Kinnard, my lawyer, who placed everything on hold to handle our case. Kinnard represented John Armstrong in a previous MELCOR-Hackett case and lost. Hackett reported Armstrong broke in at night, stole and damaged things, and then killed the security guard who caught him. Hackett charged us with the same things, minus the security guard murder. Kinnard believes Armstrong's innocent and desperately wants another shot at George Hackett."

"Are you sure we want a loser representing us?"

"He's not a loser and about our only chance for representation at this late date."

"Are we in trouble, Doc?"

"Hope not. We have proof of who started the fight, and you aren't in the video. We have video proof of what happened when Ryder let us into the plant. And the state police procured copies of the security camera footage. And they know we suspect Hackett went through our home."

"That should be enough, shouldn't it?" Merry asked in a fearful voice.

"Hopefully. Our biggest problem could be the unknown. Your video camera and the plant security system date and time stamp shots. The potential problems I see involve Hackett's claim that I stole money from the safe."

"What can we do, Doc?"

"I can't know that until we hear Hackett's charges and see the video."

"What then?"

"I'm meeting Kinnard in the morning to deliver our videos and discuss the case."

"I'm scared, Doc. I can't sleep thinking about Hackett and my father. Hackett's bad, but I don't think you understand the danger attached to my father. Even more, what if the corporate team watches our video tonight and offers me a better job to stay on at the station? Would you forgive me if I turned it down and didn't have a job for a while? I have bills but don't want to be away from you."

"Merry, please stop worrying. We'll come up with something."

"What if the court case goes against us?"

"Honey, too many what-ifs. Let's have faith in God and the court system."

"Doc, remember, you said, 'What can go wrong will go wrong?' What if my father tries to screw up our lives? I'm so afraid."

"I'd be lying if I said I wasn't concerned, but I believe we'll be all right. Something else: I'm changing my email address and password. I'll send it to you. And I plan to contact my broker and dump the MELCOR stock."

"Can we talk tomorrow night? I need it, Doc."

"Oh, Honey, yes. I need it too. Sweet dreams. I love you."

CHAPTER 36

Arriving at work early after a rough night and sitting with her head in her hands, fear clogged Merry's throat as thoughts of Hackett and her father stormed through her mind. She struggled through her video notes but discovered she was only partially ready for what might come when Maggie, Melvin Warner, and the New York group called and waited in Maggie's office. Apprehensive and wondering what this unplanned meeting was about, she hurried to meet them.

Once there, Warner began. "Merry, this video is beautiful from the elk and bears right down to the big yellow rattlesnake. You completed a lot of work during your vacation. We're impressed."

Goldstein added to Warner's comments. "You have talents we badly need. It's hard to believe someone who wasn't a camper could take these videos and put this piece together. Great job."

"This wasn't all me. I shot the material, but a knowledgeable guide took me places and set up shots."

"Is this knowing person the Doc fellow you mentioned yesterday?" Annette Labrozzi asked.

"It is."

"It seems as if Doc became more than a friend. Is that a correct assumption?" Annette asked, smiling lightly.

Merry's face reddened as she searched for answers. What to say? What not to say? "It is."

How might he fit into your career future?" Annette asked.

What now, Merry wondered. Doc says the truth will out. It might as well be now. "The video reflects his abilities to research and set up projects. We plan to be married," Merry announced, holding out her ring.

"Wow, that's beautiful," Annette said, stepping in for a closer look. "Did all of this occur during your vacation week?"

"It did."

There were smiles around the room as Foer recapped all that had happened. "Let's see, you produced an outstanding video, fell in love, received a beautiful ring, and are getting married. Did you cram anything else into your ever-so-busy schedule?"

Oh well, Merry, you might as well go along with them. "I attended a songfest where I sang in front of people for the first time, worshiped in church for the first time, learned to pray, and I'm learning how to cook. I also went horseback riding twice."

Red-faced, Merry found herself laughing with the others. She added, "If someone told me this could happen in a week, I'd think they were crazy."

"Do you always stay this busy?" Goldstein asked.

"Please let me answer that as Merry's mentor," Maggie volunteered. "As you noticed, Merry's at work early. Her ideas on video projects were the best at our meeting concerning ways to increase our market share. When she does newscasts, she looks great and speaks well. Viewers write the station concerning her warmth and professionalism. She has a bright future. I hope it's with us."

"Maggie's right," Melvin Warner agreed. "Miss Morehouse came up with ideas for videos that would interest viewers. And she acted on that idea on her own time."

"Yes," Annette agreed, "and achieved it with a packed schedule."

Laughter followed until Goldstein cut it short. "That's great, Melvin, but do you have any concerns?"

"None. How about you, Maggie?"

"No concerns but a comment. Merry has a bright future, but that future can be with our company or elsewhere. Let's remember that in our plans."

"I have two questions, Merry," Goldstein said. The first has to do with this video. Can we take this copy for the headquarters staff's review?"

"Yes, sir."

"The second question: How flexible are you as far as your future career is concerned?"

Merry had no idea how to answer this question with her life taking new directions. "I'm not sure what you might be considering, Mr. Goldstein, but with Maggie's help, I believe I can adapt to most challenges."

The meeting was soon over, leaving a concerned Merry immersed in a research project that quickly saw her through the day. That evening as she removed her coat at home, the phone rang, and the screen said it was Doc.

"Evening, Doc. I love you and miss you. I want to be home with you."

"Oh, Honey, thanks for calling this place home. I'm crazy about you."

"You say that to all the girls."

"Not even. New subject. Did you watch the video on PTSD?'

"Last night. It reminded me of a recent night we had together."

"Wanta back out?"

"Doc, stop!" Anger and frustration erupted. "I'm never changing my mind," she protested, slapping her legs. It was quiet while she gained self-control. She then continued, "New subject. I'm glad you told me about the changes you made to the site and password, merryndoc@verizon.net, with a password of merry0511. I love that. I watched some of the other stuff you suggested. It shows me why you question some newscasts. Doc, there's another subject. Sleep's been hard to come by. Love and fear. Love makes me tingle, but fear's driving me insane. I'm following your recommendations as I read my Bible. Merry-type problems fill Proverbs. It says, 'A gentle answer turns away wrath, but a harsh word stirs up anger.' I'm fighting my argumentative tendencies. Another message followed, 'A hot-tempered man stirs up strife, but the slow to anger calm a dispute.' It sounds like you and me, Doc, and should say hot-tempered woman. I'm trying, Honey."

"Merry, I find a new face slapper every time I read Proverbs. Oh, Honey, I have a call coming in. It's from our attorney?"

"Good luck with Kinnard. Love you."

"Love you too."

"Good evening Mr. Kinnard. What can I do you out of this evening?"

"Just updating you on your trial. Your video presents a different story of the Hackett attack. The police gave me a copy of the WLDZ security system video. We have every base covered except for money theft. We'll figure out how to handle that when we get more information. Can we get together Saturday morning? Maybe nine or ten?"

"Ten should be good for us. I'll let you know if there's a problem."

Doc hung up and dialed Kevin Hackett. After formalities, he mentioned the upcoming trial and explained their attorney could call Brian Ryder as a witness, and in all probability, his truthful answers would get him fired. "Kevin, Brian trained both of us. He'd be a great plant manager for you."

"If not you, he'd fit. I'll call him when we finish."

"Can you wait until I talk with him? I believe it's best if he calls you."

"We'll work with that."

A concerned Doc ran his hand through his hair before continuing. "Kevin, there's something else you should know. I met a woman, and we're planning to get married. I hope that doesn't change our relationship."

"It won't. We invited to the wedding?"

Relieved, Doc said, "I'll call you as soon as we have all the details."

The week dragged endlessly toward Friday when Merry would return. Thursday night, she talked with Doc. It was a difficult call for both of them, and she was apprehensive, having heard nothing further about the video. Extreme fear rode Merry's crackling voice. "I can't get past this Hackett trial. You have to help me," Merry whispered and began crying.

"Merry, maybe it's best if you remain in Harrisburg until the trial."

"I can't, Honey. The only peace I get is with you. I love you."

As they talked, Merry became more at ease. "I gather comfort reading the Bible. Proverbs 16:2 fits us right now, 'When a man's ways are pleasing to the Lord, He makes his enemies be at peace with him.' I'm praying that what we're doing will please the Lord. We need peace."

"Merry, peace is coming. You smile more and throw in little kidding remarks that make me want to squeeze you. Honey, we're growing together, and I love it."

"Doc, I was never around anyone like you. You're nice and so friendly. You make me feel loved for the first time in my life."

"That's because I love you, and I'm crazy about you."

After talking for a while, they ran out of things to say and signed off.

Merry was called to Warner's office Friday morning to meet with Maggie and the corporate staff. Excitement ruled as she hurried to the meeting.

"Good morning, Merry," Warner said. "Our friends have good news to share. Please have a seat."

"Merry, we must apologize for not meeting sooner," Martin Goldstein began, "but we've been waiting for information from headquarters. Our CEO desires a personal interview with you tomorrow morning in New York to determine exactly where you fit in our plans. Melvin can arrange an early morning flight."

Merry's heart sank. She counted on being with Doc, plus there was the lawyer's meeting Saturday morning. Breathing faster, she tried to think through to an acceptable answer. Deciding the truth was best, she said, "We have a meeting with our lawyer tomorrow morning. Would it be possible to postpone the meeting until next week?"

"I'm afraid that's impossible. Our CEO will be in LA. That's why he suggested the Saturday meeting," Goldstein answered. While Merry was thinking, he questioned her. "Do you mind if I ask why you need a lawyer?"

Panic-stricken, Merry answered with the first thing that ran through her mind. "I'm a witness, but the guy causing problems is lying. Could I get Mr. Warner an answer about the meeting this afternoon?"

After looking at the other meeting participants and gaining nods, Goldstein said, "Please get back with Melvin by noon. This meeting could significantly impact your future and the future of other station personnel."

They shook hands around and excused Merry. She departed, wishing to hear what they discussed when she departed. This trip to New York would end the opportunity to see Doc over the weekend, which saddened her.

She apprehensively called Doc and got his answering machine. *What now*, she wondered with chills chasing up her spine. *Man, I hope this isn't another Hackett attack or something caused by my father.*

At eleven-fifteen, she called again and, with hands shaking, left a second message. *Man, I only have a few minutes,* she noted while glancing at her watch. *Is nothing going to go right this morning,* she asked herself, before returning to her current assignment? Fear rode heavily on her heart as she rubbed her temples, trying to clear her mind.

Twenty-two minutes passed before her cell phone rang. It was Doc. She quickly explained the dilemma she faced. "Doc, I'm sorry. The bottom is dropping out of everything."

"Merry, this New York trip could be great news. The late-night return would prevent you from coming here, but it's not the end of the world."

"It's close to the end for me. I counted on seeing you all week. Maybe I should kiss this off and come home."

"How'd your trip home go?"

"What does that have to do with anything?" she asked, obviously upset.

"If it went well, there might be another solution. You could drive to the city, attend your meeting, and then come here. When you talk with your boss, you can negotiate a bit. Tell him the lawyer meeting is important. Explain that you can drive to the city and then here for a later meeting with Kinnard, possibly on Monday. Ask if you can trade Monday off for the time invested on Saturday."

"I'd have to drive your car into the city. That's scary."

"Merry, that ring says it's our car now. The decision is yours."

"I'll call you back after I talk with Warner. Love you."

Merry hesitantly met with Warner, explained the potential solution, and was surprised he supported her and her problems. "Merry, Monday off isn't a problem. This meeting is important for both your career and WLDZ. If they didn't see significant value in your video and you, they wouldn't call you to the city. You have to make this appointment. You can't miss it."

After guaranteeing she'd make the trip, Merry returned to the phone with Doc. "Doc, I have an eleven AM meeting in New York with Mr. Big and the crew that was here. It should last about an hour. Driving time home is about five hours, and I have Monday off."

"Be safe, Honey. You're what I live for."

"I'll call you when I depart the city. I can't wait to see you. Love you bunches.

"Love you too, Honey."

CHAPTER 37

Doc nervously stalked the deck Saturday afternoon, waiting for Merry's call. She planned to leave New York around noon and promised to call saying she was on her way. It was now 1:45. Time crawled. "Where is she," he muttered, with fear rising. Hackett or her father could have something to do with this.

At 2:13, his phone rang. It was an unknown number with a 212 prefix. *Oh no, what happened? Had she been kidnapped?*

"Hello," he answered in a worried, shaking voice.

"Doc, it's me, Merry. You're going to kill me. I wrecked your Traverse and —"

"You hurt?"

"No, but your car is a mess," Merry said, with fear driving her speech. "Got run over by a bus. I drove over here and missed my appointment. I should have said 'No' to this damned New York trip."

"You at a hospital?" Doc asked, with all kinds of terrible scenes running wildly in his mind.

"No. A police station."

"Can I talk with someone?" Doc asked, hoping they'd be calmer.

"Officer, can you talk to Doc?" Merry asked in a pleading voice as she handed him his phone.

"Pete, here."

"Did you say, Pete?"

"I did. James Peterson."

"Is Merry all right?"

"Physically, yes, for now, that is. She said you were going to kill her because she wrecked two of your vehicles in two weeks."

Doc laughed nervously. "I'm not killing anyone. She okay?"

"She's shook up and nervous. Merry's had a tough day. She got lost in the city when her GPS failed. Said she had an appointment with her CEO and missed it. By the time she found the place, the staff had departed. She pulled out on the street just when the bus I was riding home in swerved to miss a bicyclist who pulled out in front of us. Bus driver missed the biker but skinned up the passenger side of your car."

"She said she's at a precinct. What kind of trouble is she in?"

"None, but she's worried about you."

"Is her car drivable?"

"I drove it over here. Runs good. Looks bad. Passenger door won't open."

"Can you help her out of the city?"

"I'll get her across the George Washington Bridge and onto the Jersey toll road. It leads to Interstate 80. She thinks she can find her way from there. I'll talk her into staying at a motel overnight if she appears too nervous to drive. Quite truthfully, she's more nervous about you being upset."

"Pete, I'm not upset. They make cars every day, but I'll never meet another Miss Merry. I appreciate what you've done for us and even more for what you said you'd do. Can you put her back on the phone?"

"Yes, Doc," Merry answered in a calmer voice.

"Pete seems like a fine man. Said he'll get you out of the city and on your way. Remember the money in the vehicle manual?"

"Yes. Why?"

"When he gets you out of the city, give him a hundred bucks to catch a cab home, and don't let him give it back. If he refuses the money, throw it in the parking lot when you drive off. We're fortunate you met Pete."

"Oh, Doc, he's so helpful. He said you weren't upset with me. Thanks."

Use the money in the owner's manual if you need more money for anything. Honey, get Pete's business card and ask him to write his home address and phone number on the back."

"It's hard to tell you how much, Frosty Adams, but I love you. See you soon."

A little over five hours later, a worried Merry arrived at Ronnie's garage with cold sweat gluing her back to the seat. Doc was waiting for her and didn't seem concerned about the Traverse.

Ronnie had her Cruz and the State Farm Insurance paperwork ready to go. Doc gave Ronnie the Traverse keys, and after they discussed repairs, Doc walked Merry to her Cruz, where she walked around it, admiring the repairs and the shine. With a broad smile, she gave Ronnie a thumbs up, "Thanks, Ronnie. It looks new. I'll get this invoice to State Farm."

Ronnie returned the thumbs up. Doc held her door open, and they kissed before heading home together. When they arrived, Doc made them sandwiches, and they sat quietly on the deck eating until Merry asked, "Doc, are you sure you're not mad about your car?"

"Our car, and I'm thankful." Smiling, he added, "Material things hold little value compared to love. I love you."

"You're hard to believe. I wrecked your car and —"

"Once again, our car, and it's just a car," Doc said with a bit of 'Let's not discuss it again' in his voice. "Let me spell it out for you. I L-O-V-E Y-O-U," Doc said, spelling it out in the air with his finger.

"My father would —"

"I'm not your father. I'm Doc Adams, the guy who can't wait to marry you."

It became quiet until Doc finally broke the silence. "Kinnard's eager for this trial to start, and clearing us is only part of his game. He believes winning our trial will help secure a new trial for Armstrong."

"How's he going to handle the theft charges?" Merry asked, her voice wavering.

"Hasn't figured that out yet because we aren't sure what it involves, but that won't impact you."

"How can you say that?" She demanded as her eyes flooded with tears. "If it impacts you, it gets me too. You're all I have."

After a quiet time, Merry apprehensively began, "Doc, I'm sorry I wrecked the Traverse, but I'm not sorry I missed that meeting. I'm not moving to New York. It's a nightmare. I don't even want to go back to Harrisburg. I have Monday off to meet with Kinnard plus Thursday and Friday for the trial. I should call and ask off Tuesday and Wednesday, or maybe just quit. There's nothing down there for me. I was going nuts when I couldn't lean on you."

After thinking it over for a bit, Doc answered, "Merry. What you do about quitting is your decision, but what happens to your boss and Maggie? They stood by you, and your quitting could adversely impact them."

"I hadn't considered that," she said, shaking her head.

"You should call your boss and explain the problems you had. Mr. Big would not set up a Saturday meeting if he didn't see a bright future for you. That provides some leverage."

Nodding her head, Merry agreed. "I'll call now. Please stay with me for support."

After the call and a positive response from Warner, the rest of the weekend flashed by with church and planning for the Kinnard meeting.

Monday morning, Doc and Merry reviewed the Kinnard information before packing her car for the Harrisburg trip. She followed Doc to the lawyer's office at the appointed time, where they found Kinnard waiting in his conference room behind a table full of neatly stacked paperwork. He wore a wrinkled suit and looked up through thick, black-rimmed glasses as they entered, his brown hair looking like he had combed it with a rake.

Kinnard began with a somber tone. "Here's where I believe our case sits. I talked with Sergeant Richardson concerning the list of damaged equipment. When he hadn't received it, I called Judge Bailey. He hasn't seen it either. Hackett used that claim in the Armstrong trial, and Armstrong said it was junk MELCOR smashed before junking it so a competitor couldn't use it. I think he was going to use those old pictures and chickened out."

"As you suggested, I called Brian Ryder," Kinnard continued. "He stopped by earlier today. He doesn't seem worried about being fired. Not sure why. The DA said Hackett provided specifics on the theft charge and claims you returned later and stole the petty cash, blank checks, and other money in your safe. Said you also stole a company computer."

"I took my personal computer, which is shown in the video. Forgot all about the darned safe," Doc said, anger flaring through him as he slammed his fist into the table. "I should have opened it for Ryder. I did give him my office keys."

"Hackett can say you had copies of the keys made for later use, and it would be difficult to prove otherwise. You didn't open the safe, so the missing money's an issue we must cover in court. Maybe we can come up with something during the trial. I made copies of the stock transfer documents Catherine signed concerning MELCOR shares and the training programs. The video of the Hackett fight shows who started it, and it's machine-dated. It clears Merry because she is nowhere on it. We can call Hackett's wife to the stand if he refutes the date or time of that incident."

"I don't want Dolly Hackett involved. She's had a lifetime of problems with George Hackett, and any testimony on our behalf could get her killed."

"Okay. The video dates will have to do. What else might we need?"

"Prayer," Doc said, his anger subsiding a bit. He was worried about the safe and supposed monetary theft and couldn't think of any way to refute it.

CHAPTER 38

"All rise! The honorable Judge Howard Blackstone presiding."

When Judge Blackstone was seated, he said, "You may be seated." With news reporters, people from various county offices, Sergeant Richardson, other interested parties, and Judge Bailey packing the courtroom, presiding Judge Blackstone began by looking at the defense table. "You requested a bench trial without a jury, and you're coming to trial before me within a few weeks of being formally charged. This is a first for me in my twenty-five-plus years sitting on this bench. Know that as the judge, I'll make the final decision as to innocence or guilt. To ensure completion of this trial in the allotted time, I'll be a bit less formal in these proceedings. You will be sworn in and remain so during the trial. Is that clear, and are you ready to proceed?"

When Doc, Merry, and their lawyer agreed with the conditions, Judge Blackstone turned to the prosecution, "Is that clear with you, Mister Manners, and are you in agreement?"

After discussing it with Hackett, Manners answered, "Yes, your honor. We agree to those terms and conditions."

The court then entertained opening statements, beginning with the prosecution led by District Attorney Keith Manners. "Your honor, this case involves several charges against the defendants. In the first charge, George Hackett visited the home of Forest Adams III to discuss a business proposal. Forest Adams was his employee at the time of this incident. Mister Hackett was attacked unmercifully by Mister Adams while Miss Morehouse rode on Mister Hackett's back, holding his arms. This assault qualifies as a felony."

The judge held up his hand for the prosecution to stop. "Does the defense have a statement concerning charge one?"

"Not at this time, your honor, Kinnard replied. "We hope to present our case in its entirety after the prosecution presents its case."

"So be it. Mister Manners, please continue."

"In incident number two, Mister Adams went to the MELCOR plant in the middle of the night and stole money and blank checks from a company safe. The amount was more than seventeen thousand dollars, which is felony burglary and theft. He also stole the company computer from his old office. The security tape obtained by the police presents this crime."

Kinnard shot Doc a questioning look, and both hunched their shoulders in 'what is this' gestures. Their facial expressions and actions evidenced significant concern for this charge. What did Hackett have planned? Doc's stomach churned as he looked at Merry, her face white with fear.

The prosecution continued. "We'll also show that the defendant, Forest Adams, holds property that belongs to Mister Hackett and has refused to return it to its rightful owner."

"Explain what this property is," Judge Blackstone ordered.

"Yes, your honor. Mister Hackett gave his daughter Catherine shares of MELCOR stock, his business. He felt she would be a lifetime member of his team. When Mister Hackett's daughter Catherine discovered she was terminal with cancer, she told her father, Mister Hackett, she would return those shares to her father, said Mister Hackett. She would also complete paperwork to officially transfer ownership of training programs she completed on company time with company equipment to Mr. Hackett."

"Is Mister Hackett in receipt of said legal paperwork?" Judge Blackstone questioned.

"No, your honor. His daughter passed away before she could complete the required paperwork."

Manners related this was the end of the charges. Judge Blackstone held up his hand, gaining everyone's attention. Mister Manners, what happened to the equipment destruction charge?"

"The plaintiff withdrew the charge, your honor."

With the judge shaking his head, Kinnard began, "Your honor, the defense will offer proof that Catherine Hackett Adams completed paperwork concerning the shares and training programs in question. The defense has said paperwork, but it is not what Mister Hackett claims. The defense will show that Mister Hackett initiated the attack on Mister Adams with no involvement by Miss Morehouse. We'll show the video when Mister Adams entered the plant where he met the night shift superintendent the same night Mr. Hackett attacked him without provocation. Mister Adams removed personal items under the watchful eye of Mister Ryder. It was his sole visit to the plant that night. We're ready for the trial to continue."

With the opening statements complete, the prosecution placed George Hackett on the stand. George wore an expensive suit and tie accompanied by an I hate to do this look on his face. After the bailiff swore him in, he explained, "On the attack charge, I visited the Adams home to discuss business proposals with Mr. Adams, who served as my plant manager at the time," Hackett began. "I was shocked to see another woman in his company so soon after our dear daughter's passing." Hackett paused and shook his head as he looked at the defendants. "Perhaps my surprise at this disturbing event is what set them off, and they brutally attacked me. Mr. Adams is my son-in-law. I thought we had a warm relationship, but he surprised me with this violent attack. Ms. Morehouse jumped on my back, holding my arms down and Adams hammered me. Both of them are much younger than me. I was lucky to escape without a worse beating. I had copies made of a picture my dear wife took when I managed to get home. I want this picture entered into evidence. It exhibits my devastating eye wounds and the multiple bruises I received from the terrible beating I endured."

After entering the picture into evidence, Hackett continued. "On charge two, Mr. Adams and I were the only persons who held the combination to the safe in his office. The security system caught Mr. Adams entering the plant wearing a ball cap with a hooded sweatshirt pulled over his head."

Doc, Merry, and Kinnard threw questioning looks at each other, deeply concerned about this statement.

"Regarding the company shares, early in our daughter Catherine's marriage to Mr. Adams, my wife and I gave Catherine shares in our MELCOR company. These shares gave her something to fall back on if Adams dumped her for another woman after they had children. When Catherine discovered her cancer was terminal, she promised to return the stock and some training material she developed on company time with company equipment for the sole use of MELCOR. We want the court to mandate that Adams return that stock and the rights to the training material."

"That ends the prosecution's presentation of charges, your honor," Manners declared.

"Does the defense have questions of Mr. Hackett?" Judge Blackstone asked.

Kinnard looked at Doc and Merry, and while Merry shook her head 'no,' Doc whispered something to the lawyer that took considerable time.

"Your Honor," Kinnard began, "Mr. Adams takes exception to Mr. Hackett's comment concerning their warm relationship. Mr. Adams asserts that their relationship has been anything but warm from the first day he met Mr. Hackett. Mr. Hackett threatened Mr. Adams physically and with firing many times in front of others, spreading lies about him throughout the community. Should Mr. Hackett desire to push this warm relationship theme, the defense would like time to gather witnesses who will refute his statement and show precisely how untruthful Mr. Hackett can be."

Judge Blackstone turned to the prosecution. "Mister Manners, do you desire to have that statement remain in the record?"

After a brief discussion with Hackett, Manners turned to the judge. "Your honor, although Mr. Hackett was under the impression their relationship was a warm one, it isn't something we wish to pursue at this trial. We move to strike this comment from the record."

"So be it."

Judge Blackstone turned back to the defense. "Does the defense have any other questions or comments concerning this testimony?"

"Not at this time, your honor. We reserve the right to call Mr. Hackett back to the stand after we present our evidence."

"Mister Hackett, you may take your seat but remain for recall. With the completion of the charges against Mr. Adams and Miss Morehouse, let's take a short break. Be ready to begin again at 10:15."

Kinnard, Doc, and Merry huddled at the beginning of the break. "What do either of you know about the safe and stolen money," Kinnard asked.

Merry and Doc looked at each other with puzzled looks. Fear road Merry's face as she considered this new twist. "This can't be happening to us. It's a lie! Doc was with me all night. We didn't leave his home after our earlier MELCOR visit with Ryder present."

Doc's usually calm demeanor slowly changed. "Look, There's a lot that isn't right about this theft charge, and for that matter, this trial. I can't put my finger on all that's wrong, but I'll note questions on this tablet that I want you to ask me when you put me on the stand. I don't know what's coming, but it isn't going to work." he softly said through pursed lips, displaying all-consuming anger.

The 'All rise' communication signified that the court was called to order. Judge Blackstone began, "Mister Kinnard, proceed with your defense."

"Your honor, the defense is prepared to refute each of Mister Hackett's claims, none of which are truthful. At this time, the defense would like to begin with the final charge concerning MELCOR stock. We have copies of letters that Catherine Hackett Adams had drawn before she passed away."

After distributing copies of the papers and giving time to read them, Kinnard continued. "As shown by these notarized letters signed by Catherine Adams, Catherine Adams transferred her MELCOR stock to her husband, Forest Adams. In her transfer letter, Catherine stated she took this action to ensure there could be no doubt who owned the stock in question."

"In the second notarized letter, Catherine transferred the right to use the training videos she created with her husband, Forest Adams, to her brother Kevin Hackett. She states, 'These videos were shot in Kevin Hackett's plant in St Mary's and on our own time. We used personal equipment located in our home to create the videos. We received no compensation from MELCOR so that there could be no argument about my brother Kevin Hackett using the material.' Catherine created this letter because George Hackett and his estranged son, Kevin Hackett, have competing businesses. This statement contains photos of said personal video equipment located in her home."

The judge read his copies of the letters while the prosecution read theirs. After conferring with George Hackett, the district attorney said, "Your honor, it appears as if Catherine Adams changed her mind after talking with her father, perhaps under threat from the defendant. The prosecution elects to withdraw this complaint."

"So be it," Judge Blackstone said. "Continue, Mister Kinnard."

"Yes, your honor. The defense would now like to answer the charge that Mister Adams attacked Mister Hackett. We first have a question for the prosecution. How many times within the past month was Mr. Hackett at the Adams home?"

After conferring with Hackett, the district attorney answered, "Mister Hackett visited the Adams home one time during that period, your honor, that being the night he was attacked."

"You may continue, Mr. Kinnard," the judge said.

"Your honor, with your permission, the defense calls Miss Morehouse to the stand."

As Merry rose to take the stand, she looked at Doc and whispered, "Pray for me, Honey. I'm scared."

Doc winked and nodded as Merry took the stand and swore in. Kinnard asked, "Do you refute any parts of the George Hackett claim that you and Forest Adams attacked Mr. Hackett without provocation?"

"Yes, sir," Merry answered, her voice a mere whisper. "Nothing Mister Hackett said is true."

"Can you please speak up," Judge Blackstone requested.

Frightened with beads of sweat breaking out on her forehead, Merry forced herself to speak louder. "I can, your honor. Nothing Mister Hackett reported is true."

"Do you offer any proof for this statement?"

"We have a video of the entire event."

"Your honor," Manners angrily interrupted, 'the prosecution takes exception. We have not received copies of this material."

"Your honor," Kinnard said, "the defense brought this video to court for use only if prosecution charges proved questionable. This charge is completely inaccurate."

After considering the exchange, the judge allowed the video and told Merry to continue.

"Mr. Adams and I were sitting on his deck after dinner with my video camera ready to photograph wildlife. We heard a vehicle, and when Mister Adams noted it was Mister Hackett, he became fearful because of their recent disagreement. He asked me to go inside in case there were problems. As a news journalist, I swung my camera toward the entry steps to the deck and started it. Mister Hackett walked up to Mister Adams acting as if he wanted to shake hands to begin a friendly conversation. Then he started pounding Mister Adams in the face again and again. He knocked Mister Adams out of his chair and kicked him. Mister Adams' leg got caught in a chair and tore off when Mr. Hackett violently jerked the chair out of his way."

"His leg tore off?" the judge interrupted, puzzled at how that could occur.

"Yes, your honor. Mister Adams is a combat veteran and had a leg blown off in Iraq. He wears a prosthesis," Merry answered.

"Your honor," Kinnard began, "the defense would like to enter into evidence and show this short video of this alleged attack. It proves that Mister Hackett started this fight. Miss Morehouse had no part in this matter other than turning on her video camera as she ran from the deck after being called a dirty name by Mr. Hackett."

"Does the prosecution have questions for Miss Morehouse at this point?" The judge asked.

When there were none, Judge Blackstone permitted Kinnard to run the video that exhibited Hackett's attack. After the video, the judge asked the DA, "Can the prosecution explain the difference between what the prosecution claimed happened at the Adams home and what we witnessed on this video?"

After conferring with Hackett, DA Manners said, "The prosecution requests the right to withdraw this charge, your honor."

Anger washed over the judge's face. "Mr. Manners, is there any truth in any of the charges, or is the court to assume that Mister Hackett is trying to pull something on Mister Adams using my court as his tool?"

"Oh no, your honor. I can assure you Mr. Hackett wouldn't do that. Perhaps he disremembered this incident after he trusted Mr. Adams, and Mr. Adams subsequently broke into the MELCOR plant."

"I warn you both, the truth had better prevail in this remaining charge, or you face severe problems. Mister Manners, thus far, it appears as if you made little, if any, attempt to research these charges."

"Your honor, as you stated at the beginning of this trial, there was little time to investigate each charge adequately. Perhaps that's why Mister Adams was in such a hurry to get these matters into your court."

"Mister Manners, that's enough," the judge demanded, his face exhibiting deep anger. "Don't ever use my truths to cover for any person's obvious misuse of information. It appears the defense has it together, and the prosecution has fabricated its case."

Judge Blackstone turned to the defense, "Mr. Kinnard, if Miss Morehouse has finished her testimony, she may step down."

When Merry stepped down, the judge said, "Let's take a lunch break. Court will resume promptly at 1:00 P.M.

CHAPTER 39

With the "All Rise," command court was called to order. Judge Blackstone began, "Mister Kinnard, proceed with your defense of the final charge, theft of property."

"Your honor, with your permission, the defense calls Forest Adams to the stand."

With Doc on the stand and sworn in, Kinnard began asking questions Doc wrote on the tablet over the lunch break, hoping these questions would bring something meaningful to light. "Forest, you refuted Mr. Hackett's claim that you two had a warm relationship. Why is that?"

"From day one, our relationship was never warm and friendly. Mr. Hackett refused to come to our wedding when I married his daughter. On several occasions, George Hackett became angry and ordered me outside with the intent of beating me in front of other people. Mr. Hackett has a well-stocked home gym. He brags he was an unbeaten champion boxer in college. He wants me to be afraid of him. He initiated the fight so he could claim in court that I started it, allowing him to fire me without paying the termination clause payment."

"Were you afraid of Mr. Hackett?"

"I was afraid of what might happen if Mr. Hackett and I got into a fight. I could lose my family, and they mean everything to me."

"What do you think brought on this fight at your home?"

"George Hackett was done with me. The only thing keeping me at MELCOR after Catherine passed away was the termination contract Catherine negotiated. MELCOR would be required to pay a heavy price if we were let go for anything other than poor company performance or personal actions that brought discredit to MELCOR. MELCOR's business performance is excellent. Performance cannot be an issue."

"Could any of your actions be considered questionable?"

"Being honest, I was drinking more than I should since my wife passed away but not on the job or so that interfered with my job. Mr. Hackett called me on drinking at the meeting when he gave me a week off without pay. He said I needed to get my act together. I took his advice on that. One always has to be concerned when dealing with Mr. Hackett. He's a set-up engineer."

"Please explain to the court what you mean by a set-up engineer," the judge requested.

"A set-up engineer looks into the future to get everything in order before taking action to bring about what he wants to happen. The fight he started at my home was an effort to get me into a fight so that he could say I attacked him. Such an attack could qualify as a reason to fire me outside the termination clause. It was another step to fire me for cause after other steps he had taken failed to discredit me."

"What might those steps be?" Kinnard asked.

"After Mr. Hackett complained that my drinking impacted my performance, I was stopped that night and the next night by state troopers. Both of them gave me intoxication and Breathalyzer tests. Mr. Hackett knew I sometimes have a glass of wine with dinner on weekends. Before the nights I was stopped, I never saw a state trooper out on the hill after dark. It wasn't a coincidence. After those stops, I knew George had me in his sights to dump me without paying the termination money."

"Why would Mr. Hackett want to remove you from MELCOR employment?" Kinnard asked.

"He didn't want to employ me. Catherine insisted. When her brother quit and formed his own company, Hackett feared losing Catherine, who served as his senior engineer. She also holds several patents that are important to MELCOR's success. That's why he agreed to our termination contracts."

"If he didn't want to hire you, why would he promote you up through the ranks to General Manager?"

"I can't answer that. Brian Ryder was the most qualified person for general manager, but something came to me during this trial. Perhaps my promotion was part of another set-up operation."

"What might that be?"

Doc paused, looking at George Hackett and going back to Merry. He steepled his fingers and looked at Hackett. "Maybe he thought he would have better control over me. There was another MELCOR-involved trial going on at that time. I was one of the shift superintendents, and George and I disagreed about what occurred. That's when he became the company CEO and promoted me to Plant Manager. He insisted I take a two-week vacation before I took over. The vacation was during the trial, about which we had disagreements. I wondered about that."

Kinnard looked at Doc and then around the courtroom with an angry scowl on his face. "Anything else you want to say about that?"

"I shouldn't have said what I did. Merry and I are both afraid after the threats we've heard concerning what Mr. Hackett might have planned for us. Someone searched my home when no one was there, and Mr. Hackett, my wife's father, is one of the few people with keys. It could be an attempt to find the MELCOR shares. I'm at a loss trying to understand everything happening."

Kinnard shook his head with his hand covering his mouth. He then asked Doc to explain why he called the night superintendent to meet him at the plant door. "I retrieved my spare leg because Mr. Hackett broke the other one during the fight he initiated. I also recovered my personal computer. Miss Morehouse took videos of the items I retrieved under the watchful eye of night superintendent Ryder. The state police went to MELCOR the next morning, where they received a copy of the security video for that period."

After receiving the judge's permission, Kinnard played the video of Adams and Morehouse arriving and departing the plant with those items.

"How do you explain this, Mister Manners?" the judge asked after reviewing the video.

"We have no problems with this video, but let's review the security video." When the video was on, Manners began again. "The first evidence of Mr. Adams follows. It shows Mr. Adams and Miss Morehouse entering and leaving the plant, but that's not the problem area." After watching that part of the video, Manners requested, "Please roll the security video to 2:07 A.M. It shows Mister Adams returning to the plant and leaving with the petty cash, checks, a company computer, money advanced to him for a new project, and who knows what else."

They rolled the security video, showing someone in a MELCOR jacket and black hood unlocking and entering the building at 2:07. This person departed seven minutes later carrying a large green cash bag and what looked like a computer. The prosecution said this was Adams with the money, checks, and company computer.

"How do you reply to this, Mr. Kinnard?" the judge asked.

"Your Honor, there is no way the security image can stand as proof that person is Mister Adams. The face isn't visible, and it's so dark that no one could prove who it might be. Perhaps if there was some way we could achieve a clearer picture from the security footage, we could determine the identity of the person wearing the hood."

"Mr. Adams, you may return to your seat, but remember, you remain under oath. Mr. Hackett, please return to the stand," the judge ordered. When Hackett was seated, Judge Blackstone continued. "Mister Hackett, you remain under oath. Is there any way to enhance the security footage to properly identify the perpetrator?"

"Not with this equipment."

The judge excused Hackett and ordered the video played again, stopping it several times to ascertain the person's identity. It didn't help. "Mister Manners," the judge asked, "could we see anything in that video that proves that person was Mister Adams?"

"No, your honor, we could not?"

Doc grabbed Kinnard's arm and whispered to him, taking considerable time with the judge looking ever more anxious. "Mr. Kinnard, are you discussing something that may interest the court?"

"Yes, your Honor, I believe we are. Can we review the security tape once more?"

The judge ordered the tape prepared for another review. "Mr. Kinnard, what would we be looking for?"

"Please play the earlier section of the video that shows my clients leaving MELCOR."

When played back, Kinnard held his hand up. "Stop there. You honor, notice the entry light outside that entrance door and Mr. Adam's relationship to it. The top of his head is even with the middle of that light. Then notice the size and shape of Mr. Adams in that frame."

"That's a reasonable request, Mr. Kinnard, The judge replied. "Mr. Adams, how tall are you, and how much do you weigh?

"I'm six foot three and weigh about 225 pounds, your honor."

"What next, Mr. Kinnard?"

"Can we run the video beginning at the 2.07 mark?"

They ran the video to the point where that person was leaving the plant. Kinnard had the video stopped with the person passing the light. There was a distinct difference in height and body structure. "Mr. Hackett. How tall are you, and how much do you weigh?" the judge asked.

Hackett answered with a red face and somewhat frightened look, "I'm almost five-ten, your honor, and weigh about 247 pounds."

"Please proceed, Mr. Kinnard," Judge Blackstone ordered.

"Your Honor, the person in the 2.07 video could not be Mr. Adams. It clearly shows this person's head below the light where Mr. Adams was halfway up that same light. This person is also stockier than Mr. Adams. If we can replay the earlier part of the video, it shows Mr. Adams walking with a noticeable limp. This person has no limp. That's not Mr. Adams in the 2.07 video."

The judge looked at the prosecution table. Hackett's pale face was visibly upset. He understood what was coming.

"Mr. Kinnard," the judge barked, "Did you notice anything else?"

"I did, your Honor. The person in the 2.07 video and Mr. Hackett are about the same height and weight."

"Mr. Manners, is there anything your table might add to this discussion?"

After looking at Hackett, who was shaking his now-hung head, Manners answered, "No, Your Honor."

Judge Blackstone turned to the defense table, "Mr. Kinnard, does the defense have anything else to present in this case?"

"Yes, your Honor. As we watched the video, Mr. Adams said, 'The man at the 2:07 section walks a bit hunched over just like Mr. Hackett walks.' If you reviewed the video again, your Honor, you might also notice this."

"I think we all noticed that, didn't we, Mr. Manners?"

"Yes, your honor."

"Is there anything else, Mr. Kinnard?"

After a brief discussion with Doc, Kinnard answered. "Yes, your Honor, there is. The police officer sent to arrest Mr. Adams and Miss Morehouse for the proposed theft at MELCOR visited the Adams home around midnight with the arrest warrant. How can this be when the theft supposedly occurred at 2:07 A.M. the next morning? Sergeant Richardson can attest to this time because the arresting officer called him from the Adams home."

"Is that all, Mr. Kinnard?"

When Kinnard had nothing further to add, Judge Blackstone angrily ordered Hackett back to the witness stand, where the judge reminded him that he was still under oath. "Mr. Hackett, what do you say about the evidence just presented?"

Anger rolled over Hackett's red face. He stared bullets at Doc without answering.

"Mr. Hackett, I asked you a question," Judge Blackstone barked, his voice rising in pitch.

Pounding his fists on the witness chair, Hackett screamed, "Damn you, Cowboy, you'll pay!" Shaking his finger, his face red with anger, Hackett screamed, "You're fired!"

"What did you say, Mr. Hackett?" the judge angrily demanded.

"That idiot will pay!" Hackett defiantly answered, staring at the judge, his face bright red. "Mark my words, Adams will get his!"

"Bailiff, remand Mr. Hackett into custody and remove him from my courtroom!" the judge ordered.

"Mr. Manners, what do you say about the charges presented in this trial?" Judge Blackstone asked.

"The prosecution requests dismissal of all charges against Mr. Adams and Miss Morehouse, your honor."

"Anything else, Mr. Manners," the judge asked angrily.

Manners turned to the defense table, "Mr. Adams, Miss Morehouse, I must apologize. It became evident the charges are incorrect."

The judge said, "Is there anything the defense would like to say before this trial concludes?"

Doc whispered something to Kinnard, and he requested to speak. With permission, he began. "Your Honor, the defense requests that Mr. Manners withdraw all charges, so there's no record of these incidents. Any verdict could potentially impact on future legal actions."

The judge turned to the DA, "Mister Manners, what do you have to say about this request?"

Manners hesitated. Could withdrawing the charges give the defendants a more durable case for lawsuits against the prosecutor and George Hackett? With the judge staring at him and no way out,

Manners said, "The prosecution requests to withdraw all charges because of the mistakes made in this case, your honor."

"So be it," Judge Blackstone barked. "Let the record show the withdrawal of all charges. Courts adjourned."

Kinnard hailed the judge. "Judge Blackstone, could we have your attention for a moment?" The judge stopped while Kinnard, Doc, and Merry approached. "Your Honor, Mr. Hackett fired Mr. Adams in your courtroom. This could serve as evidence in a lawsuit regarding Mr. Adam's termination contract."

After thanking the judge, Kinnard turned to Doc, "You need to be watchful. Hackett doesn't like you."

"He doesn't like himself. And I believe the results of the video evidence presented in this trial will go a long way towards success in an Armstrong retrial."

"You sure you aren't a detective, Doc?"

"Just a poor country boy in love with this beautiful lady."

CHAPTER 40

With court adjourned, Kinnard led Doc and Merry to a side door out of the courthouse, where they were surprised by reporters. Kinnard held up his hand in a stop gesture, "Please, this has been a long, difficult day."

"Mr. Adams, I'm Debby Tompkins from the Bradford Journal. I'd appreciate answers to a few questions," Tompkins yelled, stepping in front of the others.

Kinnard started to talk, but Doc stopped him. "It's okay, Tom. We can handle a few questions. They need to make a living."

"Thank you, Mr. Adams," Tompkins said. "How angry are you about Mr. Hackett's false accusations?"

"Miss Tompkins, I'm not angry with anyone."

"You're not angry? Would you feel the same if false charges placed you in prison?"

"I can't know that."

"What's your plan, Miss Morehouse?" Tompkins asked.

"Starting a business with Mr. Adams and whatever follows," Merry answered with a broad smile.

"I'm Barbara Card of the Independent. Have your plans been in the works for a while?"

"They have. We've known each other for several weeks and wanted to do something together for most of that time," Merry answered, still smiling.

"Are you serious?"

"As Mr. Adams might say, serious as a heart attack."

"Miss Morehouse, how do you feel about the newspaper's damaging reports about you based on Hackett's claims?"

"Your papers took Mr. Hackett's claims as truth. You printed those claims without talking with us. Some may have added material to the Hackett claims based entirely on speculation. My father heads a large law firm. He can handle our lawsuits against reporters and their newspapers."

"Are you serious about suing?"

"Time will tell," Merry answered with a sweet smile.

Doc held up his hand. "Thanks for your time. We hope you have a great Memorial Day. Good day."

After thanking their Lawyer, Doc said, "Let's talk with the pastor."

They happily discussed wedding plans as they drove to the pastor's office, where Candy, Pastor Mike's secretary, met them. She explained the pastor was in but had to leave within the hour. She rang into the pastor's office, and he asked Candy to send them in.

"Good afternoon. Please come in." Pastor Mike said, smiling and standing to shake hands. As they took seats, the pastor asked, "Is court recessed?"

"Court's over," Merry answered.

"I trust the verdict was in your favor."

"Merry's going to prison for life, but I promised to visit her often," Doc answered.

"You're kidding?"

"Yeah. The prosecution withdrew all charges," Doc said.

"Withdrawn after the articles printed in papers?" Pastor Mike asked with a puzzled look.

"The charges proved baseless," Doc answered. "If your faith or conscience doesn't allow you to conduct our wedding, we understand. We prefer a church wedding, but if we can't have one, we'll get someone to marry us."

"Doc, I fully believe you're a practicing Christian. Merry, tell me again, how long have you been a Christian?"

"A couple of days after I met Doc a few weeks ago."

A questioning look slid over the pastor's face. "How do you know the Christian life is your long-term plan?"

"I read the Luke passage you recommended," Merry replied after considering the question. Looking at Doc, she continued, "I'm the seed that fell in Doc's good soil." Returning to look directly into the pastor's eyes, she began. "Pastor Mike, at the risk of repeating what we discussed over dinner, I grew up believing God was a delusion for the ignorant. My father ridiculed believers, so I didn't give God much thought. My first worship experience was here when Doc took me to church."

"And that service made you decide to be a Christian?"

"No. From day one, Doc talked easily about our Lord. He prayed before meals and encouraged me to pray. I found myself praying, and Jesus seemed to be in the room with me. Since I've known Doc, my life took on meaning I didn't realize existed. I witnessed a Christian practicing his beliefs, and I saw a life unlike any I previously knew, a life I wanted to live. I don't know how to tell you how I feel about Doc. But if you love Anita, you know."

"Doc, you're fifty, right?"

"Close."

"How old are you, Merry?"

"Thirty-one. And before you ask," Merry began with a hardness in her voice, "at Doc's insistence, we've been over our age difference and the ramifications it holds. We've covered having children, the sexual parameters it could hold over the years, and his problems with PTSD. I know he's deaf in one ear, and wearing a swimming suit, he made me look at his terrible scars. You may be wondering, so I'll tell you, we haven't had sex and won't until we're married. I'm not trying to convince you; I'm telling you how it is. If I weren't living this new life, I'd be skeptical, but I know it's real, just as I know our

Lord is real. Think what you want, but over time, you'll believe what I'm telling you."

"I believe you, Merry, but I like to see people worshiping together for some time before I marry them. I want to know they love each other and their marriage will last."

"Pastor, I love Merry in a way that's hard for me to believe. We're going to be man and wife soon, whether you marry us or someone else does. I understand how you feel, but at the same time, I hope you understand our love for each other and our desire to be married."

Pastor Mike thought about the conversation and asked, "When are you planning on marriage?"

"ASAP. I believe the way this trial concluded says God cleared the way for us," Doc said.

Another pause took place. Then Pastor Mike said, "Let's pray about this. Oh Lord, our God, show us your will in this matter. We want your guidance and will act accordingly."

It was silent until Doc began. "Lord, when we talked through our situation, it became clear you would be with us through this trial, and the outcome would tell us your plans. That trial's over. I strongly believe you ended it that way so we could become the Forest Adams team. If this is not your will, Lord, please show us now."

"Lord, I strongly believe our marriage is God-sent and in your will," Merry added.

Silence followed as the three of them thought through the situation and the prayers they had offered. Pastor Mike spoke first.

"Merry, if I offer an altar call for new believers on Sunday, would you answer that call?"

"What's an altar call?" Merry asked, her palms held out in front of her.

Pastor Mike smiled, and after he explained the purpose and importance of altar calls, Merry agreed. The pastor then said, "Here's my plan. I'm going to break my long-standing wedding requirements. Because of Memorial Day, the earliest we can plan for the marriage ceremony is Saturday, June second, but that doesn't give people much time to plan for the wedding."

"Will you announce during this Sunday's service that we plan to get married on that day?" Merry asked.

"I'll do that after the altar call," the pastor agreed. "Can you and your wedding party be at the church on Friday evening, June first, for a walk-thru service?"

"We'll be there. May we call you between now and then with questions?" Merry asked.

"I'll be waiting for calls," the pastor agreed.

CHAPTER 41

Their wedding guest list became the topic of discussion on the way home from dinner at Kitty's. Ronnie headed Doc's list as his best man and daughter Cindy, hopefully, the photographer. Since Merry's list contained out-of-towners, she suggested reservations at a motel. Doc believed otherwise.

"We have three bedrooms that aren't in use, one with two beds. We have queen-size sleeper sofas, blow-up beds, a fold-up double bed, and two fold-up singles. Invite whomever you want, and they can stay with us. That way, we can become acquainted before the wedding."

Merry had tears running down her face as they pulled into the lookout. Through her sobs, she whimpered, "Please hold me." Her body shook as they grew together. With time, her tears slowed. "Oh, Doc, I love you. You're my anchor. Everything is so screwed up. The Hackett problems. My father and what he might do. I wrecked your vehicles. I don't want to live away from you during the week, but I have so many bills I must work. I'm so scared and mixed up."

"Honey, we'll be fine."

Merry looked away and softly began. "Maybe fine with everything but my father. I think about what he did to me every day. He'd get me alone and play with me."

"Touch me."

"Sniff my neck."

"He raped me when I was fifteen. He said it was my fault and made me clean up the mess. Then he laughed at me. He said he'd kill me and anyone I told about this. I bought bolt locks and put them on my door. I tried never to be alone with him. How can you live with that?"

"Merry, I knew there was a problem and thought this might be it. You couldn't do anything about it. Let's not let it impact our marriage. We both have problems to work through. I love you. More now than before."

After her crying was under control, Merry began again. "I want Maggie at our wedding, but she'll see the stuffed animals in the great room. I'll be the laughingstock of the company when people find out."

"From what you told me about Maggie, there's no way that woman would embarrass you. Do you see any other problems?"

"My family and our wedding. I want Sunny to walk me down the aisle and possibly my mother as my matron of honor, but I don't want my father There. I can't handle more 'how dumb can you be' beat up Merry sessions."

"Call your brother and tell him we're getting married, and you want him to walk you down the aisle. How could he turn you down? He can figure out how to get your mother here."

"I don't know."

"Honey, never allow what might go wrong to be your driving force. Most worries never materialize. Let's get started and work our way through things as they evolve. It's the best we can do."

The weekend ran by with wedding planning and riding horses. Doc accompanied Merry forward on Sunday at the pastor's altar call. After a short discussion, the pastor announced their marriage plans.

It became more difficult as Sunday flowed into Monday and Merry's departure. Walking to her Cruz Monday afternoon with tears streaming in her eyes, Merry announced, "Doc, I feel like I'm twisting in a tornado with George Hackett, my father, and my job tearing at me. I hate my job. I'm quitting."

"Honey, we can work from home. You owe it to yourself to develop a career you love. Let the video project play out. That said, I'll stand behind any job decision you make."

"If I don't quit, I'm asking for Thursday and Friday off for our wedding prep and the following week for a honeymoon. This time off screws my paycheck, but so be it. "I want to do my —"

"You did your share when you gave me back my smile. Better head south before Memorial Day picnic drunks hit the road."

"I know what you're thinking," Merry teased with her first smile of the morning. "Two wrecks this month is more than enough. I'll be careful and call when I get to Harrisburg. Love you, Doc Adams. Thanks for being you.”

Finding their goodbyes ever more difficult, they kissed, holding each other tightly for some time before Merry departed. Doc and Jack watched until her Cruze rounded the curve and sadly went inside to follow their plan.

On Tuesday morning, Doc dropped by their lawyer’s office, where Kinnard said, “I called and you weren’t home. Something came up.”

“You sound concerned.”

“You will be, too,” Kinnard said with his bulldog scowl and knowing eyes peering out of steel-rimmed glasses. “I called Brian Ryder to talk about the Armstrong trial, and he’s talked with your old secretary. She caught part of a phone call and believes Hackett’s making serious threats against you. He said he didn’t have anything to lose the way he got screwed with the trial. You should consider a Protection Order.”

Doc shook his head with a worried look. “Hackett sees his life crumbling after the details that came out at the trial. I’m concerned. Protection orders often flame violent fires while offering little protection. I’ll call Sergeant Richardson for suggestions.”

“Your trial provides a solid basis for an appeal in the Armstrong case. I reviewed the Armstrong trial security video several times since your trial. That same outside light that won your case shows that it wasn’t Armstrong going into the plant and places the spotlight on Hackett.”

“Let me know if I can help. In the meantime, I have another project for you. This is my contractual agreement with MELCOR,”

Doc said, handing him a copy of his contract. "It includes a hefty separation allowance if they fire me for any reason other than cause. You heard Hackett say he fired me, and the trial proved there's no cause. I want the request for my separation money to come through you after our wedding."

After thanking Kinnard, Doc went to his truck and called Jane Boyer on her secure line. "Jane, Doc here. You probably can't talk, and that's fine. I'm on my way to pick up my last check. I heard you witnessed a threatening Hackett conversation. I'd appreciate it if you'd type out what you heard and how you heard it. Just put it in my pay envelope. You don't have to do this, and I won't use the info without your approval. Take care."

Doc stopped by MELCOR and had Jane paged from the main receptionist's position. She was soon down with his check. She whispered, "Please remember me if you get another job in the area."

"I will, Jane and I'll write a reference letter for you. Email me anything you'd like in it."

It was tough saying goodbye after years of working together, but Doc was glad to depart. He stopped at the dry cleaner and picked up his clothing. The cashier lifted the covering on one piece and made sure he thoroughly examined it. He hung the things in his truck and headed home.

That afternoon, Doc removed the winter bedding, and while it washed, he hung replacement cotton sheets on the clotheslines to freshen them. He was finishing a late dinner when the phone beckoned. Glancing at the screen, he saw it was Merry. "Good evening, Miss Morehouse. I trust all is going well."

"It would be better if I were on that end of the phone with you. Besides missing my love and being worried sick about Hackett and my father, all else is going my way. I thought the New York Team would be upset, but I gathered more sympathy than anger after they heard what happened. Everyone believes our videos have a bright future. The highlight of my day was Maggie getting me off Thursday and Friday plus all of next week. I'll have to work late Wednesday to finish everything here, but I'll be home by noon on Thursday."

"Great. I'll be waiting. I picked up my last check at MELCOR," Doc said, purposely leaving out Hackett's new threats. "Came home and worked through some of our plans. Ronnie will be our best man. I called band members for our reception and placed our order with Valley Meats."

"I asked Maggie to be our guest, and she happily accepted. The last thing she said was, 'I hope you aren't bailing out on me, Merry.' I didn't answer. Sunny will walk me to the altar, and Mother agreed to be my matron of honor. They know I don't want my father there. Not sure how they'll work that out."

Being apart was growing tougher. They spent a few more minutes with their 'I love yous' and then hung up.

Wednesday morning, Doc departed early for St. Mary's, where he purchased a queen-size bed that matched his cherry bedroom furniture, a high-end box spring, and a mattress set with a foam mattress pad. At the lamp display, he chose new dresser and nightstand lamps.

Heavy into his home conversion, he stopped at Peebles and bought two sets of light gray satin sheets and pillow covers, drapes for the bedroom and sitting room with matching throw rugs. Next came bathroom curtains and several sets of different colored guest bath towels, hand towels, and washcloths, plus throw rug sets for his bedroom, sitting room, and bathroom. He stopped at Sears and bought paint for those three rooms.

The reformation began at home. Doc started the washer with new purchases from that morning. While they washed, he made beds in preparation for wedding guests. In the room Merry was using, he turned her bed around to accommodate the bed from his bedroom and moved it in. He then began painting his bedroom.

Around four that afternoon, the delivery team arrived with the new bedroom furniture. Doc put the now washed new sheets and pillow covers on the clothesline to blow in the mountain breeze, setting his alarm for six-thirty so he'd remember to bring the bedding in before it drew damp. After eating, he began painting again.

Doc had finished the bedroom and bathroom when Merry called. He informed her of his phone calls and explained Cindy agreed to photograph their wedding and reception without explaining she appeared somewhat cold to the idea. He told his family in Texas of the wedding even though he understood it was unlikely anyone could attend. After Merry's call, he finished painting the sitting room, wondering what she would say about the new look.

On Thursday morning, Doc had the daily chores and breakfast behind him when the morning sun crept over the mountains. He finished cleaning and felt the place was ready for a new bride and guest inspections when Jack began barking excitedly as he watched Merry come rolling in.

Dust covered her car as she braked to a stop. Merry's amber hair shone brightly in the sun, hanging loosely over one shoulder. "Oh, Honey, we're so glad you're home."

"Couldn't wait to get here, Docsy. I so love you. This week wouldn't end, and it was only two days long."

After hugging tightly and a lengthy kiss, Doc suggested, "Let's get your stuff in. We have a lot to discuss over lunch. Can you handle burgers and beans?"

"Sounds like a feast as long as you eat with me."

Doc created a salad while the burgers and beans cooked. Merry changed clothes, and her charming appearance warmed Doc. "Man Docsy, you've been busy. My bedroom had a complete overhaul. It looks like the rest of the house had a face-lift too. And flowers. You have them everywhere. The place looks great and smells like a flower garden."

Doc smiled without talking. Over lunch, they discussed their wedding plans. Sunny would arrive Friday morning with his fiancee, Kathy, and their mother. He was able to arrange everything without their father knowing about the wedding. Even better, their father was out of town for the weekend. Maggie would also arrive in the morning, and everybody agreed to stay with them.

With the lunch mess cleaned up, they sat on the swing, going through wedding plans while marveling how fast they got from the wreck to their wedding. When that played out, they washed Doc's truck and Merry's car for the wedding. Looking at Doc when they completed her car, Merry said, "Man, Honey, you look beat."

"Let's eat in town? We'll pick up steaks and groceries for the weekend while we're there."

They were soon on their way to town, completing a store list. After finishing the shopping and the food in coolers, they went to

Kitty's for the evening special. Later at home, Merry put on CDs, and they sat on the screened porch. Doc explained he moved Billy's clothes into the closet in her computer room, all beds had clean sheets and pillowcases, and the flannels were washed and put away until next winter. "My bedroom is off-limits until after the wedding," Doc said.

"You've been busy, Honey."

"Had to stay busy to keep from going nuts. Got a question. Have you decided what you're going to wear for our wedding?"

"I bought a light pink suit. Why do you ask?"

"You may want to inspect your closet before we turn in."

"Okay, Frosty, what'd you do," Merry asked with a quizzical smile. Without waiting for an answer, she rushed upstairs. A short while later, she yelled down the stairway, "Oh Honey, see why I love you." A bit later, she called down the steps, "I'm coming down to show you?"

"Someone told me that's not proper. Have to wait until Saturday afternoon."

As she came around the corner, Merry said, "I have to show someone, and you're the only someone here."

"My gosh, Merry, you're beautiful. They created that gown for you."

"Do you like it?"

"Like it? I love it and you in it. Honey, are you sure you want to marry an old man?"

"Stop that! Doc, I can't stop thinking about us. I want all of you."

They stepped into each other's arms, kissing, snuggling ever closer. Doc held her tight, kissing her neck and ears. Breathing ever harder, they kissed. "Oh, Darling, I so love you," she whispered.

They kissed again, a loving embrace but with less heat. still embraced, they leaned back, lovingly looking at each other, each with teary eyes. "I love you," they whispered in unison.

With a light smile, Merry stepped back, looking into Doc's eyes, "Oh Honey, you treat me so great, and I love you." She kissed him, adding, "My new shoes go with my dress. Wait until mother sees me."

Doc kissed her lightly, and with a chuckle, he said, "Save the price tag for her."

"She wouldn't believe it. I won't show her the other tag I found pinned to it."

"I missed that."

"The original owner's note said, 'I hope this works better for you than it did me. I kicked him out for cheating two days before the wedding.'"

CHAPTER 42

Merry was drying the last pan after a busy morning preparing salads and desserts when Jack began barking. "My gosh, I think Maggie's here," Merry said, looking out the window.

"Better bring her in. She may be afraid of Jack," Doc suggested as he rinsed the soap off his hands.

Maggie was out of her car petting Jack when Merry reached the porch. After a brief welcome, they headed inside. "Doc, look who's here," Merry said as they entered the kitchen. "It's Maggie."

"Welcome, Maggie," Doc said as he dried his hands, "So glad you made it. Heard great things about you."

Maggie pushed away the hand he held out to shake, "I need a hug after a long, interesting drive." Done hugging, she added, "From all Merry tells me, you two have a lot going for you. Love your dog too. He's so gentle for a big guy."

"Jack was mine until Miss Merry arrived on the scene," Doc said. "Hardly knows I'm around now. Let's get your things in."

With her suitcase in a bedroom, they laughed as Maggie explained how key players often glanced at each other with strange looks as they watched the WLDZ copy of the video. Maggie's accolades pushed Merry to feel the need to confess. "There's more to the videos than you realize, Maggie," Merry said, pointing to the great room.

She held her breath with a wondering look as Maggie entered the animal sanctuary. Barely breathing, she tightly clasped Doc's hand until they heard Maggie chuckling.

"Merry, this is classic. It's amazing how you achieved such a lifelike video using stuffed animals. The coyote with the sausage and that yellow rattlesnake crawling away look so real. The bear shots are way too much. And then there are the fawns. How'd you do it?"

The yellow rattler and does with fawns are real. So are the elk and the bear with three cubs. The twin fawns are on the fireplace."

They were still discussing the video when Jack lit off again. "Doc, it's Sunny and his girlfriend. Oh great. Mother's with them," Merry said, heading outside.

Maggie continued looking through the great room while Doc joined Merry. The newcomers were climbing out of their car as they walked up. After hugging family members, Merry introduced Doc. As they shook hands, Sunny said, "I couldn't wait to meet you, Doc. It's hard to believe you're a human being. After talking with Merry, I thought you'd come flying out on angel wings with a magic wand granting wishes."

"Sunny, you wait. Doc is everything I said he was," Merry said with a smile. "Mother, this is Doc. Doc, this is Anna, my mother."

"Can I just call you, Mom?" Doc asked, holding out his arms.

"With a broad smile, Anna replied, "I'd love that. Hug me, son."

Merry and Sunny stared with amazement at their mother's demonstration of love as they watched the pair whisper to each other, something they had never witnessed before.

"Maybe it's the mountain air," Kathy whispered.

"Whatever, it's beautiful," Sunny returned.

Merry smiled warmly. "Let's get your things in. Mother can sleep in my bedroom. Sunny. Kathy. There's another bedroom that has two double beds. There are also several sleeper sofas. You decide. I'm just thankful you made it."

"Me too," Doc agreed. "You can arm wrestle for bunks while I fire off the grill."

"We'll have burgers and hotdogs now," Merry said with happiness written across her face. "After the rehvearsal, we'll come home and eat for real."

Merry felt her mother's hand on her shoulder as she helped carry her things to their bedroom. "Merry, we'll share a bedroom for the first time ever. That means a lot to me."

Merry noticed tears in her mother's eyes as she hung up her clothes. "Something wrong, Mother?"

Anna wiped her eyes. "No, Merry, things are right."

"Why the tears?"

"I've known your Doc for a few minutes, and he asked if he could call me 'Mom.' No one has ever called me Mom before."

"Can I call you, Mom?"

"Oh, Merry, I'd love that. Mother is cold. It's your father's idea."

"Mom, it is, Mom." They hugged tightly, something they had never before enjoyed. When they moved apart, they shared tears.

"Doc seems so caring and easy to be with."

"He is, Mom. He's a kind gentleman, not just to me but to everyone."

"Merry, I'm worried. You were never close to any man, and now you're marrying an older man you hardly know. Are you sure he's the right one?"

"Mom, Doc's it."

A knock on the door stopped their conversation as Maggie said, "Lunch is ready."

With an agreement to talk later, Merry and Anna headed to the deck, where food and beverages were on the table. When all were seated, Doc held Merry and Maggie's hands, and as people joined hands around the table, some with questioning looks, Doc offered a prayer.

The conversation at the table was cheerful but reserved as people got to know each other. By the time they finished eating, they were acting like old friends at a class reunion.

That afternoon, they departed for church with Doc, Merry, Anna, and Maggie in Doc's truck, and Sunny and Kathy followed. Pastor Mike was at the church when they arrived, and Ronnie and Sarah came soon after. After introductions, the pastor assumed control.

"Friends, each participant has a folder with a copy of the ceremony. I won't go over all of the readings today, but I'd like you to read through the entire service tonight. If Doc or Merry desire changes, we can discuss them. Any questions before we begin?"

When there were no questions, he began. "I'll start with the welcome to family and friends and continue to this point, 'Should there be anyone who has cause why this couple should not be united in marriage, speak now or forever hold your peace.'" He stopped and asked while looking at the attendees one at a time, "Are there any concerns in this area?"

Doc, Merry, Anna, and Sunny searched each other's faces before shaking their heads' no.' The pastor then worked through the ceremony, stopping in places to add additional emphasis on marriage requirements, insisting they understand marriage isn't a fairy tale without challenges or obstacles. The pastor again remarked on their importance when they arrived at the vows. When he reached the man's vows, Doc slipped Merry a look, and their feelings told everyone their marriage was right for them.

While going over the ring exchange, the pastor's eye contact with Merry was a bit longer when he said, "Merry, do you take Forest to be your husband, vowing to build together a Christian home under the Lordship of Jesus Christ?" The look in her eyes told the world she was ever so serious about her vows.

He ended with, "May the Lord bless you and keep you. May the Lord make his face shine upon you and be gracious unto you. May the Lord lift his countenance unto you and give you peace. Congratulations, you may kiss your bride." And they did, creating attendee smiles.

"I present to you, Mr. and Mrs. Forest Adams."

"I'll thank everyone for coming on the Bride and Groom's behalf and tell them again about the reception and sing-along at your place. When folks are outside, Doc and Merry will exit. And we'll shower them with birdseed instead of rice."

"Now, Doc and Merry, are there changes or additions you want to make to this program?"

Doc and Merry looked at each other and, after shaking their heads, said they had none. After the rehearsal, Doc asked Pastor Mike to share a steak dinner, explaining they would have Anita picked up at the parsonage.

"Sorry, folks. We can't but enjoy yourselves. I say that lightly because I know you will. Doc. Merry. I'd like a few moments with you alone."

Standing alone, Pastor Mike asked Merry, "Were you able to review the PTSD video Doc mentioned?"

"I was. It's scary. Not coming from a military family, I had no idea about any of this until Doc had a problem that night. And yes, there's concern. But then there's concern about living into tomorrow. Pastor Mike, I want to marry Doc more than anything else ever. You cannot know the beautiful change he brought into my life."

"Any concerns, Doc?"

"Always some concern and, especially about something as serious as marriage. I have no concern about our love for each other. It's almost beyond my ability to believe. At this point, I'm not sure how I'd face tomorrow if we didn't give this our best shot. Pastor, we know you are going out on a thin limb for us. We can't control everything that might happen, but we'll do all we can to make this work."

"To this point in my ministry, I haven't had a failed marriage."

"Ours won't be your first. Thanks so much for your efforts on our behalf and your understanding," Merry said.

"Anita and I owe Doc. He's been a blessing in many ways."

"I understand. Doc gave me life."

Later, the rehearsal group sat on the deck discussing everything from Doc and Merry stories to the wedding. Maggie talked about the video and how highly the company bigwigs thought of it, which led to Ronnie's introduction as the 'hunter and animal stuffer .' Animal stuffer stories led to real animal stories, leading to talk about these mountains and the groom and bride's plans. Merry excused herself and headed into the house for a bathroom call. When she stood, Maggie said, "I may have the same need. I'll follow you."

After the bathroom visit, Maggie asked, "Merry, what are your career plans, and how can I help?"

Merry hesitantly answered, "Maggie, the two days away from Doc this week was more like two years. I've considered submitting my resignation."

"Then what? You have talents you've just begun to explore, and the station needs you."

"Doc's no longer employed at MELCOR. We've discussed creating videos together, perhaps some around Pennsylvania like the first one, some educational programs, and perhaps advertising."

"Sounds interesting. Maybe you could both be WLDZ employees. The station needs your talents as employees, if possible, or contractors if required. I can't make any promises, but I'll discuss this with Melvin. I respect you and —"

"Hey, did you two fall asleep in there," someone yelled. "We're getting hungry."

"Guess we better get hot," Maggie said, smiling.

At the table, Doc felt a tap on his shoulder and turned toward Sunny. "You didn't hear my question, did you, Doc?"

"I'm deaf in that ear."

"Sorry. I didn't know. Merry mentioned you had a court appearance. How'd that go?"

Everybody listened as Doc provided a short version. Merry and Maggie arrived in time to catch the last of the story. Not wanting to discuss it further, Doc got up to light the grill, and Sunny accompanied him. While Doc worked with the grill, Sunny said, "Merry's a different person with you. When she looks at you, she can't look away."

"Not sure how this happened, Sunny, but I'm crazy about her."

"Merry said your first wife passed away. Did you have the same kind of relationship with her? I ask because Kathy and I are discussing marriage, and we don't want one like my parents."

"Billy and I loved each other. We worked and played well together. Liked the same kinds of things."

"What made you and Merry click?"

"A friend suggested we were God sent. Our backgrounds are very different, and our first days together were sometimes difficult. Our beliefs on media coverage, guns, law enforcement, and politics are different. I'm older than her, a combat vet who lost a leg, and a Christian who isn't going to change. I treat Merry the way I want to be treated. That's about it."

"That appears to be more than enough for her."

As they talked, the subject got around to his father. Doc said it was sad he wouldn't be at the wedding.

"Kathy and I wouldn't be here if he was."

"He's your father."

"He's also a dictatorial ass whose reputation has my life twisting in the wind. Kathy worked for his company, but he wouldn't keep his hands to himself. Tried to get her to spend time with him in the Poconos."

"That's not good."

"There's more, but I wouldn't want it repeated. When I went to work at the firm, I heard whispers that my father was part of questionable activities. Robert Peabody, another of the third-generation partners, was found hanging in his office. The coroner ruled his death a suicide, but it's questionable. After that death, Justin Rosenstein and his sister Sharon, the other partners, sold their partnership to Father and retired. I applied for a job where Kathy works, but they're reluctant to hire me because of my father's reputation. I love Kathy, but she won't marry anyone who isn't a Christian. I don't know what I believe, having grown up with no exposure to Christianity. It's an offensive topic with our father."

"Sunny, I believe in God and try to live that way. Let me get the steaks, and we can talk while they cook."

Doc took orders and began putting steaks on the grill while Sunny talked about the phone calls he received from Merry, how she was learning to cook, live in the mountains, enjoy animals, and loving life for what it could be. "She said she's learning people can peacefully discuss differences of opinion and accept each other's ideas for what they are without fighting."

With a light smile, Doc answered, "I don't have everything together, regardless of what Merry thinks. A Confederate soldier once wrote, 'I among all men, am most richly blessed.' How could I not have a positive outlook on life or not believe in the loving God who brought Merry into my life?"

Doc was turning over the last of the steaks when Sunny spoke again. "We were raised in a mansion by wealthy parents who showed little real affection toward each other and not much toward us. I'm fearful our father will wreck your marriage. He might have you ... well, something terrible could happen."

Doc stopped lifting steaks. With narrowed eyes and a hard look, he said, "Sunny, I'm concerned, but I'm not afraid of your father. I grew up among tough men who don't scare easily. He'd be making a mistake to threaten us. Nuff said."

After a quiet spell, Sunny softly said, "I see so much I want for Kathy and me, but I'm not sure how to get it."

"Pray and trust in our Lord. I had no idea how to get what Merry and I received. As the lady said, it's God sent."

The wedding party was enjoying dinner and each other when a phone rang in the upstairs bedroom. "That could be your phone, Mom," Merry suggested. "That's our bedroom window."

"It's probably a wrong number," Anna replied.

As conversations picked up, the phone began ringing again. Once more, Anna ignored it. Shortly after that, it rang for the third time, and Anna excused herself to check to see who was so persistent.

As she entered the bedroom, it rang again, and the identifier read "The Office1." It was Howard. What could he want when he was in his beloved Poconos for the weekend? "Hello. Anna speaking."

"Anna, this is Howard," he said, anger dripping off his tongue. "I've been trying to call you at home. Can't I trust you for a weekend without you wandering off?"

"Howard Morehouse, how dare you question me after the way you live your life? I know where you go and who —"

"Who do you think you're talking to? You'd have nothing if —"

"Howard, I suddenly realize nothing is what I have with you. I don't—"

"Have you gone completely nuts?"

"No, Howard, I haven't, but I'm attending an important meeting. Bye now."

Merry entered and said, "Mother, you should have taken the phone off the speaker. Everybody heard Father's big mouth."

"I'm sorry. It's so upsetting when he questions my trust."

"Does he know about our wedding this weekend?"

"How could he?"

"How he finds out things is beyond me. I don't want him ruining what promises to be my best day ever."

CHAPTER 43

"Deerman Detective Agency. Andrea Busch speaking. How may we help you?"

"Good afternoon, Andrea. Howard Morehouse."

"Mr. Morehouse, how are you?" she answered in a fake sweet voice.

"Needing information."

"I believe your agency usually works with Karl Schmidt. You can reach him at home. Do you have his phone number?"

"I do."

"Please call me if you don't reach him."

"I'll do that, Andrea. Thanks for your help."

"I'd sure like to get that chick in bed," Howard muttered as he dialed Schmidt's number.

After two rings, a voice answered, "Schmidt here. How may I help you?"

"Karl, this is Howard Morehouse. I need information, and I need it kept between us!"

"Howard, it's always between us. What do you need, and when do you need it?"

"Times short. I need the information by 4 A.M. tomorrow. I called my wife on her company phone with the GPS Tracker and located her at a remote site in Cameron County."

"If you have her location, what do you need from me?"

"It seems Merry went nuts over some hillbilly. No daughter of mine is hooking up with some nothing dorkhead. I need to know what's happening."

"Let's see; it's the weekend. The location is in hillbilly heaven, and you want me to find out all kinds of private information in about ten hours. Is that all you need, Howard?"

"Karl, you've done spectacular work in the past. Will you help me?" Morehouse asked in a more supplicating manner.

"I'll put aside the case I'm working on and get started, but I'm billing overtime for hours worked plus expenses regardless of the results achieved. Is that agreeable?"

No, it's not agreeable, Howard thought, but there isn't much I can do about it. If Karl can't help me, nobody can. "It's agreeable, Karl, but make sure you send the invoice to the firm in my name."

"Are you in your office?"

"No. I'm in the Poconos."

"Oh. Got a little hottie with you, and you want to know what your family's doing while you're busy with her."

"Don't get smart, Karl. I take good care of you."

"Yes, Howard, you do, and we take good care of you too. If we didn't, you wouldn't remain a customer. Do you have the information I gave you that explains how to hook our computers together?"

"It's in my computer case."

"Good. Hook us up. Give me a half-hour, and I'll have you call Anna back with us hooked together. I want to do some research before you call."

"I'll wait for your contact."

"Talk to you then."

"Yeah, talk to —"

The phone clicked off, and Howard sat looking at it. "Horses butt," Howard muttered.

"What's the matter, Honey?" a sweet young voice asked as she massaged his shoulders. "Does Daddy need a little lovin' to get his mind right?"

CHAPTER 44

The wedding party moved into the great room where Doc agreed to play a few songs. Anna eagerly asked, "Can we choose some songs?"

"If you'll sing along," Doc said.

Doc hit a few chords and said, "My grandparents raised me. Since they can't be here for our wedding, I'd like to begin with one of their favorites." He began picking the hymn "In The Garden," and Kathy started singing with Doc joining her. When they hit the refrain, Maggie and Anna joined in. Together, they sang through the second verse.

When they finished, Anna softly asked, "Can you play 'She's Not You' by Elvis'?"

"If you sing with me."

After Doc picked through it once, they began together, "Her hair is soft, and her eyes are oh so blue. She's all the things a girl should be, but she's not you."

When they finished, everyone clapped. Doc smiled, looking at Anna, "Your eyes are blue. Is there a story behind that song?"

Anna blushed as she softly answered. "My first boyfriend would play the piano, and we'd sing it together."

Anna's phone began ringing in the bedroom again. She ran upstairs to the bedroom to turn it off and noticed it was 'The Office1.'

This time she took the phone off speaker and answered, "Yes, Howard."

"Anna, where the hell are you?"

"Why would you care?"

"Because I want to know where you are when you're supposed to be home. We haven't discussed this trip."

"We didn't discuss your Pocono chickie trip either. That's —"

"You don't know —."

"Howard, I know more than you think. You have a good time now."

Anna turned off her phone and placed it in her purse. Sunny met her with Merry standing by. "What's wrong, Sunny?" Anna asked, sensing he was upset.

"Mother, was that father again?" Sunny asked.

"It was. Why do you ask?"

"Are you using a company phone that shows 'The Office' as the person calling?"

"I am."

"Those phones have a GPS Tracker installed. He called back to track your location. The firm's hooked up with a detective agency, and I'm betting the agency is also connected. By morning, Father will know what we're doing here."

"Sunny, you're kidding?" Anna begged.

"No, Mother, I'm not," Sunny answered, carrying a frightened look.

"They won't find out much over the weekend."

"Mother, that agency's ability to uncover information is beyond belief. How father might use the information is anybody's guess."

Anna began crying, and Merry was immediately fearful. "What if he shows up and causes problems? What then? The last time I talked to him, it was another 'How dumb can you be' threatening conversation. I'm scared."

"Oh, Merry, I'm so sorry," Anna said, sobbing harder. "I just didn't know."

Anna flopped down on the bed, crying. Sunny remained with her, but Merry returned downstairs, where Maggie told her Doc was outside saying goodnight to Ronnie and Sarah. Merry joined them with goodnights, and as they got in their car, Merry grabbed Doc's hand. "Can we talk... out here ?"

"Always. Honey, you're shaking. What's wrong?"

"Father called mother again. When mother hung up, Sonny explained mother's company phone has a tracking system installed. Sonny's afraid father is bent on causing problems. What are we going to do?"

Doc held her close and whispered, "I love you, Merry. Let's not mention this to anyone. I'll run upstairs and make some phone calls just in case he causes problems."

"Oh, Honey, he ruined most of my life until you came along."

After kissing, Doc went to his bedroom and called Sergeant Richardson at home. The call went better than expected, and Doc felt some relief as he dialed the Pastor. After their initial comments, Doc began, "Pastor, there's something you should know. Merry's father could be a problem. You heard him when you ate with us. Just in case, I called Sergeant Richardson of the State Police. He'll have a person at the wedding sitting in the back row on the left aisle. He's getting someone from another barracks, so people will think he's an out-of-town family friend."

"Do you have any indicator there will be a problem?"

"Just premonitions. Conversation with Merry and her brother suggests he can be a dangerous person."

"I believe this marriage is God sent. Unless you change your mind, Let's continue as scheduled."

CHAPTER 45

Howard Morehouse smashed his fists into the nightstand. "What's taking him so long? I expect people to be timely."

"Maybe daddy needs a little recreation to soothe his troubled mind," Sweet Thing suggested.

Morehouse slammed the nightstand again and screamed, "I told that idiot what I needed and when I needed it."

"Does Daddy need help?" Sweet Thing softly questioned.

"Please shut up while you still can," Howard snarled.

Sweet Thing rolled over and began crying. Howard shook his head and walked nude to the front room. "Man, you pay these chicks well, and they think they're the center of your universe."

As he fumed, the phone rang. Howard answered it after glancing at the time. "Hello," he snapped.

"Karl here. You sound upset."

"It's almost four-thirty. I expected a call as soon as you got your information together."

"You're getting it, Howard. I upset people and got some in trouble. I'll email my report to you as soon as I give you a brief. You ready?"

"I've been ready for hours," Howard lied, grabbing his pen.

"Cameron County has coverage from two weekly newspapers plus a daily out of Bradford. I couldn't get hold of anyone from —."

"Get on with it, Karl. Time's running short."

"Let's not get testy, Howard. I got hold of a person who works for a newspaper. She put me on the information trail. Your daughter's running with a tough customer, Forest "Doc" Adams. They recently went to court for beating the hell out of Adam's ex-father-in-law and stealing a bunch of money. Then —."

"Dammit, she's hooked up with a freaking druggie."

"There's more. This woman said they came out of court smelling like roses. She heard they were getting married in the Hill Church and gave me the pastor's name and number. I called, and a woman answered the phone. She confirmed they're getting married this afternoon. A man grabbed the phone and demanded to know who was calling. He wouldn't buy the lie I made up. The newspaper lady told me the preacher is also the pastor of the Methodist Church in town. I looked up that church which provided names and phone numbers of people serving in various church positions. I began calling, telling them I was a friend of Adams and forgot what time the wedding was. The wedding's at two with an evening reception at Adam's place. She said Adam's wife-to-be is beautiful. You're a lucky man, Howard. Pretty women in your family and that hot chickie you're with."

"Stuff it, Karl. What else I should know?"

"There's often no phone reception in the mountains. I put directions to the Hill Church and Adam's house in the report. Maybe you can bunk there tonight."

"Shove it, Karl. Anything else?"

"It's all in the report."

Howard turned on his computer, and while it powered up, he ran shower water. Things were looking better. After showering, he checked his email. When he turned on the bedroom lights to get dressed, Sweet Thing asked what was up. "My plans changed. I can drop you off at your place or give you money for a taxi."

"We're supposed to spend the weekend together. I could've gone to the shore with friends."

"Yeah, but you wouldn't have the money I'm throwing at you. Get your fanny out of bed or count on a taxi."

"I don't know what I was thinking when I agreed to spend the weekend with you. I must be —"

"You were thinking a great payday, a good roll in the hay, and maybe a promotion. Now get up and get dressed. I don't have time to fool."

Chapter 46

Doc finished feeding horses before daylight and headed in to work on breakfast. He soon had the meal ready when he heard someone on the steps. Maggie was already talking when she rounded the corner into the kitchen. "I detect delicious smells coming from down here. Got a whiff of bacon and potatoes, but there's more."

"Morning, Maggie. Grab a coffee," Doc said.

"Good morning, Doc. How can I help?"

"Knock on bedroom doors. Pancakes, bacon and sausage, and an egg breakfast dish are staying warm in the oven. Fried spuds are ready to go."

"I'll knock, but I believe everyone's awake."

Soon, everyone was seated at the table, and after Doc's prayer, they quietly passed the food. "Wow, this is a quiet group this morning," Maggie suggested. The sun's up, birds are singing, and a fabulous breakfast faces us. Even more, There's a wedding this afternoon. I'm thinking we should all be smiling."

General agreement about the wedding picked up the conversations. Wedding excitement grew, building a wonderful day. Mid-morning, the women retreated upstairs to lay out their clothes for the wedding while Doc and Sunny washed vehicles. They were working on Sunny's car when an uptight Sonny said, "Doc, I'm worried. My father remains a problem. Merry has had problems with him since she was a high school freshman. His track record carries a load of questionable activities, and he's dangerous."

"I understand the danger, Sunny, but please don't mention him to the others. I want this to be a great day for everyone, especially Merry."

Upstairs in their bedroom, Anna gazed happily at her beautiful daughter. A warm smile covered her face as they discussed how Merry and Doc quickly grew to love each other and arrived at this point in their lives. As she zipped Merry's wedding gown, she said, "This is a beautiful gown, Merry."

"Doc bought it," Merry answered without thinking.

"Really? How would he know your size?" she queried with a need to know.

"Mother, he —"

"Weren't we going with Mom?" Anna sweetly questioned.

"Mom, it is," Merry laughed. "I held the dress against me in a store but refused to try it on. The ring was enough."

"Your father will be outraged when he hears about the wedding."

"Don't tell him?" Merry barked.

"He's your father."

"In name only. No loving father would do what he did."

"Merry, what are you talking —?"

"Please let it ride!" Merry bitterly snapped. "I don't wish to think about him on my wedding day."

A black cloud hung over the room as Merry finished dressing. A light knock and Kathy's voice asking, "About ready?" broke the tension. Turning, Merry noted the tears running down her mother's face.

Anna dried her eyes on a Kleenex as she watched Merry descend the steps holding up her gown. Grabbing her makeup kit, she hurriedly retouched her tear-drawn face. Tension rode heavily in Sunny's vehicle because of the angry discussion.

The women met Pastor and Anita in a Sunday School room at church. Pastor Mike asked if there were any last-minute needs, and when there weren't, he mentioned there appeared to be some tension within the group. Merry shrugged her shoulders in a way that suggested it wasn't something to be discussed.

Anita departed to wait for the ceremony to begin, and the pastor joined Doc. Ronnie and Sarah arrived next and joined Doc. Cindy soon came with her cameras and a solemn face, quietly sitting behind them. Doc got up and hugged her, but the hug didn't hold the usual warmth.

Pastor Mike looked at Doc and asked, "Nervous?"

"Not about the wedding. My only concerns are what we discussed last night."

"We had a call last night seeking information about your wedding. When I took the phone from Anita and demanded to know who was calling, he hung up."

"Any idea who it was?"

"None."

The church filled rapidly, prompting ushers to set up folding chairs. At the appointed time, the pianist began playing wedding music. Pastor Mike and the wedding party went to the front, where the pastor began. "Welcome family and friends of Forest 'Doc' Adams and Merry An Morehouse. We're gathered here in the presence of our Lord, loved ones, and friends to celebrate one of life's greatest moments, to recognize the worth and beauty of love, and to add our blessings to the words which will unite Forest Adams and Merry Morehouse in holy matrimony."

"A Christian marriage involves a believing man and woman who pledge to live according to Biblical principles and remain solely committed to each other for life. In the Garden of Eden, God saw that it was not good for man to be alone, so He created a helper. And the Lord saw that it was good."

After a nod from the pastor, the wedding guests stood, and Sunny and Merry looked at each other with smiling faces before beginning their walk to the church's front with Merry holding his arm. After the slow walk to the front, they stopped in front of Pastor Mike, who smiled warmly.

Pastor Mike asked, "Who brings this woman to this man?"

Sunny replied, "I, Sunny Morehouse, her brother, bring Merry on behalf of her family," and placed Merry's hand with Doc's. Stepping away, he sat beside Kathy.

Pastor Mike began, "Forest and Merry, our Bibles tell us we begin life as individuals, and with marriage, we must learn to live and love together as a caring team. This becomes one of life's most significant challenges, but it must be the shared goal of married life. Only love will maintain a marriage. Humanity does not create love; God creates love. In First Corinthians 13: 4-8, we receive divine direction concerning love. 'Love is patient; love is kind. It does not envy, it does not boast, it is not proud. It does not dishonor others, it is not self-seeking, it is not easily angered, it keeps no record of wrongs. Love does not delight in evil but rejoices with the truth. It always protects, always trusts, always hopes, always perseveres. Love never fails.'"

After Bible readings, the pastor began, "Marriage is a serious, Christian union held together by the bonds of Christ and the Church. Should anyone hold reason why this couple should not be united in marriage, they must speak now or forever hold their peace."

An angry voice surprised the congregation, "I hold reasons. My daughter isn't marrying this criminal anywhere, and especially not in this godforsaken little shanty. Preacher, call off this mess, or I'll call it off for you."

Pastor Mike saw the angry man in the back of the church and grabbed Doc's arm, restraining him. He looked at Merry. "Merry, how old are you?"

"Thirty-one," Merry answered, her voice shaking with fear.

"Do you wish to marry Forest Adams?"

"I do," she fearfully replied.

"Mrs. Morehouse, as Merry's mother, can you affirm Merry's age, and do you bless this marriage."

Anna looked at her angry husband with fear flooding across her face. She swallowed hard before turning to the pastor and softly said, "I'm Merry's mother. Merry is thirty-one years old, and I bless her marriage to Forest Adams."

"Then we shall proceed with their wedding ceremony," Pastor Mike calmly stated, looking down at his Bible.

"Wait a minute. I'm Merry's father, and I run the Morehouse family," the angry voice shouted as he headed up the aisle. "I'm telling you this marriage is off. Anna. Merry. Sunny. Get back here — now!"

Pastor Mike nodded to the man in the brown sports coat sitting in the back of the room. The man sprang to his feet, grabbed Howard, and when Howard attempted to push him away, the big man quietly muscled him outside, closing the door behind them.

"Mr. Morehouse, I'm Detective Jordan Nash of the Pennsylvania State Police. The folks being married inside are of age and desire to be married. You have two choices: get in your vehicle and drive off, or I'll put you in my car and haul you off."

"Maybe you don't understand. I'm Howard Morehouse of Morehouse, Peabody, and —."

"Mr. Morehouse, it's you who doesn't understand. Your choices are leaving peacefully or with force. You have little time to decide."

Howard snorted with anger riding his white face. "Copper, that's my family in that shanty, and I run my family. You'll hear more from me, and it won't be nice."

Howard stomped around the trooper to his new Mercedes CLE Coupe and roared off, spinning gravel as he went. The detective smiled as he assumed a just-in-case position by the door.

Inside, Pastor Mike took Howard's car roaring off as the signal to restart the ceremony.

"Forest Adams and Merry Morehouse, we begin life as individuals, and with marriage, must learn to live and love together as a caring team. This becomes one of life's most significant challenges, but it must be the shared goal of married life. As I mentioned before we were rudely interrupted, only love will maintain a marriage. Humanity does not create love; God creates love. I'm rereading First Corinthians 13: 4-8 because of its importance to a successful marriage. 'Love is patient; love is kind. It does not envy, it does not boast, it is not proud. It does not dishonor others, it is not self-seeking, it is not easily angered, it keeps no record of wrongs. Love does not delight in evil but rejoices with the truth. It always protects, always trusts, always hopes, always perseveres. Love never fails.'"

Pastor Mike continued through the service to the point of oaths. "Forest Adams and Merry Morehouse, would you please face each other? Forest Adams, do you take Merry Morehouse to be your wife? Do you promise to love, honor, cherish, and protect her, forsaking all others and holding only to her forevermore?"

"I do."

The pastor went through the same with Merry and continued with a Biblical reading. "From Ephesians, we read: 'Wives, submit yourselves to your husbands as you do to the Lord' and 'Husbands, love your wives, just as Christ loved the church.' His guidance follows with 'a man will leave his father and mother and be united to his wife, and the two will become one flesh.' The Bible tells us that you, Forest, must love your wife as you love yourself, and you, Merry, as his wife, you must respect your husband."

They then recited their vows, exchanged rings, and came to the part they had been practicing. "Congratulations. Forest Adams, you may kiss Merry Adams, your bride."

After their loving embrace and kiss, Pastor Mike raised his hands to the congregation. "Friends, I present to you, Mr. and Mrs. Forest Adams. On the Bride and Groom's behalf, I want to thank everyone for coming. Please remember their reception this evening at the home of Doc and Merry Adams."

Chapter 47

At home, Sunny approached Doc and Merry, holding a worried look. "Doc, can I talk with you? It's important."

Doc looked at Merry, and she nodded to go ahead. The fear riding her face said she didn't want to be alone, but the look on Sunny's face screamed of importance.

"Let's walk out to the barn. I want to feed the horses before the reception begins," Doc said.

They walked without talking. Howard Morehouse's angry face at church rolled through Doc's mind, the only thing that could cause Sunny's panic-driven face. As they walked into the barn, Sunny grabbed Doc's arm, his hand shaking. "Doc, something terrible is going to happen tonight. Being tossed out of church this afternoon made things worse. Please call off the reception. Please. It's best for everyone."

"Sunny, your father's actions stole fifteen years from Merry's life. He robbed her of faith in herself. Her abilities. She's gaining those back. I'm deeply in love with Merry, and your father will not slam her back into his prison while I'm alive."

"I'm sure he's coming here tonight," Sunny said, his voice barely a whisper, "to kill us all."

A savage look grabbed Doc's face as he held Sunny by the shoulders. "Try to kill us. Sonny, I come from a tough family. My Dad and his brothers were heavily decorated Marines, as was their father. I hope we've seen the last of your father. If we haven't, we're headed for a difficult experience."

Doc fed the horses, and they headed for the house. The Morehouse family and Maggie stood whispering when Doc and Sunny arrived. Sunny's face announced he was hesitant to party, but guests were here, and more were arriving. Family and friends filled the picnic tables with flowers and champagne for the marital toast. The party was on!

Or was it?

"Doc, I'm so afraid," Merry said, trembling with fear as they watched out the window. "Howard Morehouse is not done with us or our wedding. If anything, he's energized to do something terrible after he was hauled out of church." Her hands shook as she held Doc's hand. "Do we have to go out there?"

"Honey, I know you're afraid. I'll tell them you're sick."

"Please, stay with me," she pleaded, tears welling as she held him from leaving. "My father will kill you."

"Honey, if we run tonight, he'll tear our marriage apart. That's not happening."

"If you're going out, I'm going too. I'd rather be dead than alive without you."

Together, they walked arm in arm out to their reception, with the others following. Merry endeavored to look calm, but her hands shook on Doc's arm.

Ronnie began the reception toasts. "Friends and loved ones, as most of you know, I'm Ronnie, previously Doc's son and now Doc and Merry's son. This beautiful woman with me is my wife, Sarah. Today, we enjoyed a wonderful wedding ceremony for a great new team, Doc and Merry Adams. Let us now raise our glasses and toast the new Mr. and Mrs. Adams. May their lives together be long, joyous, and full of love."

"Here! Here!"

When this toast finished, Sunny began, his nervousness shaking his voice." My beautiful sister, Merry, found the right man in Doc Adams. Now that I know him, I fully understand her choice. Watching them together provides a view of true love in motion. I am thankful to be part of this special day. Let us toast this wonderful couple who brought us all together today."

"Here! Here!"

After the toast, Ronnie stepped forward and said, "Now, let's hear from the new Adams team."

Doc tightly held Merry's hand, "Merry and I are honored to stand before you, pledging our forever love to one another. The love you're sharing with us today enriches our lives. We thank my daughter Cindy, my son Ronnie and his wife Sarah, Merry's mother Anna, her brother Sunny and his friend Kathy, Maggie, our friends in the Hill Church, our little band, and all of you for accepting us and our marriage. We appreciate everything you all did to make this day possible. Thanks for spending this day with us. We pray the Lord continues to watch over us this evening."

"Here! Here!"

His last comment wasn't lost on Merry as she gathered strength to make a toast. She struggled initially but continued, "I'm grateful for all who had a hand in bringing Doc and me to the point of being husband and wife. We're thankful for your acceptance of us as a married couple. I thank God for bringing Doc Adams into my life. He gave me true reasons to smile, introduced me to our Lord, and gave me love I didn't know existed. We're thankful for Pastor Mike and Anita, who trusted us for marriage. Thank you all for being so good to us. We're truly blessed."

"Here! Here!"

Bob Beck operated the fire pit grill as it burned brightly, accompanied by the delightful aroma emanating from the applewood while Ronnie and Sunny ran the gas grills. "Chows on" was soon the order of the day. Evening glided in as people finished eating, waiting for the music to begin.

Edna Mason and Bob Beck were soon tuning up with other players as another picking session was about to begin. Then, Bob announced, "Our first song for this evening is beginning without our lead guitar. Would everyone allow our newlyweds this first dance together? Our song is a Carter family favorite that Merry sang with us on her first weekend in the mountains. It's called 'The Winding Stream.' Can't you picture them alone in their canoe?"

Doc and Merry danced with arms wrapped around each other.

"O give to me a winding stream.

It must not be too wide

Where waving leaves from maple trees

Do meet from either side

The water must be deep enough

To float a small canoe

With no one else but you."

They looked at each other with the sincere, loving smile that had become a part of them, lost in the moment as they danced together.

"Oh, Merry, you brought life back to me," Doc whispered.

"Honey, you gave me a life. For sure, we're God-sent."

Tears of happiness formed as they danced together, whispering as if on command, "I love you."

The band played through the song and began another with Doc and Merry still dancing. "All right, lovers, time to share. Lines are forming to dance with you folks," Bob announced.

Looking around, they grew blushes as they saw the people waiting. Doc danced Merry to the dance lines, where Sunny took Merry's hand, and Doc searched for Cindy. He found her taking pictures and asked her to be his partner. When she hesitated, he said with a smile, "Please, Cindy. I love you."

Hesitantly, she handed her camera to a bystander, and they danced. Doc tried to hold her closer, but when she kept her distance, he realized the problem noted in church was still there. Bob called change partners, and the song changed. Cindy let loose without speaking and turned to walk away.

"I love you, Cindy," Doc said, then looked skyward with his 'Oh Lord, help me - I need your support' request.

A tap on his shoulder brought him back, and he found Sarah waiting. They danced until the change partners came up, and Sunny's Kathy took her turn. Anna was next, seeming hesitant at first and then dancing closer. And closer.

"Oh, Doc, this is so good for me. It's better than our first hug. I don't want to let you go."

Doc wondered where this was heading when the change partners came again and a new partner took over. Doc's bum leg was beginning to ache, and after a few more dances, he begged off and took his chair. Ronnie slid away and returned with Doc's guitar. "Bob said you're needed to make great music."

Doc glanced at Merry. When she smiled and nodded, he moved his chair near the fire pit where the band set up, and Merry followed. Evening slid away with Merry and many others joining in the singing. Doc listened carefully during a band break, thinking he heard a vehicle nearby. When no one appeared, he passed it off as a mistake.

Something crunched under the apple trees just past the yard. It grew quiet for a bit. Touching Doc's arm, Merry whispered fearfully, "It's him, Doc. I'm scared. My father came to kill us."

Concerned, Doc put his guitar down and sat Merry on his lap. His muscles tightened as he strained to hear anything that shouldn't be there. No animal would be this close to the party noise.

Hearing nothing further, the band began again. The fun didn't last long. A figure stood up behind the stone wall and flipped on a light. It became deathly quiet as the man flashed the light from one frightened face to another. Locating Merry sitting on Doc's lap, he slid his light to the left, back, and then to the right, finding Anna and Sunny.

"People, this party's over!" his angry voice bellowed. "I came to take my family out of this wasteland. Morehouse family, get up on the road. We're going home."

"I don't remember seeing your name on the guest list, Mr. Morehouse," Doc said in a cold voice. "You need to leave while you can."

"I'm not an invited guest. I'm removing my family."

"Mr. Morehouse, you and I are headed for a place I don't want to go. A place you don't want to be when I get there. Nuff said!"

"Move and you're dead meat, you freaking druggie."

Merry stiffened with fear. No one moved. "Dammit!" Morehouse boomed maliciously, "I said, Morehouse family, get up and get moving. That includes you, Merry. The rest of you stay put until we get out of here."

"Listen, people," Merry screamed in anger. "This animal raped me, his fifteen-year-old daughter. He said he was teaching me about real life. He finished and —"

"Shut up, Merry, or I'll shut you up permanently," Morehouse ordered, pulling a pistol from his jacket pocket and pointing it and the light at her. "Get up and get moving while you still can."

Anna and Sunny eased out of their chairs and began to edge past people moving toward the road behind them. Merry sat still and screamed. "He told me to get up and get cleaned up. Said I made a real mess. That's who this coward —"

Howard fired a round in the air. "Merry, I'm not fooling," the angry voice roared. "The next round is yours. The one after is for the doofus that hijacked you. After that, it's anyone who tries anything funny."

"Shoot me!" Merry shrieked. "Listen, everybody! Howard Morehouse raped—"

With Morehouse's pistol swinging toward them, Doc threw Merry aside and dove across the fire pit. A round hit the chair they had been sitting in, ripping into the ground. People screamed. Morehouse fired again, and the 9MM round hit Doc in the shoulder slamming him against the fire pit. It felt as if a knife stabbed deep into his back, crushing the wind out of him. A sharp pain tore through his shoulder. He gasped for air, rolling to his side, coming up on his knees. Another round hit his arm knocking him sideways. He lunged at Morehouse, grabbing the gun as Howard fired again.

Straining, Doc crushed Howard into the ground, pounding him. Holding the pistol with one hand, he beat his face and throat. Morehouse used both hands to push the gun up and fired. Straining, Doc turned the weapon. It fired again. Then, once more. Morehouse's grasp eased. His body shivered, then relaxed.

"Enough, Doc," a female voice said, laying her hand on his shoulder.

It was deathly quiet, and Edna Mason had the Morehouse light. She knelt beside Howard, feeling his neck for a pulse. She looked up, shaking her head. "He's gone.".

379

CHAPTER 48

Doc groaned in pain, and Merry's hands shook as she helped him to his feet. Her hand came away wet, and a hole in the shoulder of his suit coat dripped blood. Panicking, in a shaky voice, she asked Edna to shine her light on Doc. "Edna, help us. Doc's hurt. Bad." Looking closer, she saw another bloody hole in his coat sleeve.

Doc pulled out his handkerchief and pressed it over the shoulder wound, wincing with pain, while Merry ran to the house for first aid kits. She returned with two kits and a pair of flashlights, giving a kit and flashlight to Edna. Edna pulled out gauze pads and a roll of adhesive tape and began working on Doc's shoulder. "You already have scars on this shoulder. You a routine troublemaker?"

"Shhh. Don't tell Merry. She doesn't know it yet."

"Doc, this is serious. You need a doctor," Edna remarked as she taped triple pads on both sides of his shoulder. "The other's a flesh wound. Good thing you dove, or you'd be dead. Merry, too."

Doc's face twisted in pain as he pulled his shirt back over his shoulder, but he knew there was more he needed to do. Relying on his combat experience, he called, "Anyone hurt?"

"Gordon Mumford's down and not moving," a voice answered out of the dark.

Another voice added, "He needs help, bad!"

"Our daughter's wounded too," a woman called. "I can't see how bad."

Edna examined the wounded girl while Doc took a first aid kit and a flashlight to look over Gordon Mumford, "Can I see where you're hurt, Crissy?"

Crissy removed the handkerchief from her arm, showing the flesh wound that bled lightly. "Crissy, I'm going to clean you up to prevent infection and then place a dressing on it. It'll sting. No swearing or I'll tell your Sunday School teacher. Okay?"

"Okay."

Crissy gritted her teeth as the alcohol took effect. As the pain eased, she giggled at Edna, "Mrs. Mason, you're my Sunday School teacher, and I don't swear . . . at least not out loud."

Laughter erupted around her.

As Edna got up, she said, "Crissy, you'll be alright, but we'll get a doctor to check you."

"Who's with Gordie?" Edna called, flashing her light around.

"Over here," Doc said, swinging his light until she found him kneeling beside Gordie. "He has a pulse, but it's weak." Someone returned with the towel used to open champagne bottles, and Doc placed it over Gordie's stomach wound.

Edna got on her knees and noted Gordie shivering. "There's a blanket in the back seat of our truck. Let's cover Gordie until help gets here. Clair called 911 and the state police when Morehouse arrived. Dr. Norton should be with the ambulance crew. We'll have him check the wounded when he arrives. They should be here soon."

Flashing red and blue lights accompanied by the whoop-whoop of a siren announced the state police vehicle's arrival. Edna signaled the trooper with her flashlight when he stepped out. It proved to be Sergeant Richardson

Edna said, "Sergeant, let me show you the body so you can ask questions before anyone leaves. He took the party out of us," Edna said, shining her light on the body and the pool of blood by Morehouse's head.

The sergeant stepped forward and requested in an authoritative voice, "Folks, please stand by. We'll need answers to some questions when the coroner gets here."

The sergeant slipped on gloves and kneeled beside the body of a well-dressed man who suffered a gunshot wound to the temple. Blood pooled behind his head where the bullet exited. His eyes held a haunted look, his mouth hung open, with fear riding his face. The sergeant rubbed Morehouse's eyes closed and removed the pistol from his hand. After ensuring it was empty, he placed the weapon in an evidence bag.

With siren screaming, an ambulance rolled in. Sergeant Richardson shined his light for the driver, who struggled to turn around. The driver and his helper got out with a gurney accompanied by the Coroner, Dr. Norton. Dr. Norton examined Gordie before the crew could load him. The driver radioed a request for another ambulance to pick up the body and departed with siren screaming.

The coroner knelt beside the body and checked for a pulse. When there was none, the sergeant shined his light so the coroner could take pictures from several angles. With the sergeant taking notes, Edna explained what happened and how Morehouse began firing his weapon.

"Has the body been moved since Morehouse fell?" the coroner asked.

"Nobody touched him since Doc crawled off," Edna muttered.

Doc introduced Anna to the sergeant. "You're his wife?"

"I am," Anna sobbed.

"I'd like to remove the personal effects from the deceased's pockets while you watch. We'll give you everything not considered evidence. I'll place the rest of the items in this evidence bag. Can you handle that?"

"I can," Anna agreed, and the process began. Sergeant Richardson handed Anna the wallet and showed her the vehicle control unit; he asked if the keys might belong to the red Mercedes parked in the field. She looked the keys over and saw their house key on the ring. She identified the keys as belonging to Howard's Mercedes. Sergeant Richardson asked if he might retain the control unit to inspect the vehicle, and Anna agreed.

The sergeant then appealed to people, "Dr. Norton and I would appreciate your support by telling us what you observed happening here."

"I have something," Anna began, wiping her eyes, "We heard noises in the dark. My husband stood behind the stone wall shining a light on us. He began calling Doc and Merry bad names and threatened us."

"Father told us to get up to the road. He was taking us out of here," Sunny added. "Said he'd get the marriage annulled. When Merry began yelling about something he had done to her, he went nuts. He pulled a gun and fired into the air, warning Merry, but she kept screaming at him. He fired at her. Doc threw Merry aside and dove at him. Father fired several shots at Doc."

"Is 'He and Him,' Howard Morehouse?" The sergeant asked.

"It is."

"I have something to say," Bob Beck announced. "That guy's nuts. He got hauled out of church for raising Cain during the wedding ceremony. We could hear him hollering at the man who hauled him outside. A lot of us feared we hadn't heard the last of him. Then he snuck in here and threatened us with a gun."

"Did anyone here do anything to upset him?" the sergeant asked.

"Guess we all did," Bob responded. "He took offense to Doc marrying his daughter in our shanty church. That's his words."

"Anyone else have anything?" the sergeant asked as a siren sounded in the distance.

"Yeah," a voice came out of the dark. "That idiot ruined the celebration for two beautiful people."

The sergeant requested Doc's permission to use space in his home so people would have light to complete statements. Doc agreed, called Merry to his side, and they headed inside with the coroner to retrieve pens and paper.

"May I have your attention, please," the sergeant requested. "Docs permitting us to use their home where there's light. I'd appreciate your written statements concerning what happened here tonight. If you feel the actions at church impacted this problem, please so note it. These statements should prevent future problems concerning this unfortunate incident."

Once inside, Dr. Norton explained the type of information that would be most helpful for the police and himself. People, including Merry, described what they witnessed, signed and dated their papers, and handed them to the sergeant. Most looked exhausted from the evening's activities.

Anna was still crying when the sergeant began talking with her, her family, and Dr. Norton about the police procedures. "We'll deliver the body to Dr. Norton's office for an autopsy. It then goes to Bennett's Funeral Home, which is located a few doors down Main Street. I'd recommend the family meet with Dr. Norton in the morning for a briefing and then go to the funeral home so they can assist you with plans. Doc knows the location of everything. Please come to my office sometime before noon. We'll finish the required paperwork."

While they talked, the second ambulance arrived and picked up the Morehouse body. Unlike the first ambulance, the driver and assistant secured the body on the stretcher and left quietly.

Before departing, the sergeant said, "Doc, I'll contact the DA in the morning after I review these witness statements. I'll make copies for the DA and the coroner. It appears to be a clear-cut case of self-defense, with several witnesses calling you a hero.”

“Would you make copies of those statements and your report for Kinnard, our lawyer, just in case?”

“I will,” Sergeant Richardson replied. “He’ll have them Monday.” He shook Doc’s left hand and climbed into the police car with the coroner. Sunny hitched a ride with them out to retrieve the Mercedes.

The sergeant went over the Mercedes using the interior lights and a flashlight. The car was clean except for directions to the church and Doc’s place, three empty water bottles, a computer, and a half-empty box of shells. The trunk appeared to be unused.

After their departure, Sunny drove his father’s car back to the fire, where Merry and Anna stood holding each other. Maggie stood beside Merry with her hand on her arm while Kathy stood beside Anna. “Merry, I’m so sorry your special day ended like this,” Anna sobbed.

“Don’t cry, Mom,” Merry said in a comforting voice. “This is still the best day of my life.”

“If I had only known, Mer —”

“Mom, let it drop . . . forever,” Merry asked. “Please! It’s time to get on with our lives.”

Merry helped Doc into the truck, and they headed to town to care for his wounds. An icy silence hung over them. The circumstances of her father’s death and her screamed comments tore her apart while Doc worried about autopsy results.

In town, Dr. Norton examined Doc. "We need to X-ray your ribs and the shoulder wound."

After the X-ray procedure had been completed, Dr. Norton looked it over with Doc. "You have two cracked ribs, but the wounds look okay. Let me get something for pain so I can clean them."

The doctor soon returned with two needles filled with pain medication, a bottle of antiseptic, and some long swabs. "Hang on. This stuff burns," Doctor Norton said as he injected pain medication in two places.

While time passed until the painkiller took effect, they discussed the evening's problem and what might have led to it. Dr. Norton shook his head as Doc talked, then snapped the wound with his finger. When Doc didn't jump, he dipped swabs in the antiseptic and ran them through the injury.

When he finished, he said, "We'll watch this one as you heal. Let's take care of the other one." After scrubbing the arm wound with alcohol and drying it, he snapped Doc's arm and asked, "Can you handle a couple of sutures, or should I put another shot in there?"

"Let's try it," Doc said.

"Hold your arm like this," Doctor Norton said, showing him how he wanted it positioned, and quickly took two stitches. After dressing the wound, he helped Doc get his shirt on. "I know you're feeling more pain than you're showing. I can give you a prescription, but I'd prefer you use Aleve or Excedrin. Too many opioids are floating around. I'll get you a sling to keep pressure off that shoulder."

As Dr. Norton adjusted the sling, he said, "I'd tell you to take it easy for a few days, but today's your honeymoon. Just be careful."

With a white face and a knowing smile, Doc thanked him. Then Doctor Norton began again. "Doc, I'd like your answers to some off-the-record questions about this death."

Doc straightened to full attention, a searching look on his face. "What might those questions be?"

Before answering, the doctor looked at Doc in a wondering way, and a sad look came over his face. "I want the autopsy to be as fair as possible." As he looked at Doc, he shook his head and began again. "Doc, this has to be between us and no one else. I want the outcomes of everything to support you without getting me in trouble. You don't have to answer if you don't want to. Understood?"

When Doc nodded in agreement, the coroner continued. "What caused Mr. Morehouse's death?"

A serious look" rolled over Doc's face. "Not sure what you want me to say, but Morehouse got away with a lifetime of terrible actions, especially to Merry. If this hadn't happened, she would live in fear for the rest of her life. I love Merry. When he shot me, his reign of terror ended."

"Doc, I understand." After a few more questions, they gently shook hands, and the Adams family headed home. After a bit, Doc struggled to explain something to Merry. With palms to his face and a tight-lipped pose, he began. "Merry, I love you and want to be married to you forever."

"I feel the same way. Nothing could change that."

"Difficult things happened today. I killed your father."

"He tried to kill us, and you saved my life." It became quiet as searing thoughts burned through their minds. Merry finally spoke. "Thanks, Doc. I hated him so."

The new Adams family arrived home to find a few people standing quietly around the fire, and Anna was still suffering through a difficult time. Sobbing, she asked Merry to accompany her to her bedroom. Once there, she said, "Merry, I guess I know why you put the locks on your door and refused to stay alone with him."

"I don't know how you stood him all these years," Merry angrily announced, wringing her hands.

Tearfully, Anna replied, "I stayed because of my children. Somehow, we'll get past this. With tears running down her cheeks, Anna cried, "I'm so thankful you ran into Doc. He's good for you. Good for all of us. He freed me tonight. Freed Sunny, too, even if he doesn't yet realize it."

"What are your plans, Mom?"

"I don't even know where to begin," Anna sobbed. "Howard's calls here woke me up to my miserable life. They made me consider divorce proceedings. Now, I have to get his body back to Philadelphia for a funeral service. I can't say I won't miss him, but I'm thankful it's over."

"We'll help you through this."

"Merry, I learned a lot here in two days. Maybe I'll put that damned castle up for sale and buy a home, something with neighbors around me and a church nearby. I've missed, no, we've missed life. You're finding yours with Doc. I'm going to find mine too. I hope

Sunny sees your happiness and closes the deal with Kathy. She's a lovely young woman. New subject, how are Doc's wounds?"

"He's hurting more than he's putting on, but he's tough. The doctor stitched his arm and cleaned his shoulder. He said his shoulder should be fine with time. Mom, I can't even explain how crazy I am about him and want to be with him. I'll see you in the morning."

After hugs, Merry handed her mother tissues to dry her eyes, checked their bedroom, and went downstairs. No Doc. Looking out the window, she observed people standing by the dying fire and headed out to see who was still there. When she arrived, Ronnie and Sarah hugged her, wished her well on her new life, said goodnight to the others, and hugged Doc before departing.

Doc pulled Ronnie and Sarah close with his good arm. "Stay in touch, guys."

Ronnie smiled and said, "Hey, Dad, remember, it's your honeymoon. If you have any questions, call me. You have my number."

"Don't get smart, son. I can still paddle your behind."

"Not with one arm." They laughed together before heading to their car. Doc sat down, and Merry sat on his lap, giving him a lasting kiss. "I hope you didn't forget what today is," Merry said with a smile.

"It's Sunday, isn't it?" Doc asked with a serious look.

Kiddingly, Merry pinched him, and when he hollered, Sunny said, "Looks like she thinks it's a bit more than Sunday, Doc."

Strained laughter followed as they returned to the problems faced that evening. "I hate to change the subject, Merry, but how's your mother taking this?" Maggie asked.

"About as good as can be expected," Merry answered. "She has a lot to think about, but I suggested we wait until tomorrow to discuss it. We let it go at that."

"Kathy and I will get her and her car home when she finishes here," Sunny volunteered. "The tyrant I used to work for won't be around to complain if I miss work for a day or two."

The comment brought more ice over the night until Maggie broke the silence. "I think it's best if I leave after breakfast. With one exception, this has been a wonderful trip. I never saw so many stars as there are tonight. I never tasted water this good. Best of all, I attended the marriage ceremony of two people who are deeply in love. I hate to leave."

"We'll have you back soon," Doc said. "Count on it."

CHAPTER 49

With hands on her hips, Merry inspected the bedroom where they would spend their first night together as a couple. "What have you done?" she inquired.

"What's wrong, Honey?" Doc asked with a concerned look and hurt in his voice.

"Nothing's wrong," Merry said with a broad smile warming her face. "It's beautiful. New paint. New drapes and throw rugs. Even the lamps are new."

"So is the bed, mattress, sheets, pillows, and covers. I wanted this to be our room from day one, Honey." Feeling trapped by events beyond his control, Doc sat down on the edge of the bed, head in hands, his life slipping into nowhere. He quietly murmured, "I feel problems rolling in, Merry. I killed your father. What he did to you was strike one. His actions at the church were strike two. I knew he would come here tonight for strike three, and only one of us would leave. He's out. If that makes a difference in our marriage, we can have it annulled before there's a honeymoon."

Merry sat holding his hand, searching for words that could help. "Please stop. Do you love me?"

"More than life."

"I love you too. I feel loved and in charge of my life for the first time since I was a kid. If it weren't for you, I'd be dead. You threw me out of the way, and as I landed, I saw you jump across the fire pit. That animal was an expert pistol shot, and he was firing at you. Again and again. You took two bullets meant for me. If I held doubts about God or being God sent, they passed tonight. I'm praying his death won't impact our honeymoon or our life hereafter. What worries me is how you feel now that your family and friends know your wife was raped by her father?"

Doc stumbled for words. "Honey, this has been a terrible night for us. What people think about anything is their business. They wouldn't want to say anything about the woman I love. I'm much more concerned about what could be coming tonight."

"PTSD?" Merry asked. "Honey, we'll get through it together."

"What happens when your family discovers I intentionally killed him?" Doc asked with a tremor in his voice.

"He's a nightmare that won't hurt anyone again. I believe there'll be a feeling of relief. If not, there should be. Speaking of nightmares, Doc, How's your arm and shoulder?"

"I've hurt worse."

"Yes, but how are you now?"

" My ribs are a little tender from slamming into the firepit, and there's pain flashing around in my shoulder. Not enough to stop our honeymoon."

Merry turned on the stereo, and a disc with Elvis's love songs began. The first song was 'I'm Yours .'"May I have this dance?" she asked while helping him slip out of his arm sling.

"You may," he answered, moving into her arms.

"Doc, you're shaking," Merry said as she felt his arm on her back. "If the pain is too much, we can wait, Honey? "

Doc wiped his eyes and rested his head on her shoulder. He pulled her to him, and she held fast. "I can handle pain. Oh, Merry, I don't want to force you into something you're not ready for. I pray we're on the way to a beautiful life together."

"I'm ready for you and your love, Frosty. Thanks be to God. Hold me tight. Never let go."

They danced ever closer until they were one. Kissing passionately, they carefully undressed each other before slipping into bed to begin their life together as husband and wife.

The author is a Vietnam combat vet who was born and raised in these mountains and maintained a home there until recently. He lived through much of what occurs in this book, and the characters residing in this book might be friends, neighbors, or people he mentored or counseled over the years. These characters and the places talked about could actually exist in these mountains.

Richard S. Johnson